The *Cornish Dressmaker*

NICOLA PRYCE trained as a nurse before completing an Open University degree in Humanities. She is a qualified adult literacy support volunteer and lives with her husband in the Blackdown Hills in Somerset. Together they sail the south coast of Cornwall in search of adventure.

Also by Nicola Pryce

Pengelly's Daughter
The Captain's Girl

The Cornish Dressmaker

NICOLA PRYCE

CORVUS

First published in paperback in Great Britain in 2018 by Corvus,
an imprint of Atlantic Books Ltd.

1 3 5 7 9 8 6 4 2

A CIP catalogue record for this book is available from the British Library.

Paperback ISBN: 978 1 78649 383 5
E-Book ISBN: 978 1 78649 384 2

Printed and bound by CPI Group (UK) Ltd, Croydon, CR0 4YY
Corvus
An imprint of Atlantic Books Ltd
Ormond House
26–27 Boswell Street
London
WC1N 3JZ

www.corvus-books.co.uk

For my father,
Kenneth Eric Snelson,
civil engineer and hydrologist.

Family Tree

FOSSE

POLCARROW (Baronetcy created 1590)

Sir Francis m. 1) Elizabeth   2) Alice m. 2) Matthew
Polcarrow   Polcarrow   Polcarrow   Reith
b.1730 d.1782   (née Gorran)   (née Roskelly)
                 b.1749 d.1770   b.1763 m.1780

James Gorran m. Rosehannon   Francis
Polcarrow   Pengelly   Polcarrow
b.1765   b.1772   b.1781

Elizabeth Marie
Polcarrow
b.1794

Joseph Dunn   *Steward*

COOMBE HOUSE

Pascoe Pengelly m. Eva Pengelly
b.1739 d.1794 (née Trewarren)
b.1748

Jenna Dunn *Teacher in the School*
of Needlework
Elowyn Liddicot *Dressmaker / teacher in the school*
Mrs Munroe *Housekeeper and cook*
Samuel *Manservant*
Tamsin *Housemaid*
Billy Bosco *Errand boy*

ADMIRAL HOUSE

Sir Alexander Pendarvis m. Marie St Bouchard-Boulay
b.1743 b.1746

Captain Edward Pendarvis m. Celia Cavendish
b.1767 b.1773

Hugo Alexander Pendarvis
b.1795

Jago *Friend of the family*
Hannah *Maid*
Penro *Butler*

QUAYSIDE OF FOSSE

Pengelly Boatyard (Est.1760)

Mr Thomas Scantlebury *Shipwright*
Tom Liddicot *Apprentice*
Mr Melhuish *Blacksmith*

Bespoke Dressmaker (Est. 1792)

Elowyn Liddicot	*Proprietor and dressmaker*
Gwen Liddicot	*Seamstress*
Josie Mellows	*Seamstress*
Billy Bosco	*Errand boy*

Mr Edward Hoskins	*Bank manager*
Mrs Hoskins	*Bank manager's wife*

PORTHCARROW

Edward Perys	*Harbourmaster*
Martha Perys	*Harbourmaster's wife*
Nathan Cardew	*Superintendent of works*
Josiah Drew	*Leat engineer*
Richard Sellick	*Clay speculator*
Robert Hellyar	*Tin assayer*

Workmen's Cottages

Samuel Cooper	*Injured clay worker*
Bethany Cooper	*Mother of three children*

Fishermen's Cottages

Jack Deveral	*Fisherman*
Lowenna Deveral	*Fish cleaner / pilchard packer*
Ellen Liddicot	*Common-law fishwife*
John Polkerris	*Fisherman*

Chapel

Tobias Hearne	*Blacksmith and Methodist lay preacher*
Ruth Hearne	*Sunday school teacher*

And what if
In your dream
You went to heaven
And there plucked a strange and beautiful flower
And what if
When you awoke
You had that flower in your hand

Samuel Taylor Coleridge

'Gates open...'

Chapter One

'It's here! Honest to God, Elly, he's as good as his word. What's wrong? Ye look like the milk's turned sour.'

I joined Gwen at the window. It was a simple cart, the freshly painted rails glinting in the sunshine, the wheels scrubbed clean, all trace of mud removed. I should have been thrilled but my mouth tightened. Not at Gwen, no never Gwen; she was my rock, my second right hand. I was being summoned, that was all. I had four gowns to finish by Monday and Gwen needed to rest.

'Ye'd best take a cushion. Pack up yer sewing – I'll finish the hems.' She stretched out, placing both hands on the small of her back.

'No, Gwen, you're not to do another stitch. You're to go home to put your feet up. That cart's too early…I'll go when I'm ready and not before.' I put my hand on her swollen belly. 'He can't just send a cart.'

'He can and he has…He adores ye, Elly. Ye must know that. He's done nothin' but ask after ye since the wedding.'

3

She moved my hand so I could feel the baby kick. With a kick like that, it would be a boy; the fourth generation of shipbuilders. If it was a girl, we would teach her to sew. 'He's a good man and ready to court. He's done so well. Honest, Elly, ye're goin' up in the world.'

Was I? My stomach twisted. 'Well, I'm not ready to leave – I'll do two more hours then I'll walk to Mamm's. It's only four miles and Billy can come with me.'

I loved everything about this sewing room, part ware-house, part shop; it was so dear to me. Every drawer filled with carefully chosen ribbons and lace, every shelf stacked with high quality fabrics. I belonged here, Uncle Thomas and Tom running the boatyard, Gwen and I in the shop above. I ran down the iron steps, glancing through the arch to the boatyard beyond. It was as busy as ever. Lady Polcarrow would never allow the old sign to come down. It would stay *Pengelly's Boatyard* in memory of her dear father and she would see that it prospered.

The driver of the cart jumped to the cobbles. 'I'm not ready to leave,' I said, more sharply than I intended. 'Tell my mother I'll be along when I can.'

'Ye sure, Miss Liddicot? I can wait awhile…' He seemed disappointed, all that cleaning and scrubbing to no avail. 'Only Mr Cardew was quite particular…said I was to bring ye in Mr Hearne's best cart.' I could see now: it was not disappointment, it was anxiety.

'Tell them I'll make my own way when I'm finished.' Gwen was watching me from the large warehouse window. In my place she would have been nuzzling the pony, throwing back

4

her mass of black hair and laughing, offering the poor man a drink, but I could not help my frown — if we did not get these gowns finished, we would not be able to start on the next three. The opening of the lock was good for business, the order book full to bursting, and we were set to make a good profit, but Gwen was getting tired, the new seam-stresses were still too slow and we were in danger of falling behind.

Tom waved at me through the arch, smiling from beneath his mass of curly black hair. I loved them both so much, Tom and Gwen, so reckless, so much in love they tumbled straight into each other's arms. I could hardly believe it, my younger brother, three months married and a baby imminent. I waved back, a flicker of envy making me feel suddenly empty. What was wrong with me? I was being courted by Nathan Cardew. *Nathan Cardew.*

I climbed back up the steps, my heart in turmoil. 'Ye work too hard, Elowyn Liddicot,' Gwen said, putting her arm around me. 'Ye're all frowns when ye should be smiles. Most women would scratch yer eyes out for Nathan Cardew. Honest to God, ye should be jumping straight into that cart, not sending it away.'

A hot blush burned my cheeks. 'He's very handsome and very kind...don't misunderstand me. I'd be proud to have him as my husband. It's just...'

'Just what?' She laughed. 'Ye've got a string of men ye're not telling me about?'

'No, of course not,' I laughed back. 'It's just...I'd have to give up working here.'

Gwen searched the heavens. 'Now I know ye're with the fairies. Give up working night and day, yer fingers so sore ye can hardly hold the needle? And fer what? So ye can sit in a parlour and have a maid bring ye tea? Ye're goin' soft in the head, Elly Liddicot. There's even rumours he's to have one of the pier houses.'

I felt strangely like crying – wonderful prospects, a life with a man who offered me so much. How stupid could I get? 'How d'you *know* when it's right, Gwen? How d'you know to take such a big step?'

Her arm tightened, her smile turning suddenly conspiratorial. 'It's when they kiss ye – that's when ye know. It's when ye should tell them to stop but ye want them so bad ye can't say no!' She swung me round, taking hold of my shoulders. 'Ye will let him kiss ye, won't ye, Elly?'

'Gwen, really…I hardly know him!'

Her eyes darkened beneath her troubled brows. 'Elly, promise me ye won't go all strict and uppity. Don't put on yer airs and graces. Let him kiss ye or at the very least let him take hold of yer hand.'

The church clock struck half past eight. It was much later than I thought but the gowns were finished and I stood looking at them with a surge of pride. They were to be worn in Bath – Mrs Brockensure and her daughter would wear them at assemblies and concerts. *My gowns in Bath*; I could hardly believe it. Billy had swept the floor and was copying from a book, his tongue following the movement of his tightly grasped pen. 'Lady Polcarrow says I've a better hand than she had at my age.'

'I can believe that. I've nearly done. What's in the basket?'

'Raised rabbit pie an' potted crab – Mrs Munroe's put in calf's foot jelly an' there's a flagon of ale. Mrs Pengelly put in rhubarb jam an' a loaf of bread, too.'

I looked out of the window. The courtyard was already in shadow, the cobbles barely visible. I had taken too long. 'We'd best get going. Can you carry all that or shall we leave something behind?'

He smiled his huge grin. 'Course I can! I'm not a child no more.'

'*Any more...*' I said, grabbing my shawl.

'Honest, sometimes, ye sound just like Madame Merrick.'

'Lady Pendarvis,' I corrected again, but it was an easy mistake – even I still found it hard to call her by her proper name. 'Tell you what, we'll take the cliff path and watch the sun set – we might see dolphins.'

No, he was not a child any more. Gone was the starving, badly beaten vagrant Celia Pendarvis had found and rescued three years ago. Mrs Pengelly had brought him to Coombe House and under her nurture and care he was now a healthy thirteen-year-old who seemed to grow as we watched. No cuffs or collars to turn, just huge hems to keep pace with his long arms and hollow legs. He was nearly as tall as me and I was twenty. He grinned back at me as we locked the door, crossing the courtyard, our footsteps ringing on the empty cobbles.

We desperately needed rain. It had been uncomfortably

hot for the last three weeks and the streets stank worse than ever. The town felt hot and crowded, the stench from the sewer almost unbearable. I never passed this way if I could help it, it was the wrong end of town – too many men spilling from the taverns, clutching their tankards, wiping their noses on their sleeves, hawking and spitting on the street.

'Hello, m' beauty, come make a sailor happy.'

I grabbed Billy's hand, ignoring the lewd calls, bold looks and whistles, and left the quay with its piles of drying nets and empty crates. As we climbed the steep road out of town, the air began to freshen, the scent of wild herbs replacing the stench of the sewer, and I breathed deeply, relishing the soft breeze on my face. Gwen was right, I did work too hard, but I was grateful for my skills and would never complain. I was driven, that was all. A woman needed the ability to keep herself, to have some means to feed her family – the first clenched fist and I would walk out. Across the river, the last of the sun lingered on the rooftops of Porthruan, turning the slates a fiery red. We stopped to catch our breath, watching the seagulls screech round the fishing boats moored against the quay.

'The pilchards better be good this year – God help us if it's like last year.'

'Don't swear, Billy. You know we don't like it.'

He smiled. He always smiled, unless you caught him unawares. Unawares, a haunted look would enter his eyes and your heart would break – both parents lost to him through disease and famine, the whereabouts of his brother and sister unknown. But tonight he was so happy, running quickly ahead as I followed him up the cliff path. On the horizon, the sails of the passing ships glowed pink. 'I love it up here,' he said, stretching his arms out wide. '*Red sky at night, sailor's delight*. Mrs Munroe says ye mustn't look at the setting sun or ye'll go blind.'

We were on the tip of Penwartha Point, the treacherous headland with its jagged rocks pointing like teeth out of the water. I hardly dared look down but followed Billy round the headland, the breeze beginning to clear my head. I needed time to think; my temples were throbbing, a dull ache lodged behind my eyes. Mamm would be so glad to see me, yet the thought of staying with her gave me no pleasure at all and sharing a bed with Lowenna was the last thing I wanted. I should have said no.

Billy stopped suddenly and we stood in silence, staring down at the majestic sweep of Polworth Bay as it arced in front of us in a perfect semicircle. The bay faced east and was already shadowed by the surrounding cliffs; it looked strangely sinister, shrouded by dusk. Billy pointed to a black shape bobbing on the water. 'Is that a dolphin?'

I had to look carefully. 'It looks more like a log drifting on the tide.'

The bay might have lost the light but from where we stood, we could see the setting sun linger over the open sea, turning the horizon a brilliant red. It was so beautiful and I breathed in the smell of the salt, the scent of honeysuckle drifting on the air. I never took time off; weekdays and Saturdays were spent at work with Sundays taken up going to church and doing the washing and cleaning, but now everything had changed. Gwen had taken my place in Uncle Thomas's tiny cottage and I had a room in Mrs Pengelly's beautiful house. I still felt like pinching myself.

I had loved Mrs Pengelly on sight – the moment she walked into Madame Merrick's shop to ask for work. An expert seamstress and such a kind person, I loved everything about her: her soft eyes, her gentle manners, the way she smiled, teaching without criticizing, always patient and willing to go over things, again and again. I could barely hide my envy when the first seamstresses arrived in her school of needle-work. I wanted to join them so much but Uncle Thomas and Tom needed me in the cottage and I had to look after them.

Kittiwakes called from their nests in the cliff side. We were at the steepest part of the climb. 'Be careful, Billy, not so fast – keep away from the edge.' He turned round, smiling at my fear.

I loved Coombe House the moment I stepped through the door. Not just my bedroom, but the beauty of Mrs Pengelly's sitting room. Everything was so delicate and refined. I loved the way we drank tea from china cups and used silver teaspoons. I loved the butter knives and dainty napkins, the etched glasses and decanters for Madeira. I loved the clock in the glass dome, the delicate vases on the mantelpiece. Best of all, I loved the way we sat together in the evenings, talking as we sewed. Mrs Pengelly and Lady Pendarvis had taught me everything – and Lady Polcarrow, of course; Mrs Pengelly's beautiful, fiery daughter, so determined all women should learn to read and write.

The cliff path was well worn and easy to follow, the mud

so dry that deep cracks had formed. The stones were loose, the earth crumbling beneath our shoes. Billy was running too far ahead of me and I rounded the bend to see him standing on the highest point.

'Come and look,' he shouted, standing so fearlessly, his hands on his hips. 'Mrs Pengelly says it was the people who named the new town Porthcarrow. She said Sir James didn't want the glory.'

I edged slowly forward, standing behind him, looking down at the new harbour with its cluster of fine houses. 'That's because he's building the town for the people, not for himself.'

'But he'll get rich, won't he? Why else would he do it?'

'He wants the mines to prosper and men to have work.'

Billy's smile vanished. 'You mean men like Nathan Cardew!' He sounded bitter, turning quickly away, his arms crossed, his eyes on his boots.

'Billy...I'll only be four miles away from Coombe House – look, we're here already. You can see the houses from here.'

He kicked a stone, sending it flying over the side, and I edged further forward, slipping my arm through his. The light was fading, dark patches of seaweed swirling round the jagged rocks below us. Billy's face was rigid, his dark brows locked in a frown. 'If ye go to Porthcarrow, I'll get work in the clay setts.'

My heart jolted. 'You'll do no such thing! You'll stay with Mrs Pengelly and learn your books. If you go anywhere near those mines Lady Pendarvis will drag you back. We all will.'

His mouth tightened, the quiver in his voice returning. 'D'you like him?'

'Nathan Cardew? I think so.'

'D'you *love* him?' There were tears in his eyes, his face sullen.

'I don't know,' I replied, 'but I love you, Billy Bosco.'

He remained pouting down at the sea. 'Well, I don't like him and he don't like me.'

I left his grammar unchecked. 'Of course he does. Or he soon will – just wait till he gets to know you.' Billy was my constant companion, always willing, always smiling. This sullen pout was something new.

Immediately he stiffened, pointing down to the darkening sea. 'That's not just a log. Look, Elowyn, someone's clingin' to it.' He let go of my arm, crouching down behind the gnarled branches of a hawthorn. 'Look…there's a man clinging to it…he's headin' straight for the rocks. We've got to do something.'

Chapter Two

Through the fading light I could just make out the shape of a man. 'We'll never reach him…there's no way down… We'll have to go back and get Tom to bring his boat…Billy, he looks dead.'

Billy stayed kneeling on the ground, peering over the edge. 'There *is* a way down. Over there…See that sheep track? There's a gulley leadin' down from the ledge. We can use that.'

I looked to where he was pointing, searching the jagged cliff side with its clusters of bright flowers and wind-bent bushes. Just the smallest track was visible, criss-crossing sharply through the vegetation that clung to the rocks. 'No, Billy. Absolutely not – it's far too dangerous.'

'We can do it, honest, Elowyn. It's never as steep as it looks.'

I tried to think rationally. The sea was calm, the tide coming in. It was a warm night with very little wind. The waves were barely moving, just the strength of the tide pushing its way along the shoreline. Fear held me back, yet Billy seemed so sure. 'D'you *really* think there's a way down?' My heart was thumping.

'I'll know when we get there. It's worth a try.'

He grabbed my hand, leading me away from the well-worn path and across the clifftop, slowly, sure-footedly, weaving his way round the boulders as if he had done it a hundred times before. We stopped where rocks had tumbled down to the sea, the gorse clinging precariously to the side, but Billy was right, the smallest track led down between the bushes. Sheep's wool hung on the spiky thorns, droppings lay scattered in the dirt. Below us, a small shingle beach was just visible, sharp rocks stabbing the air like daggers. It was far too dangerous. 'I can't do it, Billy.'

'Yes, ye can, honest – it's easier than you think.' He sounded so sure, as if nothing could stop him. 'Just turn and face the cliff – like this. Hold the roots, not the branches... there's no thorns then.' He grabbed a root with his right hand, digging his boot into the cracked earth. 'Do it like this – honest, it's safe.'

'How d'you know, Billy?'

'Because when ye're hungry, ye steal eggs. Seagulls nest in the gullies and there's limpets on the rocks.' He started descending the cliff, the basket slung over his shoulder, and I caught a glimpse of his former life. He never spoke of it, but that basket hung so easily across his shoulders. Three years ago, he would have filled it for his brother and sister and they would have lived another day.

I was wearing my yellow poplin. It was one of my favourite

dresses but it was not my best. I never wore my best to Mamm's and I was grateful for that now. I stretched out my shawl, wrapping it round my hips and tying it tightly. Every fisherman's daughter knew how to hitch up her skirts and tuck them against her thighs. 'Don't look up, Billy, my stockings are showing.'

'I've seen stockin's before,' he shouted back. 'Just make sure yer foot holds. The stones will fall but take no heed… just don't let go yer hand till yer foot's sure. It's not as steep as ye think.'

I turned to face the cliff, clutching the roots like Billy had instructed, following him down the tiny track as it traversed the cliff. I could not look down but stared straight ahead, feeling for the footholds, digging my toes into the cracks until my boot felt secure. Flowers clung to the cliff side, clusters of pink thrift, sea lavender, wild carrot. Guillemots swooped in protest, circling the air with plaintive cries, but I hardly saw them. All I could do was choose the biggest roots and cling to them, slowly transferring my weight from one to the other. Stones broke free and rolled ahead but I took no notice. At the bottom, my hands were shaking and I looked up at the huge cliff towering above us. Billy's eyes were full of pride.

'Ye did that really good, Elowyn.'

'Really *well*,' I replied, smiling back.

We were at the water's edge, just a scramble over the rocks and we should see the man. I looked round in surprise. We were in a small cove, completely hidden from sight. Something was lying on the furthest rock and Billy ran across the shingle to pick it up. In the fading light, I presumed it was seaweed but he held it up, smiling broadly. 'Look, Elowyn, just what we need — a coil of rope...and look, an old crate... and a barrel. Tide must've washed them up.'

He flung down his basket, holding out his hand to help me across the rocks. The evening sky still glowed from the west but the light was dimming and it was hard to see where to step. Swathes of seaweed swirled around the rocks, some places wet and slimy, other patches dry and blackened by the sun. The smell was pungent, almost overpowering, and I edged forward slowly, the cockles crunching under my wet shoes.

'There, Elowyn. There!'

I looked up and caught my breath. The shape of the man's body looked unnatural, immediately terrifying. His arms were stretched wide along the log, his head to one side. 'He must be dead...he's not holding on to the log.'

'He might not be dead...We've got to bring him in.' Billy's voice rose in desperation. He began pulling off his boots, stripping to his breeches. 'I'll tie the rope round me...ye can follow me along the shore...That way, we'll avoid that huge rock. I'll rope meself to the man and ye can pull us round... back to this cove. The ropes should be long enough.'

I nodded, trying to calm my fear. The tide was coming in, not out. There was no strong current. The cove was sandy in places and Billy was tall enough to wade out some distance. I was panicking, that was all. I grabbed the heavy coil of rope, letting it out loop by loop, scrambling along the shore to keep Billy in sight. He was making good progress, half swimming, half wading through the darkening water, his lips clamped tight against the cold.

'I can't go any further,' I shouted. I had lost sight of him. 'Billy...can you hear me?' The rope tugged, slipping quickly through my hands and I wrapped it round my wrist, desperate it should not be pulled away. I was a child again, cold, wet, clinging painfully to the heavy rope, petrified I would be the one to let it go; a small, hungry child, hauling in the nets – the rope chaffing my fingers, the salt stinging my raw hands.

From behind the rock, I heard Billy shout, 'Pull us back. I've got him.'

I pulled as hard as I could to the sound of splashing. The rope was coarse and difficult to grab, but at last I saw them. Billy had one arm round the man and was struggling back through the inky black water but something was wrong. The man's arms were rigid, his head on one side and my stomach sickened, realizing at once that he was bound to the log. A mass of black hair swirled round his face, his shirt was torn, floating weightlessly around him. His legs dangled lifelessly beneath him and I hauled on the rope as hard as I could. Billy struck the sand and I could pull no more.

'Is he alive?' I was up to my knees in the sea, forgetting how cold it could be.

Billy was breathless. 'I don't know – he's tied so tightly.'

I was filled with anger, a terrible sense of wrong. The man was naked from the waist down, his breeches binding his hands to both ends of the log. 'Get this loose...' I cried, trying to uncoil the heavy material. His arms were looped through the breeches, wrapped so tightly it was almost

17

impossible to undo. My hands were trembling, my normally dexterous fingers numb and clumsy. 'He must be dead. He's too cold.' At last we freed him. 'Take his other wrist, Billy – we'll have to drag him out.'

Billy pushed the log away and we each grabbed a wrist, pulling him on to the sand with all our might. He was a large man, tall and muscular. His head had fallen forward, his forehead scraping along the sand, his legs dragging heavily behind him. 'Again – on my count of three,' Billy shouted. I gripped tightly, hauling again, inching him slowly out of the water.

'That's far enough. Roll him over.'

We rolled him over and knelt by his side, almost too scared to part the matted curls that covered his face. I recoiled in horror. His face was a mass of cuts and bruises, his eyes black and lifeless against the pallor of his skin. His lips were blue, his cheeks a deathly white. Across his chest, more bruises showed and on his abdomen, a band of deep purple. 'He's been beaten badly – he was probably dead when they threw him in.'

'Ye sure he's dead?'

I had seen drowned men before. He was dead, no doubt about it. I cupped my hand against the man's nose. 'There's no breath, Billy. We'll need to get him further up the sand, or the tide will take him.'

A terrible sadness filled me – sadness for Billy, despair for this man. He was young, he was strong; he had huge muscles and was in the prime of life. He should not be dead. Billy threw his shirt across the man's loins and I smiled my thanks. I had seen naked men before but not so close.

Billy stood staring down at the man. 'He wasn't dead when they threw him in. I think he used his breeches to keep him afloat – he must've hoped the log would save him. What shall we do? Leave him here and tell them at Porthcarrow?'

'We'll have to. We can't stay much longer – the light's fading...'

'There's a cave. I saw one. We could leave him there, save him driftin' off again.'

I looked to where Billy was pointing. There was nothing. 'A cave? Are you sure?'

'Yes – it's hidden in the rocks. I saw the opening. We'll drag him over – it's the least we can do.'

Billy had tears in his eyes and I, too, felt like crying. 'I wish we could've saved him,' I whispered.

Every fisherman's family lived with the fear of the boats returning with drowned men; their bodies laid so gently on the sand. It was what we all dreaded. My heart jumped. 'Billy...he just breathed...I saw him.' I put my hand against the man's chest, spreading my fingers wide. There was nothing – no movement, just the terrible cold of a lifeless body. I put my ear against the mass of tight black hairs. 'Billy, I saw a breath...honest, I did.'

The movement had been so faint, just the smallest intake of what could have been a breath, but it had definitely been something. 'Dry him. Get him warm. Quick, take off his shirt.' I put my cheek to the man's nose, desperate to feel some movement. He was so cold, no sign of a breath. I freed my shawl, shaking it so Billy could help. 'Here, use this to get him warm.' We began rubbing his body, vigorously shaking the man's chest. Once again, I put my cheek against his nose. 'Breathe…God damn you, breathe.'

The faintest breath caressed my cheek and my heart jumped. 'He's alive, Billy.' I laid my head against the man's chest, the pounding in my ears making it almost impossible to hear. There was the tiniest movement, one faint beat. 'He's alive.' I was shaking, tears in my eyes. 'Quick, get him to the cave.'

Billy smiled. Sand smeared his face, his black hair dripping onto his bare shoulders. 'Ye just swore,' he said, grinning from ear to ear. 'Ye just swore and ye can't say ye *didn't* because I heard it plain as anything.'

Chapter Three

Through the half-light we surveyed the cave. It looked dry and recently used. Footprints led to the entrance, pitchforks were stacked against the sides. Billy's face fell. 'There's axes, Elowyn, and huge great clubs. We shouldn't be here.'

His words echoed my fear. 'We've no choice, Billy. We need to get him warm. See if there's any sacking – perhaps, behind that boat?'

The entrance was narrow but the cave was large, stretching well beyond what we could see. Two rowing boats lay at the centre, rows of barrels stacked high on either side. Lanterns lay on an upturned half-barrel and fishing nets were heaped on the ground. Through the dimming light, we looked for somewhere to lay the man. Wooden crates, chains and a mass of ropes coiled at my feet, but in the distance the ground looked softer. 'Over there – where there's more sand.'

Billy reached behind the boat, drawing out some sacking and we dragged the man across the cave, laying him on the soft ground, piling the rough sacks over him. I lifted his head for a softer pillow and pushed the damp strands of hair from across his face. Sand covered his forehead and I reached for my handkerchief, gently wiping it away from his eyebrows and eyes. He had been badly burned by the sun, his lips were swollen and raw but even in the half-light they seemed less blue. The cuts on his face were white and bloodless, more like grazes, and I ran my hands through the man's hair, feeling his scalp. The bruising on his temple looked viciously inflicted but there was no open wound.

I laid my hand on his chest to feel for movement. 'His breathing's deeper, but it's still too shallow. I think his heartbeat's stronger.'

Billy struggled out of his wet breeches and hung my stockings up to dry. 'He can't die, Elowyn. Not now.' We both knew we could neither leave him nor carry him; we had no choice but to stay. Darkness was almost upon us, the moonless sky threatening a pitch-black night.

'Any chance of getting those lanterns lit?'

'Don't think so.' Billy searched the cave in the half-light. 'There's nothing but barrels...and nets...and rope.'

'We'll make a bed and leave first thing.' I did not want Billy to feel my fear. We had food, we had shelter. We were warm.

I turned at the sound of moaning. The man had begun to shake, his whole body shivering so severely I thought he was convulsing. Billy piled more sacks onto him but jumped back in fright. A fist had flown at him, the man thrashing violently from side to side, and we drew back quickly, watching in fear as he heaved himself upright. He glared at us, his eyes wild and unseeing. He looked possessed, like a madman.

'Stay back, Billy. Don't go near him. You'll get hurt.'

He must have heard my voice, for his thrashing stopped and he fell back against the cave, his head slumping forward, his black hair falling over his face. I could see he was trying to speak, opening his cracked lips as if to tell us something, and I edged forward, putting my ear to his mouth. His lips were barely moving, his words making no sense, just a string of mumbled sounds, slurring together as if he was drunk.

'You're safe,' I whispered, 'but you must lie still if we're to get you warm.'

He started shuddering again, convulsing violently, and I tried to cover him. 'Quick, Billy, we need more sacks. Is there any brandy?'

'No, I've been lookin' all over. No brandy or rum.'

The force of the man's shivering was terrible to watch. We knelt by his side, piling on the sacking as best we could. At last his shivering stopped and he lay exhausted, his chest rising and falling in long, deep breaths. I felt for his heartbeat and my fear rose. 'He's not out of danger. His heart's too rapid. It's unsteady – there's no rhythm to it.'

Billy looked up at the catch in my voice. 'He can't die, Elowyn.'

The tide had turned, stronger waves rippling against the shingle outside. It was dark, the air fresh and intensely salty. These were the sounds and smells of my childhood – and with them came the same sense of anxiety. I needed to stay calm; after all, Mrs Pengelly would think I was with Mamm and Mamm would assume I had worked late and would expect me tomorrow – no one would be looking for us. All we had to do was get through the night. 'He could still die, Billy. I've seen it happen – he's not out of danger.'

At the sound of my voice, the man's hand moved slowly beneath the sacking, reaching out as if he wanted to touch me. I slid my hand under the coarse cloth and our fingers met, his hand slowly slipping over mine. His hand was large but his touch was gentle, just the slightest pressure squeezing my fingers and a shiver ran down my spine. 'You're safe,' I whispered, trying to sound confident, 'but you need to get warmer. You must sleep and gather your strength.' Despite my brave words, my fear was rising – everyone knew a cold shiver meant the passing of someone's soul. 'Billy, we've got to get him warmer – we need to do what I've seen others do. We need to lie next to him – use the heat from our bodies.'

Billy nodded, quickly wrapping the sacking around us as we lay next to the man. He was as cold as ice and I could not sleep but lay staring into the empty darkness, listening to him breathing softly beside me. It seemed to be working; the heat under the sacking was building, the man's naked body getting decidedly warmer. I felt strangely like crying, forcing back my sudden tears. His touch had been so gentle, the merest squeeze of his hand, but I knew he had been trying to thank me. Another cold shiver ran through me and I began pleading with the shadows...*Don't take his soul. Please don't take his soul*. I reached across and felt for his pulse – it was thin and faint, no sense of rhythm.

24

I must have fallen asleep, for something roused me. Lanterns were swinging in the distance, the cave diffused in a soft yellow light. I lay rigid, watching the lamplight flickering across the ceiling, outlining the figures of two men. They were making their way towards us, the light distorting their shadows, but I could see at once that they were big men with huge, hunched shoulders, thick necks and powerful arms. Their muffled footsteps were barely audible but their stride was purposeful. Next to me, the man's body was warm, the dark sacks covering us, but what if he and Billy woke with a start?

'Stay still. Don't move.' The man's whisper startled me. He was lying so still I had thought him asleep. Relief flooded through me.

The two men had stopped at the upturned barrel, lighting the other lanterns, and my fear spiralled. With more lanterns lit, they were bound to see us and I held my breath, my heart hammering so loudly I thought they would hear. They barely glanced round but took a lantern in each hand and headed out of the entrance, their shoes crunching on the shingle. 'They must be expecting a ship,' the man whispered in my ear.

I leaned over him, rousing Billy gently. 'Billy, wake up – we're in danger. Someone's using the cave.' Billy's eyes opened wide with fright. 'Two men are hanging lanterns outside...but they'll be back any moment...stay very still.'

The man reached round us, silently drawing more sacking over us. 'We're as safe here as anywhere,' he said. 'We're well hidden behind these crates. Lay back, lad. I'll cover you. Not a sound, you understand? Not a movement.' He sounded hoarse, as if he might cough at any moment, and I held my breath, praying we would not be seen or heard. He made no more sound, piling the sacking round us, and we lay rigid in the darkness listening as the men dragged the rowing boat out to the cove.

'Oh, no…my stockings!' I whispered. 'They're just above us…and Billy's breeches.'

The man reached up, grabbing our wet clothes, covering us over with yet more sacking. As he lay back, he slipped one arm round each of us, holding us tightly in the musty darkness. He squeezed Billy's shoulder. 'All right, lad?' I felt Billy nod. 'Best pretend you're asleep.'

A small gap allowed us air but it gave us sight of the two men. 'How about you? Are you all right?' I whispered.

'I've felt better – I've a head from hell.' His throat sounded sore, his voice parched.

The ship must be anchoring, the lamps guiding them safely through the rocks to the small stretch of sand. It must be the top of the tide, the early hours. The men began dragging the second rowing boat out, scraping it across the shingle, and I lay cursing my stupidity – no moon, no wind, near perfect conditions. Everyone knew it was a night to close shutters and lock doors. Those clubs would be used. My stomach twisted as I fought my fear. Only luck had made me venture so deep into the cave; if we had stayed at the entrance, we would have been seen.

Two men from the boat joined the others, both equally stocky and powerfully built; each with his hat pulled low, a thick scarf hiding his face. I could hardly see them, their long black coats merging with the darkness. The tallest of the men pointed to the barrels and they began working in pairs, grasping a barrel, rolling it quickly through the entrance and across the shingle. They worked so fast, emptying the cave with the utmost efficiency, and I lay burning beneath the heavy sacking, the man's arm around me. His face was so close; I could feel his breath on my cheek. 'What's in the barrels?' he whispered.

'It's not fish – the barrels look too heavy. It could be lime.' Hours ago, the man had been icy cold yet now the heat of his body scorched me through my dress. I was sweating, my face on fire; his naked body was pressing against me – all of him, not just his arm but his leg as well. Not that I did not want him there. I did. His presence made me feel safe, his strength giving me much needed courage.

The last barrel left the cave and the two men returned, dragging the rowing boats back to their hiding place. They did not speak but collected up the lanterns, extinguishing all but two. Holding the lanterns high, they looked around, glancing at the entrance, at the boats, taking one final look round the cave. One of them stooped to pick up some rope, throwing it down on the pile of coils, and I was petrified he would see us. Lamplight flickered round the cave, shadows dancing like phantoms across the ceiling, and I held my breath, praying that the lamplight would fade and the sound-less footsteps would vanish like the barrels into the darkness.

Then there was nothing but darkness. The lamps had vanished and we lay rigid beneath the heavy sacking, half expecting their return. It was too hot, sweat trickling down my back, but none of us dared to move. At last, the man's arm relaxed and he threw back the sacking. 'The tunnel must go deep into the cliff.' His voice was rasping. He began coughing violently and a wave of fear flooded through me.

'Quick, Billy, get the ale – they'll hear him.'

The man heaved himself upright, coughing and hawking as he leaned against the cave. 'I'm sorry…' He coughed again, his chest wracked by painful spasms. 'I'm…William—' A further bout of coughing stopped him from saying more. He leaned forward, using some sacking to wipe his mouth.

'Would ye like some ale?' Billy reached inside the basket, quickly pulling the cork, the tremor in his voice matching my own. If the men heard us they would come straight back. 'I'm Billy and this is Elowyn – Miss Liddicot, I should say.' The muscles next to me flexed as William held the flagon to his lips. He took long deep gulps, downing the ale before he coughed again. 'Thank you, Billy. I take it you both saved my life?'

My fear might have lessened but my sense had returned – a cold, nearly lifeless body was one thing but a burning, hawking, completely naked man was quite another. I threw off the covers and moved quickly from his side. 'Billy swam out and brought you back. I merely helped pull you in. We thought you were dead but you breathed…We got you warm, that's all.'

'You're a brave boy.' His voice was still hoarse. 'Spit on your hand, lad – for you and I are bound for life.' He tried to spit, succeeding eventually, and leaned towards Billy, holding out his hand. 'You did well keeping so still. Where are we?' In the silence that followed, he sensed something was wrong. 'What's up, lad?'

Billy shrugged. 'Elowyn don't let me spit. We're just round from Fosse — Penwartha Point, to be exact. Have some more ale.'

William took another long drink. Through the darkness his voice sounded mocking: 'You don't spit, what never? What about on your tools?' He wiped his mouth with the back of his hand. 'You must spit on them.'

'Don't have no tools.' Billy's reply sounded sullen and I sensed the pout was back.

'A big lad like you?' William whistled in surprise and I felt my lips tighten.

How dare he be so familiar? We had just saved his life yet he was already criticizing us. He had no right to mock. Outside, the night sky was lifting, the first tentative streaks of grey crossing the darkness. Shapes were taking form, the upturned barrel, the pitchforks and clubs against the walls. Without the barrels the cave seemed so much bigger, reaching deep into the rock. William's voice was growing stronger, even more unpleasant.

'What about when you wrestle? Surely, you spit when you shake?' Through the sullen silence he laughed softly. He sounded genuinely amused and my stomach twisted. 'Don't tell me...*Elowyn don't let you wrestle*. She's strict, your sister, and that's a fact.'

The man was too forward — he had no need to mock us; he had no manners and no sense of his place. He seemed oblivious to my displeasure, ignoring my turned shoulder and deep intakes of breath. Billy was encouraging him. 'She ain't my sister.'

'Ah, then she must be your *sweetheart*? No wonder you do everything she says!' He started laughing, his deep chuckle echoing around the cave.

Billy laughed back, giggling behind his hand. 'Course she ain't my sweetheart!'

William leaned over, nudging Billy in the ribs. 'That's good, because I'd hate us to fight over her…not now we're such good friends.'

Again, Billy laughed, a conspiratorial giggle I did not like. 'Are ye hungry?' he said, reaching inside the basket. 'There's Mrs Munroe's rabbit pie an' potted crab – I'm hungry an' all. Can we eat somethin', Elowyn?'

I grabbed my shawl, straightening my dress as I stood up. I felt strangely disappointed. For some reason I wanted the man to be nicer. His life had been so important to me and I wanted to like him, yet he was too familiar and I did not appreciate his tone. Men had to be kept at a distance – just one smile, one pleasant look, and they would start to take liberties. He would try to touch me, slide his hand across my bottom, pretend it was a mistake. 'Have what you like,' I said, reaching for some more sacking. It was a warm night and I would be quite comfortable beneath the stars.

I passed in front of him and he reached for my hand. 'Don't mind me teasing you,' he said softly. The spittle was still on his hand and I pulled mine quickly away; I was right, he was trying to touch me, just like every other man. We had saved his life and he was welcome to our food, but that was all. He watched me wipe my hand on the sacking, his eyes black in the darkness. 'I owe you my life, Miss Liddicot, and in my book that makes us bound. Spitting and shaking's but a promise I'll always be there for you.'

I stared back at him. I neither wanted nor needed him to be there for me. He was a rough, lewd fighter and would be a bad influence on Billy. Billy had to be kept safe. First thing tomorrow, I would make that clear. At the entrance of the cave I heard them laughing and turned in horror.

'There you go, Billy — we're bound for life. Tell me, lad, would you like me to teach you to wrestle?'

Dread made me catch my breath. Billy seemed so drawn to the man. He did not answer but hesitated and I stood, silently willing him to refuse. The eagerness in his voice ripped me like a knife.

'Could ye, William? Could ye really?'

'Big lad like you would make a fine wrestler. My friends all call me Will — you're a William too. See, Billy, it's no accident you saved my life. We're meant to be friends. Did you say rabbit pie? I can't tell you how much I love a rabbit pie.'

Billy dived deep into the basket again. 'Wait till ye taste this, Will. It's Mrs Munroe's — honest, there's none better. See what ye make of that!'

Chapter Four

I woke to see William sitting on a rock watching me. His hair was wet, only the slightest attempt made to sweep the black curls from across his face. His torn shirt was open at the neck, his breeches back where they belonged. He had been swimming – to nearly drown, yet swim again? The man was clearly reckless. Billy was still asleep by my side. They had both joined me, coming to lie next to me at the entrance of the cave. The stars had been so bright, the sound of waves soft against the shingle.

Pink streaks lit the horizon. 'We better get going as they may come back.' His voice was soft but his looks were rough. Bruises showed on his face. His cuts were red and sore but there was colour in his cheeks, strength and vigour in the way he moved. He had torn some sacking into strips and was winding them round his feet in place of boots. 'Did you come down that tiny track?' He seemed impressed.

I nodded. My hair was a tousled mess, my dress creased. I never looked like this, *never*. There was sand in my hair, grit between my toes. My bonnet was all but squashed. 'Turn round,' I snapped, reaching for my stockings. He must have laid them beside me. Billy's breeches lay folded by his side and the basket was packed, ready to go. 'Have you left Mamm anything?' I asked his turned back.

'Just the rhubarb jam – *Billy don't like rhubarb.*'

I resented his joke, his assured familiarity. He had been watching me and I resented that too. My shoes were less damp than I expected. They were almost dry, packed with sacking by William to act as a wick. 'It's not as steep as it looks – you've to hold the roots but the footholds are good…' I laid my hand gently on Billy's shoulder. 'Wake up, Billy, we need to go in case they come back.'

Billy led the way and we started up the track, William insisting he should go after me in case I slipped. The thought of him looking up and seeing my stockings made me reluctant to lift my skirts and I cursed my stupidity for not insisting I went last. A sudden tug made me look round and my worst fears were realized. Thorns had caught the delicate poplin on my skirt, snagging several threads, and my skirt was about to tear. I was holding tightly to a root and could not reach down. 'Don't touch,' I shouted in frustration.

He ignored both my scowl and my sharp tone. 'Stay still… there…all done. No one will notice.' His touch was surprisingly gentle, his large fingers releasing my skirt with hardly any damage, and for a brief, unwanted moment, I remembered the feel of his hand as it closed over mine.

'People *will* notice. I'll notice.' I bit my lip. Nathan might notice. This was not how I wanted to look.

At the top of the path I stopped to shake free my skirt. The early light shimmered pink on the sea. The cliff was waking, the first tentative calls of birds greeting the new dawn. The air smelt fresh and full of moisture, of damp grass and wild herbs, and I turned to check my skirt – three threads, no, four. I just hoped Mamm had a delicate enough needle for me to mend it. William was watching me, his brows as dark as his still wet hair. He had striking looks – rough looks. His hazel eyes were flecked with green, his nose straight. Dark stubble covered his strong chin but it was not just his cuts and bruises that marked him as trouble – the angle of his chin showed stubbornness and there was arrogance in the way he stood. Stubbornness, arrogance and muscles like that could only lead to fighting.

Yet he had a power about him that was hard to ignore. Billy must have felt it too; I could see the admiration in his eyes, an eagerness to please. 'We live at Coombe House in Fosse…Elowyn's a dressmaker – she has the shop above Pengelly's Boatyard. We're going to Porthcarrow to see her mamm…Ye can come with us if ye like…I can show ye the new lock…or ye can go to Fosse. We're halfway to both.' The words spilled from his mouth in an excited torrent and foreboding gripped me. He had said too much. He had told him everything.

'William's no more need of us,' I snapped. 'He's well fed and can continue by himself. We'll say goodbye and take our leave.' I turned my back, pulling Billy roughly behind me. A layer of dew covered the ground, glistening on the long grass that edged the path. 'Billy, how *could* you – a man like that?'

'I like him, Elowyn, and so should ye.' The scowl was back, the pouting lips.

'He knows everything about us now – everything.' Billy was not watching where he was going but kept turning round, stumbling on the rough ground. 'You're wrong to encourage him. He'll bring trouble. He's rough and he fights – and you know how I feel about men like that.' There were footsteps behind us and my fear spiralled. He would follow us, pester us, and we had no money to see him off.

'Elowyn...wait.' He must have seen how cross I was but stood staring down at me – a bold, penetrating stare, stripping me of all privacy. 'I'll leave you in peace but I must have your word not to tell anyone about the cave, or the ship, or about finding me. Not a word.'

Billy nodded, but I stared back into those bold eyes. They held danger, a sense of warning. 'Who are you?' I said, knowing I sounded a bit too like Lady Pendarvis.

A slight flicker crossed his face, a definite hesitation. 'My name's William Cotterell.'

'Then you have our word, Mr Cotterell – no cave, no ship and we've certainly never met you.' I used my firmest voice, the voice I used when traders tried to overcharge me or short change me because they thought me all curls and no brain. He had hesitated too long – he was lying. He did not want to give me his proper name.

We were on the last rocky outcrop, William's eyes still boring into my back. My courage was failing, my nerves getting the better of me. I wanted to be back in Fosse; I should never, ever, have agreed to Gwen's gentle persuasion.

Spending the day with Nathan Cardew seemed suddenly too daunting and I stared down at the new harbour, wanting to turn back.

I was almost too scared to look. Porthcarrow would be a morning town, like Fosse, and I should take heart from that. In morning towns, the sun greeted you when you went to work, helping you face the day with bright expectation. Yet here, I would have no work. Billy kept turning round, but I forced myself to look at the row of newly finished houses. They were so beautiful, rising above the lock, looking far out to sea. The Piermaster's house...I would have my very own parlour, my very own maid.

My cheeks began burning in mounting shame. What was I thinking? I was Elowyn Liddicot, prim, proper, exacting in my standards and well used to keeping men at bay. My blush burned deeper, hot tears filling my eyes. William had been naked, completely naked, and I had lain next to him with no thought of the consequences. Nathan must never know – no one must ever know.

Just a short descent would take us down to the yard of Mamm's cottage. We sat staring down at the closed back door, hoping Jack Deveral would not be in. I had only met him twice but both times I had hated what I saw. Perhaps my childhood fears clouded my judgement – perhaps, he did not have fists that clenched in an instant, the sudden sideways swipe that would send me flying. Even so, just a look, a frown or a sudden flare in temper and I would be a child again, clutching Tom's hand to run and hide. I took a deep breath. *I could read and write. I had a living. I had savings. No man would do that to me again.*

'Ye all right?' Billy slipped his arm through mine. 'Only ye look so sad.'

'We're too early, that's all. We'll wait until we see some sign of life. It won't be long; Mamm always gets up early.'

Mamm's cottage lay half a mile down the beach from the new harbour – one of two ancient stone cottages lying at the mercy of the fierce south-easterly gales but sheltered and safe in the prevailing westerlies. They had once been thatched but were now roofed in fine, grey slate and stood extended and improved, their newly refurbished fish cellars stretching far beneath them. Jack Deveral and his neighbour John Polkerris may hate Sir James for his new harbour and meddling interference, but they had been the first to prosper. Everyone wanted their fish.

On the clifftop, the new battlements stood stark against the early-morning sky. Major Trelawney had worked tirelessly to ensure that no French ship would ever threaten Sir James' new harbour. The cannons were in place, the volunteer force mustered and trained, the men already mounting a watch across the bay. So much had been achieved in such a short time – not only the battlements but the harbour itself. The inner lock had been dug, the outer harbour dredged and strong granite walls built like arms to enclose it. It was already drying, a band of seaweed lying in a perfect arc across the sand.

Ships lay at anchor, their sterns pulled seaward by the

outgoing tide. Billy pointed to a boat lying wedged in the sand. 'See the lugger that's beachin' – that's Jack Deveral's new boat. He can't have gone out.'

A grand hotel now dominated the lock entrance, the harbour office was nearly complete and the weighing room was well in use. Two new yards had been fenced and even the rope-walk was finished; the bark-house had been newly roofed, the cooperage doubled in size. I took in the changes, nerves making my stomach flutter – all this achieved under the watchful eyes of Nathan Cardew.

Plumes of smoke rose from the lime kilns, cockerels heralding the new day. Yet the day had long since started. Shouts echoed across the early stillness, hoists rising amongst the rigging, the huge barrels swinging through the air. Farm boys leaned on their long sticks, still half asleep as they brought the dairy herd down for milking. We watched them cross the brickworks and amble slowly up the main street to the old farm buildings.

'There's your mamm, throwing out slops.' We watched her open the chicken coop.

'What will you do today, Billy?'

'I'll be all right – I'll watch for when ye leave.' His sullenness had returned. 'Is Mr Cardew takin' ye to chapel?'

'He said he would. He's to come to Mamm's at ten o'clock.'

Billy stood up and scowled, glaring down at me, his face puckering, his eyes filling with tears. I had never seen him like this before. 'Ye should tell him ye're church, not chapel,' he said, turning quickly to run down the path. 'Tell him ye *don't* want to live here,' he shouted over his shoulder. He was out of sight, behind the gorse bushes, but I heard him stop, his shoes scuffing the stones. 'And tell him ye don't want to give up yer business.'

'But, Billy...' I wanted to turn back. I should never have come. I should never have let Gwen persuade me. What if Nathan Cardew tried to kiss me?

Chapter Five

1 Shore Cottages
Sunday 5th June 1796, 6:00 a.m.

'Come in, Elly dear. It's only me what's up. I was expecting ye late yesterday, not this early.' Mamm stood at the door, clearly taken aback. 'Look at me not dressed yet...Come in, but be quiet. Jack's still sleepin' so mind ye don't wake him.' She was still in her nightgown, a shawl wrapped round her shoulders. Her hair was tousled beneath her cap, curling, just like mine. She had once been as fair as me but had long since turned grey. 'Go through, but quiet, lass. Don't let that catch slam – Lowenna's sleepin' too. How come ye're so early?'

I would never look like that. The fear that never left her eyes, the constant looking up, checking she was not doing something wrong. Every time I saw that look, or her hands tremble, I felt like shaking her. 'I fell asleep doing the hems but everything's finished. Mrs Pengelly thinks I came yesterday but I slept at the shop. She sent you this jam...and Gwen sends her love – she's getting very tired.'

'I'm not surprised.' She took the jam and smiled, placing

it on the dresser along with everything else. 'Sit down, my dear. I'll get ye something to drink. Only, the fire's out and I can't rake the grill – not yet awhile. Will ye have some ale?' I shook my head, trying to find a chair that would not further snag my gown. Already, she was wringing her hands, her voice barely above a whisper. 'Ye look beautiful, Elly dear, but then ye always do. Ye're such a fine lady now – every inch a match for Nathan Cardew.'

'I'm sorry I missed your birthday. Here, happy birthday.' I kissed her cheek and sat down. Three and a half hours to wait in this filthy kitchen with its rough flagstones and oppressively small windows – it was darker inside than out. The table stood littered with the remains of a meal, bread left exposed, pewter plates scraped clean and pushed to one side. Mice would have crawled all over that bread. How could I have thought to stay here? It must be that holding me back – not leaving Coombe House, not leaving the shop, but returning to what should have been left well behind.

She smiled at the silk handkerchief with her embroidered name encircled by colourful flowers. 'Oh, Elly...it's that delicate, honest.' She searched the room for something to say. 'The fishin's been good. We've the smoke house full and there's plenty of salt left for the packin'. Jack don't like the new harbour but they like his fish all right. He's supplyin' the hotel – we can hardly cope with the need.'

'Looks like he has a new boat – is that his lugger in the bay?'

She nodded but her eyes looked fearful. 'Not so loud, love. Ye do look lovely. Is everythin' well at Coombe House? How's yer uncle? How's Tom? Workin' all hours, I shouldn't wonder.' She began clearing away the plates, soundlessly creeping round the table like the mice watching her. Instinctively, I looked for bruises. She had become so good at hiding them.

'Does he treat you well?' I whispered as she finally sat down.

Her eyes flew to the door. 'Course he does. He's a full-blooded man, mind, but I like that.'

'You shouldn't have left Fosse. You had a perfectly good home – you have Tom and me and Uncle Thomas. You don't need to be here. You could be with the baby, helping Gwen.' My voice was rising and I checked myself. I was not a *fine lady*, I was a dressmaker and I worked day and night so I did not have to live like this: watching how others did it, unpicking, sweeping the floor, dusting, tidying the rolls of fabric until I was allowed to pick up a needle. Then, I had cut, sewn and stitched until my eyes were sore and my fingertips numb. And I still did.

I was not a fine lady. I had learned everything from Lady Polcarrow – Rose Pengelly, as she was then, so insistent, smiling when I got things right, shaking her head and scowling when I made mistakes. She read me Mary Wollstonecraft, taught me calculations, reading, writing, opening a whole new world to me. Thanks to her, I was meticulous at keeping books, my clear handwriting and well-drawn columns copied by every seamstress passing through Mrs Pengelly's school of needlework. Everything entered twice – what was spent, what was earned; what was due, what was paid – everything dated and clear.

'You could come back, Mamm. You could help me in the shop.'

Mamm's mouth clenched. 'Ye must understand, Elly love. I'm born a fishwife an' I'm good at it. I've been guttin' fish an' stringin' them up since I was in my cradle! It's what I do. I'm not sayin' ye should do it, but it's an honest day's work an' I enjoy it.' She sniffed, getting out a dirty handkerchief. 'Ye've come so far and I'm that proud of ye...but I'm a woman, Elly, with a woman's needs – I like a man in my bed. An' he's not like yer father – he don't beat me.'

Her words made me flinch; even now, I could see father's hunched shoulders, the anger in his eyes as his temper flared. I would lie awake at night, listening for his drunken tread, waiting for the first punch. She reached across the table, a waft of stale fish oil drifting towards me, and I must have recoiled. Her face filled with sudden sadness. It was just that smell that drove me to knock on Madame Merrick's door four years ago. Sixteen years of gutting and scraping fish, cramming pilchards and herrings into barrels, pressing them for oil. Of heaving cartloads of bones and blood to the fields, fish scales lodged beneath my fingernails; the relentless smell clinging to every part of me, my hair, my skin, my hideous brown shawl. I glanced at Mamm's hands, guilt slicing through me. It should not be like this, I should not feel uncomfortable in my own mother's home.

'D'you have a needle, Mamm? Only, I've snagged my dress.'

She rose from the table and smiled. 'I've a needle an' a comb, an' I'll bring ye a basin of water...No, don't ye go getting' up, I don't suppose ye know how to work a pump these days.' She paused at the door, turning sadly. 'When ye're in yer pier house, ye need never come here. I'll come to ye an' I won't go anywhere near yer new parlour. I'll stay in the kitchen – or the yard, if ye prefer. I won't shame ye, I promise. I'll be that glad just havin' ye near me.'

Shame made me sit still while Mamm dressed my hair. She had read my thoughts and my heart felt ripped in two. Lowenna Deveral sat opposite me, her narrow eyes not leaving my face. She had a long face, a pinched complexion and sallow skin. 'Ye eatin' here or with Mr Cardew?'

I resented her tone. Half an hour more and I could leave this place. She had scowled all through the mending of my gown, her hostile glare adding to my nerves. 'I think his sister's doing us a cold platter.'

'*A cold platter*,' she mocked.

Above us, the floorboards creaked. A man was hawking, spitting, his heavy feet stamping angrily down the wooden stairs. Mamm and Lowenna stared quickly at the door and I held my breath, my heart hammering. The front door slammed and their frightened eyes turned to mine, Lowenna with her pinched face, Mamm with her timid smile and half-shrugged shoulders. I could hardly hold back my anger. Four years ago, Uncle Thomas had come to our house, packed our very few belongings and taken us to Fosse. He had swept Mamm up and carried her to safety, yet this was how she repaid him?

'Your hands look very sore – both of you,' I said sharply. She could leave. She could just walk out and never come back. 'D'you bandage them? Have you goose fat?'

Lowenna shook her greasy hair. She looked ready to jump at her own shadow. What was she, about fifteen? There was a smudge of mud on her arm, dirt on her face. 'Goose fat's for cookin' an' we've no bandages.'

'I've got some calico in the storeroom. It would tear well and you're welcome to it. As it happens, I've got several spare rolls so I'll bring some next time.'

'Could ye, love? 'Twould help a lot. Any calico gets taken to cover the clay. There's a terrible row goin' on – the coal dust's gettin' everywhere, contaminating the clay. Now, who could that be?' The back door opened and a young woman peered round. 'Ah, it's Bethany. Come in, dear. Have ye brought young Sam?'

The woman's timid smile lit her pale face. 'Is it all right? Only I saw Mr Deveral leavin' the house so I thought 'twould be all right.' I saw her eyes widen with pleasure at my gown.

Mamm straightened her back, shaking her filthy apron. 'Hand me yer babe, lass. Look at him, growin' so big. This is Elowyn, my *daughter*.' I heard the pride in her voice and my shame returned. The woman stopped looking at my gown and began blushing, staring suddenly at the ground, unable to look me in the eye.

'It's…very nice to meet ye, Miss Liddicot…only I've heard about ye, of course.'

Her voice was gentle yet she seemed ill at ease, stammering as she spoke. She was painfully thin, her eyes shadowed by dark circles, her hair lank. She could have been so pretty. She had fine bones, a sweet, timid smile and with Mrs Munroe's pies, she would have been beautiful. Her thin hands clasped the baby and she handed him to Mamm. As they passed him in front of me, I took him from her – a pale, miserable child with a running nose. 'Where did you get his clothes?' I asked. They had been finely cut and stitched with great precision. There were box pleats, perfect gussets, faultless sleeves and collar. 'Who sewed these?'

She could barely look me in the eye. 'I did. I learned it from me mamm.' Her thin fingers smoothed over the baby's jacket, caressing the material, and I looked at her own clothes more closely. The same perfect stitching, working with the bias, not against it, her dress as well made as anything I could have done a year ago. Across the upper edge was the most exquisite embroidery and my heart soared.

'You've real talent, Bethany. Would you like to work for me? I could give you a job – we've enough work to keep you busy.' I had only ever taken on seamstresses from Mrs Pengelly's school, but Bethany showed such flair. Someone like her would be a godsend. 'My shop's in Fosse. The pay's good. You could start late and leave early – I'd let you work eight thirty to five.'

Mamm and Lowenna stared, open mouthed. I know I sounded just like Lady Pendarvis but I could not help it. I hired seamstresses all the time, dismissed them, too. I ran a profitable business and I had the means of giving this woman employment. If I sounded like Lady Pendarvis, it was because I *was* like her. I copied her every move, bargained like her, haggled like her, cajoled and encouraged like her. I chose fabrics women had no idea they should be wearing and cut patterns women had no idea would suit them. I had learned my trade from the very best, and being the very best meant customers came back for more.

'I'm sorry, Miss Liddicot.' There were tears in Bethany's eyes. She grabbed her baby who had started to cry. 'I'd love to, ye must know that. I'd love to sew an' I'd love to earn, but I can't. Not now. My husband's sick...he can't look after the bairns. I've got two others an' I'm...' She looked at the ground. 'I'm...' She could not speak. 'I'm sorry, that's all.'

Mamm hurried across the kitchen and opened her larder, lifting a package from the slate shelf. 'Don't ye worry, Bethany love. Here's yer fish, it's all gutted an' ready an' there's a couple of crabs popped in as well...an' take this bread, I baked it yesterday – best hide it under yer shawl. How's Mr Cooper doin'?

Tears welled in Bethany's eyes. 'They say he might lose his leg. It smells awful an' he's in that much pain. If he loses his leg he'll never work again.'

Mamm reached for her purse. 'Here, my love, a little to keep yer goin'. It's not much...And do yer boys like rhubarb jam? Take that an' all. Bless ye, don't ye go givin' up hope. Legs do mend – I've seen crush injuries make good, so just keep yer hopes up.' She reached under the table, drawing out a flagon. 'Give this to Mr Cooper. It's good an' strong an' will kill the pain. Can ye manage that, love? Lowenna, best go with her. Hide it under yer shawl.' Mamm was looking at me, her eyes strangely serious.

She glanced quickly down. 'Mr Cardew will be here soon. Ye'd best go down an' meet him as he'll not come to the door. He's arranged fer the cart to leave at four – I've a parcel for Gwen an' somethin' for Tom.' She looked suddenly puzzled. 'Ye didn't come by yerself, did ye? Where's Billy?'

'He's gone to the lock – couldn't wait to get there!'

She smiled as she waved me down the path. I think I smiled back but I could not be certain. Now it was happening, I felt so fearful. Gwen had known Nathan Cardew for years and Tom could do nothing but sing his praises, but I knew so little about him. We had spoken only twice since we met at their wedding.

Chapter Six

I saw him before he saw me. He was on the lock side, talking to a group of men. The men were nodding vigorously, touching their caps. He took out his fob watch and turned in my direction but a man approached, holding high a wad of papers. Nathan examined the papers and pointed to the hoist suspended over the third ship, shaking his head at yet another interruption. He shouted something to the men on the dock and ran up the steps, crossing the narrow lock gate with long, easy strides.

The last time I had seen him had been in Mrs Pengelly's parlour. Seen him through a haze of awkwardness, heard him through pounding ears. He had looked so handsome, his well-cut jacket fitting him perfectly, his breeches a fine woollen twill. His cravat had not been to my taste, but his hair had been freshly washed, his smile eager and full of hope. We had glimpsed a side to Nathan Cardew that very few must see – not the assured man of business, the supervisor of works, but a vulnerable contender for my hand. His nervousness had taken us both by surprise.

'Poor lad, did you see his hands shaking?' Mrs Pengelly had whispered the moment Sam showed him out. 'He clearly adores you and it was very polite of him to ask my permission. Proper courting! Well, there's a thing. Was I right to say yes?'

We had both giggled. A man among men, one of them, the best of them; everyone spoke of him with respect. If something needed doing, you asked Nathan Cardew. Watching him now, I felt strangely light-headed. I should have eaten at Mamm's but the thought of food had turned my stomach. Excitement tingled with fear. I had seen him watching me at the wedding, his eyes following me round the room. Gwen had introduced us and he had bowed so politely. He seemed shy of me, almost lost for words. He was so formal, so anxious to please. He did not want to force his hand, just wanted me to get to know him. He wanted to show me where he worked, where we would live. It felt like pain now, dizziness and pain, my stomach turning somersaults. Ten Sundays, he had told Mrs Pengelly, ten Sundays of *stepping out* – just like his parents and their parents before them.

He was running along the shore path, anxiously re-checking his fob watch. Under his hat, his hair caught the morning light – the colour of sand, streaked by sunshine. He looked up and smiled, a shy, almost boyish smile, and I thought I would faint. 'Miss Liddicot…Elowyn, I hope you haven't been waitin' long.' He had a square face with a cleft in his strong chin, his blue eyes alight with pleasure. 'When did you get here? Only I heard you worked late.'

'I came this morning, as early as I could…' His Sunday clothes made him look so prosperous and my anxiety spiralled. I was under-dressed, too informal. I had worn my yellow poplin for Mamm but it was so creased. I should have worn my cotton lawn, even my silk. He was dressed so well, he would think me shabby. My cheeks began burning, hot tears filling my eyes.

He held out his arm and I slipped mine through his, smiling back at him as we walked down the path. Mamm would be watching from the tiny leaded window, never guessing the shame I felt. His arm felt strong, taut, altogether unnerving. He seemed not to notice my discomfort, helping me gently down the steps. 'I thought we'd go straight to chapel; Mr Hearne's got a meetin' afterwards so Ruth's bringing a basket of food down to the office. I hope you don't mind – I suppose it's a chance for you to see where I work. ' His smile faded. 'Are you all right? What is it?' He stopped, the slight pressure on my arm making me do the same.

I had resented Billy's parting words but I knew he was right. Not about leaving Fosse, but because Nathan might expect me to go with him to chapel. They were so different. I loved everything about church, I was used to it, and the thought of chapel seemed like a gulf opening up between us. I knew I had to speak plainly before things went further. 'Mr Cardew, Nathan…I have to tell you. It's important… but it's not easy.' My stomach began twisting. 'Gwen's chapel …and she may have led you to believe that I'm chapel…but I'm not…I'm church. And with your sister being married to the preacher…I think it might put some strain between us.' My heart was hammering, I could hardly say the words straight.

He seemed momentarily shocked, his brows contracting across his handsome forehead. 'So you'd want to stay church, not chapel?' I held my breath, thinking this would be the end of his courtship, but he looked concerned, the tenderness in his voice making my heart jolt. 'There's no church in Porthcarrow but St Austell's only three miles away and Fosse is only four. It would mean a long cart ride, but I don't see why we couldn't do it.'

'That's very kind of you.' I felt suddenly overcome. I had not expected him to show such kindness.

'My family will just have to understand that's the way it's goin' to be. I don't want to change anythin' about you, Elowyn – nothin' at all.' He looked down at the calluses on his hands. 'But I understand there might be things you want to change about me.'

We started walking again, side by side. He did not seem frightening at all, far from it. He had a way of looking at me that drew me to him – intimate but not familiar, respectful, but friendly. 'Father made our name,' he said softly, 'an' we've risen high in respect and standin', but we've not long mixed in society. I've worked hard to improve myself,' he stopped, looking down at the ground, 'but I'm ready and willin' to learn your ways.' He seemed relieved by my smile, holding his arm out again and I slipped mine through his as if it was the most natural thing to do.

'I like everything in its right place,' I said carefully. 'Things have to be just so – has Gwen told you how I fussy I am?'

By his smile, I could see that she had. 'I'll be your willin' pupil, Elowyn. I'll take my boots off at the back door and I'll hang up my coat an' hat. I'll do everythin' you tell me. We'll have silver cake-forks and fine china cups – just like Mrs Pengelly.'

'And a silver butter knife?' I laughed.

'One for each day of the week! I'll never bring tools into the house – and I'll always wash and change before dinner.' I smiled up at him; that must have been Tom. What else had they told him?

We reached the cobbled road with the first of the large pier houses. Ahead of us, the lock gates stood holding back the water, the upright masts of the ships strangely incongruous against the empty sweep of sand in the outer harbour. The lock looked busy, mules and wagons crammed side by side in the dock, the men rolling large barrels along the quay-side. Heavy sacks hung suspended above the ship's holds. Nathan followed my gaze. 'Sir James is determined to make his harbour pay. We're to use every tide, night and day, even Sunday – coal and timber in, clay and tin out.'

He had definite presence. He was not tall but his demeanour was commanding. He was slimly built but seemed powerful in the way he stood – proud, shoulders back, not quite but nearly master of all he surveyed. A man and woman hurried past; the man bowing, the woman dipping a quick curtsy and we stopped, gazing across the dry outer harbour. Gigs lay beached on the sand, seagulls strutting along the glistening shingle; cormorants stood with wings outstretched on the exposed rocks. Already the sun was warm on my back.

Nathan seemed to hesitate. His voice grew intimate and my mouth went dry. 'I'm glad you spoke your mind. I'd like to think you'll always tell me what you're thinkin'.' A wave of happiness flooded through me – he was so honest, so easy to talk to. Mamm never spoke her thoughts to Father, never – I had never heard them speak to each other like this.

In the distance, a bell began to toll and he looked up, his smile turning strangely boyish. 'If we're goin' to miss chapel, I've time to show you round – I'm glad you thought to wear stout shoes.'

It was as if a weight lifted from my shoulders. So this was the real Nathan Cardew, the man behind his public image. I was thrilled by his gentlemanlike manners, intrigued by his sense of boyish vulnerability. He seemed to hold me in such respect, hoping, not presuming, I might return his love. The pressure on my arm tightened. 'Mr Perys is Harbourmaster and this is his house.' His voice was full of pride, his eyes surveying the granite house with obvious delight. 'It's the biggest of the seven houses. Can you guess how many bricks in each chimney?'

I stared up at the slate roof, the two chimneys. 'No. Tell me – how many bricks? How long did each house take to build? Who lives where?'

My questions made him laugh; he raised his eyes heaven-ward. 'You'd never believe the fuss. Buildin' the houses was nothin' compared to the wrangle I'm havin' over who's to live where! Talk about dogs fightin' over a bone.' His voice turned conspiratorial. 'Take this next house – we've two clay agents, both insistin' on havin' it. The agent from Spode and Wolfe says he saw it first, yet the agent from Wedgwood claims the larger family.' He shrugged his shoulders.

'So, who's to have it?'

'Neither, as it happens. Both lost out to Mr Hellyar, the tin assayer – the deeds are already drawn.' He pursed his mouth, showing his displeasure, walking slowly up to the next house. 'It got very heated but it doesn't stop there… This next one's under offer to Mr Drew, the leat engineer, but he's fallen foul of Mr Sellick so we can't put them next each other.'

The houses were even more beautiful the closer you got. They had perfect symmetry with deep stone sills and wooden shutters, but I was more delighted by the tone of Nathan's conversation. He was so easy to talk to, not frightening at all. 'Who's Mr Sellick?'

'He's one of the clay speculators – he's leased the bottom sett and is ready to move in.' A furrow formed across his brow. 'We'll need more houses – the last three leases are already signed. The clay's beginning to make a profit and there's goin' to be a rush.'

The last two cottages lay joined under a slate roof and I held my breath, hardly daring to look. They were also built from granite, each with a newly painted front door and shutters at the windows. An alley led between the two houses and I caught a glimpse of an iron pump with an ornate handle. Nathan seemed suddenly nervous, a flash of uncertainty crossing his face, as if fearful of getting hurt. He seemed so vulnerable and a wave of tenderness filled my heart. His eyes caught mine.

'These houses are put aside for the Revenue Officer and

Piermaster…and though I can't promise anythin', I've every expectation of bein' given this larger house.' His words were barely audible, a slight catch to his voice. 'There's a parlour and an office and there's a third bedroom over the alley – see that extra window?' I could hardly look. The windows faced the lock, just as I imagined they would. A lump formed in my throat, my heart hammering.

He reached for my hands, holding them as if he was scared he might crush them. His hands were rough, warm, burning like my cheeks. 'Elowyn, you must take your time – see whether this new life would suit you or not, but for me… well, for me, you must know how much I love you. I will take care of you an' give you everythin' within my power to give you. Every hour's toil, every day's work will be worked thinkin' only of you.' His voice was tender, a look of pleading deep within his eyes.

The lump in my throat was set to choke me. I had not expected anything so soon – his talk of devotion, his declaration of love suddenly filling me with panic. He seemed to sense my distress and let go of my hands. 'I know it would be askin' a lot of you, Elowyn…I'd be takin' you from Mrs Pengelly and bringin' you here…but you'd have your mother and maybe we could persuade Tom and Gwen to join us. But I mean what I say – no man could work harder or more willingly than I will for you.'

He held out his arm as if not expecting a reply and I slipped my hand through his, looking anywhere but at him. The terrace was yet to be finished and I was grateful for the excuse to look down at the cobbles waiting to be laid. A group of people passed and I must have nodded and smiled. I think I asked the right questions but my mind was in turmoil. He was so handsome, so attentive, it was almost frightening.

I tried to calm my fear and we walked on, Nathan proudly showing off the new town. He knew the price of everything, the quantities for each building. Pride for his work shone in his face. He was brimming with plans – two new rows of cottages, another seamen's hostel and separate lodgings for the pilots; there was enough work for another blacksmith, another cooperage, another carter.

A rough path led to an old barn with a bell hanging from the door. The courtyard was clean and neatly swept and I recognized the donkey cart standing by the gate. 'That's the makeshift chapel. My brother-in-law's happy enough with it till we've the new one built.' He began leading me across the green, pointing out his father's brickworks, and I lifted my skirts, taking care as we crossed the rough grass. Hens scattered as we approached, a tethered goat bleating in protest at her rope.

A pile of milk churns stood waiting outside the milking parlour. Dogs were barking, pigs grunting, geese squabbling. Behind us, the grey stones of the disused engine house shone silver against the blue sky. Nathan pointed up the hill. 'Behind those spoilings are the settlin' pits – see those reed thatches? That's the clay dryin'. They dig the clay further up.' I nodded, looking to where he pointed. 'The setts are allocated at random so there's no knowing if there's clay's underneath. If the leaseholder strikes lucky, he's every chance of turnin' a profit. It's their responsibility to dig safely an' clear away the spoils – Sir James is very particular about that. He says I must fine anyone who leaves a mess or constitutes a hazard.' He smiled. 'You'll be pleased to know everything's to be kept tidy and in its right place.'

I rather liked his gentle teasing and smiled back, breathing in the scent of wild herbs. Skylarks were singing above us, swathes of wild flowers carpeting the fields. There was no river, just the gentle curve of the bay, the slope of the hill and one man's determination to bring prosperity to his land. Ships were anchoring, pilot gigs racing to be the first to reach the new ships entering the bay. This would be my life – the bleating of sheep, the sound of cattle; the clatter of cartwheels down to the harbour. It was so beautiful, I wanted to stay where we were, sit down among the flowers and watch the ships. Nathan was frowning.

'Sir James is insistin' this land should stay common ground but space is tight. Four ton of coal's needed for every ton of tin – if we're to have our own smeltin' works we'll need bigger ore floors. I've got ballast from the ships pilin' up which I could use to line the floors but that's not all – we've thousands of staves for the casks and nowhere to put them!' He stopped suddenly. 'I'm sorry, Elowyn, I must take care not to bore you – I live and breathe my work. How're Gwen and Tom? When's their bairn expected?'

'They don't know exactly.'

An old oak tree stretched above us and he reached for my hand, helping me over the twisted roots. His jacket brushed against me, his outstretched hand burning me through my bodice. His face was so close, the deep furrow on his forehead,

58

the lines by his mouth. At rest, his face looked stern, yet when he smiled his eyes looked so blue. They almost dazzled me with their intensity, drawing me to him with a power of their own.

He removed his hand. 'When we cut across here, we'll have done the circle. This side's known as *the workin's* and you'll see why.' He pointed to the buildings, the sun catching the light in his hair. I was thrilled by his courtesy – his sense of propriety. I had thought he was going to keep his hand resting on my waist. Men did that. They always tried to touch. 'There's the timber store, the bark-house and the harbour office behind the weigh house – and that's the brewery.'

We joined the road down to the harbour. Most of the buildings were stone but the new hotel was brick, so too the granary, the rope house, the bark-house. No wonder Nathan's family had grown so prosperous. Their bricks were the best and everyone wanted them. We stopped outside a large stone building.

'This is the main harbour office…but my office is down this alley. It's a bit small but I've got the best view of the lock. It used to be a stable and my office is up these stairs.' He stopped in front of a wooden door, to our right, the old stables crammed with broken equipment; cartwheels and old yokes hanging on the wall. He seemed suddenly shy. 'Perhaps we should wait for Ruth?'

'Mr Cardew, come quick.' Behind us, a man was hurtling down the alley, almost too breathless to speak. 'The cows is out…they're goin' everywhere – tramplin' Mr Perys' potatoes an' ruinin' his vegetables. Buggers broke through the top fence.' He hawked and spat. 'Some are headin' for the harbour.'

Nathan swung round, reaching inside his jacket for his key. 'Dammĭt…I'll have to go.' He opened the door, shouting to the man, 'Get back to the cows. I'm coming.' He rushed me up the narrow wooden stairs, his sudden anger taking me by surprise. He threw down his jacket, disappearing behind a door. 'I'm sorry, I need to change. This was *not* meant to happen.'

A moment later, he reappeared. He looked rueful, apologetic. 'Elowyn, I'm so sorry. Ruth made me promise *best* clothes and *best* manners but I can't help it. Shoddy work makes me angry an' it's best you know me as I am – there must be no pretence.' He pointed to his corduroy breeches, his worsted wool jacket. 'I'm a builder, Elowyn, a brickmaker's son, and when work's not up to scratch, I can't help gettin' angry. That new fence has only just gone up and if the cows have broken through, it means corners have been cut. I can't tolerate sloppiness. Sir James deserves the best an' I'm determined he'll have the best.' His eyes searched mine, his mouth held tight.

His anger had startled me but I understood his determination to build the best; in fact, I would have felt the same. He looked down as if he had lost all hope of my hand.

'And I'm a fisherman's daughter,' I found myself replying. 'I too have risen through hard work and determination – my gowns are the very best because I'll not tolerate sloppiness. If the sewing's not perfect, I make the seamstresses do it again – sometimes I make them do it several times.'

Our eyes locked and we stood smiling shyly. We had both spoken from our hearts, the veneer of politeness swept aside. He reached for my hands, turning my palms upwards, bringing them to his lips. He kissed first one, then the other, a wave of excitement flooding through me. 'I love everything about you, Elowyn. I hope you know that.'

'You'd better hurry,' I said, unable to look up. 'I'll wait for Ruth. There's plenty for me to watch.'

Chapter Seven

His office was sparsely furnished, only a large desk and a small table with three chairs squeezed into the corner. He had left the door to his bedroom slightly open and I caught a glimpse of a small couch and a chest for clothes. The room was no bigger than a cupboard, the jug and basin balancing on the window sill. A large window stretched the length of the office and I stood staring down at the dock.

It seemed so much bigger from above, the huge storage cellars cutting deep into the hillside. Yoked horses and wagons stood waiting along the quayside, the ships two abreast, cranes stretching high into the air. Men were loading the clay, heaving the heavy casks high into the air and into the waiting holds. Others were balancing on the dried blocks stacked high on the wagons, their long-handled shovels sending the clay down the wooden chutes. A lock with no river – it seemed almost impossible. Every square yard cut by hand, every ton of spoil removed by cart, and Nathan Cardew at the centre of it all. He was offering me so much.

Papers littered his desk, huge leather-bound books piled high on top of each other. A stack of accounts caught my eye and my curiosity soared. How could you keep everything in order with so much going on? I edged towards his desk, unable to stop myself. The sums were incredible, the quantities almost unimaginable – hundreds of bushels of lime, tons of sand, thousands of nails. It made the quantities I used seem totally insignificant; everything in such vast numbers, so many payments – blacksmiths, carpenters, farriers.

My accounts were kept with such precision but how did he do it? Ruth would be here any moment but I was bound to hear her footsteps on the creaking stairs. I could not help myself, but edged nearer, opening the top leather-bound ledger. I stared in surprise – such a messy jumble of crossings out and smudges. I could hardly read the entries, let alone make sense of them. Nothing was entered twice. If this had belonged to one of my seamstresses, I would have put a line straight through it.

I felt immediately disappointed that Nathan could not do better, yet the more I looked at the jumbled entries, the more my heart softened. There seemed too much work for just one man. I picked up the large red rent book. The same smudges and crossings-out, yet the figures were tidier, the columns neater. Nathan's writing was small and I had to peer closely at the pale ink.

Several rents had remained unpaid, the name Samuel Cooper immediately catching my eye. It must be Bethany's husband and I looked closer, making out a list of fines. Six names were on the list, including that of Samuel Cooper, but three names had been crossed through with *payment received* written alongside. Not so Samuel Cooper, his rent remained unpaid, a sixpenny fine added to the rent.

Disgust churned my stomach. How could anyone fine an injured man with a wife and young family because he owed rent? Poor Bethany. I turned back the pages, my fingers trembling. How could Nathan do that? I could hardly read for my sense of injustice.

It seemed Samuel Cooper had not paid rent for eight weeks but the closer I looked, the more puzzled I became. Each previous week had a cross through it, the words *rent rescinded* written alongside. Other names had also been crossed through, with *fine withdrawn* scribbled by their side. Yet no money had been entered. I checked the incomings, trying to match the columns on the other page. Definitely no money had been entered, the fines and rent vanishing into thin air. It could only be an act of kindness, and for a moment I thought my heart might burst.

The stairs creaked and I closed the ledger, getting back to the window just in time. Ruth Hearne peered anxiously round the door. 'I've just seen Nathan roundin' up the cows!' I could see the family resemblance – the same light brown hair, the same blue eyes. Under her bonnet, two plaits coiled round her ears. Her gown was a plain dark grey, her shawl, spun cotton. She seemed shy of me, smiling timidly, her face full of sweetness. 'You're every bit as lovely as he said you were,' she said, holding out her hands. 'I hope you like it here. I've been that excited about meetin' you.'

'And I've been looking forward to meeting you.'

She looked suddenly startled. It must have been the way I spoke but she smiled again, stuttering slightly, 'Ah…Miss Liddicot…you're such a fine lady…you've such a beautiful gown. Mr Hearne sends his apologies but vagrants have settled in the upper wood an' he's taking food and clothes to them.' Her courage seemed to return. 'That's the second lot that's come in two weeks. Poor people, they've nothing, what with the price of bread so high.'

'Can they hope for work?'

She had beautiful eyes, full of kindness and compassion. 'Nathan would give them all work if he could, but they need to be fit – buildin's hard work and clay minin' even harder. Most of them are starvin' and too weak to work.' Her brows remained drawn, her head shaking sadly. 'They've nowhere to go. Nathan's goin' to ask Sir James if they can sleep in the top barn but he's not holdin' out much hope – he's that kind, my brother, doesn't like to see men sufferin' for want of employment.' She squeezed my hands. 'We're on this earth to serve our fellow men, not to judge them – to love each person as our neighbour and bring them succour.'

My heart was still pounding. She had very nearly caught me prying but I was glad I had seen what I had. Nathan Cardew may be a powerful man, he may get angry with his workers, but like his sister, he was charitable and kind. Ruth was busy unpacking her basket and already I knew she and I could be friends.

I could have stayed longer. The bread and cheese were delicious, Ruth's cherry cake almost as good as Mrs Munroe's. Nathan sat quietly, seemingly content to let Ruth and I do all the talking. He was watching my every move, his eyes burning me. Each time I looked his way, our eyes would meet and a shock of excitement pierced my stomach. To be sought and courted by such a man. He smiled shyly at Ruth's teasing; getting his own back by telling me she had once taken five kittens to chapel in their father's hat. Their family stories drew me to them. I felt so at home in the crowded office, the centre of Nathan's life.

Nathan checked his watch. 'Goodness, the lock's openin' in half an hour, I'd best get down there. The day's gone so quick, it hardly seems right. May I walk you to your mother, Elowyn?'

'I'd best be off too – you can lock the door behind us.' Ruth piled the plates back in her basket and folded the tablecloth. With the pewter mugs wrapped carefully in the napkins, she held the basket under her arm and stood by the window, glancing down at the lock. She looked again. 'See that man... there...the one with the huge shoulders – the one by the gates talking to that boy?'

Nathan followed her gaze, immediately frowning. The lines round his mouth set firm. 'What about him?'

'He's one of the vagrants. He came to the barn early this mornin' askin' for work. I said not on a Sunday but he looked in such need so I gave him a shirt an' some milk. He'd no boots, poor man, so I found him an old pair of Mr Hearne's. I wasn't sure they'd fit but they did an' when I came out of chapel, I found he'd dug me a trench – all the way from the leat to the garden. Said he didn't want me waterin' my vegetables with a pail. Can ye believe that?'

The furrow on Nathan's brow deepened, his eyes hardened. 'He's no vagrant – he's too well fed. That's Billy he's with...Elowyn, do you know that man?'

I could hardly speak, let alone look. William was standing by the capstan, a crowd gathering round him. He was laughing, throwing back his head, pointing first one way, then the other. 'No, I've not seen him before.' My words sounded clipped and I knew I must look flustered. The more Nathan stared at me, the fiercer I blushed. I could not help myself – if I said I knew him, he would question me.

Nathan remained glaring down at William. 'I don't like the look of him. Speak to Billy, Elowyn. The press gang are back and Billy must understand the danger of talkin' to strangers.'

Ruth seemed oblivious to the tension, smiling happily at both of us. 'No, honest, there's no need to frighten the boy – he's not the press gang.'

'How can you be so sure?' If I sounded harsh, it was to vent my anger.

She mistook my anger for anxiety. Putting her hand on my arm, her sweet face filled with reassurance. 'I give a lot of alms and I get a *feel* for people – he's rough an' he's been in a fight but I don't believe he's wicked. He's the sort that likes to give back – said he'd return the boots as soon as he could.'

My face was a furnace, my stomach twisting. I should tell Nathan, now, this very minute. There must be no pretence between us, yet how could I tell him? To sleep the night next to a near-drowned man might be forgivable but what if the smugglers heard of it? They would seek us out, make sure to silence us.

Nathan's eyes hardened. 'And I've worked with enough men to recognize those who bring trouble.'

Chapter Eight

The day had been spoiled. I did not look at Nathan but looked down, carefully stepping over the piles of horse muck. A covering of fine white powder dusted the men's jackets, their hats, their faces. It was everywhere. Nathan had obviously been missed as there were papers to sign, last-minute questions to be answered. He bowed politely, his mind elsewhere. 'After chapel next Sunday, Elowyn – if that suits you better?'

Men were shouting from the decks of the loaded ships, others yelling back across the lock, everywhere the same sense of urgency. The ropes were in position, men poised to haul the ships out of the lock. Once in the outer harbour the ships would unfurl their sails and head north to the potteries. It must be Mr Perys, the harbourmaster, standing on the dockside, his whistle to his lips. The tide was at its height, the blue sea lapping against both sides of the gates. Billy was standing on the wooden steps. 'Quick, Elowyn, we need to cross.'

'Hurry up, miss. Shouldn't 'ave left it so late. We need to open the gates.'

I held the man's hand, stepping carefully down the wooden steps, glancing quickly back. William was one of the four men positioned at the capstan, waiting to pit their strength against the huge wooden spokes to open the gates. His shoulders were hunched, his hands gripping the polished wood. His borrowed shirt glowed white in the sun, his black hair falling across his face. He was laughing with the man opposite but his eyes caught mine and an uneasy pain sliced through me. 'Come, Billy.'

'But Elowyn, we can't leave now. You've *got* to watch.'

A piercing whistle filled the air and Mr Perys held up his hand, waiting for silence. At once, his voice rang loudly across the quayside. 'Gates open...' and the men began heaving against the large wooden spokes.

'Look, Elowyn, look!' Billy was insistent.

The hot sun pricked my back. I kept my eyes straight ahead, looking along the path towards Mamm's cottage. He had followed us just as I knew he would. He had sought Billy out. 'You've less than an hour,' I said without turning round. 'The cart leaves at four. Don't be late.'

Mamm seemed strangely nervous, hardly able to look me in the eye. She smiled at Billy. 'Send my best wishes to Mrs Pengelly, an' tell Mrs Munroe I loved the jam – no need to tell her I gave it to Bethany. Ah, here's the cart now. Out ye go, Billy love. Wait in the cart.'

Lowenna had been silently watching me, the same hostility on her pinched face. She rose quickly, reaching under the table, drawing something heavy across the flagstones. 'I'm to come with ye,' she said, 'an' we're to take these.' I stared in horror. Six large bladders lay plump on the floor, each one, no doubt, filled with brandy. 'We're to strap these under our skirts an' leave 'em at yer shop.'

Fury made my eyes water. 'I'll do no such thing.'

Mamm grabbed my arm. 'Please, love, please, just fer me. It's not too much to ask. They'll not think to stop ye in the preacher's cart.' Her pleading sickened me, that quiver in her voice, the look in her eye. 'We thought...seeing as how it's ten Sundays, we just thought...'

'Well, you thought wrong, Mamm. I'll have nothing to do with this. You do what you like but I'll not abuse Mrs Hearne's trust. What if Nathan found out? How could you think I'd do it?' I pulled my arm free, reaching quickly for my bonnet while Lowenna ran like a frightened mouse, scampering to the door.

Mamm gripped my arm tighter. 'Elowyn...do this fer me.' Her eyes looked wild, her hand pulling me back with greater force. Above us, the floorboards creaked, the same heavy footsteps banging down the stairs. 'Don't make him angry.'

The door burst open and Jack Deveral's huge bulk filled the room. Shoulders rounded, fist clenched, he glowered at me from under bushy brows. Lowenna cowered behind him. 'Ye'll do as yer told. Ye'll take those bladders fer your mamm's sake, if not fer mine. I've no quarrel with ye, so long as ye do what's good fer ye.' His head was shaven, stubble covering his chin. He was a heavy man, thick set, red faced, his pig-like eyes callously cruel. 'An' next week ye'll do the same, an' ye'll keep yer mouth shut.'

I knew about backing into a corner, not looking them in the eye. About keeping my mouth shut, my eyes downcast. Shouting back would make things worse, Mamm would get hurt. He knew that too; Lowenna, Mamm, both dancing to his tune. The old fear was rising, taking hold, the child in me cowering under my bed, hiding behind my arms in make-believe protection. There would be tenderness afterwards, the belt back in place, the promise never to do it again, but I knew better.

I took a deep breath. *I could read and write. I had a living. I had savings.* 'I'm sorry, Mr Deveral, I'll say nothing – nothing at all – but I am not taking your brandy in Mr Hearne's cart – not today, not next week, not the week after.' My voice was calm, but my heart was pounding.

I thought he would strike me. Mamm reached down, picking up one of the heavy bladders. 'Please, Elowyn, please, love…it would be so easy. No one will know. Ye won't have to deliver them – just take them to yer shop. It's only brandy, love, only a drop.' She held out the bladder. 'Tie the ties round yer waist, yer skirt will conceal it – no one will know.'

I felt unsteady, almost dizzy. It was Mamm's choice to be here, not mine. She would feel his fist, not me. He was laughing, his voice mocking: 'Ye think to tell Nathan Cardew, do ye?'

I glared back at him. 'No, of course not. I'll tell no one.'

Suddenly, my fear spiralled. Fury distorted his face. His eyes had darkened, a murderous blackness sweeping through him. He clenched his fists and I thought he would strike me. I could place him now, the hunched shoulders, the thick-set neck, the slight limp in his left leg. He had been the one holding up the lantern. Those clubs, those pitchforks, he would have used them. My bravery was misplaced – he was a ruthless man who would stop at nothing. Something must have given me away, a flicker, a sudden pallor. He was born to sense fear and he knew he had me.

'Ye think to squeal to yer uncle?' He kicked the bladders on the floor. 'Pigs squeal when they get their throats cut – daughters do what they're told. Ye're gettin' on that cart an' ye're takin' these with ye.'

My hands were shaking, my heart pounding. The back door was behind me and I knew it was unlocked. If I was quick, I could do it. I reached forward, picking up the bladder, slowly walking across the room. I skirted the table but twisted quickly, knocking everything to the ground as I ran for the door. The bladder thudded on the flagstone, Jack Deveral's curses ringing behind me.

Billy turned at the sound of the slammed door. 'Get off that cart, Billy, we're walking.' My legs felt weak, my breath coming in painful snatches. I was giddy with fear. The driver of the cart looked shocked, jumping down in surprise. 'Tell Mrs Hearne we're walking home. We've no need of you,' I snapped.

'Beggin' yer pardon, but Mr Cardew won't be happy…he was that insistent.'

I wanted to cry. Dear Nathan, if only he knew how desperately I wanted to get on that cart and get back to Coombe

House. I feared for Mamm, what if Jack Deveral took his anger out on her? But I would not go back, not now, not ever. 'Don't look like that, Billy – you're always going on about being cooped up in the shop, well, now we're walking.' Billy knew to say nothing, running behind me as I stormed up the path. I was so angry, I could hardly see. How could Mamm do that to me?

We were far enough away, starting the long climb up the hill. Billy could not understand my sudden fury. 'Did you know the lock gates are no more than twenty-seven feet wide?'

'Who told you that?'

'Will did.'

'Don't say *no more than*, just say twenty-seven feet.'

'It can hold fifteen vessels at a pinch.'

'It can hold *as many as* fifteen vessels. Who's pinching whom?'

Billy was not to be stopped, his eager face shining with delight. 'And the biggest ship so far has been a five hundred tonner—'

'Five hundred *tons*.' We might be out of danger, but we had a long walk home and my shoes were rubbing. 'What's the point of learning grammar if you forget it the first sight of a lock?'

All happiness drained from Billy's face. 'Ye really don't like him, do ye?' The pout was back, the sullenness returned. 'Well, ye're wrong. Mrs Hearne likes him – he's to build her a sluice gate.'

'You shouldn't have spoken to him – I told him to go his separate way.' The hill rose steeply above us, the dusty track pitted with cart ruts. Once up the hill, we would have to make our way past the settling pits and the old engine house. It seemed so much further than I thought and I began to regret not taking the cliff path. Fear had clouded all sense. 'Save your breath, Billy, we've a big climb ahead.'

Billy turned round, his eyes wide. 'No we ain't...Look, the cart's coming.' He began smiling broadly, waving both hands, leaving my side to run back down the path. By his smile, I did not need to look round. Foreboding seized me, a terrible anxiety. William Cotterell was about to ask for money. I kept walking, striding purposefully up the dusty road, the cart's wheels fast approaching. Billy's happy chatter rose above the jingle of the harness. They were just behind me, drawing alongside.

'Will you not stop, Miss Liddicot?' His voice held the same familiarity, the same disrespect.

'How come you're driving the cart? I sent the other man away.'

'I was watching. I could see something was wrong and I can be very persuasive when I need be...' From the corner of my eye, I saw him nudge Billy who laughed appreciatively. 'Let's just say, I managed to persuade the poor man that Mrs Hearne had sent me instead.' Billy giggled even louder, clearly at ease with this man, sitting next to him like he had done it all his life. It felt like treachery, like being stabbed in the back.

'You've stolen the cart?'

His laugher was deep, genuinely amused. 'No, Miss Liddicot, I've *borrowed it*. I'll take it straight back – Mrs

Hearne may never know it's missing. Are you getting in or are you going to walk beside us the whole way back?' He drew on the reins, pulling up the horse.

What if Nathan was watching? Panic made me want to cry but Billy was already sitting next to William and I would be by myself in the back. Surely that would be seemly – I would be accompanied and if anyone saw us, it would look perfectly proper. All I wanted was to get home – desperately, desperately wanted to get home. William jumped from the seat and held open the door. The wheels were covered in fine white dust, the painted wooden seat freshly wiped. He held out his hand to help me. 'After all, we can't have the Piermaster's lady walking home.'

His words chilled me. If I was cross before, his mocking tone now made me furious; insolent man, barging in on our lives with his huge shoulders and great muscular arms, his horrible knowing eyes and taunting smile. Billy stayed by his side and I was forgotten, the horse taking his time up the steep incline. Not once did either of them turn round. I could have fallen out of the cart for all they cared.

Billy kept asking questions, his eager voice growing ever more excited. Leats, rivulets, sluices, waterwheels – overshot, undershot, shoulder shot. Which one to use and why? How did the lock stay full? How come the gates could open? Each torrent of questions was met with the same rise of the shoulders, the same smiling reply, *Think, Billy – you tell me. Leats feed the lock but you've to account for the leakage. Equal pressure on both sides.*

I watched the pier houses grow smaller by the minute, the

next batch of ships lining up to take their place. The sea was so blue, the sun still warm on my arms. I would never, ever, set foot in Jack Deveral's cottage again. Mamm had forfeited my company, she must realize that. How could she do such a thing to me? I closed my eyes, trying to recapture the good of the day. The touch of Nathan's lips on my palms, his kind gestures, his avowals of love. He wanted so much for me, yet all I could hear was talk of stemming the streams, the constant chatter of how to wash out the clay. *Think, Billy. What's heavier, rock or clay? What happens if you dissolve clay in water? Exactly so — leave it to settle then drain off the water.*

Great swathes of flowers lined the path, butterflies dancing, skylarks soaring high above us. Seagulls circled the fishing boats out in the bay, white sails far out to sea. Yet they saw none of it. *Clay's but six feet below ground...six ton of spoilings for every ton of clay. Coal's for the engines in the tin mines, Billy.* I wanted to stop the cart, jump down and pick some flowers. My embroidery designs were good but if I could only capture these colours and use them for my new dresses. William's voice kept disturbing my thoughts. That man had an answer for everything. *Adits drain water above the water level — below the water level, you need to pump.*

At last Billy's questioning came to an end. 'Take the reins, lad; know what to do?' Neither of them looked at me. It was as if I was not there. Billy took the reins, William making himself comfortable, his arm stretching along the bench as he nodded his approval. Billy held the reins loosely, copying William, doing exactly what he was told.

The Piermaster's lady — he had said it mockingly but

that would be the truth. The lock would become my life, that beautiful cottage my home. I shut my eyes, trying to picture Nathan's kind eyes, that boyish look of vulnerability, yet, once again, my thoughts were disturbed. William was singing, his rich deep voice rising joyfully into the air.

> *And I would love you all the day,*
> *Every night would kiss and play,*
> *If with me you'd fondly stray,*
> *Over the hills and far away.*

Billy was enthralled. 'Sing that again, Will.'

'Elowyn lets you sing bawdy songs, does she, Billy?'

Billy burst out laughing. 'Course she don't. Not *bawdy* ones she don't.'

I felt a stab of jealousy. It was as if I was not there, the two of them completely at one with each other. Billy loved me, he was devoted to me. I knew he was not being unkind, but I felt suddenly so empty. Perhaps his father had been like William? Something about their easy friendship made me feel strangely lonely. Mamm was a foolish woman and Jack Deveral, a dangerous man. I was not even sure I liked Porthcarrow with its white dust everywhere. And what was I doing going along with Gwen's scheming? I had a trade, a way of making a living. Why should women have to depend on men for beautiful pier houses with wooden shutters and water pumps with ornate iron handles in the yard?

The top of the moor; we were nearly home, the familiar landmarks beginning to take shape. Across the purple heather, I could see the steeply wooded riverbanks of Fosse, the church tower, the sheep and cattle grazing in the pastures above Porthruan. The river mouth would soon be visible. I would catch the first glimpse of the grey rooftops and masts in the harbour. Billy was singing along happily. 'So beggars have opera?' he said when they stopped.

William was intent on mocking me. 'Course beggars have opera. Why shouldn't they? We're all born equal.'

Through the town and along the river, the safety of Coombe House could not come quickly enough. The cart stopped and Billy jumped down, smiling up at the house with the same pride we all felt. William looked up at the fine brick building with its eight sash windows and ornate portico and I caught the approval in his eyes. He winked at Billy. 'You've a nice home, lad. You've done well.'

His words sent a chill through me. He was too friendly, his influence too strong – he would take Billy from us. He opened the cart door, putting out his hand to help me and I stared at it, not wanting to take it.

It was as if he read my mind. 'You can trust me, Elowyn. Do you really think I would harm the boy?' The look in his hazel eyes made me catch my breath. Hazel eyes, flecked with green, and I looked away, reaching for my handkerchief. It was not there, not anywhere. I had not used it since I had wiped the sand from his face. Fear gripped me.

'My handkerchief…Oh dear Lord…it's still in the cave. It's just like the one I gave Mamm…if Jack Deveral finds it, he'll recognize it and know I've been there…'

His eyes sharpened. 'Jack Deveral?'

I looked quickly down, realizing my mistake. His cracked lips parted in a smile and he shut the cart door. 'Don't worry,' he whispered. 'It's perfectly safe.' He patted the inside pocket of his jacket and bowed in mock salute, jumping on to the driver's seat to pick up the reins. Billy stood on the step, waving him goodbye, and we watched him urge the pony on, his broad shoulders swaying with the rhythm of the cart. His white shirt caught the last rays of the sun and I stared after him. Beneath that glowing white shirt were cuts and deep purple bruises.

Well, he could keep my handkerchief; he could sell it and squander the money. He could get blind drunk and start another fight. He could get thrown into the sea again and someone else could come to his aid.

Chapter Nine

Coombe House
Sunday 5th June 1796, 9:30 p.m.

Dusk had fallen, my candle long guttered. I knew I should close the shutters against the damp night air. There was a knock on the door.

'Elowyn, my dear, you're not asleep, are you?' Mrs Pengelly's greying hair was neatly plaited beneath her lace nightcap. She was wearing her cotton nightgown trimmed with lace, her finely embroidered shawl covering her shoulders. She was still a beautiful woman, even more so now her face held such tenderness and understanding.

She held up her candle, shaking her head. 'Elowyn, dearest, you've not closed your window.' She smiled her sweet smile. 'I'm sure you've far too much on your mind.' She put down the candle, unfolding the shutters, blocking out the sounds and smells of the river. 'You'll catch a chill, my dear – you must keep this damp air at bay.'

I smiled back at her, delighted she had come and even more delighted when she settled herself next to me on the bed, plumping up the pillow, drawing the cover round us. She reached for my hands, holding them softly. 'You were very quiet at supper…go on, then, tell me. How was your day and did you like Nathan Cardew?' She squeezed my hands.

I was so glad she had come. I could always speak my thoughts to her and I wanted to talk but not in front of the others. 'Yes…I did really like him – he was very attentive and Ruth was lovely. They made me feel so welcome. He's not frightening at all – not when you get to know him… He's actually quite shy and he said the nicest things…'

'Oh, Elly, I'm that pleased. What about your mamm, is she happy with Mr Deveral?' She must have felt me stiffen. 'What is it, love?'

'She's very foolish. She says he doesn't hurt her but he's a bully and I don't trust him.' I cleared my throat. 'We had a falling-out…and she took his side.' I would say no more.

The lace on her nightcap fluttered as she shook her head. 'I'm sorry to hear that. I hoped she'd found happiness. Elowyn, my love, what is it? I can tell you're not happy.'

I could no longer hold back my tears. I put my head on her shoulder, overwhelmed by violent sobbing. She smelt of lavender, of fresh clean linen, of dependability and everything I held dear. 'I'm sorry…I'm being silly…'

She stroked my hair. 'So you *don't* really like Nathan and you want the whole thing to stop?'

'No, I *do* like him…I like him a lot. I can't find fault with him – he's kind and attentive. He's a good man…he's thoughtful and merciful…and I like that. Ruth says he's too generous at times – and that's coming from her! She does nothing but good works.'

'They sound good, honest people, both of them.'

I blew my nose, my tears subsiding. 'Nathan says I can still go to church. He doesn't want me to change in any way. He wants everything I want – he wants me to fill the house with beautiful things…he wants so much for me…and…well…I know I'd be safe with him.'

Mrs Pengelly cradled me softly. 'Well, ye can't ask for much more than that, can ye?' She pushed a strand of hair across my face. I loved it when her voice took on the lilt of her childhood. It made her sound so loving and intimate – the voice of a mother I always wanted.

'The cows got out and Nathan had to go and mend the fence but in a way that was good. He was really angry that the work hadn't been done properly but it seemed to break the tension. Until then, I'd felt nervous…what with him in his fine Sunday clothes; but after that it was better. I could see we both have so much in common. We both feel the same about liking things done in the best way possible. We both have high standards.'

'Well, that's good, Elly. It's a good start, anyway.'

'He works so hard. He seems to run everything – Sir James couldn't have chosen a worthier man…' I could feel my face burning. 'Nathan believes he's to be offered Pier-master…'

She lifted up my chin, forcing me to look her in the eyes. 'That's wonderful, Elly love, but ye should be smiling, dancing round the room, not crying.'

I was being silly, I could see that now. 'It's just such a big step. How do you know if it's right?'

She squeezed my shoulder. 'Take yer time, my dear. Ye've no need to rush. Love soon follows liking.'

'A man like Nathan would be hard not to love.'

She pinched my cheek. 'Well, there ye go! It's just nerves making ye so scared.'

She seemed reluctant to leave, suddenly fidgeting with the coverlet, stroking the delicately stitched embroidery. Now I thought about it, there had been something strained in her voice all evening. She cleared her throat as if trying to pluck up the courage to speak. 'Elowyn...there's no easy way to say this.' She could not look at me, but stared down at the coverlet, examining a stray thread. 'I don't know how I'm going to tell ye this...but Rose came today.'

I held my breath, my heart racing. *Rose* not Lady Polcarrow. Something was wrong. She cleared her throat. 'The lease of the shop has run its course...and though Lady Pendarvis had every intention of renewing the lease...the boatyard wants the space back.'

'No – they can't! They can't take it from me.' I buried my face in my hands.

She was as distraught as I was, tears welling in her eyes. 'This is so hard for me, Elly. I'm quite torn in two...I love that shop as much as you – it's as precious to me as anything... But the boatyard has prior claim and you know what Rose is like about that yard.'

My business, my living, everything I held dear. Everyone I loved, conspiring against me – Uncle Thomas, Tom, Gwen, even Lady Polcarrow and Lady Pendarvis, not one of them with the courage to tell me, or even to discuss it. I could hardly breathe. I loved that shop more than anything. It was where I found happiness, where I drew my courage.

Mrs Pengelly reached for my hand. 'Lady Pendarvis has only ever held the sub-lease. My husband let it out when things got bad…but they need the space now. Your uncle must've told you how crowded they are.'

I felt dizzy with shock. 'But it's my livelihood…I own all the stock. I've bought each roll of fabric, every yard of lace… all the ribbons. I bought everything from Lady Pendarvis …and I've worked *so* hard. All my money's invested in that shop.'

'I know, my love. Don't cry, Elly, please don't cry.' Mrs Pengelly reached for her handkerchief, dabbing her own eyes. 'Rose will find somewhere else – she's already started to look – and you know what Rose is like! She'll find somewhere… but think on it, Elly…Maybe it's not *such* a bad thing. We could…' Her hands were trembling, crushing her handkerchief. 'We could join the dressmaker's with the school.' Her eyes searched mine. 'Things sometimes work out for the best – sometimes what you *think* is terrible just ends up being good timing.' She wiped my eyes with her handkerchief. 'It might be that you could sell us your stock and use the money for other things – for furnishings…things like that.'

'You'd merge my business with the dressmaking school and Jenna Dunn would take charge?' I needed to keep my jealousy at bay, the gnawing envy every time Jenna Dunn's name was mentioned. She was their favourite and always would be, and why not? She was like a daughter to Mrs Pengelly, once her most trusted and loyal maid, now the teacher in her school of needlework. She had married Joseph Dunn, Sir James' steward, and I knew her happiness was well deserved. It was just she was so forthright, that was all; her word would be law. Joining forces with Jenna Dunn would end the dream of running my own shop. I bit my lip, my aspirations fading before me.

Mrs Pengelly rose from the bed. 'We've got a month, Elly. I'll ask Tamsin to bring up a nice cup of yarrow tea. You've had a long day and a nasty shock.'

A long day and a very long night before it; Mrs Pengelly did not know the half of it. I felt numb with shock. 'No tea,' I said, shaking my head. I could not bear it if Tamsin saw me like this.

She picked up her candle, her fragile frame bending to kiss me softly. 'Remember, your home's here, Elly love, for however long you like – until you decide otherwise.' She curled one of my ringlets round her finger, leaving it coiled against my cheek. 'I've resigned myself to losing you...first Rose, then Jenna...and one day I'll lose you. You must all set up yer own homes but *only* when you're ready, Elly, not before. Try to sleep now.'

The door closed and I gripped my pillow, burrowing my head deeply to muffle my cries. Sobs wracked my body, I felt like howling. My whole life, turned upside down. Nathan's courtship, Mamm, and now my business was set to go. I could not stop the pain ripping through me. Everything turned upside down. Everything set to change.

Chapter Ten

Fosse
Monday 6th June 1796, 6:30 a.m.

I grabbed my basket, flinging my bonnet on my head as I hurried up the back stairs.

'What's wrong, Elowyn?' Billy had a hunk of bread in one hand, his hat in the other.

'I've a lot to do – there's four new fittings and those last gowns need to be packed and delivered.' He sensed my mood and kept silent, running behind me as I hurried along the road. The tide was out, the muddy riverbanks glistening in the early sunshine. Rooks screeched from the tops of the trees, herons stood silently by the water's edge. Already the street was crowded; a woman was herding a gaggle of geese, the brewery wagon obstructing her way and tempers were beginning to flare. No one must see me like this – my eyes were swollen and I knew I looked awful. I could not decide what hurt me most – Lady Pendarvis keeping so quiet or Uncle Thomas and Tom not confiding in me.

Or was it just the thought of Jenna Dunn? The brewery wagon was truly stuck, people protesting as they pushed through the narrow gap. I held my breath, squeezing in front of a man whose large belly stood no chance of getting through. Billy ran by my side and we crossed the town square. No, it was not jealousy making me bitter so much as having to join forces with her. She was a forceful woman – she would make the decisions, not me. I fought back my tears. But I possessed skills she did not have – Lady Pendarvis had taught me business and I was good at balancing the books, making a profit where others might make a loss.

We reached the cool of the courtyard, the huge warehouses rising around us. A heavily laden wagon was making its way under the arch and already the forge was blazing. I could hardly speak. I loved this place so entirely and it would break my heart to leave.

Gwen was waiting on the top of the iron steps. One look at my face and she paled visibly. 'You *knew*, Gwen...You, Uncle Thomas and Tom, you had it all arranged. How could you not tell me?' I strode across the polished wooden floorboards, hanging my cloak roughly on the hook.

'It happened so fast – it's only just been decided.'

'Does Nathan know? Is that why you got him to come courting?'

Gwen shook her head, her brown eyes with their lush black lashes, for once, defiant. 'Don't be a goose, Elly. Nathan asked after ye the moment he saw ye.' She hung up her own bonnet, glancing in the mirror as she put on her mobcap. 'Be cross with Tom – he's the one what told me not to tell ye – but don't be cross with Nathan. Go shout at yer brother. I'm as upset as ye are. I love workin' here.'

'Does Josie know?'

Gwen shook her head. 'No one knows 'cept Billy now. Come here, Billy, give us a hug. We're to join with Jenna – you're soon to have *all* of us tellin' ye what to do!'

The slammed door made me turn round. Billy was running down the steps. 'Oh Gwen, I should've told him but I just can't face this. I just want everything back to how it was.'

She tied her apron, smiling kindly. 'I know, Elly love – but look what's ahead of ye. Piermaster's wives don't sew for other people – they embroider fer themselves. Ye can sew yerself a chest full of beautiful table linen and fancy bed quilts. It's like the right thing at the right time, ye must see that. Ye can sell the stock and prepare fer yer home. It's good timin', that's all.'

Good timing, my dreams and aspirations sold at the first opportunity? I could barely look at the pristine room with its polished table and sparkling windows. Years of hard work etched on every surface – the shelves stacked so neatly, the finest fabric, the most delicate lace. Everything chosen with care and attention, at just the right price, no corners cut. Replaced with what? Beautiful linen and fancy quilts packed in a chest? 'Mary Wollstonecraft says we should be helpmates for our husbands. She wants women to know their worth – not sell their business the first moment a man shows interest in them.'

Gwen's eyes shot heavenward. Her voice softened: 'Ye *do like* Nathan Cardew, don't ye?'

I could see Nathan's fine clothes, his timid smile, the shy way he had of looking at me. The creases at his eyes, the strength in his jaw, the cleft in his chin as he bent to kiss my palms. 'Yes, I like him very much.'

'Then what's yer problem?' she replied happily.

I turned to hide my tears. 'We need to get these gowns folded and prepare for the fittings. I want the spools of ribbons in exact order...my usual sequence, the satin, the moiré, then the picot silk and the gauze...and stack the lace by size...best first – the blue French floral, then the *Toile de Bordeaux*. We'll serve coffee in the morning, punch after twelve and tea in the afternoon. Mrs Munroe's given us some macaroons.'

Gwen smoothed her apron over her swollen belly, smiling as she went through the door. I remembered my promise to Mamm and followed her into the storeroom. I would honour my promise and that was all. She had forfeited my love long ago, now she would forfeit my company. The shelves were tightly packed, stacked high with fabric. The cotton was on the top shelf. 'I promised Mamm some of that old calico. We never use it, do we?'

Gwen shook her head. 'Never touch it...there's a lot of it, mind. A good four rolls.'

I stretched up, careful not to snag my silk sleeves. Lady Pendarvis had taught me to wear the sort of gowns my customers would like to wear themselves. Not the *very best*, but better than *expected*, and it definitely worked. It let me showcase my skills and persuade my customers their money would be well spent. Gwen saw me falter and held out her arms.

'My problem is,' I said, laying my forehead on her shoulder, 'I don't want anything to change. I've been so happy here…I've had such hopes…' I could hardly bring myself to say the words. 'But…I think I've been very foolish.'

She hugged me to her. 'Ye're never foolish.'

'I have been…I've been fooling myself…I don't think any of them – Lady Pendarvis, Lady Polcarrow, not even Mrs Pengelly – expect me to continue running the business… not really. I think they're just waiting for me to marry – all that walking around with books on my head, all those deportment lessons with riding crops under my arms…all that learning and grammar. I think it was just to make a good marriage. Only I've taken too long.'

Gwen crushed me to her large bosom, her good-luck birthing talisman, a carved walnut shell with its gauze soaked in lilac oil, pressing against me. 'Elly, it's not like ye to get so upset.' She wiped my tears with her apron.

'Lady Pendarvis should have warned me. I know she's busy and hardly comes here…but she could've written.' Tears splashed my cheeks. 'I think she just wants me to get married…like you all do.'

'There, Elly, hush yer crying, come. It's just ye must secure yer future.' She dropped her voice. 'Dressmaking's all right but ye mustn't end up like Josie.' She stroked my cheek, trying to coax a smile. 'And Jenna's not *so* bad – she's just got a very direct way of sayin' things.'

I smiled through my tears. She would never understand the desire to run my own business. It was just I was good at it, I made money. I was profitable. I loved everything about it – the pride I felt when I exceeded my customer's expectation. The look in their eyes when I helped them chose colours they would never think to choose and patterns they thought would never suit them; the gratitude as I made them look their best. I did not want to sit drinking tea, embroidering for myself.

'Let's get that cotton down then...' Gwen winced and my heart jumped.

'No, Gwen – don't. From now on ask us to lift down the rolls – besides, Billy needs to be kept busy.'

She smiled. 'Why's that, then?'

I swallowed. Gwen had a habit of winkling out my secrets but this was one secret I had to keep safe.

Billy took the news worse than I expected, burying himself in the stores and hardly speaking. I knew how much my stock was worth but kept him busy, making a list of the fabrics and how much they cost. Tomorrow he would add everything together. Sunlight slanted through the huge windows, the fittings had gone well with four silk gowns ordered by women whose husbands were members of the Corporation. Gwen folded her apron.

'They all chose silk because of Lady Polcarrow's ball – she may be at loggerheads with their husbands but their wives won't give up the chance of goin' to her ball.'

Josie matched the last thread and laid it on top of the lace. She eased her back. 'There now, all ready fer tomorrow.' The four dressmaker's dummies stood tightly bound and padded to the exact measurements. Mrs Hoskins' dummy had required three cushions and a great deal of woollen wading, but the measurements were now exact and we were ready to leave. I closed my order book and looked down at the yard. It was busier than ever. Gwen and Josie had their bonnets on. 'Are you coming, Billy?'

Gwen looked tired, Josie her normal jolly self. 'Ye go on down – I'll wait till ye're back. Save ye lockin' up twice.'

Dear Josie, with her buck teeth and strange curly hair. A lump caught the back of my throat. How was I going to tell her that her failing eyesight was affecting her sewing? Her stitching had been getting worse and soon I would not be able to shield her. Jenna would never employ her. Not now her sight was going.

Chapter Eleven

I gripped my money box. 'Are you coming, Billy?'

He nodded, running down the steps in front of me, always glad for an excuse to see Uncle Thomas. The yard was bustling, the smell of tar stronger than ever. The sawpit stood empty, a bucket of newly crafted shackles cooling in a large trough of water. Behind a criss-cross of poles and planks the skeleton of the new brig was already taking shape. Tom waved his hammer in the air, not looking at me but at Gwen who waved back from under the arch.

They definitely needed more space. The increasing demand for privateer licences was good for business and two new shipwrights had recently joined them. How could I not see it coming? Three more apprentices had been signed up and Jimmy Tregony was now working with Mr Melhuish at the forge. Even the sawyers had tripled in number. War was good for shipbuilders who had a supply of wood and Uncle Thomas certainly had wood – a large log pool bobbing with seasoned, white oak. But even without the new brig and regular repairs, a steady stream of requisitioned ships lay waiting for refitting and a string of badly damaged ships lay ready to be broken up.

I waved at Uncle Thomas through the window. The ground floor had been sufficient in lean times but now papers piled high on his desk and files spilled untidily over every table. The shelves were clearly over-stacked and bulging boxes balanced on the floor. Shipwrights' plans needed to be stretched out on a table, available to be consulted at every moment. How blind could I be?

Usually when he saw me, Uncle Thomas' eyes crinkled in their customary fashion but not today. 'Elowyn, my love, what have you for me?' His round-rimmed glasses gave him an air of gravity, his grey hair cut short, his chin closely shaven. I loved Thomas Scantlebury so completely. His generosity had saved us. He had opened his door to us and became the father I always wanted.

'There's over four pounds in here – nearly five.'

He whistled softly. 'As much as that? Is it all good?'

The coins looked real enough but I could never tell if I had been cheated. Some coins felt lighter than they should and others looked clearly forged, but most of the tokens I thought were counterfeit were perfectly usable. I liked gold sovereigns – coins you could weigh and trust. 'It's just the usual lot – mostly from Truro, some from Bodmin.' I handed him the box.

He swept aside a pile of paper, tipping the contents onto his desk. 'They look fine to me. I'll be grateful for this change, no mistake. There's more wages to pay than ever – you've enough for your own wages?' I nodded. Our arrangement worked so well. His accounts were for larger sums and were mainly paid with notes or gold sovereigns and he needed small change to make up the correct wages. I, on the other hand, wanted the larger sovereigns. 'Goin' to count it with me, Billy?'

Billy smiled. 'Four pounds, eighteen shillings, six pence and three farthings – I've already counted it.' He began separating the coins, piling them up in neat rows.

Uncle Thomas laughed. 'Not cheating an old man?'

Billy returned his laugh. 'Course not. Anyway, you're not old! How's the brig coming on?'

Uncle Thomas scooped the money into his box. 'See for yourself, lad.' We watched Billy race across the yard, calling to Tom. Uncle Thomas turned back to me. 'I've only got notes, Elly. Are you all right with notes, only I know you prefer gold?'

My heart sank. I hated notes. 'How *can* paper have the same value?'

'It's proper currency whether we like it or not. Perhaps it's time to let me bank your money? I know you've a safe place to hide it, but a bank would be better. They're Mr Hoskins' notes – he issued them and he'll keep them safe.' He took off his glasses and leaned back, pain deep in his eyes.

'You mean when I sell my stock?' It was unkind of me and I regretted it instantly. He seemed tired, more drawn than usual, his brow furrowed by deep lines.

'How's your mamm, Elly? Would be lovely if you lived closer – it's all Gwen and Tom can talk about. Nathan's a good man. He asked if he could court you a good four weeks ago.' His smile was tender, his eyes downcast.

Nathan, always so proper, his manners perfect, but the thought of Mamm troubled me. 'I don't like Jack Deveral.'

The lines round Uncle Thomas' mouth tightened. He swallowed, his face stony, 'Your mamm's a loving woman and I can't find fault in that. 'Tis *her* choice. We may not like it, but what can we do? How did she look?'

'I don't think he hurts her but he's a horrible man.' I could not keep the accusation from my voice. 'She could leave him. She could just pack her bag and come home.'

He shook his head. 'She says she's happy.' He opened the top drawer, reaching for a stout wooden box. 'And he's doin' well. He's supplying the whole town with his fish. Here, lass, five pounds in notes – all done, that leaves me with two shillings owing. Keep them safe.'

I took the crisp new notes, holding the print of a ship up to the light. The name *Thomas Hoskins Esquire* was on the top, the words *I promise to pay the bearer the sum of one pound* written across the centre. They seemed so flimsy, hardly money at all. He bent to close the box.

'Have you got the two shillings, Uncle Thomas?' I asked.

'Aye, lass – you want them?' He seemed surprised.

'Yes…for Josie – she needs a pair of spectacles.'

'Josie?' A slight lift to his voice made my heart jolt and I searched his face, wondering if I had misread his meaning. Josie would be perfect for him. He looked swiftly down, fumbling in the drawer.

'Josie's a dear, sweet woman, Uncle Thomas – one of the

best, but Jenna won't employ her now her sight's going. I'm worried she'll be out of a job. Especially as she's her old mother to look after – she needs all the money she can earn.' Sudden tension in his back made me stop, a slight stiffness in the way he held his neck and a rush of hope almost broke my heart.

He seemed reluctant to catch my eye. 'Gwen's always tellin' me how good she is – how kind and thoughtful. She still lives with her mother, does she?'

'Her mother's very frail. They'll have nothing when you take back our shop.'

He shook his head sadly. 'Oh, Elly love, it cuts to the quick hearin' you speak like that…Perhaps, you could give her the two shillings from me? I'd like to pay for her glasses. Tell her if 'tis not enough, I'll gladly give more…her needing to find work on account of us taking away your shop, that is.'

I slipped the money into my purse and bent to kiss him. Dearest Uncle Thomas, somehow I knew Gwen must be behind his thoughts of remarrying, but even as my heart filled with hope, it seemed so unfair. Women should not have to keep their savings hidden under floorboards because they were denied a bank account, nor should they have to depend on kind men with steady jobs to pluck them from the streets. I shut the door. Women should *not* have to depend on men to offer them beautiful pier houses with wrought-iron gates and wooden shutters.

Billy saw me and waved. He was running across the yard, brandishing a hammer, and my heart dived. 'Look, Elowyn

– my first tool.' He held it up, spitting on it, rubbing it with his shirt sleeve. 'Tom said I could have it.'

Anger sliced through me, a terrible foreboding. He was spitting on purpose, testing my response. Soon he would be fighting and brawling, coming home with deep purple bruises. 'Take it back,' I snapped. 'Take it straight back.'

Sam shut the front door. 'Mrs Pengelly's got letters fer ye – here, give me yer bonnet…' He looked tidier than usual, his slightly greying hair neatly parted down the middle, drawn back in an unaccustomed knot. He was closely shaven, his shirt, impeccable.

My heart jumped. 'Letters?' I never got letters.

Mrs Pengelly was sitting in her favourite high-backed chair, the delicate mahogany feet hidden by her grey silk dress. Her Chinese sewing box with its spools of threads and silver scissors lay on the little table beside her, the glasses balancing on the end of her nose a sure sign that she was embroidering something intricate. She looked up, smiling broadly. 'Did Sam tell you, you've got two letters?'

Two large windows overlooked the river. In the morning, the sun would fill the room with brightness but I preferred it in the evening when the setting sun lingered on the fields opposite, turning the trees on the riverbank a golden red. I loved this room; it was exactly how I thought a sitting room should look. There were scrolls on the marble mantelpiece, a large gold mirror reflecting the glass dome of the carriage clock, but best of all was the display cabinet holding Sir James' very own china. His own clay, dug from his own pits, transported north and crafted into vases by Josiah Wedgwood.

Mrs Pengelly pointed to the silver tray. 'Take them away to read. I don't want to pry…'

I smiled back, sitting down on the chair opposite. 'You never pry.'

The two letters had very different handwriting but both were sealed with the same red wax. I slipped my finger under the first, my heart racing. Nathan's writing was neat and beautifully executed but I could hardly read it for the pounding in my heart.

My Dearest Elowyn,

Forgive me if you think me bold but I think of you as my dearest. The day we spent together is as clear in my mind today as it was last night and the day before. I barely think of anything else — I walk round in a daze, wanting next Sunday to come so quickly, praying it will pass more slowly. Last Sunday passed too soon. There was still so much I wanted to say.

I have news that will excite you. Mrs Perys wants to meet you. She saw you walking on my arm and asked me who you were. She thought you very lovely and insists we dine with her next Sunday. It seems, dearest Elowyn, that everyone is set to love you and I must learn to share you. Believe me when I say next Sunday cannot come soon enough.

I remain your obedient servant.
Nathan Cardew

An invitation to dine with Mrs Perys! I reread the letter, sick with sudden nerves. I had written to Ruth to thank her for my lunch but had not expected a reply. I broke open her seal, surprised to see her writing almost as neat as my own.

Dear Miss Liddicot,
or Elowyn if you will permit me,
Thank you for your kind note but I insist the pleasure was all ours. We've done nothing but talk about your beauty and bearing. Mr Hearne was sorry to miss you — but you've heard of our invitation? This is an honour indeed but you need not fear as I know Mrs Perys will love you.

Since seeing you, I have a new sluice gate and a ditch to water the vegetables. The water flows down the gully and into a new ditch and I can't think why we haven't thought of doing it before. The man who dug it is also going to channel the water into a holding pond so my ducks can have fresh water. He's mended my mangle and the catch on the chicken coop — what with the forge and the ministry, Mr Hearne has very little time for the house and garden so you can imagine how thrilled I am.

The vagrants are still here. I've no clothes for the children and next to nothing for the men. Perhaps you could look out for some jackets and breeches and as many boots or shoes as you can find? The poor souls are so hungry. There's no bread as the grain's all but finished — but I know the Good Lord will provide and I do His work with joy in my heart.

I write too slowly and Nathan is impatient to get our letters posted. Dear Miss Liddicot, you can't imagine how

you've brightened up our lives. I long for the day I can call
you sister. My prayers are with you. Goodbye until Sunday,
Your sister in Christ,
Ruth Hearne

Mrs Pengelly caught my eye and for a moment I wished I had taken the letters away to read. Ruth's note unnerved me. 'One letter's from Nathan and the other's from his sister.' I slipped onto the stool by her feet, handing her Ruth's letter.

'She's very neat writing.' Mrs Pengelly adjusted her glasses. 'The family's done very well for themselves. I believe his father's a burgee of St Austell and they live in a large house by the church.' I nodded. Somehow I could not bring myself to talk. 'We'll get together some clothes – Sam's old jacket for a start and there's some of Billy's he's long outgrown. She's right about the grain…I hear there's rioting outside Truro. The harvest was terrible last year – quite terrible – and we're paying the price.'

She handed me back the letter. 'I had hoped one of the letters might be from Lady Pendarvis,' I said softly, and by her look, I knew she was thinking the same. 'I'm worried about Josie – her sight's going and her stitching's beginning to suffer. Uncle Thomas gave her two shillings for glasses and she could hardly stop from crying – dear Josie. Did you know she had a fancy for Uncle Thomas?'

Mrs Pengelly picked up her sewing, snipping a thread with her silver scissors. 'Course she has. She's been in love with him ever since I've known her. And it's time your uncle married again…Josie would make a lovely companion for him.'

102

This is what I would miss; these intimate conversations, just the two us sitting in this beautiful blue and gold sitting room with the delicate furniture looking so well against the stripes of the wallpaper. Mrs Pengelly's pearl earrings swung as she searched the sewing box. 'What will you wear next Sunday – your lemon gown or your pale blue silk?'

A fresh breeze blew through the open window, the salt just discernible above the scent of the lavender in the vase on the table. I rose to close the window, watching the pack mules pick their way back to the stables. Oxen were returning to the fields, yawls drifting home on the incoming tide. A rowing boat was moored to the post outside, a man stacking it high with empty crab pots. These were the sights, the scents and sounds I loved so much. 'Were you scared when you first met Mr Pengelly? Scared of marriage, I mean, of leaving what you loved most and starting somewhere else?'

Mrs Pengelly rose to join me at the window. She slipped her arm around my waist. 'It's never easy starting up with someone you hardly know.' I followed her gaze across the river to the tiny cottage where Rose had been born. 'But I was more scared of moving from Porthruan to here. The house seemed so grand and the rooms too big!' She must be thinking of her husband, just two years buried. He had not lived long enough to see her start her school of needlework.

'Mr Pengelly would be so proud of you,' I whispered. 'Your own school and Rose married to Sir James. It's a shame he never got to see Lisbeth. Did you love him very much?'

She smiled, her voice hesitant. 'It wasn't always easy living with a man so set against everything…but I did love him and knew I'd never change him. Ye can't change a man, Elly. You might think you can, but ye can't. He was always on his high horse, demanding his rights, and we both knew he trod a dangerous path. Always fighting those in authority – I knew it would kill him. God bless his soul.'

We shut the windows and resumed our seats. Soon, Tamsin would bring us tea and a slice of lardy cake. Mrs Pengelly would sip a small glass of brandy and we would retire to bed. *I'll do everythin' you tell me. We'll have silver cake forks and fine china cups – just like Mrs Pengelly.* Why was I scared? Nathan was a good man, he would never hurt me. The clock chimed nine and as the last chime faded Mrs Pengelly folded her sewing. 'Let's have tea with Billy in the kitchen. Ye must never go to bed on a quarrel.'

I nodded, wanting that too. 'We said no tools until he was fifteen. He's doing so well with his books.'

'Celia Pendarvis thinks he should go to Truro Grammar School. She's offering to pay all his expenses.' She looked up. 'It's an opportunity very few are offered – and he's clever enough for it.'

A knot twisted my stomach, the thought of him alone, in a school so far away, was too awful to contemplate. 'We can't do that to him – he'd hate it.'

'Billy's not a boy any more, Elly,' she said, her voice catching. 'Much as I'd like to, we can't stop the march of time – a dressmaker's is not a place for a youth, we both know that.'

Chapter Twelve

'The cart's here,' called Billy from halfway up the stairs.
'It can't be. It's too early.' Anxiety had the better of
me, discarded gowns lying in a heap on my bed. Mrs Pengelly
adjusted the lace on my bodice and pinched my cheeks to
give much needed colour.

'He obviously wants you early. It's a good job you're ready.
There, that's better. Have you got the dates?'

I grabbed the delicately wrapped parcel and slipped it in
my basket. Mrs Munroe's plumpest dates, carefully stuffed
with her very best marzipan. 'What if Mrs Perys doesn't like
them?' I felt giddy with nerves.

'Course she will, they're delicious.' She glanced out of the
window and handed me my parasol. 'Billy's on the cart. Have
a lovely day and come back and tell me all about it. Take your
cloak — it looks like rain.'

I wrapped my embroidered silk shawl round my shoulders
and put my woollen cloak neatly in my basket. A break in the
heat would be most welcome. Sam opened the front door,

standing proudly in his new jacket and polished boots. Mrs Pengelly stood beside him. It was too late to run back upstairs and change my gown but I felt suddenly over-dressed – too formal, my hair too ornate.

I stopped, the blood draining from my head. I felt suddenly dizzy. William Cotterell was holding open the cart door. Billy was already sitting on the driver's seat and he turned round, smiling broadly. Mrs Pengelly sensed my reluctance and took hold of my arm, guiding me firmly towards the cart. 'You've nothing to worry about – go and *enjoy* yourself. You work too hard and the fresh air will do you good.'

She was coaxing me forward but I hardly heard her. William held out his hand and I chose to ignore it, stepping into the painted cart as if going to the guillotine. He flicked the reins and the cart pulled away, Mrs Pengelly and Sam waving happily from the door. A tapestry cushion lay next to me, a woollen rug folded on the seat opposite. I felt sick with nerves, my heart hammering.

'I'll get us through town, Billy – then you can take over. It shouldn't be too busy.' Billy turned round and waved, fidgeting and sliding on the seat in excitement. People were watching, tongues would soon be wagging. 'Steady, Billy. The horse will catch your excitement.' William winked at Billy and my heart froze. 'We managed that all right – I wasn't sure it would work.' He smiled again and my unease turned to anger – they had planned this, the two of them conspiring together to get the better of me. This man's power was absolute; he was already taking Billy from us, influencing his thoughts, leading him astray.

'Comfortable enough, Miss Liddicot?' William did not turn round. 'There's a cushion for you to sit on.'

He wore an unbuttoned corduroy waistcoat over his shirt, a scarf tied loosely round his neck, and I stared at his back, my cheeks flaming. Two hours too early. I should have made him wait. Of course, everything was not all right. The crowded streets gave way to scattered cottages, the steady climb taking us out of town and along the old drover's lane. Parts of it had been widened and strengthened but the passing places were still too few, the surface far from adequate. Only the pack horses were safe to pick their way between the ruts. Sir James had plans for this route but funds were against him and carts travelled at their peril.

William handed Billy the reins, reaching his arm along the back of the seat. Above us, wispy white clouds stretched across the sky, a soft breeze blowing from the sea. The early sunshine was gathering strength, the air smelling of thyme and chamomile, honeysuckle and wild carrot. Gorse bushes lined our path, their yellow flowers bright against the purple moorland. It was so fresh, so beautiful, until William spoiled it. 'You know what they say about gorse, Billy? They say when gorse is out of bloom, kissing's out of season.'

'Never! Do they really?' Billy laughed, looking nervously round at me.

William nudged Billy in the ribs. 'And you know why that is?' Billy shook his head, smiling despite my glower. 'It's because gorse is always in flower.'

I looked away, leaving them to laugh gleefully, childishly, like the conspirators they were. Billy was like a puppy with a new master. 'Know what you said about adits, Will? Well, I understand them now. They're big drains what take the water—'

'*That* take the water…' interrupted William.

Billy grinned, a huge, beaming smile. 'That drain the water down to the sea. Any water below them has to be pumped out – because it's now below the water level.'

'Quite so. And pumping's expensive so you need efficient engines. Some engines burn coal so fast they make the price of tin so high that the cost of running the engine is more than the price they can sell it at.'

'Like if Elowyn charges too little for her gowns, then the price of making them is more than she gets back.'

'That's right, lad.' He cuffed Billy round the ear. 'Going to be a dressmaker, are you?'

Billy blushed a deep beetroot red. 'Course not. I'm goin' to be an engineer.'

They sat in happy silence, the two of them nudging and pointing at things along the way. I sat alone and wretched, my sense of isolation increasing by the minute. To them my presence was of no consequence; I was a sullen passenger they could ignore. Billy started singing and William joined in. That hateful song, once more ringing in my ears…*And I would love you all the day, Over the hills and far away*…I clamped my mouth shut, fighting back my anger. If I complained, he would have a ready answer. He had an answer for everything.

The grassy meadow gave way to the gentle sweep of the hill and the first sight of the bay. The harbour was bathed in sunshine, the lock once again crammed with masts. Every full tide, Nathan had said; Sir James must make his harbour pay. Ahead of us was the old engine house and the disused mine, all around us, signs of testing the land to look for clay. Piles of spoil rose untidily along the track, pits worked in strips, their boundaries marked by low wooden fences.

Everywhere was covered in a fine white dust, even the petticoats and aprons left drying on the gorse bushes. We passed the hurdle thatches where blocks of clay lay protected from the weather, each block separated with sand and straw to help it dry. William answered Billy's question before he asked it. 'Summer clay takes four months to dry, winter clay as much as eight. It must dry properly or else it crumbles.'

The chapel bell began to clang, people rushing up the lane to be in time. William took the reins, urging the horse behind a pile of spoilings, and we were hidden from view. 'Good a place as any,' he said, smiling.

Billy jumped down quickly but I remained sitting in the cart. William held open the door, his bold eyes searching my face. Hazel eyes flecked with green. 'We've an hour to spare, Elowyn. I thought you might like to sit among the flowers and watch the harbour.' His voice was tender, far from mocking. 'I've brought a rug and Billy's brought some of Mrs Munroe's apple tarts. She made them especially for him.'

'She spoils him,' I said, once more refusing his hand. Swathes of flowers basked in the morning sunshine and for a moment I hesitated. 'I'll get out for a short while — only because I want to study the flowers — then I'm getting straight back in.'

His smile was rueful, his eyes full of mischief. 'It's the pink campion you need to study. The petals are longer than you sew them and slightly rounder. Your roses are perfect…your honeysuckle's good but the pink could be darker.' I looked up, astonished. 'I'll get the rug,' he said quickly, 'I know just where to take you.'

Billy smiled nervously, expecting my rebuke, but I stopped myself, raising my eyes heavenwards and clamping my mouth tightly shut. He seemed thrilled and ran ahead, his leather bag of tarts hanging from his shoulder. Had he grown? Surely he seemed taller? William led us to a boulder and spread out the rug. There were flowers everywhere, carpeting the ground, standing sentry in the wind. A wild rose bush stood entwined with honeysuckle and I stood breathing in the heady scent, my anger slowly abating.

'Keep a watch for us, Billy – over there, where you can see both ways. Let me know if anyone comes. The tarts are all yours.'

Billy looked conspiratorial yet slightly nervous, standing squarely up to William who towered above him. 'You goin' to kiss her?' he asked abruptly.

William whistled then laughed, putting his hand on Billy's shoulder. 'Kiss another man's woman and get myself beaten up and thrown into the sea again? You think I don't learn? Elowyn's quite safe – all we're going to do is sit amongst the flowers until that frown leaves her face and her cheeks fill with colour. Then we can go.'

My frown deepened. *Another man's woman*. He had done all this before, the rug, the talk of flowers, the way he made you feel somehow special. Billy ran away and I turned my back, picking some flowers, holding them carefully so I could study their shape. He was right: campion petals were longer and rounder at the tip. My honeysuckle was perfect and I should have told him but I sat letting the sun warm me, watching the water sparkle in the bay below. A sense of peace filled me. I could come here as often as I liked to walk these cliffs. I could find flowers I did not know existed and embroider exquisite shawls like the one I was wearing. I did not need to be a dressmaker, I could embroider shawls.

He sat down on the rug, his back to mine, reaching over, picking a tiny bunch of speedwell. 'As it happens, I've never kissed another man's woman and I wasn't thrown into the sea. I was forcibly thrown onto a ship and I jumped in time. It was a risk, but I knew I wouldn't drown.'

His sudden intimacy startled me, the way his voice had softened, his gentle picking of the flowers. 'Of course you could've drowned — you nearly did!' I stood up, leaving him in no doubt that the out-spread blanket was both inappropriate and unwelcome.

He smiled but did not look up. 'I might have died of cold, but I'll never drown — I was born with a cowl over my face. My mother sold it to the highest bidder. They can fetch as much as a sovereign, you know — sailors fight over them.'

Above us, skylarks were singing, cattle watching us from the fields beyond. He held up a selection of tiny flowers, carefully crafted into a small bunch. For such large hands, he had a very delicate touch, like when he removed the thorns from my gown. 'There are men who want my downfall — men particularly good at beating people up and making them disappear. They think me long gone and that's how I want it.'

111

A wave of fear made my heart race. 'Why are you telling me this?'

'Because I'll never lie to you.' He held up the flowers, obviously deciding to add more. 'Tell me, why use *French* seams? We're at war with France – surely you should be content with English seams?' He smiled up at me, enjoying my surprise. The wounds were healed on his face, his chin closely shaven, his black hair curling round his forehead. His hair had been freshly washed, shining black in the sun. 'Billy told me that's what you were doing, honestly, I know nothing of dressmaking. Do join me, Elowyn. I'll not lay a finger on you, I promise.'

My actions seemed suddenly churlish. Perhaps he did mean no harm; besides, my hem was in danger of getting dirty. I sat down carefully, pulling my gown off the dusty stones, and we sat watching the gulls circle round Jack Deveral's new boat. 'If you really want to know, French seams enclose the cut edge and stop it from fraying – I use them on very delicate material. English seams leave the edges exposed so you have to overstitch them. It depends on the material...Why are you interested?' I kept my voice sharp; he must have no encouragement. One smile at a man and it gave them ideas.

'If you like a person you're interested in what they do and how they spend their day. Here,' he said, holding up the miniature bouquet, 'I meant what I said – that frown will have to go.' He slipped the flowers under the ribbon on my bonnet, smiling at my embarrassment. 'Tinners need fresh air as much as any dressmaker – I come to the cliffs as often as I can.'

'You're a miner?' I asked, taking the flowers from my bonnet.

'Of sorts,' he replied, stretching suddenly forward, picking a leaf from the ground. 'Look at this. Look, Elowyn, a four-leafed clover – definitely four leaves.' He held up the leaf, his fingernails freshly scrubbed and free from dirt, his smile lighting his face. His shirt was freshly laundered, the same white shirt that had blown in the breeze. His scarf was tied neatly at his neck, his breeches, brown corduroy with leather at the pockets. His boots were newly polished, covered only by fine white dust. 'I wonder what Mrs Munroe would make of this?'

He leaned nearer to show me and I pulled back at the touch of his arm. His proximity, his freshly shaved chin, the dark lashes round his eyes made me suddenly uneasy. My face was on fire, my eyes filling with heat. I remembered the strength of his arm as he held me in the cave, the touch of his hand as it closed over mine. He seemed oblivious to my discomfort, smiling happily, reaching for a pocket notebook. He opened the pages, positioning the leaf carefully, pressing it quickly as he closed the book. 'This will bring us luck.' His words were barely a whisper.

This was all wrong – the man was trouble, anyone could see that; his terrible liberty, his talk of flowers, his whispered intimacies, his huge arms with their fighter's muscles. He was too strong, too capable – working his way into every-one's favour. I rose quickly, shaking the creases from my pale blue silk. What was I thinking? He was playing us, first one then the other – playing us all, even poor Ruth with her mended hen house and newly dug ditches. I threw his flowers to the ground. 'Take me to Mr Cardew. You should never have stopped.'

Billy had been running. He caught his breath. 'Someone's comin'...a man, walkin' right below us.' He turned and pointed. 'Goin' towards that shack.'

A large boulder lay between us and the shack. William took my elbow, ushering me forward. The cart was out of sight but quite some distance away and panic gripped me. Damn William Cotterell – if that *was* his name. Nathan would find out and would think me wanton. William peered round the boulder through the protection of a hawthorn. He reached out, drawing me forward, standing close behind me as we watched the man. 'He'll not see us – we're well hidden.'

Billy peered through a bush on the other side. 'What's he doing, scurryin' around like that? It's as if he doesn't want to be seen either.' The man was clearly in a hurry, scrambling over the uneven ground, bending almost double. We were far from the harbour but he kept glancing back as if fearing he was being followed.

'You're right – he doesn't want to be seen,' replied William.

The man certainly looked furtive, his long dark coat concealing his clothes, his hat pulled low to hide his face – a fleeting black figure, intent on getting to the shack. 'What's in the hut?' I asked.

William leaned forward, his hair touching my cheek, his jacket brushing against my back. 'It's a privy. It washes into the settling pits...it's for decency's sake, really – the clay maidens work up here and it serves to keep them private.' His hand burned my arm. 'Hold still, he's looking round.'

'Poor man…he's probably desperate.' Billy stuffed his fist into his mouth, throwing himself back against the boulder. 'Needs it pretty bad! Did you see him run? Man must have the gripes somethin' terrible!'

William chuckled and I found myself smiling, even repressing a laugh. I drew back, frowning at Billy. 'There's no need for bawdiness.'

'Then why are we all laughing?' He opened his bag. 'If we're stuck here, you might as well have a tart.' He giggled again, his eyes shining.

William smiled. 'Left me some, did you, Billy?'

'Just one!' He smiled back, holding out the tart, and we sat looking across the pits to the thatched shelters with their slated trestles and blocks of drying clay. William ate his tart, wiping his mouth on his large white handkerchief. Around us, gorse bushes bloomed in glorious profusion. From a nearby bush, a songbird sang. 'Taking his time, isn't he? If he was in such a hurry, ye'd have thought he'd have finished by now.' Billy was giggling again.

The smile left William's face. He tensed suddenly and I felt his shoulders stiffen. He peered round the boulder. 'You're right. What if he's not using it as a privy?' Something in his tone had changed.

'What if he's waitin' for someone?' replied Billy.

What if Nathan found me like this? The situation was unbearable. Everything about it was wrong. Not just the danger, but my appearance – my dress was in danger of getting snagged, my hem already covered in fine white dust. I could not turn up looking dishevelled again.

'He's leaving – crossing back the way he came.' William's jaw clenched. 'When he's over that stile, take Elowyn to the cart and wait for me – his behaviour's strange. I'm going to take a look inside that hut.' His voice was sharp, authoritative, and Billy knew not to question. 'Keep out of sight.'

William returned to the cart as if ready to pick a quarrel and my heart froze. Two very different faces – two very different men; one I could almost forgive, the other, angry, defiant, a man not to be crossed. A different man, a different voice; I pulled my shawl around me, a sudden chill making me shiver.

He was clearly preoccupied, answering Billy's questions with the same patience but not the same enthusiasm. The horse seemed pleased to be nearly home, pricking up his ears and shaking his bridle. The chapel bell was ringing and a steady stream of people had stepped out into the sunshine. 'I'll let you off next to that stack of barrels.' There was tension in his face, a hardening of the jaw. He pulled up the reins.

Thick woodsmoke blew across from the brick kilns, the acrid smell of burning lime. I had not wanted to get on the cart, yet now I did not want to get off. A sea of faces swam before me and I knew Nathan would be watching. I gathered up my skirt, my eyes firmly on the chapel. Fear made it hard to breathe. I started searching the crowd – if he saw me with

William Cotterell he would think me untruthful. Scattered stones littered the ground, horse dung and mess left by the cows. Behind a low wall, two sows basked in a muddy pen.

I hardly heard William. His head remained bowed, his eyes averted. 'Say nothing about what we saw – we need to keep that to ourselves.'

Another secret to be kept. 'This is the last time,' I said. 'I mean it, William. You're to leave us alone.' My legs were shaking, my nerves getting the better of me.

His reply was harsh, as dark as his mood: 'I've been watching your Nathan Cardew, and I don't like what I see. He's not good enough for you, surely you can see that?'

Chapter Thirteen

Pierside
Sunday 12th June 1796, 12:30 a.m.

The sea of faces took individual forms, some smiling, some nodding, all of them looking twice at my gown, their eyes widening as they took in the soft scoop of my neckline, the slightly raised waist, the elegant lace on my three-quarter sleeves. Embarrassment flooded my cheeks. I looked so frivolous, not high-minded at all. I was over-dressed, my gown too bright, their dark clothes and unadorned bonnets completely at odds with my colourful ribbons.

I had forgotten how blue Nathan's eyes were – the lightest blue of a summer sky. They were smiling across at me now, alight with pleasure. 'Elowyn, here you are.' He came to my side. 'Let me introduce you…' A rush of pride made my heart leap. He looked so handsome, his distinguished clothes and air of authority marking him out from those around him. 'You're in time to meet Mr Hellyar.' The crowd parted, their expectant gazes following us as we passed. 'He's Viscount Vallenforth's chief assayer and what he doesn't know about tin isn't worth knowin'.' Nathan seemed so proud of me, holding my arm, nodding politely to people as we passed.

I had forgotten his strong jaw, the dimple in his chin, the way he held himself. He was dressed the same as last week but his cravat was more to my taste, neatly folded and held in place with a silver pin. A stout, short man stood with his back to us and Nathan waited by his side, smiling at me. The sun caught the light in his hair, the fine lines around his eyes, and I smiled back, swallowing my nerves. That such a man had singled me out.

The barest flicker crossed Mr Hellyar's thin lips. 'Mr Cardew,' he said, bowing. His piercingly intelligent eyes looked the sort to take everything in at first glance; the whiskers of his sideburns almost meeting under the folds of his chins. His clothes were good quality, his waistcoat embroidered with fine, gold thread. His cravat was shot silk, his shoes, soft leather. A gold chain stretched across his bulging belly, an eyeglass hung from a gold chain round his neck. He picked up the eyeglass, examining me in greater detail. 'May I introduce Miss Liddicot? Perhaps, you've met before at Sir James Polcarrow's? Miss Liddicot's a particular friend of Sir James' wife.'

Mr Hellyar's eyes strayed straight to my bodice and remained there. 'From Fosse?' I had expected better and disappointment filled me. It was always the same – the leer, the wetting of the lips, the hand accidently touching me. I could feel my cheeks redden, my mouth turning to dust.

'Yes, here for the day...'

Mr Hellyar nodded curtly, drawing out his fob watch. He turned without a word, heading quickly down the lane ahead of everyone else. Nathan smiled but a flash of irritation crossed his face. 'I'm sorry, Elowyn – he's a difficult man to pin down.'

'Why does Sir James let Viscount Vallenforth ship coal to his harbour? Mamm said the coal for his engines is contaminating the clay – shouldn't Sir James insist he builds his *own* harbour, to keep the clay and coal apart?'

Nathan seemed surprised. 'Importin' coal for Viscount Vallenforth's mine brings good money, and exportin' his tin makes even more sense. Polmear Mine's just the other side of the hill and Sir James has brokered a good deal. Sir James' harbour dues aren't cheap – he's set to profit from Polmear Mine though he's not invested a farthing in it.'

He smiled happily, pointing to a thick-set man standing at the chapel door. The man was dressed in sober clothes, a large black hat and two white bands hanging stiffly from his collar. 'That's Tobias Hearne, my brother-in-law. He's a blacksmith by trade and the only lay preacher we've got… and the man standin' next to him is Josiah Drew. He's the leat engineer and he's comin' to lunch, so you'll meet him later.' He stopped. 'Did you get my letter?'

'Yes, I did. Thank you.'

He seemed suddenly shy. 'I've been counting down the days, Elowyn…honest, I barely know what I've been doin'…' His timid hesitation made my heart jolt. His outward appearance was so assured but deep inside he seemed so vulnerable. 'Shall we stay here or take a stroll?' The tide was out, the lock gates holding back the water. Already, the strange incongruity seemed so familiar – the tall masts crowding the lock, the beached boats lying crookedly on the sand. Small boys were running along the shoreline, men fishing on the rocks. Nathan's eyes held mine. 'We're not due at Harbour House till two so at least we've got some time to ourselves.'

The wind felt colder all of a sudden. I wrapped my cloak round me, looking across the bay to the black clouds stretching across the horizon. The sky had darkened, the sea turning an ominous grey. I nodded, walking slowly down the lane, our unspoken thoughts leading us as surely as an invisible thread. The new cobbles had been laid and glistening iron railings lined the road. I hardly dared breathe, let alone look. A plate had been fastened to the iron gate, the name *Piermaster* painted in fresh blue paint.

'They've finished the back yard an' there's a gate that leads straight to the fields. I've fenced a small patch for vegetables an' I've ordered apple trees to be planted. Shall we have plums as well – though it would be best to plant them in autumn?' He stopped, closing his eyes in painful embarrassment. 'I'm sorry, Elowyn,' he said, 'I'm gettin' ahead of myself. Forgive me, the plums can wait.'

I glanced down the alley separating the two cottages and caught my breath. A beautifully crafted iron arch stood begging for a climbing rose and I stared at it, aching with pleasure. I could see yellow roses hanging in glorious abundance – masses and masses of yellow roses. Tears pricked my eyes and I forced them away. My childhood dream – how could he have guessed? 'I'm very fond of plums,' I said.

The pressure of his hand increased. Callused hands, scrubbed clean yet not entirely free from dirt. 'You'll be pleased to hear I've checked every yard of the new fence and those cows won't be breakin' out again!' His tone was tender, used only for me. 'And I've sorted the leases – Richard Sellick's takin' rooms behind the hotel and his wife's to stay with her mother.' He raised his eyes, pursing his lips. 'You should've heard him trying to negotiate the rent! Honest, we're not givin' away the houses – though he obviously thinks we should!'

The cottage seemed to be holding out its arms to me, wanting to keep me safe and I swallowed the lump forming in my throat. Roses round the back gate, a room to sew in and yet another room for people to stay. Billy could come whenever he liked. Nathan reached for his watch. 'We've another hour...time enough to walk down to the lock so I can check the imports. There's a bench on the harbour wall where you could sit and watch...We'll be next to my office if this rain comes.'

He seemed so happy, tucking my hand under his arm, leading me down the cobbles towards the lock. I felt suddenly safe, cherished, quite content to let my future be dictated by the rhythm of the sea. He seemed to read my mind.

'I'm only busy today because I've no claim to a day off but it won't always be like this. When I'm Piermaster, I'll have every other Sunday off and during the week, I'll work opposite Mr Perys. He'll do the high tides – the harbourin' and getting the ships in and out, and I'll do the low tides – the unloadin' and loadin'. He smiled, nodding to a man who passed. 'We'll not get time off together, me and Mr Perys, not when I'm Piermaster.' His look grew somehow bolder, not boyish at all, and a shiver of excitement shot through me. 'I'll have plenty of time to keep you company – you'll be kickin' me out the house – sendin' me on my way.'

I understood his meaning and my heart pounded. Half of me wanted him to draw me to him, show me some intimacy. For the first time in my life I was ready to let a man kiss me but he showed no sign of impropriety, remaining stiff and formal beneath his Sunday best. If only he would rest his hand on my back or lean closer against me. If only I could feel his cheek brush against my hair.

Harbour House rose majestically above us, twice the size of the house next door. We were to fit in with the tides and eat in the afternoon but my appetite had long gone; my lips felt dry and my mouth parched. I had been to many fine houses and should not feel so nervous – Coombe House was just as grand, in fact, grander; Harbour House had only five windows, whereas Coombe House had eight – and that did not include the attic windows. It was meeting the people who might form my new life that caused me such dread.

Nathan seemed to sense my fear and held my arm, helping me up the five stone steps. 'They'll need this storm porch; without it, the force of the easterlies will damage this paint.' He knocked on the gleaming front door. 'This house will stand the test of time. It's as solid as a rock.'

I breathed deep for courage, inhaling the smell of wax polish and rosemary. The hall was dark and oppressive, the flagstones hidden under a swirling red carpet. A huge painting of a ship hung on the wall, a heavy oak mirror absorbing rather than reflecting any light. It looked cluttered and cramped, a large barometer hanging at the bottom of the stairs and a long case clock with a polished brass dial squeezed into the corner. It felt forbidding and severe, such a contrast to Coombe House. Only the alabaster vase on the hall table and the silver filigree tray for calling cards seemed to welcome us.

An ornate wooden banister curved extravagantly from the right and I glanced at Nathan, catching the pride in his smile. The clock chimed two and Nathan pointed me forward, following the maid to the open pine door. It was polished to a shine, the handle a smooth, deep ebony. 'Mr Cardew and Miss Liddicot,' announced the maid with no trace of a smile. She looked nervous, far too thin, her petrified eyes darting to Mrs Perys.

'Come in, my dear.' Mrs Perys moved away from the window and the room filled with light. Her voluminous skirts swished as she came towards us and I dipped my best curtsy. She merely nodded in return, the feathers in her hair barely moving. Her deep purple dress looked dark and severe, her smile clipped. She had been watching us from the window and obviously did not like what she saw. 'How very kind of you to come.'

'No, Mrs Perys, it is you who are very kind to invite me. A small present to say thank you.' I handed her the little parcel. 'They're marzipan dates. I hope you like them.'

She looked up, surprised. My voice had clearly taken her by surprise. '*Marzipan dates?*' she repeated, looking at me with greater interest. Women looked at my gowns in two ways: either with envy or with delight. Her look was envious, calculating, and my disappointment soared. She was wearing satin, I was wearing silk, and though it meant nothing to the men in the room, I caught her obvious displeasure. 'This is my husband, *the harbourmaster,*' she said, leaving me in no doubt I had offended her.

Mr Perys bowed and I recognized him as the man with the whistle. Everything about him looked authoritative, his grey side whiskers, strong jaw and austere bearing instantly commanding respect. A disciplinarian, no doubt about that, yet I liked the way he was smiling and I knew Nathan liked him, too. There was kindness in his eyes, genteelness in his manner. Snapping shut his fob watch, he smiled politely. 'You're very welcome, Miss Liddicot. We've heard a lot about you.' He seemed ten years older than his wife, maybe more.

This room too was dominated by heavy furniture and more paintings of ships in full sail. Only the window saved the room – the polished pine shutters framing a beautiful view of the lock and the harbour beyond. Two portraits hung either side of the large fireplace and a gold mirror balanced on the mantelpiece. Mrs Perys saw me look at them. 'Mr Perys' parents. We're to have our own portraits painted soon...' She threw a coy look at her husband who smiled back in adoration.

'How wonderful,' I replied, smiling as warmly as I could.

The maid coughed politely. 'Mr Sellick, if you please, and Mrs Hearne.'

The sight of Ruth gave me much needed courage. The two women were clearly friends, Mrs Perys immediately smiling, holding out her hands to clasp Ruth's. Mr Sellick bowed. He was a short man, smartly though soberly dressed, his greying hair worn short, his complexion sallow.

'Mr Sellick has just taken the lease on the top clay sett – an' this is Miss Liddicot.' Mrs Perys' voice sounded curt, her words brusque, as though he, too, had offended her.

I took a deep breath to steady my nerves. The maid was balancing a tray of five glasses with what looked like lemonade and I took the nearest, glancing over to Nathan who was smiling broadly. Of course, no alcohol, I had forgotten Methodists did not drink. Mr Sellick was one of Sir James' new speculators, his investment bringing much needed employment, yet he looked far from prosperous. There was an air of nervousness about him, his hands shaking as he took his glass. His collar and cuffs had already been turned and a badly sewn darn was visible on the sleeve of his jacket.

'So, once again, we've to make do without Mr Hearne,' came Mrs Perys' reproachful teasing. 'No, Ruth, no matter – if Mr Hearne believes the vagrants warrant a service, I'll not be the one to interfere. In fact, I've sent them a sack of potatoes – the ones trampled by the cows last week. Come, sit here...Tell me, Miss Liddicot, d'you like our little community? D'you think ye'll feel at home here? I believe ye're a *seamstress*.' She turned abruptly. 'Mr Sellick, ye weren't in chapel this morning?'

He seemed surprised, looking up quickly. 'Alas, Mrs Perys, I'd much paperwork to attend to. I've a great deal to get sorted – what with the agents comin' tomorrow, I've a mound of work to see to.' His accent was not local – Cornish, but not from here.

'You're confident you'll get the Wedgwood contract?' Nathan spoke quietly, an edge to his voice I had not heard before. 'They're determined on the best and I've heard Lord Falmouth's clay's the purest – he's leased the Goonvean pit. I thought you'd hit a seam of discolouration – a tinge of rust?'

The two men stared at each other, the colour rising in Mr Sellick's face. 'No…not at all. The top twenty yards had a touch of discolouration but for months we've been diggin' the whitest clay – they'll be fools not to take mine.' He wiped the sweat from his forehead. His cuffs needed washing as well as replacing; there were further signs of wear on his elbow and a dark stain showed on his breeches. It looked like clay had been recently scraped from his boots. 'There's a lot at stake – you'll have to forgive me.'

Mr Perys tucked his fob watch back into his jacket pocket. 'Mr Joseph Drew, if you please.' The maid bobbed a curtsy as a middle-aged man entered. He was short and thin, with watery eyes behind round-rimmed glasses, his frame stooped, as if the weight of the world rested on his shoulders. I felt drawn to observe him. He was the engineer responsible for the lock, the man who designed the leats – the drainage channels that fed the lock. William had told Billy even the best lock gates leaked and a constant flow of water was needed to keep the lock full. Mr Drew seemed so slight, bowing stiffly, blinking at us through red-rimmed eyes.

Mrs Perys rushed forward. 'Mr Drew, let me help ye.' She

looked angrily at Mr Sellick. 'The speculators *must* come to some arrangement – the dust must be dampened – or the very least, the clay must be shipped in barrels, not loaded as blocks.' She had fierce eyes, a deeply puckered mouth. 'Nothin's been done, though ye know my mind. An' while I think on it, nothin's been done about the horse muck. It must be picked up sooner an' taken to the fields. Am I right, Mrs Hearne? And somethin's to be done about the wagons – they come hurtlin' two abreast where there's only room for one. A woman can lose her skirt to the passin' wheels. Or a leg…I believe several men have had accidents, have they not, Mrs Hearne?'

Ruth nodded vigorously but Mr Sellick looked weary. 'What you say is of great concern, Mrs Perys. Believe me, Sir James is as anxious as you to increase the safety of his port. You've everything in hand, I believe, Mr Cardew?'

I felt a rush of pride as Nathan nodded. 'I've a list as long as your arm and can vouch everythin' will get resolved.' He smiled at Mrs Perys, his voice softening as he continued, 'Drags will be fitted to the wagons to slow them down and we're to widen the road to the harbour. I've ordered leather bags to catch the horse muck an' we're to move the dries further uphill – to catch the wind. Sir James has ordered a doctor to come from St Austell once a month to check the maidens' eyes, and we'll open the sluice gate to swill the harbour between loadin' and unloadin'.' His voice was respectful, his tone serious. 'But we need your opinions, Mrs Perys. Any concerns you have will be dealt with straight away – that's my promise.'

Mrs Perys nodded. Ruth was nodding too, her beautiful eyes looking anxiously at Mr Sellick. She coughed. 'I'm glad about the doctor, but the maidens still need protectin'. That dust goes everywhere.'

'Maidens?' I asked.

Ruth smiled. 'You've not seen them, Miss Liddicot, because they don't work on a Sunday. They scrape the sand and straw off the dried blocks – you've seen the thatches? The grit gets everywhere – in their eyes, down their necks – it's hard enough work without all the irritation.'

Loud clanging sounded in the hall and Mrs Perys seemed delighted at our obvious surprise, glancing coquettishly at her husband for his returning smile. 'It's a gong, from *China*,' she said proudly. 'Mr Perys picked it up when he was a master of *Fortune*. Now then...' I was surprised she did not clap her hands. 'Mr Perys will escort our lovely Mrs Hearne...' She glanced sideways at me. 'A bride of six months *always* takes preference. Mr Drew, you must take my arm and Mr Cardew can have the pleasure of escortin' Miss Liddicot. I'm afraid, Mr Sellick, ye must follow behind. Is your wife never to join us?'

I put my hand on Nathan's arm and he squeezed it gently. He seemed so at home, never guessing my discomfort. We followed Mrs Perys along the hall, and I took a deep breath. Immediately, I regretted it. A strong smell of boiled cabbage wafted from the kitchen.

Chapter Fourteen

I sat between Mr Drew and Mr Sellick with Nathan and Ruth opposite me. Mr and Mrs Perys commanded each end of the table, Mrs Perys closest to the door so her nods and frowns could be directed to the maid waiting in the hall outside. It seemed the cabbage was the least of my problems; a mound of tripe lay covered in a congealed sauce, potatoes and dumplings as grey as the day outside. Only the pie looked promising; though if it had been Mrs Munroe's, it would have been glazed to a golden crust.

Nathan's list was growing longer. Mrs Perys hardly took her first mouthful before she began again. A Sunday school was needed, a bowling alley, a wrestling green. Everyone *must* agree that dissipation followed idleness – too many visiting sailors were restless and unoccupied, thinking only of the sort of pleasure that gave the town a bad name. She lowered her voice: 'Supply follows demand – the linhay *must* be guarded, day and night. The girls rounded up and expressly forbidden – it's a wicked sin. *And* so close to the settling pits…' She pursed her lips. 'Ye know my mind – there's danger in letting things slide.'

Mr Sellick braved an interruption. 'The settling pits are soon to be re-fenced—'

'It's the children I worry about,' interrupted Mrs Perys. 'Spendin' their days handin' staves to the coopers. A school's needed – and not just on Sunday.'

'The school's to be built,' replied Nathan, 'but at the moment, the casks must be made. Clay, vinegar, beer, pilchards – it all needs to be barrelled. Sir James has procured a teacher – the children will have lessons in the mornings and stack the staves in the afternoon. That way, they'll still get paid.'

Mr Perys smiled kindly. 'Ye're doin' a good job, Mr Cardew – after all, Rome wasn't built in a day. The new lanterns on the harbour are a great improvement.' Another kind smile, a nod of respect. 'There's only so much ye can do at once.'

Nathan returned his smile. 'And you, Mr Perys? Have you told the owners of the seine boats not to block the entrance?'

'That scoundrel Jack Deveral's kicking up merry hell. He'll not pay his dues an' refuses to anchor elsewhere. In the easterly last week, his boat lay right across the bay – blockin' the brig from Norway. Nigh on three hours it had to wait. I've fined him, but he says he'll not pay.'

I felt myself blush, my cheeks burning in shame. The mutton pie turned to salt in my mouth. Mrs Perys was clearly enjoying my discomfort. *Fancy clothes and jumped-up speech but you're nothing but a fisherman's daughter – and your mother, living with a man like that.* I hated this stuffy room with the view of the back yard; hated the heavy creamware plates, the ugly figurines, the hideous gravy boat in the shape of a bull.

Nathan saw my discomfort. 'You can't really blame the man. Jack Deveral and John Polkerris have had the bay to themselves their whole lives – living an' workin' here with just five cottages in the whole bay – and now…well…now they must share it with hundreds. Jack Deveral's showin' his anger and I can't blame him. Leave it with me. I'll make sure he pays his fine.'

Mr Perys wiped his chin with his large pink napkin. 'Aye, ye've a way with these men, Nathan. Get him to see reason and I'll not bother him again.'

Mrs Perys sniffed at my still full plate. 'Ye see, Miss Liddicot, we've a way of helpin' each other in our little community – that's how it works. I believe I might ask you to look at my gown that needs readjustin'.' She smiled sweetly, barely taking breath. 'Mr Drew, we've not even begun discussin' the opening of the lock. Ye must be so proud – yer vision soon to be the envy of the whole of Cornwall.'

Mr Drew blinked, taking off his glasses, putting them back on again. 'Not so much *my* vision but that of Sir James. I merely draw the plans.'

Mr Perys shook his head. 'Come now, ye're too modest. Ye've worked for Lord Falmouth and I believe ye worked with Mr Smeaton on the Birmingham Canal – quite an achievement. Ye've not done a lock before?'

'I've done harbour walls, waterwheels, artificial lakes, but this is my first lock…' He seemed hesitant as if not wanting the praise. He glanced at Nathan. 'Drawings are one thing but it's the building that counts. What are engineers without builders? It's a good Supervisor of Works what's needed – a man who gets things done.' He nodded respectfully at Nathan who seemed dismissive, not wanting the attention.

'As Mrs Perys says, *we help each other*.'

The room was getting unbearably stuffy, my cheeks were burning. Mrs Perys nodded to the maid to clear the plates. 'Well, the grand openin's to be quite the cause for celebration. Sir James wants *two* hogs roasted – though I believe one would do quite well...and I've heard he's providing *both* beer *and* cider, which is most unwise. He's goin' to ask Miss Lilly to judge the pie competition.'

Mr Sellick had finally finished eating, working his way steadily through his piled plate. Some colour had entered his grey cheeks and he was smiling, resting back on his chair. 'I think we all know who's goin' to win the pie competition,' he said, his hands on his belly. 'There's none finer pie than that...'

'Exactly so,' echoed Mr Drew, 'a foregone conclusion.'

Nathan nodded. 'I've had none better.'

Mr Perys smiled fondly at the praise lavished on his wife. 'Sir James is bringin' Mr Lilly and his daughter on his ship. They're to sail in with the tide and leave as it ebbs. Major Trelawney's to provide a marchin' band.'

I knew it was my turn to praise the food but I was still smarting from Mrs Perys' comment. I was a trained dressmaker, I charged good money for exquisite gowns, but a free service – was that how she saw me, hers to call every time she needed a new gown? 'Have you always been a good cook?' I managed to say.

'Yes…an' I'm willin' to teach ye.' Here it was – her offer in return for my free services. 'Next time, I'll give ye some of my recipes. Ye can come here and write them down. Ye do write, do you, Miss Liddicot? Only, my recipes are like dear friends an' I know them by heart. It's easier for me to speak them – that way I can tell ye exactly what to do.'

Nathan's eyes hardened. Even if Mrs Perys could really write, he was clearly not going to let that pass. 'Elowyn's very clever,' he said quietly. 'Lady Polcarrow's taught her everythin' she knows and Lady Pendarvis has been most particular. Elowyn teaches the accounts in Mrs Pengelly's School and she's very well thought of.' He smiled warmly, lovingly, as if we were the only two people in the room, and my heart swelled – gratitude, love, it was hard to tell. He had come to my rescue over Jack Deveral and now he was singing my praises.

Mrs Perys sat bolt upright. 'Lady Polcarrow and Lady Pendarvis?'

'Elowyn's known the family for years – back when Lady Polcarrow was Rose Pengelly. She lives with Mrs Pengelly and Lady Polcarrow often drops in for tea. And Lady Pendarvis is Elowyn's staunchest admirer and her dearest friend. Don't be shy, Elowyn – they love you, you know they do.'

I was lost for words, stammering excuses, not wanting this at all. 'I do know them…I often take tea with Lady Pendarvis and Lady Polcarrow likes to come to her childhood home… but I hardly know Sir James…Usually, I'm just at home with Sam and Mrs Munroe – she's Mrs Pengelly's friend…We sit together, sometimes we all eat together…'

Nathan's eyes burned with pride. He sat back, smiling as Mrs Perys delved deeper. 'Mrs Munroe? Mrs *Elys* Munroe what worked at Pendenning Hall? You surely don't mean she's Mrs Pengelly's friend? You mean she's her *housekeeper*. Does she still cook?'

Housekeeper, friend, what did it matter? The room was far too hot, this sudden interest in me completely overwhelming. 'Well,' said Mrs Perys, smiling through piercing eyes, 'yer days as a seamstress are soon to be over – homes don't run themselves. Ye'll need help with your drapes and yer linen will need airin'...ye'll have a maid who *must* be watched. Give them an inch and they take a yard.' She sniffed and shook her head. 'There's much to learn and I'll teach ye the *proper* way of goin' about things – though, no doubt, Elys Munroe's tried her best.' She smiled at Nathan who smiled back.

His eyes were burning, his face flushed with pleasure. Ruth, too, seemed delighted, her sweet face reflecting her brother's joy – Mrs Perys had every intention of taking me under her wing. At last, the sweetmeats were cleared from the table, the pale pink blancmange removed untasted. Mr Perys snapped shut his fob watch as the clock struck four.

'Tide's soon to turn. A wonderful meal, my dear...yet again, you leave me thinkin' how thankful I am. Fifteen years married an' every day a joy. I'm a lucky man, indeed.' He smiled at Nathan. 'Marriage makes a man, lad. Marry a good women and yer days are blest.' He seemed suddenly shy and my heart jolted. A stern disciplinarian and feared by so many, yet still so in love with his wife.

Nathan rose from his seat and disappointment shot through me. I was used to good manners, Uncle Thomas' courteous ways, but perhaps Nathan did not know to pull back Ruth's chair? Perhaps my expectations were too high? Beside me, Mr Drew belched and Nathan smiled. I pushed back my own chair, gathering my skirts. 'That was a lovely meal, thank you, Mrs Perys,' I managed to say.

Her smile did not reach her eyes. 'Ye must join me for the openin' of the lock.'

'But I'm—'

'No, no. Don't be shy. I know my mind and I'll not hear otherwise. We're to stand on the quayside and Mrs Hellyar's to join us.'

Nathan came to my side, slipping his arm through mine. 'That's very kind of you, Mrs Perys. We'd consider that the greatest honour.'

Mrs Perys pursed her lips, her satisfied nod making my heart hammer. I was screaming inside. It was going to be such a special day and I wanted to spend it with Gwen and Tom; Sam and Mrs Munroe were coming and Josie and Mrs Pengelly. All of us, planning to spend the day together. Nathan and Ruth were clearly delighted and I stood staring at Mrs Perys, nerves wrenching my stomach. Yet Nathan had told me to speak my mind.

'Mrs Perys…I'm so sorry…but I've a prior invitation. Mrs Pengelly's asked me to join her…'

Her eyes hardened and I saw at once they were the eyes of a woman who was never crossed. 'I'm sure it's nothing ye can't change.'

She stood stiff faced and flushed, her curt tone leaving every-one in no doubt I had offended her. I could hardly breathe. I was a child again, facing the bullies. I was on the streets, facing the lewd calls, the hands that grabbed. Nathan's arm stiffened. He stared ahead, his mouth tight, but Mrs Perys had not finished. I was caught on her line and she was reeling me in. 'I've no doubt Mrs Pengelly will release ye from yer obligation when she knows ye're to join me on the quayside.'

Chapter Fifteen

I had upset them. I had not intended to snub them, far from it. Nathan and Ruth's hurt faces and brave smiles made me feel so wretched – they must think me awful. Nathan had gone out of his way to praise me, coming straight to my rescue over Jack Deveral. They had wanted Mrs Perys to accept me and I had let them down.

They walked silently beside me as we crossed the lock and skirted the workings, taking the long way back to the chapel courtyard. Finally, Ruth broke the silence. 'What Mrs Perys didn't tell you is there's to be dancin'…and catchin' the oiled pig…and tossin' the bales. It's goin' to be that much fun.' She put her arm through mine, squeezing it gently.

Nathan took my other arm. 'I think I'll give catchin' the oiled pig a miss.' He smiled, and my heart jolted. He was so handsome, his smile lighting his face. They had clearly forgiven me. 'And I'll definitely make sure there are *two* roasted pigs – the vagrants can have some taken up to them.'

The clouds that had been threatening all day now gathered

angrily above us but I felt so happy. They were showing me such friendship, taking my side, any disappointment they may have felt clearly forgotten. We reached the courtyard and I waved to Billy who stood waiting by the cart. He looked so happy, his face and hair covered in white dust, his clothes dishevelled. Thick mud caked his boots.

My smile vanished. Mamm and Lorwenna were sitting on the water trough amidst a profusion of cloaks and baskets. Their skirts were bulging and fear gripped me. How could they think to smuggle their brandy in front of Nathan? He stepped forward, bowing formally. 'Ah, Mrs Liddicot, Lorwenna, this is a pleasure. Are you hopin' for a ride? There's plenty of room and you'd be more than welcome.'

The outlines of the bladders were as clear as day and I made to stop them. 'I don't think you should come...you'll get soaked. Look, it's going to pour and you'll get drenched.'

Mamm stood up. 'Ye think I wouldn't risk a drenchin' fer the sake of talkin' to my daughter and visitin' my son? Ye don't know a mother's love, Elly. And we've stronger cloaks than ye have – we'll not feel the rain.'

'You're more than welcome, Mrs Liddicot.' Nathan was going out of his way to be pleasant, showing her as much courtesy as he had shown Mrs Perys. His only thought was to be pleasant, yet she was abusing his goodness. Footsteps sounded behind me and I dared not turn round. The tripe lay uncomfortably in my stomach and I thought I might be sick. The driver drew alongside and I breathed a sigh of relief. Not William Cotterell.

Nathan held out his hand, helping Mamm and Lorwenna

into the cart. He handed them their baskets and turned, the kindness in his eyes almost taking my breath away. All that work, all that responsibility. Men deferred to him, treating him with respect and awe, yet he had been so proud of me, defending me, telling everyone I was clever and educated. He was offering me so much – his love, his fierce protection. He would never hurt me and in turn, deserved never to be hurt. I felt so wretched, wanting him to know I had not intended to slight him.

But I could say nothing, just stand awkwardly by the cart under the watchful eyes of Mamm and Lorwenna. I wanted him to know of my growing regard, to understand I was grateful for his kindness. I pulled out my handkerchief pretending to dab my eyes and as he helped me into the cart I dropped it to the ground. He would know. He would understand my gesture and recognize that by refusing Mrs Perys I had not meant to slight him. The driver cracked his whip and we jolted forward.

'Wait!' Nathan shouted, bending down to retrieve the handkerchief. He shook it firmly to remove the dust and held it up for me to take. 'That's a bit of luck,' he said, smiling. 'You just dropped this.'

Mamm saw me bite my lip. 'Ye look beautiful, Elly. Did ye have a good time? I'm that proud of ye, supping at the great house.' I stared away, unable to speak. 'Elly, look at me… always so angry? Such a scowl!' She bent forward, whispering so Billy would not hear. 'Others need what ye've got – ye're well accounted fer but I've another to think of.' She sat back, her lips pursed, nodding her head beneath the hood of her cloak. 'There's another needs my attention. An apprentice wage's not enough to keep a wife an' bairn.'

Lorwenna was glaring at me – Jack Deveral's eyes and ears staring straight at me. Mamm's voice took on a firmness I hardly recognized. 'He'll be waiting fer this – just like he was last week an' will be the week after this. What's wrong with ye, Elly, don't ye want yer brother to have what ye have?'

I turned my face away. 'You know very well I want nothing to do with it. You were wrong to ask me.'

Her eyes sharpened. 'Ye've not said a word?'

'Of course not, what d'you take me for? I'll say nothing.'

We jolted on in silence, neither of us saying another word. Drops of rain began falling and with four miles to go, we were going to get wet. I reached for my basket, balancing it on my lap to retrieve my warm cloak and a small black note-book caught my eye. I stared in disbelief, a sudden jolt in my stomach making me feel queasy. My heart began thumping, knowing I should throw it straight from the cart and let it lie among the spoilings.

Yet there it lay in my basket, every lurch bringing my eyes back to the black leather cover. A terrible need was urging me to open it. I would glance at it. Glance at it and throw it away. I put my hand back into the basket, keeping it hidden so that the others could not see.

On the first page there was an etching of the lock with the gates both shut and open. I turned more pages, recognizing everything in turn – the waterwheel, the engine house, the row of pier houses. The drawings were very delicate and finely executed, and my mouth turned to dust. I turned the next page and my heart missed a beat. I was staring out of the page – ten, maybe twelve drawings of me. They were my features exactly, the cut of my gown, the exact ribbons on my hat, and I stared back into those reproachful eyes, a terrible emptiness flooding my heart. In each drawing I was scowling or looking angrily away and I shut the notebook, suddenly wanting to cry. He had made me look so unpleasant.

As if compelled, I opened the notebook again, slipping my finger further along the pages. This time, the pages were covered in drawings of wild flowers, each one so complete in their likeness that I recognized them at once – buttercups, roses, honeysuckle. There were pages upon pages of delicate etchings – vetch, campion, sea thistle; each one a perfect template, each one able to be copied and embroidered. Pressed between the last two pages was the four-leaf clover.

To twist the knife deeper, Billy began to sing.

'That's lovely,' cried Mamm. 'What's that, then?'

'It's the *Beggar's Opera* – we're all born equal, did ye know that? Even beggars have opera – it's not just for the gentry.' His voice rose, imitating William's, and I shut my eyes, fighting my tears.

Sam held my dripping cloak at arm's length. 'I'll take that… Mrs Munroe wants ye both downstairs with yer feet in steaming water.' He took my bonnet, shaking his head. 'Least ye're back before the storm – Mrs Pengelly's stayin' over at Polcarrow tonight.'

Billy ran down the stairs but my eye caught sight of Mrs Pengelly's finished bonnet. She had made the brim larger, stiffened it with wadding, and I picked it up, staring at it with sudden realization. This was what the clay maidens needed – added protection, a thicker brim. I could start a new business; I could sew protective bonnets for the maidens. I would make the brim stand proud and add a flap to cover their ears. I could attach a protective scarf to pull over their mouths and noses to protect them from the dust and the wind – even the sun and rain.

Sam called up from the kitchen: 'Mrs Munroe says ye're to come *now* – she's not havin' ye come down with a chill.'

Bethany could make them. We would use the rolls of cotton in the storeroom – calico for the hood, thicker cotton round the face. We would make the bonnets beautiful so the maidens would be proud to wear them. We could make aprons as well. I sneezed and reached for my handkerchief, suddenly so happy. Nathan was a builder, his instincts too practical for frivolous love tokens – he knew I would need my handkerchief. It was Mrs Perys who had upset me, Mrs Perys and Mamm. Not Nathan. Nathan was a good man, as solid as his houses.

Chapter Sixteen

The kitchen of Coombe House
Saturday 18th June 1796, 6:30 p.m.

Mrs Pengelly put her hand to her back, staring down at the cut pieces on the meticulously scrubbed table. 'Make this a bit wider to allow for the cord…and you'll need to stiffen this with webbing.' She reached for the pins. 'Use several rows of stitching to join the flounce to the crown… you can pleat it in like the top of a sleeve – then overstitch it so they can be boiled and starched.'

Mrs Munroe rocked in her chair. 'I've seen somethin' similar used up on the moors. Not white, mind. The ones I remember were sackcloth but they're good as the same…' Mr Pitt, her big black and white Tom cat, lay stretched against her ample bosom. 'White's prettier, mind – it'll match their aprons.'

'We're nearly finished. I'm sorry we're taking so long.' We had promised five minutes.

Mrs Munroe's plump hands gripped the side of the rocking chair; behind her was the warm hearth and the spit that had stopped working. Rows of pans hung gleaming on their

144

hooks, jelly moulds and huge tureens sitting neatly on the shelf above. Bunches of thyme and sage were drying round the hearth. There were hams in the larder, jars full of jam and pickle. Mr Pitt watched through half-closed eyes.

'I'd not be sittin' like this if I'd work to do. I've the potatoes to peel and Tamsin's got the peas to pod but I'm all right fer another five minutes.' Mr Pitt stretched out a paw and she smiled fondly. 'It's not often I get told to sit down!'

'Do you know Mrs Perys?' I asked. 'She seemed to know you.'

Mrs Munroe rocked slowly. A large cap covered her greying hair, her spotted sprig dress and apron spilling over the chair beside her. She shook her head. 'Can't say I do.'

'I think you must. She said you worked up at the Hall. Her name's Martha Perys and she's the harbourmaster's wife in Porthcarrow.'

Mrs Pengelly took the pins from her mouth. 'She was Martha Ellis before she was married.'

Mrs Munroe stiffened. 'Martha Ellis? *Miss* Martha Ellis, too high and mighty to lift a finger...too busy runnin' after any man who'd so much as look at her? Harbourmaster's wife, is she? Well, I'm not surprised.' She clasped the chair arms, sending Mr Pitt jumping from her lap. 'Martha Ellis. Yes, I know Martha Ellis, but I've not seen her in years. Too good to be a cook! Huh, well I can tell you, she was given her marchin' orders and that's God's honest truth. Fired fer laziness and makin' eyes at the men.'

We turned round amazed. Mrs Munroe was used to her word being law and had very decided opinions but this was different. She seemed genuinely upset, her usually jolly face with its dimples and rosy complexion looking like she had seen one of her ghosts.

'She still can't cook,' I said. 'Her pie wasn't a patch on yours...And she's planning on teaching *me* her recipes!'

Mrs Munroe's lips clamped tight. 'Is she indeed!'

'I told her you were a friend of Mrs Pengelly and Lady Polcarrow and she didn't seem to like it.'

'Don't suppose she did.'

The large kitchen clock chimed seven. Mr Pitt jumped onto the window sill and sat glaring at the swallow's nest, his tail flicking from side to side. 'There's to be a pie competition at the lock opening and Mrs Perys believes she's going to win.'

'Does she indeed!' came the furious retort.

Mrs Pengelly caught my eye. She raised her eyebrow and shook her head, recognizing my mischief.

'Let's make Billy a new waistcoat for the opening,' I said, trying not to blush. But why not? Mrs Munroe's pies were so much better, and Mrs Perys was so sure of herself. 'What about that last quarter of red silk – the one from India?'

Chapter Seventeen

Fosse
Sunday 19th June 1796, 10:30 a.m.

Footsteps echoed across the hall, followed by the sound of the front door opening. Mrs Pengelly looked up but I kept on sewing. Further scuffles followed, and then there came a knock on the door. 'The cart's here, Elowyn. I'll get your cloak.' Billy dashed away.

Mrs Pengelly took off her glasses. 'It's early again,' she said, folding her newspaper and putting it on the table beside her. 'But at least the weather looks fine – though there's definitely a breeze.' She seemed puzzled by my lack of movement.

'The cart's two hours too early – he'll have to wait. I'd rather stay here than be kept waiting outside the chapel.' I reached for a pale yellow ribbon. 'I think I've mastered this.' I held up my embroidery. 'Look, I've twisted the ribbon into a petal.'

Billy peered anxiously round the door. 'Are you comin', Elowyn? Only, the cart's here…'

'It's too early, Billy. Tell the driver to wait.'

He looked horrified. 'But Elowyn, it's a lovely day...and it's not *really* too early...We can go across the moor. We can take the long way round...'

'I'd rather not,' I said, snipping my thread carefully. 'The driver will have to wait. The cart's far too uncomfortable to go the long way round.'

Mrs Pengelly was watching me, a puzzled look on her face. 'Perhaps you could offer the driver a drink, Billy? Ask Mrs Munroe for one of her dumplings and tell him to return in two hours.' She blanched at the sound of the slammed door, rising slowly to walk to the window. 'It's the same driver,' she said, peering round the shutter. 'It must be the one who taught Billy that song.'

Of course it was the same driver, and he would have to wait.

Billy knocked on the door again, his furious eyes accusing me of treachery. 'Can I have some paper, Mrs Pengelly? Something I can write on?'

Mrs Pengelly nodded. 'There's paper in the desk upstairs. Don't waste it, Billy. There are pens as well...'

'Thank you, Mrs Pengelly...it won't be wasted.' He scurried away, racing up the stairs. The clock on the mantelpiece chimed half past ten and I reached for another ribbon – a deeper yellow this time to add depth to the rose, a light orange for the base, sage green for the leaves.

'It's not *such* a bad idea, Elowyn,' Mrs Pengelly said. 'A breath of moor air is always good. I'm half tempted to go myself but the jolting would hurt my back...I like the new way you've dressed your hair – it's quite lovely.'

I smiled my thanks, adjusting my thimble. The curls I usually pinned back so severely had been allowed to fall round my face. I was wearing my yellow lawn, edged with local lace and pearl buttons at the sleeve.

'I'm really not dressed for the moor.'

The clock chimed the half-hour, then the hour. Mrs Pengelly went once more to the window. 'They're sitting on the rock – I've never seen Billy so still. They've been like that for over an hour... Sam's taking out another pile of dumplings. What can they be doing – is it suitable, d'you think?' I did not look up. The rose was completed and it was perfect. Mrs Pengelly walked softly to the door and peered tentatively round. 'Sam, what are they doing?'

'Drawin' leats an' waterwheels an' any amount of stuff ye'd never imagine,' came his awed reply.

I put down my sewing and went to the window, glancing casually across the river. William and Billy sat on a rock at the water's edge, hunched over spreading papers, both with their black curls and freshly laundered shirts. Billy even wore a scarf, next he would be keeping a pocket notebook, sketching everything he saw. 'Tell the driver we can go now,' I called after Sam.

Mrs Pengelly was watching William. He had thrown back his head and was laughing, his smile lighting his face, and her eyebrows shot up, her half-smile concealing her sudden doubt. 'Is it safe to send you across the moors with such a man? Who is he, Elowyn?'

I, too, had caught a glimpse of his straight white teeth, his smile as his huge hands gently gathered together his drawings.

149

'He's called William Cotterell. It's all right, I'll be perfectly safe – he does nothing but talk about watercourses.'

'Watercourses? He's educated, is he? An educated cart driver?' Her eyes searched mine and I shrugged my shoulders.

'He talks to Billy about leats – I don't really listen.' I reached for my basket. 'I'll take the cut pieces of calico to show Bethany. I hope she'll agree to sew the bonnets.'

She held my gaze. 'I'm sure she will, my love. It's a wonderful opportunity for her.'

The cart swayed as I waved goodbye. Billy sat next to William and, once again, I sat straight-backed and solemn, smiling at neither of them as we made our way along the riverside. Their sideways glances were not lost on me. They could smirk as much as they liked. I hardly knew which was the man and which the boy. 'You seem very happy today, Miss Liddicot,' William said, winking at Billy.

'Why wouldn't I be? I'm to spend the day with the man I intend to marry. I think I'm allowed to be happy.'

We passed the old mine shaft and William frowned, stiffening his lips. The bay was glinting in the sun, the landscape already beginning to look familiar; the scarring of the land, not quite so ugly. William urged the pony behind a large pile of spoilings and pulled gently on the reins. Of course he would. Well, this time I would speak my mind. He turned round. 'At least you've allowed me half an hour! I suppose I should be grateful for that.'

'You leave me little choice,' I replied, the warmth of his smile catching me off guard.

He laughed softly, jumping down from the cart and reaching over to open the door. He nodded at Billy. 'Follow that stream a hundred feet up – then you should see the feeding lakes. Quick, lad, we've very little time.' Billy glowered across at me. 'Go, on, lad. I didn't bring you up here to glare at Elowyn.' As Billy hesitated, he cuffed him round the ear. 'She's quite safe. Never kiss a woman who won't kiss you back. That's the second lesson to learn...'

Fire filled my cheeks, a frisson of excitement making me turn quickly away. His talk of kissing, the way his shirt billowed in the wind. He was so physical, his strength frightening. His words hung in the air as he knew they would, planting thoughts in my mind, making me wonder what it would be like to be kissed by such a man. His skin was browned by the sun, a sheen to his hair, no trace of the cuts and bruises on his face. He looked wholesome, clean, his newly laundered shirt smelling of lye.

He smiled. 'You've dressed your hair differently – it would suit you if you weren't still frowning.'

I turned away. 'Those drawings were very unflattering.'

He laughed, reaching across the hedgerow for a rose. 'I'd prefer to draw you smiling but I draw what I see.'

I took a deep breath. 'Billy's soon to be offered a place at Truro Grammar School and though it would break our hearts if he does go, I'm scared of your influence over him. I'm worried he might turn it down...he might even run away. I can't tell with Billy any more...' He was staring at me, smiling kindly, not interrupting or contradicting, just listening to what I had to say. If only he would get cross, be offended, seek to justify himself. 'I want you to stop seeing him...please...leave us both alone. You've no obligation... What we did for you we'd have done for anyone.'

He raised his eyebrows, reaching for another rose. 'You really think I'm a bad influence? I'm a miner's son, Elowyn, I'm self-taught. At Billy's age, I'd quarrelled with my teacher, the parson, and just about everyone else. I was down the mine watching the engineers. I'm self-taught because others didn't teach me right. At fifteen, I could see the mistakes. At seventeen, I'd worked out an answer.' He stooped down, picking a handful of long grasses, twisting and plaiting them into a circle. 'You really think I'd tell Billy to do the same?'

I stared across the glistening sea. If only he would shout at me, raise his voice instead of speaking so softly. 'Who were you in a fight with that night?'

'Who was I in a fight with?' His laugh was scornful, at complete odds with the man who laughed and joked with Billy. 'Who am I not in a fight with? Every damn one of them. Tinners are expendable, did you know that? Profit must come before safety.'

There was something about William Cotterell that seemed so complex, his mixture of strength and gentleness. He had woven the long grasses into a circlet, his deft fingers threading the roses through the plaited stems. As a child, I had longed to wear a garland. He held it out. 'A woman as beautiful as you should wear roses.' He shrugged as I turned away. 'It wouldn't harm you to let your guard down just once in a while – let your heart rule, not always your head.'

I glared back at him. 'I don't want Billy growing up to be in a fight with everyone.'

He held the garland in his hands, turning it slowly. 'If Billy asks my opinion I'll give it to him...but you'll need a lot of ribbon if your apron strings are to reach Truro.' I stared in astonishment. His words had been kindly said, no trace of mocking. 'We've no need to quarrel, Elowyn, no need for that hard shell of yours. I was in a fight but I was not the one to start it. I know my strength and I *never* fight. I wrestle, but if I were to fight, there's every chance I'd kill a man. You think I'd risk that?'

I glanced at the cart and he must have thought I meant the blanket. He reached over and spread it quickly on the rough grass, sitting down with the garland beside him. Billy was nowhere to be seen and I stood staring out to sea, knowing I must not sit down. He looked up, holding his hand to shield his eyes. 'The vagrants in Porthcarrow know nothing of Billy's brother and sister...nor the large group just moved to Pendenning land. There's no sign of them. Billy will never run away – he'll stay where they last saw him – he expects them to come looking. '

'Did he ask you to search?'

William shook his head. 'He didn't need to. But I told him I had asked.'

I swallowed the lump in my throat, a jealous stab adding to my disquiet. Billy never spoke to me about his family and I always felt shy to raise the subject. I should talk to him more, try not to shield him. Yet I felt drawn to shield him, just as I had done with Tom. Three pilot gigs were racing across the bay to a new ship, the sun glinting like a thousand pieces of broken glass; the breeze was westerly, blowing our hair. The scent of wild roses filled the air and I shut my eyes, feeling suddenly fearful. Would I ever sit like this with Nathan?

It was as if he read my mind. 'Does Nathan Cardew know you love yellow roses so much?' He had my handkerchief in his hands, my delicately embroidered roses held between his fingers.

'Of course he does. He has the exact same handkerchief.'

His face was stony, his eyes burning mine with a ferocity that scared me. 'No he doesn't – he gave it straight back to you. I was watching.'

I stared back in horror. 'He didn't need it…he already had one…the exact same one…' By his look, he knew I was lying.

'Does he know you use lavender soap? That your hair smells of lilac? That you wear your thimble on your left middle finger? That you have the strength of an ox and can scramble up a cliff path as nimbly as a goat?' My heart was pounding, my face flushing. Why spoil everything? Give them an inch and they take a yard. I had been too friendly, our talk of Billy too intimate. 'Or does he just want to parade you round and play you like a puppet, make himself look good because he has such a beautiful woman on his arm – a friend of the Polcarrows…How good is that for his detestable self-importance?'

How dare he be so familiar, so rude about Nathan? I walked

quickly past him, intent on sitting in the cart but he jumped up, moved to block my way. He put his hand on my arm, his touch soft, like when his hand had closed so gently over mine. 'I draw as I see and speak as I see. Don't marry him, Elowyn. He'll imprison you in that pier house and you'll never be free…'

He spoke as if wishing me a good day but I knew not to be fooled by his soft talking. His disregard for authority was blatant. He was a dangerous man – he spoke his mind and paid the price. Tinners had a reputation for rioting and disorder. They were violent, they looted; they forced bakers to give them bread by putting nooses round their necks. He began folding up the blanket, putting it carefully in the cart.

'We serve harsh and greedy men but the days of serfdom are over. Men must know their worth – you above all should know your worth. Be your own mistress, don't always feel the need to bend to other people's will—' He looked up. Billy was running down the hill, jumping the large boulders in his way. 'What's wrong, lad, you being chased by a bull?'

Billy doubled up, breathing so hard he could hardly speak. 'The lake…the diversions…the channels…the sluice gates…they're all choked up with weeds.'

William's face hardened. 'All of them?'

Billy heaved himself onto the cart. 'Just about…thick as a carpet in places.'

The anger returned to William's face, the same stony fury. 'Well, there's a surprise,' he said, gathering up the reins and urging the pony forward.

'There's little or no flow…thought you said there must be a constant flow, Will?'

'I did – there should be. It's a sea lock, not a river lock. Without a constant flow of water, the level will drop in low tide. Those gates are good, but there's always seepage – the water flowing in must match the water seeping out, or else the ships will ground. The whole lock could silt up.'

Chapter Eighteen

I left Billy talking to William and started walking down to the lock. A large crowd was gathered – it seemed everyone was there, even Sir James Polcarrow and his attorney, Matthew Reith. Sir James was clearly furious, striding along the quayside, his tall hat head and shoulders above everyone else. Nathan walked by his side, a quill in one hand, a large ledger in the other. His shirtsleeves were rolled to the elbow, his hair dishevelled. Men were pressing forward, clearly affronted, shaking their heads. It was not a riot, no one was shouting, just glaring at Nathan with their mouths clamped hard.

Ruth was making her way through the crowd, her eyes full of tears, and I picked up my basket, running straight to her. 'Ruth, what's happening?'

She grabbed my arm, hurrying me away from the mass of angry men. 'They've found clay dust in a flourmill in Truro… People are very ill – some might even die. Clay dust's been mixed with the flour…Honest, how *could* they?' She wiped her eyes, her hands trembling. 'Dr Trefusis has been worried for some time. He told Mr Reith and they found clay in the bread. They've traced it back here. Honest, Elowyn, someone's been shippin' clay to a flourmill in Truro *from this very harbour.*'

'Ruth, that's awful.'

'It's terrible. It's a disgrace for Sir James but it's a disgrace for humanity. Honest, Elowyn…there's no bread – people are riotin' because they're starvin' yet someone thinks to profit from them. It's a wicked, wicked world. People might die. *And from this harbour.*' She started crying again. 'Poor Nathan doesn't deserve this.'

'But it's not his fault. He's blameless – everyone must see that.'

'He's taken it that bad…he's meant to account for every barrel…and someone's been cheatin' him. He's no idea who shipped it or when it was shipped. He's got lists of where people *said* the clay was goin' but that's of little use. Sir James is furious. Oh Elowyn, I don't need to tell you how Nathan's sufferin'.' I caught her fear and my stomach twisted. 'Nathan's good name could be ruined.' She wiped her eyes. 'He says people are castin' him sideways looks like he don't know his job…like they don't trust him.' Her eyes filled with pleading. 'Could you talk to Sir James…tell him Nathan's not to blame? Please, Elowyn…'

'Ruth, I hardly speak to Sir James. I've nothing to do with him…'

'Could you, though? Nathan loves you so much and Sir James knows you'd only speak the truth.'

The crowd was thinning. Sir James had left the quayside and was now in Nathan's office. We could see them through the window, Nathan shaking his head, holding up more ledgers, Sir James sitting at the desk, studying them carefully. Ruth looked so distraught and I wanted to comfort her. 'I'll do my best...I'll tell Mrs Pengelly – she'll talk to Lady Polcarrow.'

She squeezed my hand. 'God bless you, Elowyn. Nathan won't be free for a while – not until Sir James has gone...' Her watery smile was full of anguish. 'It's just he loves you so much...and he'd hate it if you were to think badly of him.' Her hands shook as she wiped her eyes. 'I'm afraid I must leave you, only I'm wanted back at the chapel. Will you be all right?'

I nodded. Anchored ships were awaiting Mr Perys' instructions, shouts ringing across the water. 'There's plenty for me to watch.'

I needed to find a place to sit. My basket with the folded calico weighed heavily on my arm and I looked around. Ruth was halfway to the chapel, waving at me from the row of worker's cottages, and a thought struck me. I could take the material straight to Bethany – after all, I knew where she lived. Nathan's rent book had listed the Coopers as living in one of the granite cottages. Nathan had already pointed out their guttered slate rooves and red brick chimneys, their clay pots pointing away from the prevailing wind.

Most of the front doors were shut but halfway along, two women sat making lace in an open doorway. I was surprised by their faded clothes, the many darns and patches, but even more surprised by the pinched look in their faces. They looked hungry with gaunt cheeks and sallow complexions. Both had missing front teeth. I forced a smile, both of them staring up at me with unveiled dislike, their fingers whirling, their bobbins flying, and I held up my basket. 'Could you tell me where Bethany Cooper lives? I'm hoping she might sew something for me.'

It was as if they loathed the sight of me. 'Last door.'

I took a deep breath, walking quickly along the row of doors, knowing they were still staring at me. Someone else was watching me from the top window of the end house but when I looked up, they slipped from sight. I knocked loudly on the door and when it opened two huge eyes stared up at me. 'Could I speak to your mamm?'

The door slammed then opened again. Bethany stood with her baby in her arms, the other small child clinging to her skirts. Once again, I was struck by how pale she looked, her eyes shadowed by dark circles, her hair hanging lank. Both the baby and the child had running noses and I caught my breath wanting to step back. Somehow, I stood my ground. I had smelt that smell before – the stench of a purulent wound.

Tears sprang to her eyes. 'Please…Miss Liddicot…if ye've something to say…please, not here.' She looked distraught, stammering, looking quickly over her shoulder. There was fear in her eyes, a desperate pleading.

'Who is it?' Bethany paled even more as a man's voice shouted from inside. 'Who wants us? If we've company, don't keep them standin' at the door.' An older boy came running down the hall, peering round the other side of Bethany's skirt.

'Could you sew for me, Bethany? Here, in your home? I've an idea for bonnets to shield the clay maidens...Can I show you what I've got in mind?'

Her eyes widened. 'You want me to sew?' She seemed relieved, her shy smile making her look quite beautiful.

'Can I come in?'

She nodded, leading me down the narrow hall and into the crowded front room. Samuel Cooper was sitting on a chair, his leg propped up on a stool. A wooden mirror hung on the wall, a row of iron hooks with nothing on them. Straw cots had been piled to one side of the room, blankets folded in a pile. Apart from the smell, the room looked tidy and clean; dishes were stacked neatly on a small table, the floor newly swept.

Samuel winced in pain as he tried to stand up. 'I'm sorry...I'd no idea...Very pleased to meet ye, Miss Liddicot. This is an honour we'd not expected.' Like Bethany, he looked thin and drawn, his clothes hanging from his shoulders. He was as young as Bethany but looked twice her age, pain and worry etched across his face.

'Please don't get up. You may think it strange but I've an idea for a business. I've four rolls of good calico which I'm not using...' I picked the cut pieces out of my basket, looking round, not knowing where to lay them. 'It's good and strong and just the thing for protective headwear.'

Bethany handed the baby to Samuel, lifting a basket of clothes to make room on the floor and I began laying out the cut fabric, pointing to a paper pattern to show which piece went where. They both looked so eager, Samuel leaning

161

forward to get a better view. 'Once you've sewn them, we'll see about selling them...' I looked up. 'We'll have to make sure everyone wants one...or at least they think they need one.'

'They need them, right enough,' said Samuel slowly. 'There's more an' more gettin' scratches in their eyes – there's many can't work for injury...' He sounded bitter but smiled. He had kind eyes, auburn hair and freckles across his face and hands, and I liked him on sight.

'You should have enough material to make about twenty – but take your time, they must be perfect. I've brought as much as I can carry but I've another three rolls in my shop. You can start with this.' I lifted out the folded cambric. 'Be very careful – just one loose thread and others will think they can do better. Make each different and make them pretty... add whatever you think fitting. Once people have one, many will think to copy so you must have plenty to sell – then take orders.'

Bethany nodded, understanding everything, feeling for the movement in the fabric with soft fingers. She looked up, her face radiant. Samuel fought to stop his mouth from quivering. 'You're bein' very good to us, Miss Liddicot.' He was obviously a proud man, his ability to feed his children taken from him. 'You and Mr Cardew...' His voice faltered. 'Mr Cardew's been that good to us – lettin' us off the rent, givin' me time fer my leg to heel. I'll do everythin' I can to make these bonnets fer ye. Everythin'...me and Bethany will sit up all night if needs be. We can do it, can't we, love?' He reached out, taking Bethany's hand, bringing it to his lips.

I saw the glance of love that passed between them and guilt sliced through me. Their gratitude was misplaced, they had nothing and I had so much – I was not giving, I was taking, thinking only to profit from their hard work. I felt suddenly so wretched, seeing myself through those hostile stares – a fisherman's daughter, dressed in fine clothes, neither fish, nor flesh, nor good red herring. Was that how people saw me? How William Cotterell saw me?

I had originally paid only three shillings for each roll, less than half-price and I felt suddenly so ashamed. I had become consumed by making a profit, driven by my desire never to go hungry, yet this family was starving, their need so great. 'I can lend you these scissors but I'll give you the first four rolls – it can be *your* business…the cotton's no good sitting on my shelf. If you profit, I'll sell you the next rolls at cost price.'

'Ye'd do that for us?' Bethany hunched forward, hiding her face in her hands. Her shoulders began heaving and Samuel, likewise, covered his face. They seemed incapable of speech, the small children gaping, burying their faces in Bethany's skirts.

'Do you bathe that wound?' I asked, desperate to break the awkward silence.

'No…I've been told to leave it be…'

'I think you should bathe it – twice a day in the sea. And wash your bandages in the salt water. I've seen injuries like that get better – Mamm should have told you.'

The boy clung to his mother's skirt, the youngest child tottering on unsteady legs as Bethany led me along the hall to the front step. Once again, a sudden movement in the window above made me look up. 'Could other members of the family help you?'

She shook her head. 'We've nothing to do with them, upstairs. That's another family. We've the two rooms downstairs and half the yard – most of the houses are doubled up.'

I ran down the hill with sudden wings. I *did* have a heart and I listened to it. I felt so happy, my gift to the Coopers filling me with elation. William Cotterell had no need for his taunts. From now on, I would do good works – like teach in the school. Perhaps, I could help Nathan with his accounts. I felt suddenly so happy. I *could* smile – see, I was smiling now.

It was much later than I realized. Nathan was still in his office, watching me run down the hill and I looked up, the smile immediately falling from my lips. It must have been the shadows, the glass in the window distorting his features, or the sun making him squint. His look had seemed so severe, like Father in one of his rages.

Chapter Nineteen

The back door was unlocked and I climbed the stairs in sudden dread, yet Nathan was smiling, his face full of pleasure. 'Elowyn, at last...' He held out his hands and I hoped he would not feel the slight tremor in my fingers. I had acted like a child, running when I knew I should walk. I felt like a child now, that same sense of doing wrong.

'I went for a walk up the hill. I didn't realize how late it was...'

His eyes pierced mine with their brilliant blue. 'You've heard?'

I nodded. 'Ruth told me and I saw you with Sir James.'

'Yes, well, he's been gone a while now – but I'm pleased you found somethin' else to occupy you.' He let go of my hands, trying to make order of the jumbled accounts. 'This is not how I planned to spend our day.' He spoke softly, his boyish vulnerability cutting through his strong jaw and cleft chin. 'Sir James is gettin' that close to the smeltin' deal but he's worried they'll not invest if the harbour's tainted with scandal.' My heart thumped as he shut the huge ledger with a slam. 'Forgive me if I sound preoccupied – my reputation's on the line.'

'I'm very good with accounts…I'd be happy to help—'

'I've no need of help.' He must have realized how sharply he had spoken as he reached for his jacket, buttoning it quickly. 'What I mean is, I've had enough of searchin' these books and I'd rather walk. Those two men talkin' to Mr Hellyar are thinkin' of investin' in the mine an' I'd like to catch them…' He held open the door, pointing me down the stairs, locking it behind him. On the path outside he held out his arm. 'Sir James knows I'm not to blame but I feel I've let him down. He puts so much trust in me.'

His voice was intimate, full of anguish, and I felt guilty that I had kept him waiting. 'I'll mention it to Mrs Pengelly…I'm sure she'll talk to Lady Polcarrow – Sir James will know it's not your fault.' He seemed not to hear me, his mouth drawn tight. 'I'll…I'll tell them of your loyalty…how hard you work.'

'I suppose a good word never goes amiss. People can be very malicious – like kickin' a dog when it's down.'

He sounded shaken but at the dockside he seemed to regain his confidence, his conversation growing more cheerful. 'Mr Sellick's been granted the Wedgwood contract and several new investors have made enquiries about obtainin' a lease. There's plenty want to dig for clay. We've been that busy, sep-aratin' the land into setts, and Matthew Reith's been drawin' up new contracts. I've been measurin' it all exactly and mar-kin' out the land – won't be long till the new setts are fenced and ready.' He helped me up the steps of the lock gates and stood looking up at me, suddenly hesitant. His eyes searched mine, his voice dropping to a tender whisper. 'It'll always be thus, Elowyn – this pride I feel...the joy you bring me. I want so much to cherish you...to keep you safe...to give you everythin' you deserve. I love you so much, it almost hurts.'

Kittiwakes were circling above us, their plaintive cries piercing my heart. His words were kindly spoken and his smile tender, yet his severe look had left me fearful and growing unease gnawed my stomach. The same feeling I got when tradesmen tried to sell me spoiled silk, the sudden certainty that if I looked beneath the first few turns, I would find inferior fabric. He was smiling, staring across the bay, his handsome face showing nothing but pleasure. 'We must hope for good weather for the lock opening.'

Something in his tone made my heart pound. He picked up a shell, dusting off the sand. 'I believe Mrs Pengelly is now to sail in with Sir James and Lady Polcarrow.' He handed me the shell. 'So...in a way that solves your problem – you'll be able to join Mrs Perys on the quayside while you wait for Mrs Pengelly. You'll be there when she alights...an' you could introduce Mrs Perys to Mrs Pengelly. That way, she'll know you meant no disrespect...'

I heard him through pounding ears, knowing exactly what he meant. His reputation was on the line and if I was not with him at the lock opening, people would talk. Malicious rumours would circulate that I thought him unworthy – *like kicking a dog when it was down*. He wanted me to be there. He wanted the whole town to see me with him. That slight firmness in his voice, the frown, everything telling me I was to pin my colours to the mast. I must let everyone know where my allegiance lay.

He held out his arm and I took it slowly, walking past Harbour House, looking up at the window. Nathan bowed to the window and I saw Mrs Perys smile back at us. 'Mrs Perys is that taken with you, Elowyn. She told Ruth you were a real lady an' she hasn't stopped singin' your praises ever since. I think you know what an honour it would be for us all if you were to join us on the quayside.'

We walked slowly up the cobbles, an icy hand beginning to grip my heart, twisting it with long cold fingers. He was a good man and loved me so much yet I could not shake off my growing unease. A long tunnel led down to the beach and though I seemed so calm, inside, my heart was screaming. He should grab my hand and take me to where no one could see us, ask me like a real lover would ask. He should cajole me, tease me; make me want to be with him. He should press me against the wall and kiss me, deeply, passionately, like I had seen Tom kiss Gwen. I would let him kiss me – I would allow him such intimacy. I knew the passion that stirred a man and I wanted that. I wanted the kind of love that ignited flames and set me on fire. I wanted him to do anything but bow formally and walk me on his arm.

We continued in silence, the invisible thread no longer pulling me to the last house in the row. I stood staring up at the window that would be our bedroom, William's words ringing like a warning bell in my mind – did Nathan want me for my connections, my friendship with the gentry or for myself alone? My unease was increasing by the minute, a growing sense of suffocation. Nathan's love was so powerful yet he did not treat me like a lover should – he treated me like a porcelain doll to be propped up on the sill and left to look out of the window.

'I've planted you roses, Elowyn, an' plum trees. I've been waterin' them day an' night and I'm certain they'll take.' He was smiling so happily, my hand on his arm, nodding across the lock to the group of men watching. 'Mrs Perys has been bringin' them on. She's got real flare – especially with roses. They've taken root an' Ruth's planted them out for you.'

My silence seemed to go unnoticed. He smiled, bowing to another group of men. 'Looks like we've missed Mr Hellyar…Never mind, I'll make sure he gets to see you at the openin'.' We walked up the hill, towards the chapel. 'I'm sorry to cut short our walk but I'm sure you must understand – I've to make a list for Sir James of everyone who's shipped clay. He wants it straight away. Our future may depend on how I handle this.'

The knot in my stomach twisted. 'What colour are the roses?'

Nathan shrugged, seemingly surprised at my question. 'I think she said they were red.'

My voice gave no notion of how my heart was beating. I was a child again, staring dry-eyed at the moon, imagining a cottage with roses spilling in profusion from an iron arch – yellow roses, like the sun, not roses the colour of blood. Why did he not know that, or even ask? *It would always be thus*, a puppet on his arm, no voice of my own. He did not mean for me to speak my mind. He had spoken for me – he had accepted Mrs Perys' invitation without a second thought and was now pressuring me into honouring the obligation.

Ruth was talking to the cart driver. A group of hens scattered as we approached and she looked up with obvious pleasure, holding out her hands in greeting. In the shade of the overhang, two familiar figures sat hugging their shawls. Ruth was oblivious to their bulging skirts but I saw at once, and fear churned my stomach. 'That's very good timin'',' Ruth called sweetly. 'And look, here comes Billy, too.'

Billy was running down the lane, his boots caked in mud. William was following him some way behind and Nathan looked up, immediately frowning. 'Keep Billy away from that man, Elowyn. Tell him to keep his distance. He's nothin' but trouble – he's an agitator, stirrin' up unrest amongst the men. He's a fighter – people neither like him nor trust him.' Ruth waved at William and Nathan's frown deepened. 'My sister gives him work but I've warned her to keep her distance.'

William stood glowering back at Nathan with reciprocal dislike, his head held in that proud and defiant way of his. His shirtsleeves were rolled to the elbows, his polished black boots covered in thick white clay. His eyes were blazing with anger and I had to look away, look anywhere but at the two men staring at each other like stags about to fight. Mamm and Lorwenna did not see William but smiled contentedly, squeezing their hidden bounty around them as they settled into the cart. Nathan held my fingers to his lips, kissing the tips softly, lingering over them as if he knew William was still watching.

He helped me into the cart, his hand burning me through my dress, and stood attentively by the cart door, wishing us a safe journey. I could not hold his gaze but sat straight-backed and stiff. It was as much as I could do to hold back the furious blush burning my cheeks. I knew with a sudden clarity that it could never be – I would never marry Nathan, not now, not ever. Wanting hazel eyes when I should want blue – my whole marriage spent aching for another man's touch, another man's laughter.

It was too late for Billy to keep his distance, certainly too late for me; too late to stop my heart from leaping every time I saw William Cotterell. He drew me so completely – his smile, his drawings; the way he talked, his powerful body, his clever mind. I had made him wait but I had longed to get on that cart, my nervous excitement hard to keep hidden. Nathan had never made me laugh, he brought me no joy, quite the opposite; I felt restrained in his company, as if I was about to do wrong. He was courting me, yes, but it did not feel like love. He should have kept my handkerchief. He should have asked me about the roses. He should have shown me some passion, shown some interest in my business. I was not an asset to be paraded on his arm.

Mamm leaned forward, prodding my knee. 'Ye've not heard a word, have ye? Too busy thinkin' of yer man to pay heed to yer mamm!' She sniffed. 'Ye've done well, Elly – ye've done us that proud. And with the boatyard, Tom's set to go far.'

My thoughts were all consuming; I must have misheard her. 'Boatyard?'

'It's as good as settled. When you've wed Nathan, he says the lock will be ready fer another boatyard. He's to offer Tom the lease. Honest, Tom's that made up.'

I thought I might choke. 'But Tom's only an apprentice – he's got years more to go. He's in no position to have his own yard.'

Mamm sniffed again, pulling her cloak around her. 'What's wrong, don't ye want yer brother to have what ye have? This is his chance. There's many wantin' that boatyard...Tom knows his good fortune even if others don't.'

'But he can't possibly leave Uncle Thomas – not for years. And Uncle Thomas will never desert Lady Polcarrow. Tom won't stand a chance on his own.'

Mamm's mouth tightened. 'Ye think yer uncle doesn't want his name above that arch? Course he does – Pasco Pengelly did nothin' but make mischief. Who built all the boats? Yer uncle, that's who. Well, Tom wants his own yard just as much, an' there's no reason he shouldn't...'

The pony was burdened by his heavy load, stumbling in places up the steep incline. I could hardly breathe – Tom and Gwen, setting up my marriage so they could profit? It felt like pain, like the worst kind of treachery. 'Tom's reaching too far. No one will give him work.'

Mamm's eyes were like iron. 'Jack's ships need repairs an' Tom's done a lot fer Jack. Believe me, he'll not be out of work – there's money to be made, Elowyn, an' Tom's the one to make it.' Her smile hardened. 'A mother does what she can fer her child an' so does a sister – ye're well accounted fer, Tom now needs yer help.'

172

I gripped the side of the cart, petrified by my sudden thought. That furtive scurrying around to clear the table – that fear in her face. What if Mamm had not been afraid of Jack Deveral? What if she had been afraid I would see the dirty plates left by hungry men? I could hardly breathe, fear wrenching my stomach. That night, those heavy barrels …It was clay they were shipping – my mother and brother, working alongside Jack Deveral – poisoning the flour with their filthy clay. All of them profiting from the starving, making children ill with tainted bread? It was as if the blinkers fell from my eyes, the truth blinding me. Mamm and Tom were working for Jack Deveral and I was part of their plan. They needed a boatyard as cover, a daughter married to the Piermaster so no one suspected. She might as well take us all by the hand and lead us straight to the gallows.

She must never, ever, suspect me of knowing about the flour. Never. I breathed deeply, steadying my growing panic. I knew the rules – see nothing, hear nothing, join them or live in fear. People disappeared without trace, were found face down in shallow water. I tried to keep my voice calm. 'Does Gwen know?'

Mamm's eyes were as sharp as knives. 'About gettin' the yard? Course she does. She's that pleased, what with the bairn due so soon – and Thomas knows. Ye're goin' up in the world, m' girl, and ye're taking us with ye.'

I stared at her through a wave of absolute hatred. She could have stopped my beatings, taken us sooner to Uncle Thomas. Childhood memories filtered through my anger – the strange irregularities, the locked stores, the barrels that never smelt of fish. All that made sense now. I should have shielded Tom from her, not from Father.

'Does she know...anything else?'

'No, an' that's the way it's goin' to stay – nor does yer uncle. Ye're not to say a word, especially not to yer uncle.'

Tears of anger stung my eyes. I was so full of rage, I could have hit her. 'I want nothing more to do with your brandy, nor Jack Deveral, do you understand?' I did not care that Lorwenna was gawping at me. Billy was talking to the driver and I knew I must keep my voice low. 'I'll not carry...I'll not store...I'll not lie to others...You've my solemn promise of silence – I'll say nothing – ever – but if you think I'll join you, or encourage you to involve Tom in any way, then you need think again.' My voice was rising. I had never been so angry; all my life, bending to her will, her sharp pinch on my ear, her quick slaps when no one was watching. For the first time, I was speaking my mind, not just trying to please her. 'Never ask me again. Never. You disgust me, thinking I would be so underhand – marry Nathan just so Jack Deveral can use Tom to get a boatyard? You think I'm going to let him take me with you to the gallows?'

She smiled slowly, her eyes iron. 'Time ye climbed down off that high horse of yers, Elowyn Liddicot. Ye're family – the same blood runs through ye as it does me an' Tom. 'Tis time ye grew up, my lass, an' stopped actin' like a child. Ye're one of us an' ye always will be.' She wiped her nose with the back of her hand, her eyes like daggers. 'Tom wants that brandy brought to yer storeroom – there's a room at the back. Ye think no one knows? Ye never wondered what that room's fer?'

Lorwenna sat white faced with fright. Poor girl had no chance but I, at least, had got away. I took a deep breath. *I could read and write. I had a skill. I had savings.* 'I want nothing more to do with you – or Jack Deveral,' I whispered firmly. 'I may have your blood, but I'll not be part of your—' Billy turned round, smiling at me, but I could not smile back. I was frightened for Gwen.

Those iron eyes glinted. 'Ye help us, or ye go down with us. Ye think we haven't already put yer names on our books – the books waitin' fer them to find the minute they start nosin' around? Believe me, my girl, we've got lists an' lists with yer name written so clear, even those that can't read can tell it's ye – all the runs ye've done fer us, all ye've taken fer us, what ye've earned from yer dealin's with us. Ye've amassed a tidy pile, Elowyn…Do ye really think the revenue will believe yer invoices and declarations of where ye bought yer fancy French silks? All that Brussels lace? It's all listed in our books an' they'll find it. Have no doubt, if any one of ye on that list squeals, ye all go down. Ye can protest yer innocence as much as ye like but they'll not believe ye.'

I stared back yet she had not finished, her voice turning thin and cruel. 'An' don't even *think* to go runnin' to yer uncle. Ye say one word of this to him an' his name will go down on the list. This isn't a game, Elowyn – as well ye know. Yer uncle's been good to you, an' that's no way to repay him.' She thrust her head back, nodding over her shoulder. 'An' Billy's name will go in the books – plain as anything for them to find.'

The driver was cursing the pony, cracking his whip with excessive strength. My stomach was retching; I thought I would be sick. How could she do this? Putting her greed above the safety of her children? To threaten me like that? Expect me to marry Nathan and demand I lie to him?

'Stop,' I shouted. 'There's too much weight in this cart. I'm going to walk – come, Billy.' Billy jumped to the ground and I vomited on the dusty tract, heaving uncontrollably, my whole body shaking. My mother, my own mother... I wiped my hand across my mouth. She was watching me from the retreating cart, her eyes piercing mine, and I took a deep breath. That was how they worked – how they got you living in fear, never knowing when the list might be found. Never knowing when you might get arrested. Join them and keep silent, or those you loved would live in fear too.

Billy stared at me in astonishment. 'Ye feel better now?'

'Hardly.'

'We've been up at the leats – Will says—'

'Billy, I don't want to talk...Let's just walk.'

Billy began skipping sideways like a crab. 'Will says ye're as clever as ye are beautiful. He says ye're to know yer worth. He says times are changing and ye should get them to come to you – that's what he said.'

I stopped, my hands still shaking. Everyone I loved was now in danger. 'Billy, I don't want you ever to mention his name again – never, do you understand?'

I drew my shawl around me, looking down at the river. The new street lamps were lit, pools of light shining on the deserted cobbles. Burning seal oil mingled with the smell of seaweed, the night dark, the water black. Only the softest wind blew against my face. It was one in the morning, one moment my fear subsiding, the next rising, ripping me apart. It was a threat, only a threat. There would be no list, or if there was a list, my name would not be on it. My accounts were approved. They were signed and sealed – the excise officer knew me well. Mamm was threatening me, scaring me into doing her will. Like sending me down dark alleys to do her errands.

The water was so black, with not a breath of wind. Everywhere was quiet, the tears splashing soundlessly down my cheeks. If William had been driving the cart he would have known something was wrong. A terrible longing tore my heart, the pain so intense, I almost cried out. *He's been stirrin' up unrest. People neither like him nor trust him.* I could never marry Nathan Cardew; I was too much in love with William Cotterell – too completely, utterly, agonizingly in love. He was disliked, a troublemaker, a man who courted danger, yet I felt so drawn to him. I loved his smile, his gentle manners, the way I felt safe with him. That terrible wrenching jealousy when Billy had been free to spend the day with him and I had not.

Of all my long nights spent staring at the moon, none had seemed so lonely. I loved the way he picked me flowers, the way he called me beautiful. The way he teased me, the passion behind his stare. The way he believed in me, made me think to believe in myself. Most of all, I loved the way he had held me so safely under the sacking in the cave.

I wiped away my tears, slamming the notebook shut. I was not going to be bullied by Mamm and nor was I going to fall into the arms of William Cotterell. I knew how to dig deep. I had fought back on the streets and I could fight back now. I needed to stay firm, grow a stronger shell. But one thing was certain: I was no longer going to bend to other people's will. *I was Elowyn Liddicot, proud dressmaker. I had a skill others needed.*

Shells were there to keep you safe, frowns to hold people at bay.

Chapter Twenty

Thick fog smothered the town, blanketing the houses, obscuring the banks. Ships' bells tolled across the river, the splash of unseen oars coming towards me. Lanterns cast no light, just solid spheres suspended in mid-air, and I shivered, pulling my cloak more firmly around me. As a child, I hated fog – fog kept Father at home or sent him straight to the tavern – but this morning the eerie silence suited my mood.

Through the office window, I saw the familiar sight of a burning candle. Uncle Thomas and I often snatched time together before the yard erupted and the day's sewing began and I knew he would be there. His plans hung over the desk, the last inch of candle flickering across the room. A blast of cold air followed me in but he did not look up. His head remained bent, his steady hand continuing his careful drawing. I stood behind him, always awed by the complexity of his plans.

'The Admiralty want heavier guns on their frigates...

an' that requires heavier scantlings. It's well overdue, mind — these eighteen-pounders give as good as they get. I've long stressed the need to thicken the hulls.' He stopped and smiled, looking over the rim of his glasses. 'They can penetrate forty-two inches...and that's through solid white oak. A twelve-pounder can penetrate thirty inches.' He started drawing again. 'Twenty-six inches between the scantlings should do the trick — an' thickening the sheathing...'

His silver fob watch lay on the table and I picked it up, swirling it to catch the light. The silver glittered. It was Pasco Pengelly's watch, lovingly given to Uncle Thomas by Lady Polcarrow. 'What if I don't want to marry Nathan Cardew?'

His smile faded. 'Are you sure, Elly love? He's a solid choice of husband — is it nerves, or has he done something to stop you liking him?'

'No...he's a real gentleman...I just don't love him. I like him and I've tried very hard to love him...but I'd only be marrying him to please others.' I glanced at the closed door, summoning my courage. 'Did you know Nathan's thinking of offering Tom the boatyard in Porthruan? It's just...well... surely, Tom's years away from that?'

His sigh sounded heartfelt. He put his hands over his face, speaking through his cupped fingers. 'It's not what I want, Elly, but Tom's grown somewhat stubborn of late — just like your mamm. Between the two of them, I hold very little sway.'

'But that's not right — Tom needs you. He needs your advice not Mamm's!'

'That's what I keep telling him, Elly love.' He sounded

almost bitter and I knelt beside him, my hand on his arm. He shrugged his shoulders. 'A while back Jack Deveral and John Polkerris bought a French war prize and your brother took it upon himself to do the repairs. Jack Deveral paid two hundred and ten pounds for the vessel – though that's not common knowledge so keep it between ourselves.'

'Two hundred and ten pounds! He can't have that sort of money!'

'Aye, well, Jack Deveral and John Polkerris together – they paid cash and spent nigh on another two hundred on materials. Tom received no payment but he's to have a percentage of the sale.' He drew his hands away from his face. He looked tired, thick stubble covering his usually shaven chin. 'Now, they've bought another prize and Tom wants the same arrangement – so you can see why he needs the boat-yard. The turnover's good, especially as there's talk this war's set to continue for quite some while.'

'I'm not going to marry Nathan just so my brother can get a yard.'

Uncle Thomas looked older, with no trace of his usual humour. He shook his head, resignation deep in his eyes. 'No, of course not – but you must understand boat build-ing's a competitive business. There's many with their name down for that lease so you can't blame Tom for seizing his chance. He's after making it into a repair yard and that makes good sense – after all, the lock's never going to dry…The ship's will come in an' out with the tide so there's no need to beach. And Tom's good at his job – he's a fine craftsman with a good knowledge of structure. You know as well as I that his work's second to none. If Nathan *were* to offer him the lease, there's a real chance he could make his name – a real chance to prosper.'

'But he's years away from being a qualified shipwright. He can't just—'

'He doesn't need to be fully qualified to do repairs – not really, besides, there's plenty who'd join him and continue his apprenticeship. It's *who* you know, Elly, that gets you a boatyard – it's favours or family ties. Sir James will sanction the lease but it's Nathan with the power to offer the contract – he's master of works, soon to be Piermaster. He's a powerful friend, no mistake.'

'It's wrong – it's like they're bartering with me. I'll not have it.'

He shook his head. 'Don't blame Nathan for your brother's scheming – the man's clearly in love with you so, of course, he's goin' to offer the yard to your brother. But surely 'tis early days?' He held my hands in his. 'Most women would jump at the chance. He's handsome and affable…his prospects are excellent. Sir James thinks very highly of him and if Tom's right, he's substantial savings. He's not a man to turn down lightly.'

The love in his voice brought tears to my eyes. My dearest uncle; I loved him so much. I bit my lip, desperate to tell him Tom's share would be in smuggled goods not the sale of the ship, but Mamm's threat still rang in my ears and I knew to keep silent. He must never, ever know or his name would be put on that list. 'Mamm says you want your own boatyard…I thought you were happy here.'

'Back a while perhaps I did, but I'll not desert Lady Polcarrow – not now, but if you'd asked me at Tom's age, well, then I'd be as anxious as him to have my own yard. Very few get that sort of chance.'

Sudden fear made my heart race. 'It sounds like you *want* Tom to get the yard.' He looked down, his silence the last thing I expected, and I felt suddenly deserted, betrayed, as if it was not what *I* wanted, but what was best for Tom. If only I could tell him about the flour. If only he knew. 'You do, don't you?'

He sighed again, shaking his head as if ashamed of his thoughts. 'Oh Elly, 'tis very hard to say this…but 'tis so different without you at home…'tis not the same at all. What with Tom being a grown man – 'tis difficult. I'm always thinking to keep him in check – he can be quite quarrelsome, you know. Two men in the same house…an' with the bairn expected…Aye, well, I can't help thinkin' 'twould be better for him to set up home nearcr your mamm. They've always been so close…'

I nodded, trying to smile. *Always so close.* If only I could tell him.

Gwen hung her bonnet on the hook and stared at me in horror. 'Course not! Tom would *never* ask Nathan – no, 'twas Nathan asked Tom. He loves ye so much, Elly, an' he wants ye to have yer family near. Tom helps Jack with his repairs an' Nathan knows 'twould be easier. Honest to God, it was *him* suggested it, never Tom.' She grimaced, clutching her belly. 'Money's tight, Elly, and once this babe comes…'

'Gwen, Tom mustn't go out at night. The press gang's back – if money's short, get him to join the Fencibles – that would give him a shilling a day and he'd be safe. Don't let him go out at night.' I tried to keep the panic from my voice.

She shrugged her shoulders. 'Ye think I haven't told him? He won't listen…says it's not my place to question.' She looked suddenly scared. 'Where's Billy? They'll take him in this fog.'

'He's safe with Mrs Pengelly. She's to make him a new waistcoat.'

It was lunch before the fog lifted and sun streamed through the windows, evening before we knew it. Slipping my needle into my pincushion, I went through to the storeroom to turn the muslin bags. The scent of lavender filled the air, my special mix of cloves and cedar wood, a hint of mint. Not one single moth. Almost at once, Billy called through the shelves. 'Elly…quick, Lady Polcarrow and Mrs Pengelly are here.'

It was as if we had turned back the clock; Rose Pengelly frowning at the bureau as she sifted through Madame Merrick's untidy accounts, Mrs Pengelly, sitting at the table, patiently teaching me how to sew. Lady Polcarrow was frowning. She was wearing her cream shot silk, the jacket collar and buttonholes embroidered in swirling black thread. She was so tall and elegant and it fitted her perfectly. Her large hat sat jauntily to one side, her thick ringlets framing her oval face, burning red in the evening light. She was always beautiful, even in her threadbare clothes her beauty had shone through.

She smiled but her dark eyes were flashing. Getting up from the bureau, she strode angrily across the floor. 'That old trout's having none of these fabrics. I'd rather you burned them than let her have them.'

Mrs Pengelly raised her eyebrows. 'I'm afraid she means Mrs Hoskins – we've just met her on the way –'

'She knows *nothing* of dressmaking yet she stands there, smiling in that particularly stupid way of hers…telling me that *as the lease is about to end*, her husband proposes to start his own dressmaking business. Can you believe it! He's to invest in a shop and expects to employ you. Her impudence is quite staggering – they would seek to poach the very seam-stresses that Mother trains! What barefaced cheek!'

Josie scraped back a chair and stood smiling broadly. 'Sit ye down, Lady Polcarrow. Ye no doubt have a plan – ye're never one to let someone get the better of ye.'

Rose Polcarrow sat on the proffered chair, smiling back at Josie. 'Well, *as* it happens, I have found the perfect place – it has very big windows and adjoins both the top road and Fore Street, which would be very useful. Jenna thinks it's perfect and Sir James will see to the lease. But Elowyn, are you *absolutely* determined to leave us?'

She took my silent confusion for her answer, smiling sadly. 'Well, all I can say is Nathan Cardew's a lucky man. His gain is our loss…but I'm happy for you – really I am. Sir James speaks very highly of him but you're breaking our hearts, Elly, you know that, don't you?' She rested her chin on her hands, just like she had done three years ago when she had taught me to read and write. 'I'll buy *all* your stock and Jenna can merge the business with the school. Mrs Hoskins can try all she likes but she's not getting anything – not *one* single thread – not one roll of fabric and *none* of Mother's seamstresses. We'll employ them all. She's certainly not getting you, Elly!'

I could not find my voice but smiled back, trying not to cry. She sounded so sincere and I felt suddenly so happy. She was not waiting for me to get married – quite the opposite. She could see I was floundering. Suddenly, she smiled, her usual mischief returning. 'Elowyn Liddicot...you're not thinking Mrs Hoskins will offer you a better price, are you?'

'No, of course not...' I laughed. 'I promise, not a single thread.'

My thoughts were in turmoil but she was smiling again, this time rather shyly. 'Elly...have you time to make me just one more gown before you pack up your shop? One that's looser round the waist?' She reached forward and I grasped her outstretched hands. She blushed deeply, smiling coyly. 'Sir James says we've another six bedrooms to fill and... well...he's not one to hold back!'

As we stood by the carriage to wave them off, Mrs Pengelly reached into her basket, leaning quickly out of the window to hand me a letter. 'Elowyn, I nearly forgot...this came today. It's so dirty the address is almost unreadable. It must have been dropped in some mud...'

It was the letter I had longed for and I ran back up the steps two at a time. The address was difficult to decipher, dirt and mud smearing Lady Pendarvis' immaculate writing

— no wonder it had taken three weeks to reach me. She had not deserted me, far from it. *I was on no account to worry*, she was as concerned as I must be and as soon as she returned to Fosse she would come and discuss the matter. All I must do was concentrate on the gowns for the lock opening.

I left it on the table and went through to the storeroom, running my hands along my rolls of fabric — my Mechlin lace at thirteen shillings and ten a yard, the brocaded satin at eighteen shillings and sixpence. Each one chosen with such care, haggled over, searched for. I had stood on freezing-cold quaysides, waiting from dawn to be the first in the queue. Watching for the ships that I knew would have *boutis in broderie*, Marseilles Vannes, the last of the Mantua silk… my Brussels lace. Even the Spitalfields silk was precious to me, each bought with such plans.

I checked behind me. A sliding panel led to a tiny room behind the end wall and I released the catch, slipping quickly into the confined space. It was no bigger than eight feet wide but room enough for a small couch and a table with two chairs. Lady Pendarvis had shown me the secret room and the loose floorboard where she kept her money, and I thought no one else knew of its existence. Now Mamm would have me fill it with brandy. I reached for a candle and struck the tinderbox, sliding the panel door shut before pulling back the carpet.

I lifted the loose floorboard. No one knew the extent of my savings — not Gwen, nor Josie, nor even Uncle Thomas, but there they lay, fourteen crisp pound notes tied with a satin ribbon — my fabrics were worth another twenty-seven pounds and the finished gowns two pounds each. After wages, I would be looking at nearly forty pounds. *Forty pounds*, it seemed almost inconceivable! I was the daughter of a drunken fisherman yet I had worked so hard to hold this money in my hand. Each roll of fabric had an authentic bill of sale – all my accounts were perfectly above board. I drew a deep breath, summoning my courage. I would not be bullied by Mamm. I would not marry Nathan Cardew. Yet just the thought of Mrs Hoskins brought tears to my eyes. She would take my profits to line her own pockets and pay me the bare minimum. Another bully bending me to her will.

Lady Pendarvis had given me so much; she had sold me her fabrics for less than half price and for the last two years she had paid my rent. Not a day passed without me recognizing my good fortune – she had set me up, handed over her business, taught me everything and I had grasped every opportunity, working long, backbreaking hours to justify her belief in me. If I joined Jenna's school, I would lose my independence – it was her school, she would be in charge. My heart thumped in defiance. I would *never* work for Mrs Hoskins, but neither could I expect Lady Pendarvis to go on paying my rent.

The notes lay in a fan on my lap. Not there by right, but there through merit. Long hours spent bent over my sewing often in poor light, my fingertips aching, yet there was laughter in those notes, the look in my customers' eyes each time I exceeded their expectations. There was respect in those notes, the merchants with whom I traded knowing I was not to be cheated. They were there because I knew what was needed and ran a profitable business. I breathed deeply, William's words pounding in my mind. *Know your worth. Let them come to you.*

But a lease of my own, was that reaching too far?

'Free Flow...'

Chapter Twenty-one

The Dock Side, Porthcarrow
Saturday 2nd July 1796, 2:30 p.m.

Across the dock, Gwen waved her flag high in the air. Josie and Uncle Thomas were beside her, the top of Tom's hat just visible behind them. Tom had rowed us round the headland and many had thought to do the same. People were dragging their boats high onto the shingle, their voices ringing across the water in excited expectation. I turned back to Mrs Perys. 'No, I've not met Mrs Hellyar. Not yet.'

'She's not as grand as those ye're used to, but she's high standards and don't choose to mix with many. Ruth, ye told the children not to run about?' She shook the feathers on her parasol, opening it against the burning sun. 'If the wind stays this calm, we'll be here all day.' I had joined her with a heavy heart but Nathan and Ruth had been thrilled, and this way I had offended no one. Mrs Pengelly would soon be here and I would politely take my leave of Mrs Perys and be under no further obligation. I need never see her again.

Ruth suppressed her smile, her simple dress adorned by a red shawl, her straw bonnet with its two small ribbons

193

making her look so joyful. I was wearing my yellow silk and had my own matching ribbons. Today was the day for flowery bonnets and ribbons, for flags and marching bands. It was not a day to stay cross with Mrs Perys.

A group of local dignitaries stood talking on the quayside. They were to greet Sir James as he stepped off the ship and Nathan had arranged them in the order he deemed proper. He began rearranging them – putting first Mr Hellyar, then Mr Sellick, finally Mr Drew – and the more I watched the more uncomfortable I began to feel. It was as if I was seeing him through new eyes, his *detestable self-importance* at first irritating but now embarrassing. His constant fawning round Mr Hellyar seemed almost repugnant.

Some of the men were clearly affronted yet he seemed not to notice and I took a deep breath, trying to hide my discomfort. At the end of the day I would kindly but firmly tell him I could no longer accept his courtship and I would never come back. Never.

Major Trelawney's band was playing and I turned to watch. Their red coats were blazing, their white sashes brilliant in the glare of the sun. The tune was so joyous and I knew I must not let my discomfort spoil my enjoyment. It was a day for cheering and laughter, a day to remember. Ruth was hardly audible above the pipes and drum. 'Look…sails – that's them coming now.'

She began waving her flag. The feathers in Mrs Perys' hat fluttered as she turned to watch. There was enough wind to keep the flags flying and the sails filled and I searched the glittering bay, my excitement growing. A group of children broke free and ran along the quayside, standing up on the railings to get a better view. The lock gates were open, both harbours brimming with sparkling blue water; the top of the tide and a perfect day – Sir James could not have asked for more.

Mrs Perys scowled. 'Mrs Hellyar's just arrived – see, over there. What's she doin'? She's no business stayin' with the men. She should come here an' stand with us. I specifically asked her to join me…'

Everyone was dressed in their best, the dockside newly swept, no trace of horse muck. Even the barrels looked neatly arranged, the ropes and chains coiled in perfect circles. Bethany saw me and smiled but did not wave. She was holding her children's hands tightly in the crowd. Samuel was sitting beside her on a wicker chair, the baby on his lap, and I could see Mamm push her way to the front of the crowd. A delicious smell of roasting pig filtered through the air – a clear blue sky after a week of constant rain, everyone recognized it as a sign for good.

Mrs Perys was still glaring at Mrs Hellyar and Ruth leaned nearer. 'Mr Hellyar's *very* important,' she whispered. 'Nathan says what he don't know about tin ain't worth knowin'. But it's Mr Lilly we need to impress – did Nathan tell you Sir James is gettin' that close to securing a smeltin' deal? Mr Lilly's a very rich man – an' if they can persuade him to build his smelter here, they'll be plenty more work for the men.'

'They'll smelt the ore here, in the harbour – rather than ship it away?'

'It's what Sir James wants – 'twould be that good for the town – and very prestigious for Sir James. Viscount Vallenforth won't need to pay for his ore to be shipped – Mr Lilly will buy it straight off him, smelt it here, and ship the tin direct. Everyone profits. That's why Sir James has asked Mr Lilly to be his guest today.'

A cheer rose – then another and another, the sails on Sir James' cutter arching in the soft breeze. The cheering grew louder, the sudden shouts drowning the sound of the pipes. Those standing on the outer harbour began waving their hats high in the air and Ruth leaned nearer. 'Mr Lilly's daughter Angelica is goin' to be guest of honour at the dance – she's to sit under the bower an' they're goin' to dance round her. They do say she's very beautiful.'

Sir James' cutter was close enough for us to see Mr Lilly and his daughter standing on the deck. Mrs Pengelly was next to Joseph Dunn, Billy's red waistcoat a brilliant splash of colour. Everyone was cheering, Ruth reaching high on her toes. 'Where's Sir James and Lady Polcarrow?'

I caught a glimpse of Sir James on the helm; Lady Polcarrow was beside him, the daughter of the man who had built the boat. For her there seemed a greater cheer, everyone straining forward, ignoring the ropes. At once, a collective gasp echoed round the quayside, the men gaping in sudden disbelief though smiles lit the faces of every woman watching.

'He's never handed her the tiller!'

'She's never goin' to—'

'Good God, he's lettin' her bring her in.'

Lady Polcarrow held the tiller in one hand. Smiling broadly, her emerald-green gown and matching hat fluttering softly in the breeze, she shouted to Sir James to take down the sails and a huge cheer went up from every woman present. Sir James turned and bowed, stripping off his jacket, throwing down his hat to grab the ropes. Joseph Dunn did likewise, stripping off his jacket and smiling back at Sir James as they began letting down the sails. Miss Lilly was clearly delighted. She stood clapping her hands at the prow.

A lump caught my throat, a sudden pang of jealousy. That was true love: James Polcarrow showing the new town so publicly how much he loved his wife. Ruth felt it too, smiling back at me through the tears in her eyes. Lady Polcarrow stood tall and upright, smiling back at the cheering women, waving at the astonished men, as she steered the cutter effortlessly through the narrow gap and into the harbour.

Sir James bowed to each dignitary in turn; Mr Lilly did likewise, nodding and smiling as he was introduced. His voice was gruff but his manner friendly. His smelting deals had brought him great prosperity but while his clothes were good quality and fitted him well, there was no pomp about him – a complete contrast to Mr Hellyar with his gold chains and embroidered silk waistcoat. Miss Angelica Lilly looked to be enjoying herself; her father may be a sober dresser but his daughter had no such scruples.

Her gown was straight from London, the cream silk elaborately embroidered, gathered into a raised waist. Her neckline was scooped and edged with lace. She wore a large cream hat with coloured silk flowers, her extravagant Brussels-lace parasol fluttering in the breeze. The children gaped in awe and I liked her on sight as she stood smiling back at them, winking mischievously at one when she thought no one was watching.

Mrs Perys was still glowering at Mrs Hellyar and I searched the mass of people for Mrs Pengelly. The hot sun burned me through my dress, my parasol more decorative than useful. Ruth was herding her dancers into a group. 'Sir James is to make his speech on the green – so the children can play an' we can use the shade. Oh, an' Nathan's lookin' for you.'

She ran on to another set of people, pointing them up the hill, and I looked round. Billy was dashing along the dock and my heart jolted in sudden envy. William was waiting for him, smiling, cuffing him round the ear, no doubt teasing him about his bright red waistcoat. I watched him throw back his head in sudden laughter, Billy beaming with pleasure as the two of them started walking side by side up the path. People stopped to watch them and a sudden hollowness emptied me of all joy.

I could see Nathan searching the crowd. He would proffer me his arm and I would never get free. He had been so busy arranging the reception committee that we had hardly spoken, but now he would claim me. Mrs Pengelly was nowhere to be seen and I knew he would suggest we go in search of her. My panic was rising. Once I was seen walking on his arm everyone would presume – he would presume. I had to avoid it. Everyone had to stop presuming.

Mrs Perys had her back to me and I saw my chance to slip away unnoticed. People were quickly leaving the lock and I darted between them, heading up towards the green. I would go to the tent and find Mrs Munroe. She would be keeping a close eye on her pie and Tamsin and Mrs Pengelly were bound to join her. The thought of ending Nathan's courtship seemed suddenly so petrifying. He would put pressure on me to change my mind – he was so persuasive, never taking no as an answer, and I knew I would have to stay strong. I would wait until the last moment and tell him as I left.

I was thirsty, my mouth as dry as dust. A table lay groaning under the weight of barrels and as jugs were being handed out, I took one gratefully. The beer quenched my thirst and was just what I needed. First, there would be the dance, then scattering the pennies, then catching the oiled pig. Miss Lilly was sitting under the bower, her jet-black hair curling under her huge hat. She had striking looks, dark laughing eyes. The children were each presenting her with a single flower and she smiled back at each in turn, collecting the flowers into a large bunch. The sky was the colour of cornflowers, the children clutching their maypole ribbon as they waited for the fiddler. The first chord sounded and they began to weave in and out. A maypole in June, but nobody minded.

They were all in the tent, even Josie and Uncle Thomas. Mrs Munroe sat nervously on her chair. There were seven pies in all and the competition looked fierce. The winner's rosette lay ready to be awarded and even Mrs Pengelly raised her eyebrows at the colour – purple, the same colour as Mrs Perys' dress. Sam came to my side. 'Here, lass, have a drink

199

– no, don't say ye won't. Just fer once, let yer hair down.' He gulped down his own, wiping his mouth with the back of his hand. 'Reckon I can take me jacket off yet?'

On the table next to the pies were an assortment of knitted shawls and gloves. Mrs Pengelly smiled. 'Look, Elly – there's a table with lavender bags and cedar balls. They would be useful…'

From the corner of my eye, I saw a flash of red and Billy came rushing to my side. He was breathless, his eyes sparkling. 'Ye've got to come, Elly. Will's wrestling – he's through to the last round. He's goin' to win. Honest he is.' He grabbed both my hands and started pulling me away.

'I hate fighting. You know I hate it…' I had to steady myself as the beer was strong and I felt strangely dizzy.

'It's not fighting, it's wrestling, and ye've never seen any. Honest, Elly, ye've got to come.' He began pulling me again, dragging me across the tent and out to the green. A large crowd had gathered round a marked circle and as we grew nearer, I saw Sir James had brought everyone along to watch. All the dignitaries were there – Mr Lilly, Mr Perys, Mr Hellyar, even Mr Drew with his rheumatic eyes and round glasses. I hardly recognized Mr Sellick; he was wearing fine new clothes and a tall hat and was carrying a cane.

Sir James held out a hat, shaking it in front of the gathered men. 'Thank you, gentlemen – I'm sure you'll all agree the winner deserves a good prize.' The men dived deep into their pockets, filling the hat as the onlookers cheered. Sir James' voice rose: 'Sixteen good men, now down to two.' He waited for the cheer to subside, nodding to the judges standing in the ring. 'So, here we have it – all betting must now cease. Let the best man win.' He raised his arm, the hat high in the air. 'Twelve guineas prize money – I give you Mr Joseph Dunn and Mr William Cotterell.'

The crowd parted as Joseph and William made their way through the mass of men. They raised their arms amidst the whistles and cheers and spat on their hands before shaking firmly. They were wearing short, loose jackets, their heads uncovered. Billy's eyes were wide with excitement. 'They've already won three rounds each – Joseph wins everything round these parts but I know Will's the stronger.' He waved and William turned.

Our eyes caught and a searing pain made my heart jolt. His sail-cloth jacket was tied with loops in the front, the sleeves loose, ending just short of his wrists. He stood tall and upright, sweat streaking down his face. His hair was ruffled, his shoulders squared. He was taller than Joseph and not so stocky. His eyes lit with delight when he saw me and my heart burned.

I turned away. 'I can't watch. You know I hate it.'

Billy pulled me back. 'It's not fightin'. Look Elowyn, fer once let go of yer stuffiness – all they do is take hold above the girdle and throw the other to the ground.' His words caught me. I wanted to watch, of course I did. I wanted more than anything to allow myself a glimpse of William, but to watch him so intently would bring me nothing but pain.

I turned back to look. William's movements were slow and graceful; he was skirting Joseph, gradually getting the measure of him. He seemed the lighter on his feet but

201

they were equally matched. My heart silently urged him on. The crowd was shouting, cheering every move, even Sir James and his party had their elbows bent and their fists clenched. Jenna stood at the front of the ring shouting for her husband. She looked so happy, a small boy on each hip, her blond hair foaming round her shoulders. Lady Polcarrow was by her side, watching intently but remaining poised and dignified.

Sweat streaked down the two men's faces, their muscles shaking under the strain. Each time one of them made a throw, they had to keep the other pinned down in a hold. 'They're to get three pin-downs, Elly. That's shoulders or hips – but ye need three fer a win. If the stickler gets his stick under, then it's not a pin-down. Needs be tight to the ground, ye understand?'

I nodded. The three men had long sticks in their hands, nodding or shaking their heads as they tested every hold. Any space at all and it was not a pin-down. William made another throw, Joseph straining hard to force him back. Billy's clenched fists flew to his mouth. 'He'll do it next time. I know he will.'

My heart was racing – the crowd, the excitement, the respect of the watchers. It was not fighting; it was simply one man pitting his strength against another. They looked so noble and dignified, their movements graceful. Two strong men with perfect muscles like the Greek gods in the painting on Lady Pendarvis' wall. I felt flushed with pleasure, my growing excitement making it hard not to cheer William on. 'Will he win, Billy?'

'That'll do it…That's the one…' Billy was almost hoarse from shouting. 'He's got him now.'

I could barely watch. William was straining to keep Joseph down, Joseph pushing back with all his might. The cheering was deafening and I started shouting, urging William to keep his hold. The muscles in his arms were shaking, his thighs trembling. Sweat dripped from Joseph's face, his mouth drawn tight; the tension on both their faces was almost painful to watch. The three men came forward with their sticks.

'That's a pin-down…that's another…three pins. Gentlemen, we have a winner.'

Billy threw his arms round me and I hugged him back. William was smiling, shaking Joseph by the hand. Joseph waved back at the crowd, patting William on the back. Sir James stepped forward, adding his congratulations as he presented the prize, and I felt suddenly so happy, for once, at one with the cheering crowd. I was laughing, clapping, smiling across at Jenna who immediately ran to Joseph. He caught her up in his arms – all three of them, Jenna and his twin boys, holding them high in the air as he swirled them round.

I fought back my jealousy. Jenna had it all. She had the man she loved, she had prior claim to both Lady Polcarrow and Mrs Pengelly. She was so forthright and outspoken, she had a sharp tongue and I knew she often made the new seamstresses cry, yet they all loved her. The crowd parted and I saw William staring at me. I wanted so much for him to come and sweep me up in his arms. I wanted to laugh back at Jenna, be swirled round like her in the arms of the man I loved.

My envy turned to deep emptiness. He filled my days, my

nights, my every sleepless hour spent torturing myself with the memory of the touch of his hand under the sackcloth, the touch that had sent sparks through me. I turned away and froze. Nathan was staring at me.

The dancing would soon start, the fiddlers were already playing. People were lining up to take their place and I searched for Mrs Pengelly. I had seen her in the crowd and knew she was somewhere close. Mrs Munroe had a purple rosette pinned securely to the front of her bodice and I ran to her, throwing my arms round her.

'You won…Mrs Munroe, you won…I knew you would.'

She clamped her mouth tight, trying not to smile. 'Yes, well, Martha Ellis can still be taught a thing or two, though she wasn't havin' it. Said there'd been a mistake…said the rosette got shifted, but I soon told her.'

'She must have been furious…'

Sam shook his head. 'There was quite a to-do. Ye should've seen the crowd, all of them shaking their heads, tellin' Mrs Perys in no uncertain terms that the rosette was right where it had been placed.'

'She tried to cheat? That's awful!'

Mrs Munroe tied the strings of her bonnet tightly. 'Yes, well…pride comes before a fall. She made a fool of herself standin' there in all that rage. Not that I'm gloatin'. 'Tis a sin to gloat.'

Sam smiled and held up his arm, leading her proudly out to dance. She looked so happy and my heart filled with love. Uncle Thomas was already leading Josie by the hand but Gwen was shaking her head, refusing to dance with Tom.

Sir James and his party were leaving and I glanced back – Nathan was taking his leave of them, his eyes fixed firmly on me. He had nearly reached me.

'There you are, Elowyn. I've hardly seen you all day. The others are just leavin' so I thought we'd go an' wave them off.' He put out his arm and my hand trembled. He was smiling, giving me no sense of reproach. 'A good bout, don't you think? I'm sorry Joseph didn't win but it's fairly obvious he lost on purpose. Can't have Sir James givin' a prize to his own steward...' He began steering me towards the lock. 'Mrs Pengelly's sailin' back with Sir James so I've told Mrs Perys we'd join her for tea. Ruth says she's distraught about her pie.' He shook his head. 'The pies should've been named... She was humiliated, shouted at by the crowd, an' she's taken it that badly. It's best we don't upset her any more.'

I turned to look back over my shoulder. The positioned couples were smiling in anticipation, Mrs Munroe retying her new bonnet securely in place. I was desperate to join them. 'Do you dance, Nathan?' I asked.

I felt him stiffen. His face clouded. 'Do you want me to dance? It's just...a man in my position...well, it doesn't look seemly...mixing with the men. I keep my distance, Elowyn – that way I keep their respect.' He began leading me away again, the same icy hand clutching my heart.

'Elowyn...wait! Ye can't go.' Billy was smiling from ear to ear, his hair rumpled, falling over his face; his shirtsleeves were rolled to the elbows, his waistcoat undone. He stood holding out his hands, grabbing mine. 'Ye have to dance...ye have to.' I began laughing, pretending to protest.

Billy started pulling me away but Nathan held me back. People were turning round and as Billy pulled harder, Nathan had to release me. I slipped gratefully from his grasp. 'Nathan…why don't you go ahead and see the boat off? I'll have one dance with Billy and come and join you…Billy, stop, you'll have me over…'

Nathan was no longer looking at me. He was staring over my shoulder, his mouth set hard, and I turned round to see William, washed and changed, his hair falling in damp curls around his face. He was walking straight towards me, his eyes piercing mine. He put out his hand.

'Winner's rights, Miss Liddicot; I believe you have no choice. I can ask any woman to dance with me.' He smiled, his hazel eyes flecked with green, looking at me with a power of their own. 'And I believe she cannot refuse.'

Chapter Twenty-two

William led me down the line of waiting dancers. We were to take our place as the top couple, dance three times down the centre then form an arch for everyone to dance under. My cheeks were burning, my heart thumping. I could not believe this was happening. The fiddler banged his bow against his fiddle and William smiled down at me.

'I don't know how to dance,' I whispered.

His grip tightened. 'We'll manage.'

The music began and he started hurtling me backwards and forwards, his eyes never leaving my face. He knew exactly what to do. I could barely feel my feet touch the ground but whirled round, getting dizzier and dizzier. He was laughing, going too fast, one minute lifting me off the ground, the next hurling me up and down the line, his hand on my waist. He was so light on his feet and I threw myself into the dance trying to keep up with him. For the first time in my life I was dancing – dancing like everyone else.

The fiddlers quickened their pace and the dance grew

faster, William's strong arms crossing in front, behind, never losing their grip. It was as if I was flying. Ever since I was a child, I had longed to dance like this, longed to be swirled round, my feet hardly touching the ground. I was in a dream and soon I would wake up. His hands were warm round my waist, lifting me up. It felt dangerous, exciting; something that happened to other women, never me.

The dance came to an end and William held me tightly, smiling down at me. His face was flushed and I rested my hands against his heaving chest. My head was spinning. 'You're a born dancer, Elowyn.' He was breathless, his hair ruffled.

'I never dance. You must've noticed how I didn't know the steps.' I was breathless too, sweat pricking my back. Everyone around us was laughing, catching their breath.

His arm slipped round my waist. 'Come,' he whispered, leading me away from the crowd, his thighs brushing against mine, his hand burning me through my gown. This was disobeying every rule but I could not hold back. I went willingly, breathlessly, eager for what was to come. His pace quickened and we ran across the green, dodging the beer wagon and up to the stables. Once in the courtyard, he drew me to him, swinging me round, smiling broadly as he pinned me against the wall.

'I love you, Elowyn...I adore you.' His eyes were fierce, devouring me with their intensity. He leaned down, his lips a fraction from my own and a deep yearning filled me. I could not hold back. He lifted my chin, our lips fusing, and I kissed him, deeply, passionately, giving myself to him so completely.

His arms tightened, crushing me to him, and in that instant I understood what Gwen meant – the inability to stop, the terrible need to be one with a man.

His lips rested against mine. 'Marry me, Elowyn. I've twelve guineas – we can start with that.'

He began kissing me again, lightly, softly, down the side of my neck, up to my ear. My throat, the nape of my neck, my eyes, my forehead, and I found myself laughing. I could not help it. His audacity thrilled me, his body so powerful, drawing me to him.

'Of course not,' I whispered, 'you'll need more than twelve guineas—' I could not finish. His kiss grew deeper, more passionate and I kissed him back, lost to a wave of desire I could not control.

Behind us, footsteps came to a sudden stop and we drew quickly apart. 'Get your filthy hands off my sister.' Tom was walking towards us, his hands clenched, his eyes blazing, and I froze, hardly believing what I saw. Tom looked just like Father – the same hatred, the same hunched shoulders. Everything about him looked like Father and a wave of terror shot through me. He grabbed a pitchfork, thrusting it at William. 'I said get your filthy hands off my sister.'

William stood clear of me, his hands in front of him, backing slowly away. 'No need for that. Put it down, Tom.'

'No need? Ye think ye can force yerself on my sister? Take her for yer prize – treat her like some alley cat!' He stepped closer, the fork inches from William's face. He was jabbing the air, making him back away. Anger distorted his features; his mouth clamped tight, his eyes black and unseeing.

'Tom, stop. You've no right...' It was as if I was pleading with Father. 'Put that down...I'll come with you.'

Tom took no heed but continued thrusting the pitchfork, forcing William back. 'I wouldn't do that if I were you,' said William slowly.

'Think ye can have yer way with her? Take another man's woman?' He was consumed by fury, spitting his words out with rage. 'It's disgusting. Get back, Elowyn. Stop snivellin'. I saw you – behavin' like those women in the linhay.' He lunged quickly, jabbing the pitchfork at William.

'That's enough!' William grabbed the fork, snapping it quickly over his knee before throwing it to the ground. 'Leave us,' he said. 'I've no wish to quarrel.' He took a step forward, towering over Tom. 'I understand your concern but you've no need to speak to your sister like that. Show her some respect.'

'Respect?' fumed Tom. 'Ye dare speak of respect?' He grabbed my wrist, forcing me to go with him. The same fierce hold – the same burning pain. I knew not to try to break free. He jerked me forward and I looked round at William, desperate for him not to intervene but he was already by my side.

'Let go of Elowyn. Never lay an angry hand on a woman.' His eyes were blazing but his voice remained calm.

Tom took no notice, his grip tightening. He seemed possessed. 'Get out of here, William Cotterell. Get far away and never bother my sister again.'

William's voice remained calm. 'I said *never lay an angry hand on a woman*. Let go of Elowyn.'

Tom swung round. 'Or what?' He jerked me angrily towards him.

'Or you'll get a soaking.' William reached forward, grabbing Tom by the jacket, swinging him to the ground in one quick movement. Tom lay sprawled on the cobbles but William had not finished. Swooping down, he grabbed Tom's wrist in one hand, his ankle in the other and flung him straight into the water trough. He reached for my hand.

Tom's splashing wet the cobbles. There were more footsteps, someone else behind us. Uncle Thomas looked horrified. 'What's this all about, Elly love?'

Nathan was next to him. He looked incredulous, pain deep in his eyes. Our eyes met and he turned abruptly away.

Tom thrust the oars into place, glowering back at me in his wet clothes. Uncle Thomas took Josie by the hand, helping her down the shingle and onto the plank. She had dressed with such care, looking so happy in her spotted sprig and knitted shawl. Her cheeks were glowing, her basket full of spoils – a bunch of lavender tied in a bow, an ebony whale whittled by one of the sailors. Only her quick glance at Tom gave away her fear.

'There's no need to stop everyone's fun – it's hardly fair. Josie and Gwen don't have to leave just because you're cross with me,' I snapped.

Gwen looked pale, her eyes darting between the two of us. 'No, I've had enough…honest, I'm quite ready to go home…'

Josie kept her eyes down. 'And I must get back to Mother…I've already left her too long…'

Tom scowled at Uncle Thomas. 'Cavorting like that with a man she doesn't even know. It was disgusting…I saw everything…She's no better than the women in the linhay.'

Uncle Thomas pointed his finger at Tom. 'I said that was enough, Tom. Keep a civil tongue. I know you're angry, but there's no need for language like that.'

'Angry?' Tom pulled at the oars, the boat slicing quickly through the water. The wind was picking up, a fine spray blowing across the waves. The hogs had been roasted, the meal just beginning. Across the green, the flame-throwers and jugglers were setting up their stalls. There would be entertainment long into the night and I was being taken home like a naughty child. 'Angry doesn't touch it. She's just lost me the yard – ye know that, don't ye?'

Gwen's voice faltered. 'Perhaps Nathan didn't see. Perhaps it can all be forgotten – no harm done.'

Tom's rowing was furious. 'Getting drunk an' throwin' herself about like some village whore! Nathan saw all right. The whole town saw. She disgraced us.'

Uncle Thomas put his jacket round Josie. 'I said that was enough, Tom. Just row us home.'

Chapter Twenty-three

Coombe House
Sunday 3rd July 1796, 10:00 a.m.

Tom demanded I write a letter apologizing for my wanton dancing – I was to stress that my unaccustomed consumption of strong beer had been the cause of my outrageous behaviour. I had lost all sense of propriety and was truly ashamed. William Cotterell had taken advantage of me and I was to beg Nathan's forgiveness. Tom would collect the letter at ten.

I reread my letter, the tremor in my hands making the paper tremble.

Dear Nathan,

I treated you very badly yesterday. You did not deserve such thoughtlessness and I apologize most sincerely. I understand that you will now want to withdraw your courtship and I believe this would be for the best. My feelings for you are that of friendship and respect, and to pretend otherwise would be to lie. You are a good man who deserves a wife who will love you as much as you love her. I can never be that wife but

I hope you find her soon and I hope she brings you all the happiness you deserve.

Elowyn Liddicot

The floor was littered with my failed attempts. Nathan must have seen me kiss William and I would not wish that on anyone. The clock on the mantelpiece struck ten and I glanced out of the window. Tom was walking down the cobbles and just the sight of him made my hands shake. My younger brother was turning into a man like Father. It was Father's face I had seen, Father gripping me so tightly. My wrist still hurt, the bruise deepening to a thick purple band.

I sealed my letter and ran downstairs. The house was quiet, Mrs Pengelly was staying the night at Polcarrow and Sam and Mrs Munroe were both nursing sore heads. Even Tamsin was with her sister. A dull ache made my head throb. I would pay dearly for my behaviour. Even now, tongues would be wagging. I heard Tom's knock and opened the door just wide enough to thrust my letter into his hand.

I slammed the door shut, climbing the stairs in mounting dread.

Mrs Pengelly smiled as I joined her in her sitting room. 'Goodness, three o'clock. What time do you call this?' She was sitting in her favourite chair, holding out her hand. I would have to tell her soon enough, but for the moment her face was a picture of happiness. 'Mind you, they're only just up in Polcarrow. The last guest left at dawn and Miss Lilly still wanting to dance! Not that I was up that late – I'd long gone to bed!' She smiled at Sam who stood hang-dog at the door. 'Is Mrs Munroe ready? I hope you're hungry – we've a lot of pie to get through!' She laughed happily, shaking her head. 'Dear Mrs Munroe – fancy making four pies to choose the best! Any one of those four pies would've won!'

Sam shook his head, putting his hand to his forehead. 'We've only the one left – I've took one to the almshouse and left t'other at the church door. The vagrants are back an' Reverend Bettison will take it round after church.' He turned abruptly, immediately frowning. 'Who's that then, knockin' on the door?'

Mrs Pengelly took off her glasses and folded her sewing. I would tell her everything once we had eaten. I knew she would listen and understand – not judge me wanton like my family had done. She was looking at me now, her eyes quizzical. 'I can't tell if that's a smile or a grimace, Elly love. You look troubled; are you all right?'

Through the door we heard the sound of rattling, a heavy bag being lowered to the floor. Sam stood at the door, a look of sheer astonishment on his pale face. 'It's Will, the cart driver – the wrestler – the one what won.'

Mrs Pengelly's eyes went straight to my face. My heart was jumping, thumping in my chest. 'Mr Cotterell?' she said. 'Well, you'd better show him in, Sam.'

I could hardly see for the blush burning my face. William's huge frame took up most of the doorway. He was freshly shaved, his hair neatly brushed. He looked so handsome, wearing a new jacket with leather elbows and a thick leather

215

collar. His white shirt had been freshly laundered, his boots newly polished. He bowed politely, his hat in one hand, a large bunch of roses held in the other. The scent of roses filled the room and he smiled shyly, his hazel eyes returning Mrs Pengelly's quiet stare. 'I hope I don't disturb you, Mrs Pengelly.'

Mrs Pengelly's back remained straight, her mouth unsmiling, but I could hardly breathe, my heart was hammering so fast. *Please, please like him. Please ask him to stay*. 'And what brings you to my door, Mr Cotterell?' she said at last.

William's eyes held hers, a slight smile. 'I'm in love with Elowyn. I thought it only right to tell you.'

I thought I would faint. Sam was watching open-mouthed at the door and I could hear Billy racing up the stairs. If Mrs Pengelly was shocked, she hid it well. 'Then you'd better give Elowyn her roses,' she said, smiling.

William smiled back at her. 'The roses are for you,' he said, stepping forward, handing them to her. 'And the bag in the hall is full of tools. Billy tells me the spit needs fixing – I thought I'd take a look.' He turned to me. 'That's if you're not averse to me teaching Billy how a spit works?'

I could hardly bring myself to look at him, let alone speak. Through the open door, I saw Billy standing over the bag of tools, already loosening the strap. 'Can he, Mrs Pengelly?'

Mrs Pengelly inhaled the sweet perfume from her roses. 'Are you hungry, Mr Cotterell?' she said, still smiling. 'Only we have rather a lot of pie to get through and we could do with some help.'

We walked down the stairs and into the kitchen, Billy running ahead with the heavy bag. Sam's admiration for William was plain to see, Billy's adoration impossible to hide. Under Mrs Munroe's watchful gaze, they stood examining the spit jack, William following the chains and pulley, testing the ratchets and interlocking wheels. Billy was spellbound, watching William undo each piece and lay them in order on the hearth. They knelt down, the pieces in front of them, William explaining how one moved the other.

'I think that's the problem,' he said, reaching inside his bag for a small bottle of oil. 'The cogs on the flywheel are blocked. Clean it well, Billy – give it a good scrape then give everything a thorough oiling.' Mr Pitt watched from his basket, his tail thumping, and William reached over, stroking the huge black and white cat firmly on his head. 'No need to glower, cat – we'll not be long.'

Mrs Munroe tied the ribbons of her apron tightly. Her sleeves were rolled up, her smile as wide as the river. 'Take no heed of Mr Pitt...Here now, Mr Cotterell, there's a basin of hot water to wash yer hands...an' here's a towel. I'll lay another place – there's plenty needs eatin'.' She had her rosette pinned securely on her breast, bustling round the kitchen with plates, knives and forks. She put the golden-crusted, raised rabbit pie on the table. 'Ye've come at just the right time.'

William dried his hands, staring down at the pie. 'Looks too good to eat, Mrs Munroe.'

Mrs Pengelly put her roses in a jug of water and placed them carefully in the centre of the table. Sam was polishing each glass, laying them down as if fit for the king. The kitchen seemed alive with excitement. 'We usually eat in the dining room but...it's just...' The scrubbed pine table had been transformed with delicate napkins and embroidered place settings. 'We like to eat together when there's no one else here.'

Mrs Munroe stood with both hands on her hips. 'Leave that awhile, Billy, an' wash yer hands.'

I could see they liked him. Perhaps it was because they had seen him win the wrestling, perhaps it was when they saw us dancing or when they had watched him teaching Billy by the river; either way, I thought my heart would burst. It was as if he belonged with us, his huge frame dwarfing the kitchen, his eyes lighting up as Mrs Munroe cut into her pie. He barely looked at me, but when he did, my heart seemed to stop, his shy smile making every bone in my body weaken.

'Thank you, you're very kind,' he said, standing by the chair Mrs Pengelly offered him.

He was so tall and handsome, immediately stepping behind Mrs Pengelly's chair to draw it out. She smiled her thanks and he looked quickly at Billy who drew back my chair, smiling proudly. I looked up in astonishment – Sam was doing the same for Mrs Munroe, all three of us taking our places with smiles on our faces. My heart brimmed with happiness and I knew I would not be able to eat; he was so polite, he had excellent manners – everything about him made me love him more and more.

There was no end of things to discuss – the lock opening, the wrestling, the judging of the pie. Mrs Munroe told us

Miss Lilly had whispered her pie was the *clear* winner. She was so happy, insisting William should have another large portion. I could not eat but listened as Mrs Pengelly began quizzing him. He was from Penzance, his father a mine captain; his mother still lived there with his sister-in-law and her two young boys. A mining accident had left both of them widowed and he had fallen foul of those responsible for the safety of the mine.

It seemed he had quarrelled with everyone. He spoke softly, shrugging his shoulders, smiling ruefully when Mrs Pengelly shook her head. He was an engineer, he had good prospects, yet he had quarrelled with both Lord Entworth and Viscount Vallenforth over the tinners' riots. Even worse, he was barred from stepping foot anywhere near an engine designed by Mr Watt and Mr Boulton.

'Mr Watt and Mr Boulton have taken out an injunction against me. They've banned me from every mine where their engines are being used – and believe me, that's most of Cornwall.'

'I don't understand. How can they ban you from their engines?'

'I've been accused of tampering with one of them, and they see that as a threat.'

'Are they that powerful? Surely they can't stop you?'

'They're that powerful, and that determined. Once they developed their engine, they took out a patent forbidding anyone to change or copy it. The patent is legally enforced – it stops anyone copying their engines or altering them…or *tampering*, as they call it.'

'And yet you obviously believe Mr Watt and Mr Boulton's engines need altering?'

'It's not just me. There are others who believe the engines could be made more efficient – there's plenty in agreement but no one willing to go to court to challenge the patent.'

Billy's eyes widened with sudden fear but Mrs Pengelly merely raised her eyebrows. 'You'd think all those with shares in the mines – even mine owners like Lord Entworth and Viscount Vallenforth – would welcome your interference. If you believe the engines could be altered to be more efficient, then, surely, it would benefit everyone. Are people justified in their condemnation of you, Mr Cotterell?'

William nodded, looking her straight in the eye. 'Legally, Mrs Pengelly, the law's on the side of the patent owners – as it is on the side of every wealthy mine owner who puts profit before the safety of the men who produce their wealth. The *law's the law*, put in place and implemented by those who think only of profit – who don't give a moment's thought that their workers are starving and most too ill to work. But as things stand, it's Mr Watt and Mr Boulton who benefit most. They have powerful friends in parliament who have backed the patent and they're lining their pockets...and believe me, their pockets are deep.'

'Did you tamper with the engine?'

'I did.' William wiped his mouth with his napkin, putting it next to his finished plate. 'I wanted to bring attention to the terrible injustice we people of Cornwall face – the outrageous greed of two men. Watt and Boulton are crippling the mines with their inefficient engines – they're preventing progress, holding Cornish mines back. Forgive me if I sound angry, Mrs Pengelly.'

'You sound like my husband, Mr Cotterell. He learned to his cost it's a dangerous path to fight those in authority. He would be with us now had he not chosen to tread that path. Was it wise, Mr Cotterell, to do what you did?'

William's voice softened. 'Most likely not, but they left me no choice. Mr Watt and Mr Boulton need to be challenged – what they're doing is neither right nor moral. But it's not just the principle of unfairness making me stick my neck out – men's livelihoods are at stake.'

'You mean mine closures?'

'I do…If we don't alter the engines to burn less coal, the Welsh mines will take our business. Cornish mine owners need to import coal, which adds to the cost, but the Welsh have it on their doorstep. If we, as engineers, can't make the improvements needed to increase efficiency, our Cornish tin will be too expensive and our mines will close.'

Billy looked furious. 'That's awful – for how long?'

'Boulton's friends are very powerful. Parliament's extended the patent to thirty years – it will last until one minute past midnight as the century changes. That's another three and a half years.'

'And in the meantime?' Sam pulled his chair forward.

'In the meantime, no one can improve the efficiency of the old engines or build new ones because they'll be in breach of copyright. Progress is being hampered and Cornish tinners are paying the price.' William smiled his thanks as Mrs Munroe cleared away his plate. 'Boulton and Watt's new engines were better *at the time*, yet that's twenty-six years ago. Since then our knowledge has grown considerably. The old engines use far too much coal and that makes the cost of mining unnecessarily high.'

'Like the old Polcarrow mine – Wheal Elizabeth. The price of mining copper was too high so the mine closed. Many lost their livelihood.' Mrs Pengelly nodded at Sam to fetch the brandy. 'My husband joined the tinners in their protest.' She poured brandy into a sparkling crystal glass, handing it to William. 'Why are Mr Watt and Mr Boulton being so stubborn? Why not let their engines be altered?'

William took a sip and smiled with appreciation. 'Greed, Mrs Pengelly. They make money because they only *lease* the engines to the mine owners and those leases remain binding until the patent expires. Not only that, they earn a levy from every engine. They charge for the coal their engine *saves* over the old engine it replaced. I think they do nothing but sit in their office and send bills to the mine owners – even Lord Entworth and Viscount Vallenforth are not exempt.'

William's voice was gentle, kind, going over everything again, explaining it in a way we could all understand. Mrs Munroe put a lardy cake on the table and Mrs Pengelly cut William a slice. 'No wonder Mr Watt and Mr Boulton seek to stop you building more efficient engines – they'd lose the income that's making them very rich.' She smiled slowly. 'I can understand your frustration.'

William leaned back in his chair. 'Mr Watt offered me every kind of inducement – a whole raft of sweetmeats from his table. He offered me well-paid employment in their Soho foundry and expected me to join them in lining my pockets, but I'm born of Cornwall – I'm a Cornishman and I care only for the welfare of my fellow Cornishmen. Tinners' families are starving and I'll not seek comfort for myself whilst others starve.'

Mrs Pengelly's smile was full of tenderness. 'I've heard all this before, Mr Cotterell. We need men like you, but you tread a dangerous path and you must take care. What brings you to Fosse?'

The sudden tension in her voice was not lost on William. His eyes held hers. 'Do you believe in destiny, Mrs Pengelly?'

'As a matter of fact, I do. But I also recognize a man in hiding.'

William's eyes sought mine, tender, honest eyes. 'I'm not in hiding, Mrs Pengelly. I would've gone back – but my destiny is keeping me here.'

Billy jumped from his chair. 'I'm going to mend that spit…I'm going to be an engineer – just like you, Will.'

Chapter Twenty-four

Billy began scraping and polishing each bit of the spit, while Mrs Pengelly talked excitedly about the previous night's ball in Polcarrow. She flushed with pleasure, describing the music and sumptuous food. 'Your gowns were beautiful, Elly – a real credit to you. Miss Lilly was clearly taken by them. She asked me where we all got them!' The large kitchen clock struck five and Mrs Munroe jumped in surprise.

'Goodness, is that the time? I'd best get cleared.' She heaved herself out of her chair. 'I'll make some butter buns – d'you like butter buns, Mr Cotterell?'

'Very much, Mrs Munroe, but I think I've already trespassed too long on your hospitality.' He stood up, helping Mrs Pengelly with her chair.

'Not at all, Mr Cotterell – perhaps you and Elowyn would like to sit outside until Billy finishes? It's a beautiful day – you can sit on that rock by the river.' She began ushering us out of the kitchen. 'Billy will soon let you know if he gets in a muddle.' My heart was hammering – to be alone with

William, to have the chance to talk. Mrs Pengelly must like him to allow us such intimacy.

Sunlight sparkled on the river, the tide ebbing. Two rowing boats lay moored in the fast-flowing current, seaweed streaming against their bows. William took off his jacket and laid it on the stone and I felt suddenly nervous. 'It was kind of you to give Mrs Pengelly the roses.'

'She made me very welcome. Are Sam and Mrs Munroe married?'

I laughed. 'No, they're brother and sister. They've been with Mrs Pengelly for nearly fifteen years. They're family, really. They love her – as we all do. She's not really *Mrs* Munroe – at least, I don't think she ever married.'

He sat beside me, stretching out his long legs. 'Was Mr Pengelly a good shipbuilder?'

I loved the way he asked questions – loved the softness in his voice, the way he wanted to know things. 'His ships were highly prized, though it's well known my uncle was the one who kept the yard going. Pascoe Pengelly was always quarrelling with the Corporation. He was a Radical and he didn't mind who knew.'

He picked up a stone, skimming it across the water. 'How did he die?'

'He was imprisoned for bankruptcy and his health never recovered. But it didn't stop him. He kept going to meetings and was arrested as an agitator. Mr Reith got him off but he died soon after in Mrs Pengelly's arms. I think he should have taken more care.' I felt suddenly uneasy. William's talk of protecting the miners had sounded so noble but Radicals scared me – were those his politics? I knew nothing about this man who drew me so completely.

My tone made William look up. A sudden breeze blew from the sea, ruffling his hair. There were soft lines by his eyes, a hardness round his mouth. 'I'll not be so reckless,' he said, taking hold of my hand, 'but I'm with Pascoe Pengelly – in spirit at least.' He turned my hand over, his own hands warm and gentle, bringing my fingers to his lips. He kissed them softly. 'I'll not bend my knee to any man – the march of time heralds a new dawn and those of us who can speak must speak. We must be the voice for those in poverty – those in need and those in neglect. I'd be lying if I led you to believe otherwise.'

Sheep were grazing the fields opposite. Such fighting words, yet spoken by him they sounded right and honourable. I understood them, believed them – they were my own thoughts yet I had never dared to voice them – the imbalance of rich and poor, so many suffering poverty and neglect. Like the vagrants starving in the woods around us, like wanting my own lease, not wanting others to profit for my hours of hard work. 'Why did you fall foul of Lord Entworth and Viscount Vallenforth?'

The lines round his mouth hardened. 'My father warned them not to blast so near the disused mine shaft. He repeatedly told them to drain the old shaft first, yet they took no notice, ordering the men to light the fuses. My father was an experienced mine captain and he knew the danger. He rang the bell to bring everyone to the surface but he was moments too late.' His voice faltered. 'My brother was working the

226

lower shaft and was the first to get flooded. My father went after him but they stood no chance. Twenty men died that day. Twenty widows left unable to feed their families.' His hands gripped mine.

'When was this?'

'Two years ago. It should have been me, Elowyn. I'll never drown, remember? I'm a strong swimmer – I swim every day and have done since I was a child. It should have been me down there, not my brother with his young son and new-born baby. I was so angry I organized a march – all the tinners, protesting, demanding the mine be properly drained.' He sounded cold, hard; his face full of fury. 'Viscount Vallenforth was waiting with his team of thugs – they used whips, clubs...anything they could lay their hands on – thrashing unarmed men. It was brutal, cruel. I'll never forget the look on Viscount Vallenforth's face. The man's a monster – he has no morals, his dealings are corrupt.' His laugh was bitter. 'I should've known it would be futile to expect humanity from a man like that.'

'He'd gallop straight over you if you were in his way – is that why he banned you?'

'He swore I'd never work again – but many were hurt and I must take that responsibility. The march achieved nothing, just brutality and pain, each man threatened with the loss of his livelihood. They went straight back to inefficient engines and masters too greedy to put their safety first.' His hazel eyes burned mine. 'But I learned my lesson – marches and riots are met with violence and brutality, it's only through the courts that my cause will be served.'

227

'So that's why you disobeyed the injunction and altered the engine? So you would be summoned to court and could draw people's attention to the inefficient engines?'

His smile scorched my heart. 'Legal proceedings are widely read – especially in London.'

'William...it frightens me. There are so many people against you – Viscount Vallenforth and Lord Entworth believe you to be a dangerous radical and blame you for the riots...and Watt and Boulton are afraid you're showing up their engines as inefficient. What if they find you?'

'That first morning, when you stood scowling at me and asked me my name, I thought to hide my identity. I had a new name on my lips but I couldn't lie to you, Elowyn. I knew I could never lie to you. When I looked into your eyes, I knew I had to risk them finding me so I could tell you the truth.'

The front door was flung open and Billy raced across the cobbles, two fly wheels gleaming in his hands. 'How do these go again, Will?'

'They inter lock, one clockwise, one anti-clockwise – like this.'

Sam was close behind him, holding out my shawl. 'Mrs Pengelly says ye're not to forget the evenin' air.' He smiled shyly, hovering above us. 'So how do these engines work then, Will?'

William shifted closer so Sam could sit next to us, reaching into his pocket to draw out another notebook and I sat hugging my knees, watching him, my heart burning with love. 'The coal heats the water in this boiler here...then

228

steam escapes through this valve...and that in turn moves this piston.'

'Well, I never,' said Sam. 'And what does that do?'

'That turns the wheel to pump out the water – just to the adits, mind. No need to bring the water all the way up to the surface.'

'What's an adit, then, Will?'

'They're man-made drainage – big underground tunnels, Sam. Cut through the rock to drain the water out to the sea. Above sea level, these tunnels allow the water to drain from the mine, but once you go below sea level...well, then you've got to pump the water out.'

'To the surface?'

'Not to the surface – just to the level of the first adit...You need to pump until the water reaches the drains – then you let nature take it away to a river or the nearest shore.'

The day I watched William and Billy by the river I had felt so hollow, as if I knew I should be with them. Now, my heart brimmed with happiness. William's power over me was absolute, his warmth, his humour, his great strength and gentle manners. He drew us all to him like the pull of a magnet, Billy, Sam, even Mrs Munroe. She was standing on the front step, her bonnet tied with its huge red ribbon. A basket swung on her arm. 'There now...just a little something to keep ye goin'.'

William jumped up at the sound of her voice. She handed him the freshly baked buns glistening with butter. 'No... no, stay as ye are. I'll just leave this an' come back with a rug. Mrs Pengelly's to join us. She says it's a long time since she sat by the river. I won't be long. Make a start on them buns.'

We sat eating the buns, all of us giggling, catching the dripping butter with our tongues, licking our fingers like naughty children. The last of the sunshine caught the tops of the trees. Billy had never seemed happier. 'Go on, Will, do one of yer drawings – draw Mrs Pengelly...then Mrs Munroe. Honest, ye're goin' to love these.'

'Let Mr Cotterell be, Billy. Don't go bothering him.'

William smiled back. 'Not at all – stay just as you are, Mrs Pengelly.'

Each sketch brought laughter and smiles. Sam shook his head as if to protest but we all knew he wanted William to draw him. After each sketch, William tore out the page and handed it to the sitter, all except mine. Mine he kept, and I caught a glimpse of it, my heart bursting. I was smiling, my head held high, round my hair a garland of roses.

The setting sun glowed red against the sea. William helped Mrs Pengelly to her feet. 'I can't remember when I last did this – I feel like a young girl again.' She was laughing, dusting down her skirt, taking Mrs Munroe's arm as Sam folded the blankets. The evening breeze was picking up and I felt suddenly chilled. I sneezed, once, twice, making Mrs Munroe frown and Mrs Pengelly shake her head. 'Time to go in. Come, Billy – you must give William back his bag of tools.'

Billy picked up Mrs Munroe's basket and we were alone again. Not for one moment did I want this evening to end. Nor did William, I could see it in his eyes; both of us were filled with such longing. 'I've paid my lodgings for a week – after that, I'll come to Fosse.' He smiled, and I wished we were out of sight of the house. 'I think you'd like Mrs Burrow, she runs a very neat house – she likes everything tidy and in its place. Coats and hats under the stairs, boots on the rack. There's not a thing out of place, not a speck of dust.'

He was so close, his jacket almost touching my shawl. His voice dropped. 'But before I leave Porthcarrow, I need to talk to Mr Drew. I believe there are dangerous short cuts in the water courses. Maybe it's just shoddy work but there's next to no flow. The lock requires replenishing at low tide and the water pressure has to be higher. He needs to know my concerns.'

'The leats are clogging up?'

'Almost certainly. There's insufficient flow – the incline's not steep enough and the ditches are too shallow. The flow's too sluggish, nowhere near strong enough to reach the lock with enough pressure. I'm surprised neither Mr Drew nor Nathan have noticed.' He stopped and looked round. 'I'm also waiting for a letter. When that letter comes, I'll know if another concern is justified.'

My heart jolted. 'You mean the clay in the flour…?'

'No, I think we both know who's behind that. It's something else. I remember hearing a conversation between my friends. They're chemists and I wasn't really listening.' He took hold of my arm, staring down at me. 'Remember that man in the privy? When I examined the ground, I saw drops of deep blue fluid. I didn't tell you at the time but it got me thinking…I may be wrong…but I think not.'

'What d'you mean?' His voice, his manner, everything about him seemed tense.

'I believe a blue dye could be used to whiten the clay – no one would see it dissolved in the water but once it's in the settling pits, I believe its effect could be quite considerable.' He spoke quickly, glancing over his shoulder.

'Only the whitest clay gets the best contracts?'

'Exactly – there's a lot at stake. Either someone's cheating for their own gain or someone wants to discredit Sir James. But I need confirmation – I can't go to Sir James with nothing but suspicion. Keep this to yourself, Elowyn – don't tell Billy.'

The bag of tools jangled behind us. 'Thank you, Billy. You did well.' William was back to his jovial self. 'I'd never have got all those pieces back properly!' He patted Billy on the back, slinging the bag over his shoulder. Taking both my hands, he lifted them to his lips and kissed them softly. 'Goodbye, Elowyn. Look after Elowyn for me, Billy, and thank Mrs Munroe for the buns.'

He walked briskly down the road, turning twice to wave back at us. Billy was still smiling but I wanted to run after him. *The whitest clay gets the best contracts*. Richard Sellick had won the Wedgwood contract, one of the most acclaimed potteries in the north. Everyone wanted the Wedgwood contract yet at Mrs Perys' meal Nathan had said he thought Mr Sellick's clay was tainted. Richard Sellick had missed chapel that morning – he had a dark stain on his threadbare clothes which could easily have been blue dye. I felt suddenly fearful. I should have remembered sooner, I should have warned William.

A sudden chill made me shiver. I had sneezed twice. Two sneezes — Mrs Munroe had frowned, Mrs Pengelly had shaken her head. Two sneezes meant bad luck. They knew it. I knew it. I should have told William.

Chapter Twenty-five

Fosse Monday
4th July 1796, 6:00 a.m.

Gwen was waiting for me on the top step. As we hung up our cloaks, I showed her the bruise on my wrist. She looked horrified, tears springing to her eyes. 'Ye made him that angry, Elly. Nathan's a good friend to Tom and Tom knows how much he loves ye.'

'Or was it because he'll lose the yard?' I never wanted to quarrel with Gwen. I loved her and I loved Tom, or rather, I loved the brother I had known.

She was clearly distraught. 'Course not. It's because he saw ye kissing that man. Why, Elly? Why go kissin' one man when you're as good as engaged to another?'

'I'm not engaged to Nathan and never shall be. I can't marry him no matter how good he is or how much he loves me – anyway, he won't want me now.'

'Oh, but he does, Elly, he's forgivin' ye. He says the beer was too strong an' William Cotterell forced himself on you. He still loves ye.'

I stared at her in horror. 'Gwen, he can't…I don't want

him to. I've written and told him...I made it quite clear.' She turned, biting her bottom lip and the same icy hand gripped my heart. 'Tom *did* give Nathan my letter, didn't he? He did deliver it? Gwen, answer me!' By her silence, I knew the truth and fury filled me. 'William Cotterell did *not* force himself on me. I'm in love with him – I wanted him to kiss me.'

She gripped the side of the chair, sitting quickly down. 'No, Elly, no! Ye don't know what ye're saying. The man's trouble – he's hated. How can you love him when he fights an' brawls? Elly, ye must stop this. It's not the yard – I don't give tuppence fer the yard – it's the man himself.' She took hold of my hand, kissing the deep purple bruise as if to make amends.

'Tom had no right to open my letter. It's hateful...How dare he not deliver it? William's intelligent and kind. He's got high morals and he's honourable. I love him, Gwen. I love him more than I can tell – more than anyone.' My cheeks were burning, tears of anger filling my eyes.

'You can't mean that! He's blinded ye, Elly...ye need to see him as he really is. It's like he's bewitched ye – closed yer eyes to his real self.'

How could she speak like that of a man she had not met? 'I know I've hurt Nathan...but William's not how you think. He's polite and charming – he's kind and generous...He wrestles...but he doesn't fight. You just don't know him – when you know him, you'll see him as I do.'

The colour drained from her face; she looked haunted, her hands trembling. 'Tom hates William...Nathan says William's not to be trusted…Elly…it's like I'm losing ye and I don't like it. We can't quarrel…we must never quarrel…I want ye there with me…' She clasped her walnut birthing charm tightly in her hands.

I knew her fear; she had often spoken of her beloved mother, lost to her as a child, and I felt suddenly terrible, shouting at her when she was so vulnerable. 'Gwen, we'll never quarrel…and it's going to be all right. You're strong and healthy…Mrs Cousins will come the moment your pains start. I promise I'll stay with you. I may be furious with Tom, but never with you.' I cupped my hands over hers, kissing her cheek. 'It can't be long now, and you'll see I'm right.'

Josie and the new seamstresses were on the steps, their happy chatter sounding through the open door, and we knew our conversation must end. Gwen blew her nose as she hurried into the storeroom and I dusted down the table with angry swipes. I would write once more to Nathan and this time my letter would be delivered. But for now, we had so much to do. Mrs Hoskins' daughter was getting married and she had ordered two new gowns, both with bags to match. We had the mannequins to set up and the fabric needed to be cut. Each gown was to be embroidered with satin ribbon roses and mother of pearl.

A flash of red caught my eye. Billy was halfway across the courtyard. He rushed up the stairs, almost knocking Josie over. 'Elly, Elly…Lady Pendarvis is back. She says she's sorry to be a nuisance but could ye come an' help with some alterations on Hannah's gowns?' I went to grab my bonnet but stopped. *Know your worth — let them come to you.* I hung it firmly back on the peg.

'Billy, tell Lady Pendarvis I'm very busy. Tell her I won't be able to come until four – if that's convenient.'

Behind me, I heard an intake of breath. Josie was staring at me from over the rim of her new glasses and I stared back, lifting my chin in defiance. I was Elowyn Liddicot. I had a skill others needed and I had to remember that.

The clock struck the half-hour and I put away my scissors. Billy handed me my basket and we hurried down the steps, crossing the yard and into the town, the sun still warm as we linked arms across the square. Loud shouting by the steps drew our attention. Men were gathering on the quay-side and we stopped to watch. 'Perhaps they're looking at Admiral Penrose's new war prize – the French frigate,' I suggested.

It was certainly a large crowd, men shouting, pushing their way forward. Billy looked intrigued. 'They must be landin' the prisoners. D'you think they'll take them to Bodmin?'

'They take the French prisoners to Falmouth – they don't bring them ashore here. That's where Lady Pendarvis and Sir Alex have been. He's in charge of their welfare.'

'Let's take a look.' Billy ran towards the crowd and we stood watching a rowing boat draw near the steps. There were three men in the boat, all scowling and shouting to the bystanders to clear some space. As they tied alongside, the crowd started jeering, throwing rotten fruit, and Billy strained forward to get a better look. 'They're bringing out a body.'

It was too late to turn away, both of us reeling as the bloated body of a man was heaved onto the quayside. The men at the front began surging forward, needing to be restrained, everyone jeering, cheering, or staring grim faced at the blotched purple body. It was so gruesome, the hatred in people's eyes quite horrible to witness. The men from the boat rolled over the corpse and I started to retch, unable to control my sudden revulsion. A deep red line circled the man's neck but most horrible of all was the gash gaping across his cheek.

'Billy, don't look. Turn away!'

Billy's face was ashen, the same hatred in his eyes. 'That's Phillip Randal,' he said. 'He's been lynched.' I could hardly bear to watch the men line up and take their turn to spit on the body. Phillip Randal, the most hated man in Fosse and Porthruan; Sir Charles Cavendish's steward, the man who evicted tenants and whipped vagrants – a man grown rich through cruelty and oppression. Billy's eyes were like iron, his mouth drawn tight. 'Are ye all right?' he asked.

'Yes, I'm fine. Are you?'

He nodded, but he looked far from all right. His lips were pursed, all colour drained from his face. 'Don't judge me, Elly, but I'm glad he's dead.' He took a deep breath. 'They'll not find who did it – there's not one man who'll talk.' He stood rooted to the spot, staring at the crowd. 'It's the people's justice. It's what he deserved.'

'Come, Billy,' I whispered, 'we mustn't keep Lady Pendarvis waiting.'

We passed the town hall, taking the cliff road, my nerves beginning to get the better of me. I should never have put Lady Pendarvis off – I should have gone straight to her. My defiance was misplaced, my action churlish. I remembered the morning she told us she was no longer Madame Merrick but was now Lady Pendarvis. She had said her *work* was *finished* and she would be moving into Admiral House to live with her *husband*, Sir Alexander Pendarvis. Just like that. No explanation, no further discussion. She asked us not to speculate and not to gossip. We were to trust her and never talk about it again.

There had always been rumours she was a French spy. The Corporation wanted her gone from Fosse but their wives had wanted her gowns. Some, like Mrs Hoskins, had been barely civil yet she had put up with their rudeness, raising her exquisitely arched eyebrows, rustling her silk petticoats as she peered through her lorgnettes at them. They must be regretting it now, timidly currying favour, hoping she had a short memory. I had been terrified of her when she first gave me work, petrified of doing wrong, but I had always admired her. Now, I loved her.

The sight of her magnificent house brought the sparkle back to Billy's face. Admiral House was the newest house in Fosse, only Polcarrow was grander, though many would say the views from Admiral House gave it the edge. Sir Alex had ordered a huge brass dolphin as they had intended calling the house Dolphin House but the men building the house had other ideas, so too did all the residents of both the house and the town. Despite the brass dolphin, it remained Admiral House.

Made of fine red bricks, it had perfect symmetry – eight sash windows and a large portico above the front door. There was a circular window above the portico and four servant's windows in the attic, all delicately arched like Lady Pendarvis' eyebrows. In fact, the whole house reminded me of Lady Pendarvis – tall, elegant and extremely commanding.

Sudden barking and a loud shout made us turn round. 'Get back here…wretched dog.' A streak of wet fur was streaming towards us.

'It's Endymion…Oh no! He's loose again.' Billy braced himself as the huge dog jumped up to greet him, his muddy paws landing straight on Billy's new waistcoat. 'You've been swimming again, have ye?' Billy said, trying to hold the dog off. 'Get down…no honest…ye stink really bad…get off…'

A man rushed to his side. 'Damn dog. He's done it this time – he'll be sent packin', no mistakin'.' Jago had served as bosun and ship's officer from boy to man, and would never leave Sir Alex; he was weather beaten and gruff, his dark blue jacket stretching across his broad shoulders, his master's cap pulled low over his wispy white hair.

Billy looked horrified. 'He can't go…he can't. Honest, Jago, Lady Pendarvis need never know…I'll help you bath him…Where's he been, he smells terrible?'

'Rolling in the sewer!' Jago grabbed the protesting dog by the scruff. 'She'll know all right – damn dog will smell fer weeks.'

Billy removed his soiled waistcoat and I grasped the tail of the huge brass dolphin.

'Ready, Billy?' I need not have asked. Billy was always ready to see Lady Pendarvis.

Chapter Twenty-six

Admiral House, Fosse
Monday 4th July 1796, 4:00 p.m.

The hall was bright and spacious, even more so today as sunlight flooded through the round window, glinting on the marble floor. A staircase curved elegantly to the right, the mahogany banister polished to a shine. Portraits of the family hung on the walls, the two new paintings of Captain Edward Pendarvis and his wife Celia looking particularly fine. Billy looked up with pride. 'Look, Elowyn – it's like she's really there.'

The gold clock on the table chimed four. 'You're to go straight up.' Pedro led us stiffly up the stairs in his blue livery. He was not a real butler but one of the many sailors who would not leave Sir Alex. It was hardly a house at all, more like a ship on land, everything running with naval precision, everywhere gleaming, polished and shipshape. There was a flagpole in the garden to signal ships, a large brass bell for the first sign of invasion.

'Elowyn, my dear, how *lovely* to see you.' Lady Pendarvis returned her gaze to the river mouth, the ostrich feathers on her turban barely moving. She was wearing a green silk gown, which shimmered in the light, an emerald brooch at her neck. 'Sir Alex is just leaving for Falmouth.' She held out the telescope for Billy to look. 'A fine prize but that's another *seventy* prisoners and nowhere to put them – certainly not Pendennis Castle as it's *woefully* overcrowded. The conditions are quite *terrible*.'

Billy held the telescope to his eye. 'Where are they to go?'

'Sir Alex has arranged for a farmhouse to be fortified but it is *far* from suitable. A *temporary* solution while we await the new prison.' She put her hand on his shoulder. 'Billy, be a dear and help Jago take the last of the blankets to the alms-house – there's quite a pile. And when you come back, help him wash that great brute of a dog.' She pursed her lips, her hawk eyes unsmiling. '*Or he will have to go*.'

Billy smiled nervously, handing her back the telescope and making quickly for the door. Even after three years he could not understand how she seemed to know everything.

Whatever the weather, the room was always bright and airy, the view from the two large windows stretching right across the river mouth and far out to sea; it was the turn of the tide, the river at its busiest – the Danish brig carrying wood for Uncle Thomas, the Prussian brig with its cargo of fish. Barges of lime lay anchored in the creek, two more brigs with their timber from Norway. A side window looked down over the church and across to Polcarrow. I could see the quay, the market square, the bright red coats and white sashes of the volunteer force beginning their parade.

It was not just the room's view I loved but the elegant

furnishings – the chaise longue in the corner, the delicate mahogany tables, the chairs upholstered in blue and cream silk. Miniatures hung on the wall, small silhouettes and paintings of ships. A gold clock sat on the mantelpiece and two huge Chinese vases stood either side of the fireplace. 'Chin up, child, let me look at you.'

Lady Pendarvis was studying me through her lorgnettes. 'You've changed the way you dress your hair – I like it. It suits you.' She herself was immaculate, her still brown hair curled neatly beneath her turban, her eyebrows carefully pencilled, her high cheekbones with their touch of rouge. '*Two* new gowns for Mrs Hoskins, so Billy tells me. I hope that woman has given you enough time to complete them both without needing to rush.' She seemed to glide across the room, taking hold of the bell pull, pulling it once. '*You* must dictate the timing, not her. Never forget that, Elowyn.'

She had taught me everything – business, manners, poise. I walked like her, tried to hold myself like her. Without her, I would be nothing. 'I've got three weeks until the lease runs out.'

She looked up. 'I am very sorry about the lease. It is highly *regrettable* but not *insurmountable*.' Her French accent was barely discernible, her choice of words often new to me; most of the time, I guessed their meaning. On the desk by her side lay an open newspaper. 'I've seen a very *suitable* property on the top road,' she said, 'which I believe will do very nicely – it has large windows and adjoins both Fore Street and Upper Street. Sir Alex will do his utmost to obtain the lease.'

I looked down, summoning my courage. A maid came to the door, not a young maid, but a woman well into her fifties. 'Ah, Hannah, Elowyn is here – could you bring us some tea and frangipane cake, then she can make a start on your gowns?' It was as if we were back in the sewing room, Madame Merrick looking at me in her most knowing way. She smiled at Hannah who smiled back. 'I almost faded to nothing when I first fell in love – no need to look so surprised, Elowyn. You clearly have not slept or eaten since I saw you last – so, I am to believe the rumours, am I?'

Her chiselled chin remained poised in the air. Yes, I was in love, yes, I had hardly eaten. She took my silence for her answer. 'Nathan Cardew is a very *lucky* man, as I am sure he *must* know.' She closed the newspaper, her mouth tightening. 'You will, no doubt, sell your stock to Jenna – I presume Lady Polcarrow has offered to buy it?' There was a catch to her voice, a tinge of disappointment and my heart soared.

'I'm not going to marry Nathan Cardew…I can't.' She looked shocked, almost relieved, staring at me with her hawk-like precision. 'I don't love him. He's a good man and he's offering me so much…I like him, but it's not enough. I don't want to live in Porthcarrow and I don't want to give up my shop.'

She returned to the table, calmly reopening the newspaper. 'In that case, you must expect a higher rent – to profit you will need to increase your takings by at least a *third*. That means no credit *what-so-ever* and payment on *delivery*. You must be firm, Elowyn, and *insist* on a twenty-five per cent deposit from all *new* customers. Sir Alex will do his best to secure the lease…though in truth, properties are scarce and competition is fierce.'

She was being so kind, wanting to help and I felt so disloyal. 'Lady Pendarvis…did you know Mr Hoskins wants to invest in a dressmaking shop?'

'That odious little man? Whatever does he know of dressmaking?'

'He must think it worthwhile…a good investment, I mean.' I had to ask her yet I could hardly form the words. 'I was wondering…it left me thinking…it's just, would you think me very foolish—' Her eyebrows rose and I stopped. I was reaching too high, getting above myself.

'Speak up, Elowyn. You are never foolish.' The kindness in her voice spurred me on and I held out the list I had quickly prepared, talking her through my earnings, my profit, and the amount I thought I could raise. She stood frozen like a statue. 'Forty pounds is a *considerable* sum of money, Elowyn.'

I hardly dared speak. 'Forty pounds would buy me a lease.'

'Is this your uncle's idea? I take it he knows?' Her voice was measured, showing no emotion. A pulse throbbed in her neck.

I shook my head. 'He wants me to marry Nathan…they all do…'

She shook her head slowly, resignation flashing across her eyes. 'Most women hold leases as *widows*, Elly…or wives or sisters or daughters. You would be granted a licence *to trade* – in fact, I believe Sir James would go out of his way to help you obtain another licence – but a *lease*?' She shook her head again. 'Not without your uncle or brother.'

The same indignation filled me. The same fury when Mr Hoskins refused me a bank account. She caught my look of frustration, shrugging her elegant shoulders in sympathy. 'Your uncle must advise you. Talk to him — make sure he knows how important this is to you. Leases run for ninety-nine years or for the lives of *three* people. He will probably suggest you put Tom and Gwen on the lease, not himself. See what your uncle suggests.'

I felt suddenly desperate. Uncle Thomas had no idea how much my savings were worth. If he had, I felt sure he would suggest I help Tom secure the boatyard, both of us wanting leases at the same time but only enough money for one. It was as if Lady Pendarvis could read my mind.

'Single women may be granted leases in towns like Truro and Bristol but we are talking of *Fosse*, Elly.' Her voice hardened, a slight tightening of her mouth. 'I doubt you would stand any chance at all as a single woman — remember, it is the Corporation who control the town's leases. What chance do you have if Mr Hoskins wants to invest in a dressmaking shop? He is a burgee, a long-standing member of the Corporation — he will do everything in his power to see you out of the race.'

I fought back my tears. The seamstresses Jenna and Mrs Pengelly taught were highly accomplished; any of them could soon get as good as me, if not better. Mrs Hoskins was bound to flourish — she would own the best shop in the best part of town and I stood no chance. I was the daughter of a drunken fisherman, to be kept in her place — neither fish nor fowl nor good red herring.

Lady Pendarvis put her finger under my chin, drawing it up so my eyes met hers. There was iron in them, the same determination that had seen her shop prosper. 'If you do not want your brother's name on your lease, then *wait* just a while...If Gwen's baby is a *boy*, no one would turn a hair if your uncle sought to buy a lease in the child's name. An investment for his sister's grandson? I am sure your uncle would go along with that. The Corporation could be *led* to believe the premises would be used for the growing demands of the yard – cordage or storage, or perhaps to house new apprentices.'

My heart was racing. 'And if Gwen's baby turns out to be a girl?'

She pursed her lips. 'Then you must discuss it with your uncle, but Elowyn, be warned. Forty pounds is just the beginning. There will be ground rent to pay and refurbishing to fund. Your new premises must look *elegant* from the *start*. You must allow for a new sign and you must put aside the *whole* of next year's rent either in a lump sum or in regular instalments – or else expect to go *bankrupt*. Tell your uncle, I will buy *all* your stock and sell it back to you, *roll by roll*.'

She closed the newspaper, the diamonds flashing in her ring. 'I have a free room in the attic that would perfectly store your fabrics. I shall have an agreement drawn up – I will pay the *current* value of your stock and sell it back to you at the *same* price. Roll by roll.'

I could hardly speak. 'But, Lady Pendarvis...the continental blockade's making silk very hard to come by – the price of French fabric goes up by the day. I can't buy my stock back from you for today's price – even in a month it'll be worth more. You'd lose money.'

She smiled. 'Merely a helping hand, Elowyn, from a friend – we women need to look after one another. Heaven knows it is hard enough to be a woman in business.' She smoothed a non-existent crease from her gown. 'But I must speak plainly. My advice to you would be to keep your money in your *fabrics* or else every unscrupulous man will beat a path to your door. As soon as you marry, your husband will own all your assets. I know this is not what you want to hear, but my advice is this...let Sir Alex secure another lease and let me only *store* your silks but not buy them.' She walked elegantly to the window, picking up a large white handkerchief to wave at the departing frigate. 'Your silks are your livelihood.'

Hannah brought in the tea, glancing nervously at me. Her gown swamped her, and I saw at once what was needed. Lady Pendarvis smiled, holding out her hands. 'We will have them done in no time.' She turned to me. 'You don't mind, do you, Elowyn? I thought two pleats down either side of the back and two down the front with extra pin tucks on the bodice. The other gown merely requires a new hem.'

I smiled back, reaching for my basket, bringing out my pins. Of course I did not mind. It was always such a pleasure to take tea with Lady Pendarvis. I loved her beautiful room and Hannah looked so grateful. 'It'll be my pleasure to do your alterations – it won't take long.' The French frigate had left the river and had reached open sea, unfurling her sails to catch the easterly breeze; she would be in Falmouth long before I finished. I put my silver thimble on my finger.

'Goodness,' Lady Pendarvis exclaimed as we heard footsteps racing up the stairs. She reached forward, carefully placing her Sèvres cup back on its saucer. 'It can only be—'

Billy fell headlong into the room. He was crying, his eyes wild. 'They've arrested William…they've taken him…he's been charged with murder. They say he's going to hang.'

Chapter Twenty-seven

Sudden dizziness made my head spin. The floor began swirling beneath me and I had to sit down. Tears streamed down Billy's face. He stood gripping his cap, twisting it in his hands. 'He never did it. Never.' He covered his mouth with his cap. 'Will wouldn't kill no one...'

I could not speak, a terrible faintness making my head swim. Someone was coming up the stairs; I could hear laboured breathing, a heavy tread. Jago rested his hands against the door. 'There ye are, Billy...' He turned and coughed.

'He's never done it – never.' Billy's eyes were wide with terror. 'Tell them, Elly...Will's no murderer – they've got the wrong man.'

Lady Pendarvis put her hand on Billy's shoulder. 'I take it this man is a friend of yours – a man you trust and like?' She was watching me, missing nothing. 'How do you know this man, Billy? How *long* have you known him?'

'He's an engineer – he's in love with Elowyn and she loves

him too. Mrs Pengelly likes him and so does Sam...We all like him, especially Mrs Munroe because he mended her spit. He's no murderer.'

A steely note entered her voice. 'Is this true, Elowyn?'

I nodded, trying to breathe deeply. 'William's *not* how people think he is. He wrestles but he doesn't fight... He's got a reputation for trouble but it's injustice he's fighting...people have him all wrong.' I was talking too fast, jumbling my words. 'He's kind...he's gentle. He'd never kill anyone.'

Lady Pendarvis' grip tightened on Billy's shoulders. 'Then I am sure all this will pass and he will be released. They often arrest the troublemakers first. Take heart, Billy.' Her words were clipped, her eyes never leaving my face. 'How did you meet this man?'

She saw the look that passed between us. 'He's the cart driver...but he's an engineer and he's between contracts... he's spending time away from Penzance...' I wanted to cry – even I knew it sounded all wrong. I gripped my hands together, my heart pounding.

Breathing heavily, Jago removed his hat, wiping the sweat from his brow. 'William Cotterell's wanted fer the murder of Josiah Drew – the lock engineer in Porthcarrow. It's as good as confirmed – there's plenty witnessed the fight...'

I had to sit, put my head between my knees. Lady Pendarvis' voice sounded far away. 'Witnessed the *murder*? Was it self-defence?'

'There was a heated argument an' a fight. Mr Drew was found drowned in a settlin' pit early this mornin'.' His voice softened as he saw Billy's face. 'William Cotterell's in St Austell held on charge – Sir Thomas Treffry's the Justice who's takin' the case.'

'Go, quickly...inform Sir James – the sooner he knows the better. Billy, you must leave this to Sir James. It is his harbour, the man was his engineer.'

'But Sir James is in Truro – he's gone for some time.' Tears streamed down Billy's face. 'Will's no murderer – honest, Lady Pendarvis, they've got the wrong man.'

'In that case, I will send an express to Sir James.' Lady Pendarvis walked briskly to her desk, picking up her quill, dipping it in the ink. Her pen scratched the paper. 'In the meantime, there is *nothing* more we can do. Billy, go home to Mrs Pengelly. Stay with her and on *no* account leave the house. Do I have your word? Sir James will not let an innocent man hang.'

Billy wiped his eyes with the back of his fists. He looked as if he had seen a ghost. 'She's with Lady Polcarrow. She's staying late to keep her company...'

'In that case, stay with Jago. Take this to the post office and then I suggest you get that wretched dog *washed*. Dry him by the fire. You are *not* to be on the streets – do I make myself clear?' She held out the express, nodding to Jago. 'Keep him safe, the poor child can barely stand. Here, hand me your sewing box, I think I'd better make a start on these pleats – Elowyn, dear girl, pass me your pins.'

With my pincushion on her wrist, her fingers began to fly, tucking the spare material into six long pleats. She worked deftly, smiling at Hannah who shook her head.

'No please, Lady Pendarvis, 'taint right fer ye to sew this fer me…Please…ye mustn't…'taint right…'

Lady Pendarvis took the last pin from her mouth. 'Nonsense, Hannah…there, all ready to tack — that did not take long.'

I threaded my needle with black cotton. 'I'm sorry. I feel better now.' My head was thumping, going over what William had told me — he was going to tell Mr Drew about his concerns, they must have had an argument but he would never fight. He was not a murderer. Lady Pendarvis threaded another needle.

'How well do you know this man, Elowyn? An engineer has no reason to be a cart driver. Engineers are in short supply — they do not wait for employment. They are poached from others and paid well for their expertise.'

I knew she had been biding her time and I must tell her everything. 'William's banned from the mines. There's an injunction against him because he tampered with an engine. He's not liked but he's not a murderer. He never fights because he's too strong and he worries he might kill someone.' It was hard to keep myself in check. 'He's disliked — even hated… He started a riot…but that's only because his brother and father were drowned and the mine still posed a danger.'

'I see.' Her voice was clipped. 'Who banned him from the mines?'

'Viscount Vallenforth and Lord Entworth.'

She held her needle in mid-air. 'Most people know *not* to make an enemy of Viscount Vallenforth. Is it wise to love such a man?'

My stitching was everywhere, my hands shaking. I could hardly see through my tears. 'I can't help it...it just happened...I love him so much...he makes me smile and makes me believe in myself. When I'm not with him I feel empty inside...And it's not because he's so handsome...'

'A handsome troublemaker – oh, Elly dearest, take heed! He is a *stranger* and for all you know, he may be lying. Your family obviously do not like him or else they would *not* want you to marry Nathan.' She leaned forward, snipping her thread.

'No...he's not lying, honestly, you would like him. He's telling the truth, I know he is. I feel it. It's only natural my family want me to marry a man they know and respect but William is...' I paused, my hands shaking. 'William's worthy of just as much respect. I was wary of him at first – of course I was...I was just like everyone else. I mistrusted him and thought him no good but then he stopped the cart so I could study the flowers—'

'Ouch.' Hannah jerked quickly away.

'I'm so sorry.'

Lady Pendarvis took the needle from me. 'Yet he is disliked by so many – you said that yourself.'

'He's made enemies of Lord Entworth and Viscount Vallenforth. And there are many others who want his downfall...'

Lady Pendarvis stiffened. 'If they want a man's downfall, they will get it. People stop at nothing – nothing. Remember that, child.' She turned to Hannah. 'I believe we must finish now. We can do the hem another time.'

Hannah nodded and curtsied, tidying away the cups and saucers. 'I'm that grateful…honest I am. It's like ye treated me like a real lady…but I've tallied long enough. I've the kitchen to clean. That dog…honest…and Jago's no better. Muddy boots all over me clean floors. Between the two of them, they'll have me moppin' all day.'

Chapter Twenty-eight

I ran down the steps. No one was at home and I was grateful to have the kitchen to myself; only Mr Pitt peeped at me through half-closed eyes. I saw the mended spit and my pain grew so fierce I could hardly breathe. William was innocent, he was not a murderer. Sir James must see that justice was done. I drew a deep breath, trying to calm myself. Sir James would understand – he himself had been falsely accused, imprisoned and tried for a crime he had not committed.

Clothes for the vagrants lay bundled on the table and I pushed them aside, crying onto my folded arms. Now I was alone, I felt so desperate. William would be behind bars in some filthy prison; he would be lying on the floor, his clothes spoiled. I had to stay calm. He would hate the filth; he was always so immaculate, his boots always polished.

Hannah's words came suddenly back to me. *Muddy boots all over me clean floors.* The banks of the settling pits were always muddy, the clay so thick and wet it clung to people's boots. If William had been up there, his boots would have been thickly coated with heavy clay, impossible to clean in such a short time. William told me his landlady was very particular – everything tidy, all the boots in their proper place. I felt a surge of hope. She would have seen they were clean. William had mentioned the rack in her kitchen...his boots would have been on the rack and they would have been clean. Billy's boots were always getting clogged but what if no one thought to ask William's landlady? What if, in a week's time, she could not remember?

Sir James must be told; someone must take her testimony, record the truth, but Sir James was away. I looked up as the clock chimed – six o'clock, light yet for another five hours. I could go. I could take the cliff path and be back before I was missed. But even as I grabbed my shawl, I hesitated. Billy was not with me and to go alone would be foolish. I stared at the pile of clothes; Sam's old jacket was on the top and I would fit Billy's boots. There were plenty of breeches and shirts in the bundle and if I pinned up my hair tightly, I could hide it beneath Sam's hat. The large brim would cover most of my face.

No one would stop me if I was dressed as a man and no one would recognize me. Not Nathan, not even Mamm.

The waves were breaking against the rocks below – Penwartha Point, I was halfway there. The clouds were building from the west, blowing across the sky. The wind smelt of salt and freshly churned seaweed. My borrowed clothes were rough against my skin, Billy's boots cumbersome, but

I was making progress. Mrs Burrow — that was the name of William's landlady.

The wind pulled at my hat, tugging my collar; the path was dry, the loose stones crunching beneath my boots. Flowers clung to the cliff side, lining the path, blowing in the breeze, and I looked back at the gathering clouds. The day was already darkening, the visibility lessening. A grey haze had swallowed the ships on the horizon and I needed to hurry. At the turn in the path I stopped to catch my breath, staring down at the harbour now shrouded in mist.

Mamm's cottage was just below me and I peered down, checking to see if the path was clear. I pulled straight back, hiding quickly behind a hawthorn. The back door was open, a man striding purposely to the privy and I stayed crouched down, concealed behind the bush, knowing he would soon return to the kitchen. I peered through the gnarled branches, determined not to risk being seen. I kept expecting to see his shadowy figure cross the garden but he seemed to be taking his time and I wondered if I had missed him slip back to the house.

It was getting darker, dusk falling, and this unwanted delay was making me anxious. I must have missed his return. I looked again, immediately drawing back. Another man was heading for the privy. Gulls were screeching around me, making it impossible for me to hear their footsteps. The garden was in shadow and though I was sure both men had entered the privy, I had seen neither of them return. I hardly knew what to do — wait or risk being seen? If they were both back in the kitchen, I was wasting valuable time.

I decided to carry on down the path but heard the back door shut and another fleeting shadow crossed the yard. Sweat pricked my back, my heart suddenly pounding. The privy must hide a trapdoor leading to the stash, or perhaps it was the way down to a tunnel. Men were silenced for knowing less than that.

Lowenna and Mamm would be watching from the window and I knew I must wait. I had no sense of time but when Mamm closed the shutters I finally saw my chance and slipped quickly from the safety of the hawthorn, placing my heavy boots on the loose stones as carefully as I could. I had chosen the darkest clothes, the biggest hat, and in the gathering dusk, I just had to hope I would pass unseen.

I shut the gate making no sound, starting quickly down the lane. My hair was well concealed and I knew to walk with my shoulders back and take large strides. Mrs Perys might be watching out of her window so I pulled my hat lower, raising the collar of my jacket. The harbour was more sheltered than the clifftop but there was still a breeze, the rigging knocking against the masts in the lock. The cranes were still, the suspended chains hanging in the air. In the distance dogs were barking, men talking as they walked. Two men stood the other side of the lock gate and I crossed the lock, standing with them by the capstan. As their conversation ended I lowered my voice. 'I'm looking for Mrs Burrow – do you know where she can be found?'

The larger man nodded, both of them ships' masters by the look of their hats. 'Down the alley past the old stables then right – green door, but most go round the back.'

I nodded politely. The old stables – that was the alley behind Nathan's office. I knew where to go from the walks we had taken, but I had to hurry. It must be gone half past eight, the dusk was falling, the light already fading and I glanced up, fearful I might bump into Nathan. Candles were burning in his office and I willed myself on, walking quickly round the lime kiln and past the weighing room. I knew to walk, not run. Running would draw attention and Nathan might be looking out of his window. All I needed was for Mrs Burrow to sign a written statement and I could go straight home.

I knew to get things in writing. Everything written down and signed for – then no one could cheat you or say they had asked for something different. It was already dark at the alley entrance, the narrow sides looming above me. Broken glass lay scattered across the cobbles and I hesitated, taking a deep breath. The old stables were open to the alley, the cartwheels propped against the wall. The wooden stalls lay hidden in the darkness, the old nets and rope hanging eerily from the beams. I walked faster, relieved to see Nathan's door was closed, and I passed it quickly – if he opened it now, he would only see my back.

The lanterns on the hotel had just been lit. Their faint glow beckoned ahead and I walked quickly towards them, turning right to look for a green door. I hardly saw the colour as everything was merging into grey and I glanced round, scared I would lose my sense of direction. The windows were shuttered, casting not a chink of light, but a wooden gate led round to the back and I followed the cobbled path hoping it was the right place. I saw another door and light coming through a leaded window and relief surged through me. I knocked loudly, stepping sideways to peer into the kitchen.

It was just as I imagined – an open hearth, a small fire burning beneath a grid. A black kettle stood on a rack, three brass pans hanging from a shelf. A row of stone jars were neatly stacked by size and pewter tankards hung from hooks. Two high-backed chairs faced the dying fire, an oak table with a vase of flowers. Everything was neat and tidy and I rushed back to the door, knocking louder.

I looked in again. A lantern stood flickering on the table, coats hanging neatly on hooks under the stairs, and I held my hat, peering through the glass, squashing my cheek against the window. There was definitely a boot rack. There were also signs of life: a portmanteau stood on the flagstones with a heavy travelling coat draped over it. Either someone was leaving or they had just arrived. I rushed back to the door, knocking louder still, trying the handle to no avail.

An iron pump stood in the middle of the yard with a bucket beneath it. There was a washing line, a large barrel full of water. Doors lead to an outhouse with a sloping roof. I could hear voices from the inn next door and smelt woodsmoke coming from the fire. A three-legged stool stood against the wall and I pulled it towards me, sitting by the window to catch the first sign of movement. Already the mist was closing in. What time was it? Nearly nine o'clock?

The mist settled round me just like it used to do. I had not sat in mizzle for nearly four years and even in Sam's old jacket I could feel the penetrating dampness taking hold. Surely someone must come soon – a burning lamp meant someone must be coming back. Yet even as I reasoned, I felt my courage fail. Time was passing, the night growing darker. I moved my stool to under the overhang and sat back in the shadows. I would wait just a little longer.

Sudden footsteps made my heart leap, the confident steps of a man coming down the path. He stopped at the back door, looking over his shoulder, not seeing me in the darkness. He reached up to the overhang, opening a stone jar, removing the key to turn the lock but jumped back as I leapt from my stool. 'Excuse me, sir, I'm looking for Mrs Burrow.'

I had clearly startled him; his voice was wary when he spoke. 'Mrs Burrow's not here but I happen to know all her rooms are taken. There's a seamen's hostel round the corner but it's very busy.' He walked through the door and was about to shut it, but I ran forward, my heavy boots scuffing the cobbles.

'When will she be back? It's very important I see her.' I was so pleased to see him I had completely forgotten to disguise my voice. He turned sharply, moving to one side so he could see me in the lamplight. 'I'm not looking for a room,' I said as his brows contracted. 'I just need to talk to her.'

He pulled me nearer the light, turning me swiftly to lift my chin. 'Her sister's ill – I doubt she'll be back tonight or tomorrow. I'm sorry, but are you in some sort of trouble, my dear?' He stood back, allowing me some space.

His kindness threw me, his gentleman-like manner and obvious concern making me want to cry. My journey had been wasted and I was fighting my disappointment. 'No…I'm not in any trouble…Are you sure she won't be back tonight?'

He was smartly dressed in good quality clothes. He had kind eyes and an air of gentleness – not unlike Uncle Thomas. Even his round glasses looked the same. He put out his hand, helping me to the chair, and I stared at him, biting back my frustration. 'I'm sorry…it's just I'm pinning my hopes on seeing Mrs Burrow. Was she here yesterday, do you know?'

He removed his hat and nodded. He had grey hair, parted down the middle, tied neatly behind his head in a black bow. 'Yes, she was. Forgive me, my dear, but you look rather shaken. Can I get you some ale? I know where Mrs Burrow keeps it.' He opened the dresser, bringing out a flagon, pouring it into a tankard. 'Not everyone is privy to this information…but I come here rather often and I've winkled out some very useful secrets.' His eyes creased as they smiled. 'My name's John Berryman. I'm a clay agent; I'm afraid I've a boat to catch so I'm in rather a hurry, but can I walk you home, my dear? I'll not ask any questions – neither do I expect you to furnish me with any answers.'

He had a different accent, which I knew was from the north. He reached for his travelling coat, throwing it over his shoulders, fastening the buttons. He was clearly dressing for a journey. His hand dived beneath the capes and he brought out a fob watch. 'I'm sorry, my dear, but I really need to go.'

I leaned forward, reaching out to stop him. 'Mr Berryman, how long have you been staying here? Were you here last night? Do you know William Cotterell?'

'So that's what it's all about….' He sat quickly down, his face growing stern. 'My stay is brief this time, a mere twenty-four hours – in with one tide, out with the other.

264

I did not meet Mr Cotterell, so I'm afraid I can't help you. Please, young lady, let me take you home...' He glanced at his watch again. 'They'll not wait. They'll sail without me – I like to think I'm important but the truth is they'll not wait one single moment.'

'But you came last night?'

'I did. We docked at eleven but by the time I got to my room it was half past, at least. Mrs Burrow was in her night-clothes.' He gave a half smile. 'Standing there in a very becoming nightcap and embroidered velvet slippers – not that I looked, of course.'

My heart pounded. 'Mr Berryman, when you came in last night was the boot rack full? Were *all* the boots there...no gaps...no muddy boots?'

I had clearly got his attention. He leaned forward, suddenly serious. 'The rack was full. Mrs Burrow doesn't allow any boots past the kitchen door. We've to take them off whether they're clean or dirty. I know the rack was full because there was only just enough space left for mine. Room four. Mrs Burrow always gives me room four because it's the biggest.' He paused. 'I took my boots off and then the rack was full. All of them clean.'

'So the other men's boots were already on the rack and none of them were muddy?'

'Yes.' By the gravity in his face, I knew he understood.

'It's just so important – they need to know William had retired to bed by eleven thirty.'

He nodded. 'Young lady, I have to go. I'll give you my name and address. I'll be back in three weeks' time. Mrs

Burrow will vouch for that. Here...' He opened his large portmanteau and drew out a notebook and a pen, scribbling in his haste, *Johnathan Berryman Esq., Clay Agent. Stoke China Pottery, High Street, Stoke.* 'There,' he said, tearing out the page. 'Three weeks and I'll be back.' He shut his bag, balancing it under his arm. 'I hope William Cotterell deserves you.'

At the door, he stopped. 'I have a daughter your age. Take a father's advice – lock the door behind me and sleep in my room.'

Chapter Twenty-nine

I could hardly believe it. Before I left, I had wished for success on William's four-leaf clover and it had brought me straight to Mr Berryman. He was obviously trustworthy and his testimony would be invaluable. The heavy oak clock on the mantelpiece chimed eleven and I looked up in surprise. I had no idea it was so late. I drank the beer, quickly wiping the froth from my lips, and slipped the key back in the jar, following the way I had come. I turned in the direction of the alley, peering into the blackness, my eyes not yet accustomed to the dark.

Rowdy voices rang across the stillness, men shouting from the direction of the inn. The sound of a fiddle echoed across the town, footsteps ringing on the cobbles, stopping and starting, getting lost on the wind. I could hear the hooves of a carthorse, the clatter of wheels, drunken singing coming from further up the hill, and I stopped to get my bearings. The lamps of the hotel were behind me, their soft glow giving me just enough light to see the entrance of the alley.

There was no moon, the stone walls of the alley engulfing me in darkness. My hands were lost in front of me and I walked slowly forward, running them along the wall for guidance. I heard footsteps racing towards me, the sound of sobbing, and before I could dodge, a woman hurtled against me, nearly knocking me over. She screamed in terror and I fought to keep my balance, grabbing her cloak to stop us both from falling. She screamed even louder: 'I've nothing... nothing...' Her hands trembled against me but I could not see her face.

Her basket had fallen and she bent down, reaching blindly across the cobbles for the spilt contents. 'I've only got this bread...take that...it's all I have.'

'No...no...You're quite safe – I only grabbed you to stop myself from falling.'

She remained on her knees, searching the darkness, and I bent down, trying to help her. There was something familiar about her voice, I was sure she was Bethany. I ran my hands over the uneven cobbles, searching for the bread. The stones were wet, the stench of urine making me want to wretch. My hands were getting soiled and when I handed her the bread, we both knew it would be ruined. She sat back, her piteous crying wrenching my heart.

'Bethany, it is you, isn't it?' She instantly recoiled, gasping in fright. She did not recognize my voice and why should she? It was dark and I was dressed as a man. 'It's me,' I whispered, 'Elowyn.'

Her hands flew to her hood. She must have been covering her face though it was too dark to see. 'I'm not Bethany...

Ye've the wrong person.' She was on her knees, rising, running quickly away from me, and as her footsteps receded, I stared blindly after her. Something had clearly frightened her and I searched the darkness, a pulse throbbing so loudly in my ear that I could hardly hear. I thought I heard something – just the faintest tread, the softest sound – but as I stared into the darkness, I saw nothing at all. I was being fanciful, catching Bethany's fear. This was the darkest part of the alley and once round the bend, I would reach the old stable. There would be light from the oil lamps, men on the quay.

I started walking quickly, trailing my fingers, once more, along the wall. I was a child again, counting the steps in my head. I had done this before and could do it again. I was Elowyn Liddicot, daughter of a drunken fisherman, sent to find him and fetch him home. I knew how to run from men who tried to grab. I turned the bend, relieved to see the outline of the stable. Lamplight flickered against the wall, casting shadows across the alley. Once past the stable, I would be safe.

The interior of the stable was pitch black, the cartwheels blurred and indistinct. I hurried past them, glancing quickly back at the sound of the same soft tread. A shadow darted across the alley and I began running furiously towards the entrance, my heavy boots in danger of tripping me up. I hurtled forward, stopping only to catch my breath on the steps of the weigh house, my heart pounding so hard I thought it might burst. No one was behind me. No one followed me out.

The weigh house was locked and the quayside strangely

quiet. The lock gates were open, the ships slipping silently out to the open sea. Men were pulling the ships on ropes and I leaned against the capstan to calm my nerves. Mr Berryman might be watching from one of the ships and I must not let him think me scared. Besides, I was safe. There were plenty of people to hear my calls and perfectly good light from the oil lamps. A water trough stood by the weigh house and I went back to wash my hands. It was probably just a cat I had heard, or a stray dog making me so jumpy.

I looked back to the alley entrance and stifled my scream. A man was leaning against the wall watching me, the lamp-light flickering and casting shapes on the wall beside him. I could barely see him in the shadows. He was dressed in black, a large hat pulled low over his face. Around his shoulders he wore a long cloak and I froze with fear. It was as if he wanted me to see him. He could have hidden in the shadows but he was leaning into the glow of the lamp, slowly, deliberately, letting me see him. One look and my fear turned to terror. His face was covered by a black scarf, his eyes concealed behind a black leather mask.

The lock gates were open and I knew I would have to walk the long way round. The water was inky black, the cranes silent. Voices drifted across the quayside, the men hauling the last ships out of the lock. Mr Perys was shouting commands by the gates and if I hurried, I could be away before the lock was empty. I began walking quickly down the cobbles, voices coming out of nowhere, footsteps receding into the blackness. The hulls of the ships were creaking, the timbers moaning. I needed to walk quietly but my boots were heavy

– if I ran, I would make too much noise and he would know my whereabouts.

I stayed in the shadows, avoiding each pool of light, glancing back over my shoulder. Barrels lined the quayside and I hid behind one, listening for his silent tread. But even as I peered into the blackness, I knew I would neither hear nor see him. He had stood in the lamplight on purpose; he had wanted me to see him. Now he would remain silent, unseen, creeping behind me with the stealth of a cat. No wonder Bethany had been so scared.

The ships were leaving too quickly, the lock growing quieter. Even Mr Perys had stopped shouting his commands and I glanced round, horrified to see the last ship slipping through the gates. The lock was now empty, just inky black water lapping against the sides and I hurried on, running across the slipway of the new boatyard, turning back along the quay. This side was darker than the other, the large stores stretching deep beneath the road. Each store was locked and barred with heavy grilles, like a row of dungeons, and my fear deepened.

The last ship was raising her sails in the outer harbour. The quayside was empty, the water still and silent, but I was nearly at the steps and would soon reach the path. I would go past Harbour House and straight up the cliff path. The wind was swirling the drizzle beneath the lamps, the men walking swiftly home. I could see their lanterns swinging as they climbed the road. Even Mr Perys was nowhere to be seen. The lock was deserted and I leaned against the wall, peering back across the sudden stillness, aware of the danger I was in.

A fleeting black shape flashed through lamplight, one moment visible, the next swallowed by the darkness. He was on the slipway, darting through the light as if he wanted me to see him. Yes, he did. He was enjoying my terror, playing with me like a cat plays with a mouse, and my fear deepened. He must know I was a woman. He would never do that to a man. Two men with barrows began picking up the horse muck, their shovels scraping across the silent dock, and I knew it was my chance to run. The masked man was far enough behind me, the steps in darkness so he would not see me. The path to Mamm's cottage was hidden from his view and if I ran quickly, he would not know which way I had gone.

The ships' lanterns danced across the bay, yet I had no time to look, running quickly past Harbour House and up to the path. Mamm's gate was closed, her windows shuttered. From now on, there would be no light. I must stay on the left of the path and run my hands along the bushes. Splinters I could remove but if I slipped, I would tumble down the cliff and be washed away by the tide. I was a child again, watching from the clifftop, told to return the moment I saw the lanterns. This was not new to me – I had done it before and could do it again.

I heard the sound of stones rolling down the path and turned in terror. The man was behind me, his cloak billowing in the wind like a vengeful spirit and I felt faint with fear. I could hardly breathe. If I ran to Mamm's, he would get there first. I would have to run further up the path and hide, yet I could not move. My legs seemed frozen to the spot. I could see him laughing, throwing back his head in evident enjoyment, and my blood seemed to curdle. The sky was shrouded with thick black clouds, his laughter drifting over on the wind. He was watching me, no doubt about it. Suddenly he raised his right hand, lifting it high in the air, his cloak blowing around his outstretched arm. It was as if he was bidding me farewell and terror gripped me. It was so deliberate, so menacing, as if part of his game.

I saw him leap off the rock and disappear and fear filled me. He would let me think I was free, then he would jump at me again from out of nowhere. I began to run, scrambling with my heavy shoes up the path into the darkness. The path was uneven and difficult to follow and I stumbled and fell, turning round in panic. Any moment, I expected the grip of his hand on my shoulder but there was nothing. No movement, just the black swirling mist and the sound of the waves against the shore below.

I pulled myself upright, glancing back in fear, but he had not followed me, or if he had, he was hiding in the shadows of the last overhang. I looked down at the harbour, at the row of lamps, and held my breath. A fleeting movement caught my attention, the slightest motion in the lamplight by Harbour House, and my hands began shaking. He was down there. He had been waving me farewell, deliberately letting me know he had allowed me to go free.

I should have been relieved but sobs wracked my body and I gasped for breath like a drowning person, gulping down air. My shaking grew worse, a tremble in my legs. It had been so deliberate, so menacing, so completely terrifying. But the game was over, he had stopped playing. The mouse could go free.

The ships were leaving the bay, their lanterns hardly visible across the black sea. The incoming ships would soon arrive to take their place in the lock and I breathed deeply, trying to steady my shattered nerves. I had done this for William, for the man I loved. I tried to calm my fear – I was safe now. I would go and show everyone my evidence.

Across the clifftop an owl hooted. A cuckoo called back and a shiver ran down my spine. I had not heard that call since childhood.

Chapter Thirty

The wind was freshening, blowing a steady stream of rain across my face. The path would soon get slippery and already my borrowed jacket felt damp. Mud was clinging to my boots, making them more cumbersome, and I stopped to listen, straining my ears above the wind. Owls hunted on pastures, they nested in woods – they did not hunt on cliffs, certainly never on a night like this. One fear gave way to another. No moon. What was I thinking?

I had never mastered that call. Mamm had sat for hours teaching Tom, holding her cupped hands over her mouth, blowing softly through her bent thumbs. *Like this*, she would say, the fingers on her hand slowly rising and falling. I had tried to learn but there was no reason to teach me. I could see that now – it was Tom who needed to learn. Not me.

It must be the top of the tide, the men waiting in the cove with the rowing boats ready. I cursed my stupidity. Of course, they would place lookouts on the top, keeping watch across the cliffs and taking no chance now Major Trelawney's volunteers were on the alert. The trapdoor in the privy must join the tunnel that led to the cave – no wonder Jack Deveral and John Polkerris hated Sir James and his harbour. They were ruthless men, their organization under threat, and they were not taking chances.

I walked slowly forward, ducking low, keeping close to the bushes. Thorns snagged me in the darkness and I was grateful for my sturdy clothes. The cave was this side of Penwartha Point but it was well away from the path. Billy and I had run quite some distance before we reached the tiny track, so surely they would only watch that part? I would stay on the public path – my clothes were dark and they would not see me.

I edged forward in the darkness, keeping close to the hedgerow. Waves were breaking against the rocks below, a steady rumble as the shingle rolled. I heard another hoot and caught my breath. The reply had come so quickly and I wanted to cry. Two men were up here. They were just ahead of me, walking to the track – one ahead of the other. I tried to stay calm. They were calling to each other, signalling their whereabouts, and I could judge their distance from their calls. One was quite close to me, maybe fifty yards, no more. I would wait and let him get ahead.

I should have guessed, part of me probably had but I hid from the truth – the two of us sent up to the cliffs as children to watch for the boats. I never questioned the catch was not fish, just closed my mind and looked away. Tom had mastered his call – two calls, to be precise: one soft and cooing, the other loud and strident. Mamm had been coaching him all that time, showing him how it was done. I should have known.

The cliff dipped and rose. I recognized the gate. Soon they would turn towards the tiny track and it would be safe to continue. The path narrowed, a sheer drop to my right, and I knew to take extra care. A hawthorn bent beside me, a thicket of gorse. Rain stung my cheeks now, dripping from my hat, and I stumbled on a root. My boot caught yet another root and I sprawled headlong in the path, my hands sinking into the thick wet mud. Immediately, I heard the hooting of the owl – this time the strident call for danger and my heart froze. I would have to hide, quickly find somewhere they would not see me.

There was nowhere else to go so I started scrambling through the roots of the gorse, the thorns scratching my jacket, catching my hat and face. I squirmed through the mud, flat on my stomach, pulling myself with my arms, pushing deeper into the jumble of roots and broken branches. The gorse was thicker than I'd imagined but there was just enough space to crawl deeper into the thorny thicket. I heard the answering call, once again, the call for danger, and knew they must have heard my boots kick against the root.

I was only six feet off the path but could go no further. The trunks of the gorse formed a thick barrier and I knew that would have to do. I could see the path through the thinnest of the branches but my clothes were dark, the thicket very dense, and unless they had a dog, they might not see me.

My cheek pressed against the fallen spines. The earth smelt dank and woody. Someone was coming back along the path, his heavy footsteps stopping in the mud beside me. He was looking round, waiting for his companion. I could hear laboured breathing, a cough, but they did not speak. They were signing to each other, pointing to show which way to look. Next to each pair of boots, a thick wooden pole rested on the ground and my stomach sickened. Fear gripped me. They were the clubs from the cave, each one hewn from a single tree trunk, each one with a bulb the size of a man's head – just one blow and a man's skull would smash wide open.

I lay too petrified to breathe. They were searching the other side of the gorse, kicking through the bracken, using their clubs to hold back the thorns. They would use those clubs the moment they saw me. I knew the rules – no witnesses, no one to point the finger. You were one of them or you were dead. I would have to cry out, give myself up and face the consequences. I heard a sudden rustle, the frantic bleating of sheep.

'Nowt but bloody sheep.' The bleating got louder, the disturbed sheep scrambling through the bracken on the other side of the fence.

'All the same, won't be long before Trelawney's mob start sniffin' about. They're workin' their way along the cliffs. Get back to yer post. I'll stay here.'

It was Tom's voice and my blood turned to ice. Gwen did not deserve this, she deserved so much better. Of course, times were hard and people were starving – Bethany was starving, her kids going hungry because of the spoiled bread, but they did not stand on the cliffs with a club that could kill.

Fury filled me, disappointment ripping my heart. Gwen was loyal and loving, she trusted Tom. She was my best friend — if Tom was caught, he would hang and she would be left to struggle with a new baby.

I caught the smell of his tobacco. He was sitting on a rock, smoking the pipe I had given him as a present. He was living rent free with Uncle Thomas, he was an apprentice ship-wright and had good prospects, but bad blood flowed in his veins; the same blood that flowed in mine. Well, I was not going to let them drag me down. I was Elowyn Liddicot, not daughter to a vicious drunk, not smuggler's daughter, but Elowyn Liddicot, proud dressmaker, one who had vowed to raise herself. I would never, ever, let Uncle Thomas make me put Tom's name on my lease. When the baby was born, I would make sure it had a proper future. I would look after Gwen and never let her suffer because she bore the name Liddicot.

The rain was penetrating the branches above me but the ground was still dry. The dead branches were sharp with thorns and painful to lie on. My hands were sore, my finger-tips bleeding, my arms stretched out uncomfortably in front to me, but I would wait all night if need be. Mrs Pengelly was staying at Polcarrow and would not miss me, and Billy would be curled up next to Endymion by the fire in Lady Pendarvis' kitchen. Tamsin might think to knock on my door but they would see my cloak and bonnet and think I had retired early to bed and would not disturb me.

Tom coughed and spat, refilling his pipe from the pouch in his jacket, and my blood ran to ice again. Father must have been one of them. I had felt numb at the news of his death, assuming it was his own doing – that it was only a matter of time before he stumbled and fell, or had a fight, or was too drunk to get home and would freeze to death, but perhaps I was wrong. Everyone knew a drunk talked in his cups – perhaps he had been silenced.

I could no longer smell Tom's pipe, nor see his boots. Stars shone brightly through the break in the clouds and I lay straining my ears, not daring to move. Something had alerted me, sounds drifting on the wind. Men were shouting and I looked up. A dog was barking, lanterns swinging along the path – Major Trelawney's men must not find me. If they found me, they would assume I was with the smugglers or in hiding from them and would ask me questions.

The barking was getting louder and I knew I stood no chance. A huge dog began pushing through the gorse, forcing his way through the thickest thorns and I shut my eyes, bracing myself for his bite. He was sniffing round me, slobbering over me, licking my face, his huge body swinging from side to side as he wagged his tail. 'Endymion,' I cried, sobbing with relief.

His frantic barking made the lanterns stop then start to go faster and I began inching backwards out of the gorse. Endymion was slobbering over me, getting hold of my collar, trying to drag me, and almost at once, I heard running footsteps. Billy hurtled to a stop, bending down to help me to my feet. He could not speak but hugged me tightly and I clutched him for all I was worth. 'Endymion's going to need another bath,' I whispered, trying to laugh.

Billy was not laughing. He was almost crying. 'Why'd ye go, Elly? Where've ye been? Honest, we've been that worried.'

'Who noticed I wasn't in bed? Did Tamsin notice?'

'No...it was Lady Pendarvis who thought to check – she had a sudden feeling ye might go to Porthcarrow and she wanted to know ye were safe. Don't know how she knew but she woke up everyone an' when she saw ye weren't in yer room, she came back for me and Endymion – and Jago, of course.' The lanterns were only a short distance away. 'Mrs Munroe's boiling water for yer bath. Honest, she's that worried. Why'd ye go, Elly?' He wiped his hand across his eyes.

'Because I knew William's boots would be clean – and I've been so lucky...I've got the name of a man who can swear William was in bed by half eleven. And he can swear William's boots were on the rack and they weren't muddy.'

Billy's hug tightened. He sniffed loudly, wiping his nose on his sleeve, smiling at my lack of reproof. 'All the same – ye should've got me to go with ye.' He started to smile. 'Honest, Elly, wait till ye see this – ye're never going to believe it. That's Lady Pendarvis...and she's wearing *Jago's* clothes. Least I think she is – unless she's a jacket and breeches of her own! That's Lady Pendarvis alongside Sam and Jago. Mrs Pengelly's still at Polcarrow, they've not told her yet, but ye should see Lady Pendarvis run. Honest, ye'd never believe it.'

I smiled back. 'I do believe it. I believe anything of Lady Pendarvis.'

One look at her immaculate jacket and breeches and I knew at once they had been tailor-made for her. Her hat was at a jaunty angle, her long legs encased in elegant boots. She wore fine kid gloves, a cravat neatly folded at her neck, held in place by a fine silver pin, and I stared in admiration. She was barely out of breath, only her flushed cheeks giving away the fact that she had run along the cliff path. Her lips tightened, her eyebrows rose and I found myself smiling back into those hawk-like eyes.

'I had to go...there was no one else I could ask.' I dug deep into my pocket, holding out the torn page. 'I was so lucky... I've got a name of a witness...he's Mr Berryman, he's a clay agent – he said he'll give us evidence that William's boots were clean and he was in bed by half eleven.'

Lady Pendarvis merely nodded, holding out her elegantly gloved hand to take the torn page. 'I will make sure Sir James gets this.' The wind was blowing her hair. She looked so at ease in her breeches and jacket and I knew she must have done this many times before. The rumours must be true. She smiled, walking back along the muddy cliff path. 'You should have had asked *me*, Elowyn – Jago would have gone for you.'

Chapter Thirty-one

Coombe House, Fosse
Tuesday 5th July 1796, 8:00 a.m.

I had to be firm, insist my scratches did not hurt. The truth was that my wrists and several of my cuts were extremely painful but I was already late for work and had to hurry. Mrs Munroe would keep me there all day. 'That feels much better...no, honestly...I'm fine.'

She pursed her lips, placing her carefully cut potato slices against my bruises, rubbing copious amounts of arnica salve and witch hazel into my skin. Even this morning she was still scowling and shaking her head. 'Ye're to come straight home – eight o'clock at the latest. Bring yer sewing back here...Though what Mrs Pengelly's goin' to say when I tell her. Honest, gadding about in Sam's jacket an' breeches...' She blew her nose, wiping her eyes. 'That demon's goin' to come straight back an' get ye. He's still out there. He'll not let ye go again.'

I had told them I was running from a masked man, Mrs Munroe crossing herself, insisting it must have been a demon chasing me. She had lit candles with shaking hands, determined to ward off his evil spirit, but Lady Pendarvis had merely raised her elegant shoulders. 'He was probably a nightwatchman, or one of the men Sir James has placed on watch. And I believe Major Trelawney has stepped up his surveillance.'

'Or he could have been Mr Drew's murderer,' I had replied. 'He was menacing and cruel – I could tell he enjoyed instilling fear in me.' She had nodded, taking me seriously, telling me Sir James would hear of it on his return.

I glanced at the clock. It was already eight o'clock and we had to hurry.

I had hardly slept and nor had Billy. He walked beside me, the new morning promising to be a fine day. I smelt of rosemary oil, witch hazel and honey, but I had too much to do to stay at home. I needed to finish cutting out the gowns and I had to teach Gwen my new ribbon embroidery. Besides, my long-sleeved dress covered most of the scratches and with a slight adjustment to my hair I had hidden the worst on my face.

Billy smiled at me for encouragement but his smile vanished as we entered the yard. Mr Hearne's pony and cart was standing by the steps. They must have only just arrived as Nathan was helping Mamm and Lorwenna out, but it was already too late to turn away. Our eyes met and a terrible blush scorched my face.

Nathan hurried across the courtyard, bowing formally. 'Elowyn...forgive me, I had to come.' He was smiling, trying to dispel the frown that creased his brow. He was dressed in his Sunday clothes, a cane under his arm, his boots polished to a shine, and though he stood with his cleft chin raised slightly in the air, I could see the same look of boyish vulnerability deep within his blue eyes and my heart hammered in fear. He still loved me, dear God, he still loved me. He had never received my letter and I had not written again – I had yet to refuse him. Agony churned my stomach, a terrible feeling of guilt.

He smiled shyly, glancing at Billy's frown before offering me his arm. 'A moment in private?' he whispered.

I took his arm, fighting my fear, and we walked in awkward silence through the arch towards the boatyard. Mr Melhuish's forge was blazing and already the sawyers were busy in the saw pit. Men were wielding their hammers on the scaffold of the new brig and I searched for Tom, knowing he would be watching. My heart hardened. Tom may hate me now, but he would be better off away from Porthcarrow. They all would. Mamm and Lorwenna were watching us from the steps, their voluminous cloaks barely hiding their swollen skirts, and my discomfort turned to anger. How dare they abuse Nathan's kindness and bring their brandy in the same cart?

Nathan seemed to hesitate, his eyes searching mine, as if he was trying to find the right words, and remorse gripped me, a terrible feeling of wronging him. 'I should've come to see you sooner,' he said softly. 'I'm so sorry, Elowyn...all this is my fault and I beg you to forgive me.' A quiver in his voice made me look up. There was pain deep in his eyes and my remorse spiralled. 'When you asked me to dance I should never have refused you. It was wrong and I've been blamin' myself ever since.' The pressure of his arm increased, he was leading me to the office door, Uncle Thomas watching us through the window.

A new note of sadness entered his voice. 'My upbringing's been very strict, Elowyn – I watch others havin' fun an' I've often longed for the freedom they enjoy. The truth is I can't dance – I don't know what it's like to dance... but I want to, Elowyn. I want to be joyful...' His hand was shaking, the plea in his voice almost unbearable. '*If only* I'd taken your hand...*if only* I'd danced with you, then none of this would've happened. You're not to blame – it's me at fault.' He held my fingers to his lips, brushing them softly. 'I need you, Elowyn...I need you to teach me to be joyful. All work and no play has left me very dull but you can change that...'

He looked so eager, like a puppy not knowing whether to expect a rebuke or praise, and I felt suddenly so wretched. Perhaps, if I had never met William, perhaps, if we had met sooner or known each other longer I might have loved him, but not now. I could never love him now. He stretched out his hand, tentatively brushing back a lock of hair from my cheek. 'Elowyn, ye've scratches on your face...Ye're not hurt, are ye? Ye must have had a fall...?'

His look was too tender, too protective, and I felt like screaming. He was not letting me speak yet what could I say? That I could never teach him to be joyful because it was William who made me joyful – William who gave me wings and set me free? There could be no joy with Nathan – he would swamp me with his protection, imprison me in his beautiful pier house and bleed me of all joy. I had to speak plainly, make him understand I no longer wanted his courtship.

'Nathan...I'm sorry. It's not that you don't dance...and it's not that I don't think you're a good man. You deserve to be happy and loved deeply...but...'

Pain wracked his face. 'Please, Elowyn...Please don't say what you're goin' to say...please, please, give me another chance...I can't lose your love – not over this...I want to change...an' I believe I can...' His body was taut, his eyes begging me not to say the words he so dreaded to hear. Maybe he had not seen me kiss William – maybe he really thought I was punishing him for not dancing.

Uncle Thomas stood in the doorway, a smile lighting his face. Gwen was looking down at us from the top of the steps, Mamm and Lorwenna staring across the courtyard, pretending to pet the pony. They were all watching, waiting for us to be reunited, and my heart lurched. To be so publicly refused. The same icy hand was gripping my heart, the same sense of guilt, the need to please him, and I felt like gasping for breath. 'Nathan...I'm so sorry...I've enjoyed our days together. It's been very nice getting to know you but you must understand...I can't...I don't...'

He let go of my arm. 'It's all right, Elowyn.' His face was stony, his voice hardly above a whisper. 'I understand – I'll never stop feelin' the way I feel about you...I'll always love you but I'll leave you be. I'll not pester you any more with unwanted suits.' He bowed politely, stiffly, his mouth clamping tight as his eyes fought his heartbreak. 'I wish you well. Thank you for your time. If I can ever be of any assistance, please don't hesitate to ask. I'll do anythin' to help you, anythin'…please remember that.'

I could see him fighting to keep his shoulders back yet all I could think of were the merchants that tried to cheat me. Uncle Thomas looked away, turning with Nathan into the office, and sudden emptiness made me want to cry. Not Uncle Thomas as well. I was becoming estranged from my family, yet why did they not listen to me, even ask about William? They were so set against him – why could they not see William was innocent? Why believe such wrong of him?

Billy scuffed his boots as I stared back at Mamm's furious face. 'How long are you staying?' I asked her.

'Long enough to see my son, and pick up a few provisions. We've some errands to run then we'll be back to help with the catch. Nathan's stayin' fer a meetin', not that ye care.' Her eyes hardened, leaving me in no doubt of her anger. 'He's been asked to attend the adventurers' meetin' – they're after new investors in the mine. Tom says they've hit a rich seam an' they're goin' to expand. It seems Nathan's as good a chance as any fer gettin' his name approved. Not that ye care…'

I shrugged my shoulders, wincing in sudden pain, but seeing her was fortunate as I had done nothing but think of Bethany since I had seen her last night. I needed to get the remaining rolls of cotton to her as quickly as I could. Lady Pendarvis was right, a helping hand, from one woman to another. 'Can you take some rolls of cloth back with you for Bethany?'

She looked surprised, her eyes sharpening. 'Bethany Cooper?'

I nodded, stepping onto the steps. 'Yes, she's going to sew something for me. I'll send Billy down with the rolls – he can wait with the cart until you come back.' I was halfway up the steps when a sudden thought struck me. 'Is there somewhere in Porthcarrow where you can get bread at night?'

She looked puzzled. 'The hotel puts out bread they've not used – there's a table round the back. About eleven or twelve at night, dependin' on the number they're feedin' an' the time they stop cookin' – Mr Hendra don't let it go to waste. He's a good man but he's makin' a fortune so 'tis no skin off his nose.' Her eyes hardened. 'Why d'ye ask?'

'No reason – just something I heard. It's good – too many people are starving.'

If I thought Mamm was sullen Gwen was far worse, striding across the floor, sharply shaking her apron. I pulled down my sleeve in fear she would see my scratches. She looked tired, dark patches under her eyes. 'That poor man; honest, Elly, ye'll destroy him. A man like that only loves once – he's putting on a brave face but underneath, he's a broken man.'

There was no need to tell me that. I was not all hard shell and frowns; I had a heart and recognized one that was breaking. 'I can't help it, Gwen. I don't love him. Maybe… well, perhaps, I could have loved him. Perhaps, I might never have known that I didn't really love him. I might have spent my whole married life *thinking* I loved him when really I didn't. But it's too late now – I know what real love feels like. It makes you want to sing and dance and breathe the air…

and sit among the flowers. It makes you look forward to the next day, not feel trapped by a terrible sense of suffocation, the sense of never being able to please.'

Despair gripped her. 'Elly, ye can't *still* mean William Cotterell? The man's a murderer. What's wrong with ye? Why can't ye see what's so obvious to others? It's like we're losing ye…it's like he's takin' ye from us…makin' ye hate us—'

'He's not! How can you say that? He's good and honest. I ache when I'm not with him, Gwen. I love him so much …for *who* he is. I don't care if he doesn't have standing or money…I don't love Nathan and I can't pretend to – not just for a beautiful pier house, nor money, nor for him growing rich with his investments. It would be like telling you to leave Tom and marry someone else…' She gripped her belly in sudden pain. 'Gwen, sit down…Are you all right?'

She nodded, her hands reaching for mine. 'I'm that scared, Elly…' Her hands were shaking. 'Sometimes I feel it's ready…but it's passing…the pain's goin'.' She looked up, her hand flying to her mouth.

Tom stood framed by the doorway. 'Go after him, Elowyn. Go straight down and beg him to take ye back. Ye don't know what ye're doin'…ye'll loose us the yard…an' far more besides. Go down now – for Chrissake, stop yer selfish nonsense an' get down there an' apologize.'

He was scowling, shoulders hunched, hands clenched, and I stared across the room at the brother I was only just getting to know. How had I not seen it before? The boy I had loved and protected had long since gone – in his place, Father's bullish shoulders, his neck and head bent forward, ready to strike. I was looking at Father.

My heart pounded. 'I'm sorry, Tom, but that won't be possible. I don't love Nathan and I'll not marry him.' I was Elowyn Liddicot and must believe my worth. I needed to remember I could read and write. I had savings and soon I would have my own lease. I had to stand up to him, never let him guess my fear. I kept my shoulders squared, my chin in the air, my fists unclenched. 'Was there anything else or can we get on with our work...?'

'Ye'll get straight down there. I mean it. Go and say ye're sorry or—'

'Or what, Tom? You'll use your belt on me, like Father? Get out of my sewing room...it's not yours yet. We've two more weeks until my lease runs out and we've work to do.' I turned away, my chest heaving. He must not see me so scared. I heard the door slam and turned to Gwen. 'Does he hit you, Gwen?'

She looked appalled. 'No...of course not. He's not like that...It's just ye've made him that angry, that's all. He's set his heart on the yard...ye must know that.'

I could hardly breathe. 'Promise me you'll tell me the first moment he hits you. Promise me?'

She looked horrified, tears springing to her eyes. 'Elly, what's wrong with ye? How can ye say that? It's like William Cotterell's poisoned yer mind to us...I hardly recognize ye no more.'

Josie was standing at the storeroom door. She, too, looked pale, tears stinging her eyes, and I knew what Gwen had said was true. I hardly recognized myself any more. I was filled with such purpose – William made me believe in myself, made me see who I really was. He had opened my eyes to my own self-belief, given me wings and I was ready to fly. Why could all women not feel like that? Why were we all kept so low?

Josie came forward, slipping her hand through my arm. 'Let's make the last two weeks count...let's make them the best we've ever had.'

Dearest Josie, with her smart new spectacles and her beautiful mother-of-pearl brooch Uncle Thomas had bought for her. I drew a deep breath, smiling back. 'It may be our last two weeks *here*, but it's not going to be our last two weeks together. I'm not going to marry Nathan but neither are we all going to join Jenna in the school...and we're certainly *not* going to be bullied by Mrs Hoskins. We're all going else-where – all of us, even the new baby will have a cot. Lady Pendarvis is going to help us – she's going to store my fabrics in an attic room and we're going to find another lease...'

It was not lying – it was telling the truth, only I knew to keep my plans to myself. Uncle Thomas and Tom had no idea of my savings and I needed it to stay that way. I had made enquires – the rent for the shipyard in Porthcarrow was twenty pounds a year so my money would buy Tom nearly two years. Tom would never agree to his name on a dressmaker's lease – he would wrangle, force me to use the money for his boatyard. He would force it from me and I would be left with nothing. No, my mind was made up. I would keep the exact amount of my savings to myself.

Josie looked up. 'There's a man outside, lookin' up at the sign. He's comin' up the steps...Now why'd a man want to come to a dressmaker's?'

The man's dark clothes and tricorn hat looked official. Greasy brown hair spilled over his collar, his huge belly protruding from under his waistcoat. His boots were scuffed and he had a large leather bag slung over his shoulder. He held a notebook in his hand and my heart froze – it was William's notebook.

There were fresh stains down his waistcoat, beer on his breath. He breathed heavily, a slight wheeze as he spoke. 'There's no denyin' it's ye.' The notebook lay open in his hand, my face smiling up from the page. William had sketched flowers in my hair and pain sliced through me. I looked so happy, my smile loving and gentle, and tears filled my eyes. I could barely look up.

'Where did you get that?'

'We'd a warrant to search William Cotterell's room. This is ye, I believe? A couple of people have identified ye as Miss Elowyn Liddicot. Is that yer name?'

I nodded, unable to speak.

'So I'll take that as yes. Ye've been associatin' with William Cotterell, held prisoner for murder, an' in my official capacity as constable I'm summonin' ye to intend the inquest of Mr Josiah Drew. Ye might be called to give evidence.' He reached into the scuffed leather bag, rummaging until he found the right document – a scroll with a large red seal.

'The coroner's presentin' his findings an' everyone who's been associatin' with William Cotterell or was witness to the crime must attend or face a fine.'

He thrust the scroll towards me and I took it with shaking hands. I felt sick with fear. 'He's no murderer...William's innocent.'

The constable sniffed, wiping his sleeve across his nose. 'Friday at the Market House in St Austell — be there fer ten in the mornin'. Sir Thomas Treffry's the proceedin' Justice an' he don't tolerate lateness. If William Cotterell's found guilty, he'll be detained for trial at the assizes.' He had not been looking at me, glancing over my shoulder to the others instead, but his eyes finally held mine and a shiver ran through me. 'Ye're lucky, he might've killed ye next. He's a dangerous man...'

I hardly made it to the chair. He must have left and Josie must have given me a drink but all I could see was the room spinning round me and the hateful glee in the constable's eyes — the absolute belief in William's guilt.

Chapter Thirty-two

Coombe House, Fosse
Thursday 7th July 1796, 8:00 p.m.

Lady Pendarvis held up the bottle of cognac, pouring it swiftly into Mrs Pengelly's fine glasses. 'A present, Eva dear – I know Sir James is *very* generous but this is my *brother's* brandy and his *finest* at that.' She raised her eyebrow, handing Lady Polcarrow her glass with a smile of deep affection. 'This is like old times – not that I wasted my *finest* brandy in the punch. And before you have me scurrying round for the receipts, Lady Polcarrow...we *have* paid the full tax.'

The lace on Lady Polcarrow's sleeve flashed as she waved her hand. 'No thank you, Lady Pendarvis – I'm too queasy to drink. I don't believe I shall ever eat or drink again. I can only just manage Jenna's raspberry-leaf tea – that seems to stay down.' She looked far from ill, a little pale perhaps, but more beautiful than ever, the red tints in her hair complemented by the hand-painted ruby roses on her gown – not my silk, but the best Marseilles silk given to her as a present from Lady Pendarvis.

'Surely not, my dear?' Lady Pendarvis handed a glass to

Mrs Pengelly. 'You must keep something down – *bouillon de poulet*, at the very least…' Her dark blue silk exactly matched the large sapphire brooch on her bosom. She was wearing matching earrings, which glinted against her long neck, a fine collection of feathers. 'And *flan aux œufs* – I believe I lived on that when I was expecting Edward.'

'Or something simple, my dear, like a clear chicken broth… and egg custard. That's what I ate when I was expecting you… and there's always porridge. You must eat something, Rose dearest.' Mrs Pengelly held up her glass and I took mine from Lady Pendarvis, my hands trembling. I never drank brandy. It was too strong and besides, I felt as sick as Lady Polcarrow.

Lady Polcarrow smiled at her mother. She had beautiful, mesmerizing eyes until you crossed her. When you crossed her, they darkened to thunder as many of the Corporation had learned to their cost. 'Elly, are you all right?' I nodded back. 'Sir James says he'll pick you up at seven tomorrow morning – you're to ride with him in the carriage. He's agreed Billy can go too. He's to ride with Joseph.'

'Joseph's going?' Mrs Pengelly spoke for us all; it was a long time since Joseph had driven Sir James' coach.

'Just a precaution. There's been more rioting. The vagrants are being rounded up and forced off the land. Phillip Randall's lynching has made everyone nervous.'

The feathers in Lady Pendarvis' headdress jerked. 'Sir James is surely not forcing them *off* his land?'

'No…not at all – far from it. Sir James has long ordered the spare barns to be left open and he provides what he can…but there's just too many and St Austell isn't under his jurisdiction. The vagrants are on Viscount Vallenforth's land – he's the one clamping down.'

All three of them had concern in their eyes, their smiles designed to encourage, and I sipped my brandy trying hard to smile back. The fiery liquid burned my tongue. 'Has Sir James heard back from Mr Berryman?' I managed to say.

Lady Polcarrow shook her head. 'Not yet. He's given all the documents to Matthew Reith. He's to take on the case – not that there *will* be a case,' she added quickly, 'but *if* there's a case.' Her eyes softened. 'James says it's far from simple. You've chosen a man who most would never dream of defending...Honest, Elly...he's got the courts clamouring after him. You do know that, don't you?'

I nodded, fear churning my stomach. If Sir James had asked Matthew Reith to take the case, he must be expecting the worst. The reputation of his harbour was at stake – first the clay in the flour, now a murder. 'William's made a lot of enemies. There are those who want his downfall.'

'That's what James says.'

Mrs Pengelly reached for my hand. 'Sir James has himself been falsely accused – he knows how the law can be...we all do...' She held her handkerchief quickly to her eyes. 'Sir James will see justice done.' Her voice hardened and I knew she was thinking of her husband. 'We may all believe William to be innocent but it must be proved. If the coroner finds evidence or there are witnesses to the murder then that's justice. Ye understand that, don't you, Elly?'

I nodded. 'William didn't do it, I know he didn't...' Mrs Pengelly had liked William and she was a good judge of character; she was just stating the facts and I had to stay strong. 'I'm sorry about Hannah's gown, Lady Pendarvis. Does she still need the hem doing?'

Lady Pendarvis smoothed another non-existent crease from her gown. 'It took a surprisingly short time...I had not realized Hannah was such an *accomplished* seamstress. She just needed someone to pin them and she was *quite* happy to do the rest. I had forgotten how much I missed altering gowns like that.' She smiled at Mrs Pengelly, lifting her basket from the table. 'They were charity gowns, Eva, ill-fitting but of very fine quality. Hannah looks quite the lady now.'

Chapter Thirty-three

The carriage to St Austell
Friday 8th July 1796, 8:00 a.m.

Sir James Polcarrow looked up at the sudden lurch, smiling across at me. I smiled back and as the coach steadied, he resumed his reading, poring over the tightly written pages with a deepening frown.

At first I thought him too severe for Rose, always frowning and stern, yet since his marriage his face had softened, the stiffness round his mouth giving way to smile lines. Every woman in Fosse would agree he was handsome, although it was not his fine features that marked him as striking, but his piercing blue eyes. They never mocked; they were kind and understanding, the eyes of a man who knew suffering.

We were picking up speed, leaving the cliffs above Porthcarrow, heading down to the valley. I had never sat alone with Sir James, nor so close. His clothes were the finest quality, his well-cut jacket stretching without a crease, his boots highly polished but plain and unadorned. His hair was worn short, black like his brows, his chin closely shaven. His kid gloves lay on the seat next to him but he never carried a cane – no buckles, no gold chains and no cane. He was hardly like a baronet at all, but was polite and courteous. He knew the names of all his servants and even those who disregarded his liberal views treated him with respect. Best of all was his love for Rose, the passion he could never hide. I glanced across at him, anxious his frown had deepened.

'Another half-hour – maybe less. We're going well. Are you comfortable, Miss Liddicot?'

I nodded. 'Very comfortable, thank you, Sir James.' How could I not be comfortable on such plump leather seats? The wood was highly polished, the brass fixtures gleaming in the early sun. The carriage was very spacious, with beeswax candles in the lanterns and blue velvet curtains embroidered with the Polcarrow crest. As a friend of both his wife and his mother-in-law, Sir James was showing me such considera-tion, his insistence I travelled with him such an honour.

The gorse and bracken began to thin, hawthorns giving way to sturdy oak. Green pastures took the place of purple heather, scarlet poppies standing like regimental soldiers along our route. Oxeye daisies and chamomile blanketed the fields, wispy clouds drifting above us. It was so beautiful. Any other time a journey like this would fill me with such pleasure, but anxiety twisted my stomach and I could not enjoy it. The carriage lurched again; the road was narrowing, branches arching above us, blocking out the sun. We were nearing St Austell and soon I would see William.

Sir James remained silent. We were all silent, even Billy who was riding with Joseph on the driver's seat had stopped his chatter. We had not seen any vagrants and even if we did, there was a basket of turnips and potatoes on the back, freshly baked bread, milk and cheese. Joseph was merely a precaution as Sir James was known for his mercy. 'Tell me you don't have too many more suitors,' he said, tidying the papers into a neat pile, putting them back in his leather case. 'It's time-consuming enough running the estate and building a new harbour...any other suitors may well have to wait!' He smiled and I tried to smile back.

'Other suitors?' I managed to ask.

He raised his eyebrows. 'Nathan Cardew?'

His smile showed no notion that his words had just ripped me apart. My cheeks were on fire, tears filling my eyes. 'We...we only courted for a few days, Sir James...he wanted me to marry him...but—' I stopped, trying to draw breath. 'I think I misled Lady Polcarrow...I believe she thought I was as good as engaged but that was never the case...'

He looked at me through those intensely blue eyes, his mouth drawing tight. 'It was not Lady Polcarrow who told me but Mr Cardew himself.'

The carriage was going faster, both of us swaying with the steady rhythm. Cottages scattered by, cattle watching us from the fields. Sir James was still staring at me, his words too awful to contemplate. The very idea of Nathan discussing our engagement filled me with horror. How could he? William was right, Nathan only wanted me for my connections, or at the very least, was prepared to use my connections to further his prospects. I took a deep breath. 'But I've only just met him – it was my family's wish...' I reached for my handkerchief, blowing my nose. I wanted to scream. My heart was thumping, my cheeks burning.

We were on the outskirts of the town and I leaned forward, peering through the window. There were granite buildings, a large town hall and a beautiful manor house next to the church. Some of the houses were thatched, some in great need of attention. Others looked newly built, lining the road as it snaked through the town. The turnpike from Truro to Plymouth; no wonder it was so busy. Yet the pavements looked in need of repair and there were potholes everywhere, large muddy holes.

Coaches stood waiting outside the inns, the harnessed horses restless to be off. Alongside us, a coachman cracked his whip and the stable boys jumped back as the wheels began to turn. We must be nearing the market; I could hear geese squawking, pigs squealing. Men were pushing barrows, boys bent double under huge bulging sacks. The horses slowed to a walk and we came to a halt. A group of people were standing outside a granite building and a man stepped forward to open the door. Sir James looked up.

'You've nothing to fear, Elowyn. Just answer Mr Reith's questions – tell the absolute truth.'

I knew I must ask him. My mind was spinning, a terrible anxiety gnawing my stomach. 'Sir James…I've no right to ask and you've no reason to answer…but when did Mr Cardew tell you we were engaged?'

He seemed puzzled by my question. 'I can't remember…I believe it was about two months ago.'

I could hardly breathe. 'Were you discussing the Piermaster's job?'

He looked up, understanding me at once. 'Don't be too hard on him, Elowyn – he's a good man and a man in love only wants the best for the woman he loves. And love can be a cruel mistress – you know that, don't you?' He picked up the heavy leather bag. 'Here's Mr Reith. Remember, you've nothing to fear and nothing to hide. If you're called, just speak the truth.'

Chapter Thirty-four

The Market House
Friday 8th July 1796, 10:00 a.m.

The room was already crowded, everyone crushing together, peering over the shoulders of the man in front. Mr Reith had told us to make our way to the reserved seats — not that we had a seat, but because he wanted me at the front in case I was called. The room was plain and unadorned, the lime-washed walls shabby, the light from the two small leaded windows blocked by men crowding against them. Lanterns were being lit in the front and I tried to calm my fear. It was already too stuffy, the air hard to breathe.

Billy grabbed my arm. 'We mustn't be separated...' He started weaving through the solid mass of men, smiling and nodding as they let us through. 'Witness for the next case... Excuse me, sir...witness coming through...' He sounded so authoritative and my heart swelled with pride. Five chairs stood on a raised platform; beside them, the dock rose like a pulpit in a church. It was intricately carved with oak steps twisting up to a stand with a shelf and huge Bible. My heart dived. A space was cordoned off by a wooden rail and I stared at it, knowing that was where William would stand.

'We'll go there,' Billy shouted over his shoulder. My panic was rising. If I was called, I would have to answer truthfully and I felt faint with fear. If I told them about the cove, word would get out. 'There's a bit more space...' Billy's leather bag hung from his shoulders; he began steering me to a gap behind the reserved chairs and I saw at once the name on the chair in front. My hopes soared – Mrs Edith Burrow.

The constable called for silence but the men at the back could not hear and the noise remained deafening. He was standing by an open door, his stained waistcoat puckering under the pressure of his tightly fastened buttons. He wore the same dark jacket and breeches and a cravat that might once have been white. The brass bell in his hand clanged. 'Silence,' he repeated, vigorously ringing the bell, 'the session will now start.'

The door opened and three men walked stiffly onto the raised platform. Sir Thomas Treffry was older than I expected – late sixties, perhaps – slightly stooped and walking with a cane. He was the only one wearing a wig. The other two were soberly dressed, their hair drawn back in a bow. The younger of the two must be the clerk, the other, the coroner, Dr Guinislake. All three looked impatient and seated themselves quickly. Sir Thomas nodded to the constable who unrolled a scroll.

'This is the inquest into the death of Mr Josiah Drew,' he shouted, and I put out my hand, steadying myself against the back of the chair in front. William would be acquitted, he was innocent; I just had to stay strong. The jury were taking their places, shuffling along the benches in what seemed a tight fit. They looked ordinary men – shopkeepers, clerks, blacksmiths, even farmers by the look of the mud on their boots – and I searched their faces, hoping they were good and honest men. Not one of them was smiling, each taking his place with an air of gravity.

The chairs in front were beginning to fill – Mr Hellyar, Mr Sellick, Sir James, Mr Reith and Mrs Burrow. Why were Mr Hellyar and Mr Sellick here? William had nothing to do with either the tin mine or the clay pits. Why call them as witnesses? 'Are ye all right, Elly? Ye look awful,' whispered Billy.

I nodded, trying to fight my sudden giddiness. I should have eaten. I could not breathe; the room was so crowded, the air foul and stale. Mrs Burrow was wearing a straw bonnet, a red shawl round her shoulders. She had a long, thin face but she looked kind and as she slipped off her shawl, the sight of her squared shoulders lifted my spirits.

Sir Thomas leaned sideways to speak to Dr Guinislake. He was frowning, shaking his head as if he found it difficult to hear. The noise level had risen, the excitement and anticipation horrible to hear. It chilled me, making my stomach churn in fear. Sir Thomas was finely dressed as I thought he would be. He was a wealthy landowner and I had heard of his friendship with Viscount Vallenforth. His shoulders sloped in a despondent fashion, his lips were thin. Only one eye seemed to open, the other remained tightly closed and slightly weeping. He held an eyeglass against his good eye, searching the room, and as the noise began to lessen, he nodded curtly to the constable.

The constable's voice filled the room. 'Bring in William Cotterell.'

I stared at the doorway, summoning my courage. William must not see any doubt in my eyes. He saw me straight away, his hazel eyes widening in pleasure, his shy smile bringing tears to mine. I had not thought he would look so smart. I expected him dishevelled and unkempt – he had been four days in a dungeon yet he was smartly dressed, his shirt freshly laundered. His cravat had been neatly tied and even his hair looked newly washed and brushed. He looked honest and respectable, only his pallor and the dark patches under his eyes showing the strain he was under. That and the heavy iron shackle clamping his hands so tightly together.

I watched him take his place behind the polished rail and reaching into my basket, pressed his notebook to my heart. This was the second time I had wished on the four-leaf clover and my hands trembled. How many wishes could I make? I just hoped I had not used up all the luck. Mr Reith got to his feet, staring indignantly at Sir Thomas. He held his right hand in the air and the room fell silent. Above the beating of my heart, I heard the constable wheeze.

Matthew Reith was tall and slender, a slight stoop to his shoulders. His brown hair was cut short, greying at the temples. He was wearing the long black jacket and breeches of an attorney, his white cravat tied neatly and held in place with a simple pin. His authority was instant yet as he stood, Sir Thomas stared past him, addressing Sir James.

'Do you bring Mr Reith here to intimidate me, Sir James?' His voice was waspish.

Sir James stood up, his face every bit as stern. 'I make no apology for asking Mr Reith to attend this inquest, Sir Thomas. The reputation of my harbour is at stake and I take this matter very seriously, as I believe does every other person here today. If Mr Cotterell is found to be guilty, Mr Reith will represent my interests in court. Therefore, I believe it right he should be here today.' He glanced at Matthew Reith's impassive face. 'Mr Reith is merely asking—'

Sir Thomas waved his hand in a dismissive manner. 'I know very well what Mr Reith is asking. I know him by his reputation.' He nodded at the constable. 'Unlock the shackles – *innocent until proven guilty*.' He turned, muttering something to Dr Guinislake and reached for a glass on the table in front of him. 'I am aware of the law, Sir James.'

The constable fumbled with his keys, unlocking William's shackles, and Sir Thomas turned to the jurors. 'Members of the jury, some of you I recognize, others are strangers to me. Thank you for giving up your valuable time. Dr Guinislake is the coroner here today. He is a highly professional and experienced doctor and we are indeed honoured to hear his testimony. First, you will hear his report and then you will hear the testimony of the witnesses.' His voice was thin, like his lips, his one eye closed, the other piercing, staring straight at the jury. 'At the end of this inquest you'll be asked to consider what you have heard very carefully and you must give a verdict on two counts – first, the cause of Mr Drew's death, and second, the judgment of guilty or not guilty of Mr William Cotterell, held on charge of Mr Drew's murder. Is that clear?'

The jurymen nodded, all of them replying, 'Yes, Sir Thomas.'

'If Mr Cotterell is found to be guilty, he will be detained for trial by the criminal courts in Bodmin. Can you all now confirm that none of you is known to either Mr Cotterell or the deceased, Mr Drew?' He watched the jurors nod in turn. 'Thank you. Feel free to stop the proceedings to ask a question. If you need something clarified, just raise your right hand. Again, is that clear?'

The jury nodded again, some of them removing their jackets in the heat. A steady trickle of sweat pricked my back and from the corner of my eye, I saw Mr Hellyar wipe his handkerchief across his brow. I could not tear my eyes away from William. He seemed so confined, like a bear in a cage. The constable cleared his voice. 'I call upon Dr Guinislake.'

Dr Guinislake carried a wad of papers with him to the stand. He was a severe-looking man in his early fifties with a long, thin face, bushy eyebrows and hooked nose. He glanced up at the still murmuring crowd, both grievance and displeasure the natural lines of his face. He was wearing sober clothes with no adornment, only lace at his wrists and throat. Putting on a pair of spectacles, he pulled free the first wad of paper.

'My examination into the death of Mr Josiah Drew shows *death by drowning* – of that there is no doubt.'

Sir Thomas nodded. 'Did you see any marks of violence on the body? Any sign of a struggle?'

'None, Sir Thomas. The body was lying head down in a settling pit above the harbour. I was roused at three o'clock in the morning. By the time I reached the body, it was gone four. There was no sign of a struggle – and by that I mean no evidence of purpura or any contusions that would lead me to believe an assault had taken place.'

'And your opinion on the time of death, Dr Guinislake?'

'Between one and two in the morning.'

'And this is based on what evidence?'

'The body had yet to stiffen. When I arrived, there was no stiffness in the jaw. In my experience, stiffness of the jaw usually sets in after three hours. None was present when I made my examination.'

'Could Mr Drew have been held under the water?'

'Yes – most definitely. I saw considerable damage to the bank as if there had been more than one person involved.'

'And yet there was no sign of a struggle on the deceased's body? No bruising or a knock to the head, no sign of strangulation?'

'Absolutely none.'

'In your opinion, could this have been murder or could it be accidental?'

'Both, Sir Thomas, I have no reason to put one cause above the other. The damage to the bank could have been caused by those viewing the body. All I am saying is that there were heavy indentations on the bank that *could* have been the result of a struggle.'

'Yet there were no signs on the body to indicate he was forcibly held down? No mud in his nostrils? His face was not pushed into the thick clay at the bottom of the pit?'

'No, Sir Thomas. The settling pits, as you know, contain

clay suspended in water. The clay had yet to settle so the water in his lungs and nostril contained clay, but there was no evidence that his face had been pushed into the thicker clay that had already settled.'

'So he could not have been drowned on purpose?'

'That is *not* what I'm saying. A man can drown in one inch of water whether he is held under or not. I'm merely confirming he was not pushed into the clay.'

'Thank you, Dr Guinislake.' Sir Thomas nodded, turning to the jury. 'Gentlemen, you will have to decide whether Mr Drew's death was accidental death or whether it was death by misadventure – and by that we mean Mr Drew drowned as a result of doing something he should not have been doing or was participating in something that could put himself in mortal danger. Or you must decide whether his death by drowning was a wilful murder by person or persons unknown – or whether his death was death by suicide.' He waited for each of them to nod their heads in understanding. 'Dr Guinislake has told us this is a clear case of death by drowning but the question you must now consider very carefully is *why* did Mr Drew drown? You will now hear the evidence of the witnesses. If you want to ask a question or if you want the accused to answer any questions, you must raise your right hand. Is that understood?'

Sir Thomas turned to the constable. 'Call the first witness.'

The constable cleared his voice. 'I call on Mr Richard Sellick.'

Chapter Thirty-five

Mr Sellick rose from his chair, mounting the steps slowly to take his oath. *The truth, the whole truth, and nothing but the truth, so help me God.* I hardly recognized the man who had sat in such threadbare clothes, eating Mrs Perys' meal with such a voracious appetite. He looked so different, his short grey hair concealed under a brown wig, his new clothes witness to his new prosperity. Only his complexion remained pinched and grey, even more sallow under the darkness of his new wig.

Sir Thomas did not look up. 'Mr Sellick, you were witness to the quarrel, I believe? Please tell the jury *exactly* what you saw and heard. Take your time, be explicit.'

Richard Sellick cleared his throat, glancing at his sheet of paper propped against the Bible. He was a short man, the lectern higher than comfortable. 'I am Richard Sellick, lately clerk to the White China Company but recently clay speculator an' investor in Sir James Polcarrow's clay mines. I have acquired the lease for the top clay sett and it's my good fortune to have struck the finest clay. I have been granted the Wedgwood contract, which I believe speaks for itself, gentlemen. There's none finer clay than mine. I used to live in Polperro but now I live in Porthcarrow – to oversee my interests an' run my business.' He cleared his throat. 'On the night of Saturday third of July I was witness to an argument between Mr Drew and the prisoner – at the Sailor's Rest in Porthcarrow.'

'And what time was that?'

'At about eleven o'clock at night.'

'Continue, please, Mr Sellick. Don't wait to be prompted.'

'The inn was full – must've been round twenty or more to witness the argument. They was sat alone in the corner, talkin', then before we knew it, they'd begun to argue. It was getting' fierce an' I looked round, wantin' to know why such a big man would pick on such a slight man like Mr Drew. It weren't right to watch.'

'In what way wasn't it right to watch?'

'The prisoner is a big man in the prime of health but Mr Drew was slight an' given to rheumy eyes. Was like a bear picking on a mouse.'

'So the argument turned aggressive? You heard the prisoner make threats that made you uneasy?'

'Very uneasy. Yes, it turned aggressive, yet as people stopped to listen, the prisoner seemed to clam up. Said he'd finish it outside. Said he didn't want people hearin' what he was saying. That's when they took it outside.'

'And you followed them?'

'I did, Sir Thomas. Mr Drew was a neighbour an' I was

313

getting' to know him very well. I knew he'd not stand a chance with a man like that.' He glared at William. 'The prisoner's a troublemaker, known for fightin', an' I was worried for Mr Drew's safety.'

'What was their quarrel about?'

'The prisoner was threatening him, tellin' him he was no good at his job. Tellin' him he should resign. An' we all know why. William Cotterell wants that job. Dead man's shoes – that's what this is all about. Mr Drew was in the way an' William Cotterell wanted his job – that's why he killed him. He's not been long in Porthcarrow but he's not liked – he's known to stir up trouble. He's sly an' deceitful. He killed him all right.'

'You saw William Cotterell acting aggressively to Mr Drew? Did you see him throw a punch at Mr Drew? When they took their argument outside, what did you see and hear?'

'Threats – terrible threats. Said it weren't over. Said he wouldn't let it lie. As God's my witness, said *he was comin' after him.*'

I gasped along with everyone else. It was the way he said it, the venom in his voice. It was as if he hated William. Behind me, the murmur rose to horrified shouts. Billy grasped my arm. 'That's never true. William wouldn't kill anyone.'

William was staring straight ahead, slowly shaking his head. Billy looked like he was going to cry and I fought down my own rising sob. The jury were also shaking their heads, their mouths clamped in firm disapproval. Sir Thomas held up his hand for silence. 'Thank you, Mr Sellick. Have we any questions from the jury?'

A man nodded. He looked like a farmer. He was middle-aged with a ruddy complexion, his jacket discarded, his brown waistcoat buttoned over a white shirt. 'I've two questions, Sir Thomas. Had the two men been drinkin' and could we 'ave some clarity on the nature of this argument? It seems important to know what led the accused to murder.'

Sir Thomas nodded. 'Mr Sellick, in your view, was Mr Cotterell worse for drink – had they both been drinking?'

'I believe so, Sir Thomas. It was late an' both had several tankards in front of them.'

Sir Thomas turned to William. 'Mr Cotterell, explain your argument. The jury would like to know what your quarrel was about and why it ended in murder.'

William nodded, his voice gentle, almost humorous. 'Our quarrel did not lead to *my* murdering Mr Drew. Someone else might have held him under the water but it was not me.' He sounded so much calmer than I felt. My heart was thumping, my hands sweating, and I reached for my fan.

'Explain your quarrel with Mr Drew to the jury, Mr Cotterell, and keep a civil tongue, if you please.'

'Begging the jury's pardon, but I'm not at liberty to explain my quarrel – it was between myself and Mr Drew and I'm afraid it must remain so.'

Sir Thomas slammed his hand against the table amidst the cries of shock. He looked horrified, his voice thin with rage. 'Mr Cotterell, don't play games with this court – perhaps you do not realize that your life is in the balance. You were heard, quite clearly, by a respectable man, who is *under oath*, saying you were coming after Mr Drew. Is that not a threat to murder?'

'Mr Sellick speaks the truth. I did say those words and I meant them in anger. But I did not mean I was coming after him *physically*. What Mr Sellick omits to recall is that I also told Mr Drew to go to Sir James *first thing in the morning* and I meant to leave him in no doubt that I would be coming after him to make sure he did.' He looked at the jury. 'My freedom may lie in the balance, but not my life. Not yet. *If* this leads to a trial for murder, then of course I will furnish the exact details of my quarrel with Mr Drew.'

I could not believe it. William was speaking so calmly yet he had every man in the room booing and hissing, yelling obscenities. Sir Thomas Treffry drew a deep breath, his sudden fury making his cheeks redden. 'I suggest you tell us now.'

William squared his shoulders. 'My concerns do not belong in the public domain. With great respect, Sir Thomas, my concerns are between myself and Sir James Polcarrow. It is his harbour and his town.'

'You murdered Mr Drew for his job, didn't you, Mr Cotterell?'

William shook his head, his hair ruffling, losing its tight hold. 'What would be the point? It was only a matter of time before Mr Drew was dismissed – I had no need to murder the man.' The room erupted, everyone shouting, yelling at William, and I found myself blushing at his words. What was he doing, talking like that?

'You are very arrogant, Mr Cotterell.' Sir Thomas' thin lips remained tight with disapproval. 'Arrogant and rather too sure of yourself. Believe me, you are doing nothing to endear yourself to the jury, nor any other man in this room. You are not helping your cause.'

William waited for the whistles to stop. 'With great respect, Sir Thomas, engineers have no need to be endearing – they have need only to be accurate. They need to calibrate and be exact, not cut corners and take risks. Livelihoods depend on their calculations. The safety of men, women and children depends on their experience and skilled reckoning.' He shook his head, his hands held in front of him. 'Engineers build viaducts and waterways. They draw the plans for harbours, locks and lighthouses. They build and maintain engines to drain the water from mines. Believe me, I've never sought to be *endearing* and never shall. I seek only to be accurate. Large investments fall or stand on good engineering. Who would you rather trust, an engineer who smiles and promises all is well or an engineer who scowls and argues all is not well?'

A few of the jurors raised their eyebrows, some shrugging their shoulders. They had obviously not expected William to speak so passionately and my heart swelled with pride.

'He's right,' whispered Billy. 'Sir James has invested heavily in his harbour. William says if his lock fails, the whole town will fail. Sir James trusted Mr Drew...he was relying on him. If the lock fails, he's likely to go bankrupt.'

Sir Thomas raised his hand for silence, his finger pointing at the jury. 'Mark that down well. The accused has refused to answer the juror's question – a downright refusal to disclose the nature of the argument.' He looked furious. 'Call the next witness and I must remind the accused to keep a civil tongue in his head. I will not tolerate insolence.'

The constable looked equally furious. 'I call Mr Hellyar,' he shouted.

The embroidery on Mr Hellyar's silk waistcoat matched the gold eyeglass he held up to survey the crowd. Rings glinted on his fingers, his stout belly filling the stand. I remembered the way his eyes rested on my bosom and my dislike spiralled. 'I am Mr Robert Hellyar — Viscount Vallenforth's chief assayer of tin.'

Billy's frown matched mine. 'Why's he been called?'

'That's what I was thinking. Has he even met William?'

Sir Thomas put down his glass of water, fanning himself with a large wad of paper. 'Mr Hellyar, you know the accused from old, I believe?'

'I do, sir, although it has never been my misfortune to meet the man in person…but his reputation goes before him. He is a rioter and a looter. He is in contempt of the law and wanted by the courts. He's banned from the mines for sedition and violence and has an injunction against him, forbidding him near any engine house.' His voice was strangely high pitched, certainly angry. He pointed his finger at William. 'Behind that soft voice there's aggression and danger. Don't be fooled by his smart appearance and false manners.'

'You believe him to have murdered Mr Drew? Explain yourself, Mr Hellyar.'

'The man's arrogant and wilful and a danger to men and women.' His voice rose above the taunts and whistles. 'He believes himself above the law — as indeed, we've all just witnessed. You saw his contempt for your authority. Yes, I believe him to have murdered Mr Drew because it is my firm belief – and the belief of many – that he has murdered, not once, but twice. His first victim was Mr Phillip Randall, late steward of Pendenning Hall.'

Sudden dizziness made me grab Billy's arm. It was so hot and stuffy, the tobacco smoke choking me. Billy held me upright but Sir James had heard us and turned round, getting up from his chair to usher me towards it. I sank gratefully down, leaning forward to stop myself fainting. To accuse William of murdering Phillip Randall! That was outrageous.

Sir Thomas stopped fanning himself. 'And your evidence, please, Mr Hellyar? Speak slowly so the jury can hear.'

'I have six names – no, more than six – on this list. All of them waiting and willing to swear *on their lives* that they saw William Cotterell assault Phillip Randal two days before he was found drowned in the river.' He had hard eyes, a stern, unforgiving face. He nodded to the jury, his sideburns insufficient to hide the wobble in his chins. 'In full daylight, William Cotterell assaulted Phillip Randal – no provocation, no reason, just sheer, wilful aggression and determination to stir up riot. Then he went back and finished the job...'

The noise was deafening, loud shouts and jeers rising to fever pitch. Mr Hellyar kept nodding his head, his lips pursed. Beside me, Matthew Reith rose to his feet, his hand firmly in the air. Sir Thomas nodded. 'You wish to say something, Mr Reith?'

'I do, Sir Thomas. This encounter was *two* days before the lynching. *Two* days, gentlemen. I believe it's obvious to every person in this room that this accusation of a second murder is based on speculation and rumour. And as such, it should be dismissed as hearsay. It will never stand in court, as well you all know. Mr Randall may well have been lynched but he was alive and well after Mr Cotterell left him...Indeed, he was alive and well two days after the encounter of which we speak. I ask that the jury disregard this testimony as unreliable rumour and speculation.'

Sir Thomas once more waved his hand in dismissal. 'Continue your evidence, Mr Hellyar. Please stick to facts. Why is William Cotterell in contempt of the law and why is he wanted by the courts?'

Beads of sweat glistened on Mr Hellyar's forehead. He stared at Matthew Reith. 'William Cotterell has a subpoena served against him and his arrogant refusal to appear in court is an act of contumacy – he shirks every law by his refusal to attend. Well, he can't shirk *this* court. He's a dangerous agitator and he's been caught at last. He incites riot. He's aggressive and dangerous – the man behind the tinners' riot. He's a man with no scruples.' He flicked the lace at his sleeve. 'I was asked to give a reference as to his character and I've done so. The jury can disregard my testament as *hearsay* if they wish, but they must live with their consciences. My conscience is clear.'

The clerk shuffled some papers, leaning over to Dr Guinislake who nodded in agreement. Sir Thomas sat fanning himself, glaring at Matthew Reith as he raised his hand again. 'You have another question, Mr Reith?'

'I have, Sir Thomas. Could we please seek confirmation

from Mr Cotterell as to whether this allegation of assault is true? I believe the jury is owed an explanation from the accused.'

Mr Hellyar stormed angrily back to his seat, a waft of stale tobacco and hair grease trailing after him. I glanced at William. He had been shaking his head slowly during Mr Hellyar's testimony and our eyes caught. I tried to smile.

'Is there any truth in this allegation, Mr Cotterell?' asked Sir Thomas.

Chapter Thirty-six

William's reply was instant. 'There is, Sir Thomas, but I assaulted the man's whip, not the man himself. I merely took the whip out of his hands and snapped it over my knee.'

Sir Thomas held his eyepiece to his eye. 'Assault is assault, whether to a man or to a man's property. Why did you assault Mr Randall?'

'Because he was whipping a vagrant and it was not to my taste.'

'And so you instigated a riot and had the man lynched?'

'Not at all, Sir Thomas, I merely told him starving people needed help, not cruelty, and I turned my back and walked away.'

'You snapped his whip – is that not provocation enough? You had no reason to be on Pendenning land, you were trespassing like everyone else.'

'I was looking for the brother and sister of a friend of mine – a young vagrant separated from his family three years ago. I had previously written to Mr Randall requesting permission and my request had been granted. I was there on legitimate business but I acted under provocation.' He hesitated, his frown deepening. 'No decent man can stand by and watch a man being whipped because his only crime is to be homeless and starving.'

'And your contempt for the court?'

'I hold no contempt for the court. I was on my way to court only I was waylaid and never reached there.'

A hoot of laugher echoed through the room. 'What delayed you, Mr Cotterell?'

The corners of William's mouth lifted in a slight smile. 'I was delayed by a group of thugs. They wanted me silenced as I believe others do. I only just survived.'

Sir Thomas drummed his fingers on the armrest of his chair, nodding at the constable who wiped his brow with his sleeve, calling for silence. He went unheard so he rang his bell. Another nod from Sir Thomas and he shouted, 'I call on Mrs Burrow.'

Mrs Burrow stood up, her hands fumbling with the cloak on her lap, and I took it from her, smiling in encouragement. She looked round, as if searching the crowd, but my spirits were soaring. William was honourable and upright. Surely everyone saw that? Her evidence would clear him and his ordeal would be over. The poor lady looked flustered, her ample bosom heaving as she reached the top of the stand. She was about fifty, her greying hair tied neatly in a bun beneath her straw bonnet. She held her handkerchief to her mouth, coughing quietly. 'I'm sorry…Mrs *Edith* Burrow, widow of the late Mr Charles Burrow, clerk to the weighing room.'

Sir Thomas looked up from his papers. 'You run a respectable lodging house, I believe, where the accused man has been staying? The accused has, himself, asked that you give a reference as to his character. I believe he was only with you a short while?' Sir Thomas resumed his slow fanning, his one eye remaining shut, the other glancing across at the jury.

Mrs Burrow was obviously scared, her eyes darting to the jury. 'I hardly know Mr Cotterell, though I can tell you he was always very neat and tidy…He never made a fuss…he mended the pump in the yard when I thought 'twas dried up.' She was talking very quickly, nervously clutching her handkerchief in her hands. 'It weren't dried up, though, it were seized up…Mr Cotterell took it to pieces an' made it pump again.' She glanced briefly at William, holding her handkerchief up to her nose. 'There's not much more I can tell. I don't mix with my lodgers on account of them gettin' familiar.'

'What can you tell us of the night in question, Mrs Burrow? We know the accused was out until after eleven o'clock but can you tell us when he came back to his lodgings? What were his movements that night? We've been told by Dr Guinislake that a muddy skirmish may have taken place. What were Mr Cotterell's boots like when he returned?'

She shook her head, her voice rising. 'I don't rightly know …I went to bed…my lodgers come an' go. Sometimes they arrive on a late tide, sometimes they leave early…I can't always be up an' I must've gone to bed…I've no recollection of his whereabouts until they came the next mornin' and arrested him…' I stared at her in horror; her words were making no sense. 'He might've been out all night or he might've been in bed...I'm sorry, that's all I can remember...'

She was lying, blatantly lying. A scream rose in my throat and I fought against it. I wanted to yell at her, to run up and shake her. She was lying. She knew full well William's boots were on the rack. I turned round, reaching up to Sir James, clutching his sleeve to grab his attention. 'She's lying...she *was* awake...' I tried to keep my voice low but panic gripped me. 'She was there when Mr Berryman arrived. He told me she was wearing *a becoming nightcap* and *embroidered velvet slippers* – she knows full well William was in his room.' My heart was hammering, a desperate plea in my voice.

Matthew Reith saw my panic and slipped to my side, kneeling on the floor in front of me. 'He told you that... those were his exact words...?'

'Yes...she *must* have seen the rack was full. Someone as particular as her would always think to look...' I was furious. Furious and scared. How could she lie like that? Matthew Reith urged me on. 'Her lodgers know where the key is kept but that night she was still awake...' William was watching me. So was Mrs Burrow. The woman was a liar and the court must know.

Matthew Reith sprang to his feet and Sir Thomas sighed. He sat back, crossing his arms as he addressed the jury. His eyebrow rose. 'Do not be put off by having one of our foremost barristers glare at you so severely. Your questions are as valid as his. I may have a reputation for being curt and disagreeable but I believe in justice. Speak out if you have a mind.

325

Ask questions. Once you've made your decision, there's no going back. You have *another* question, Mr Reith?'

Matthew Reith smiled at the jury. 'Believe me, gentlemen, I've no desire to intimidate. If I scowl and look severe it's because I seek the truth, as do you.' He turned to Mrs Burrow. 'I believe, Mrs Burrow, you run one of the best boarding houses in Porthcarrow – if not *the* best. Please, don't be coy because your reputation is well known. I believe you turn away more people than you take, such is your desire to keep things genteel.'

Mrs Burrow seemed more nervous than before, glancing back at the crowd. 'I do, sir. I'm very fussy with the likes of who I take.'

'And yet you took Mr Cotterell and you told him the secret place where you keep your key?'

'I did, sir...'

'Your lodgers come and go, leaving you free to retire to bed – you do not always wait for their return, so you must have trusted Mr Cotterell. It must mean you had no qualms about his character and believed yourself quite safe in his company?'

She looked like a rabbit caught in a trap. 'Yes, I did...'

'Splendid, Mrs Burrow. I may well ask to stay at your establishment next time I come. I'm up all hours and to be able to come and go as I please would be very helpful. Not least because of how clean and tidy you keep the place. I believe no boots past the kitchen door. Am I right?'

The flowers on Mrs Burrow's straw hat bounced as she nodded. Two bright plums shone on her cheeks. Mr Reith smiled, turning to Sir Thomas. 'Mrs Burrow may not remember seeing William Cotterell's clean boots on the rack that night but I have the sworn affidavit of another guest who can testify to that very thing. A man willing and eager to attend any court to swear that he saw William Cotterell's clean boots in their correct place at half past eleven on the night of the third of July.'

He smiled at Mrs Burrow who stared back at him open mouthed. 'Mr Johnathan Berryman was lodging with Mrs Burrow on the night of the third July. He is the foremost agent to Mr Spode of Stoke and is, I believe, well known to Mr Sellick. He is a highly respected man,' his voice hardened, 'and the evidence he offers is wholly irrefutable. It proves Mr Cotterell went straight home after the quarrel. There was no time for him to follow Mr Drew up to the settling pit and no time to drown him. Mr Cotterell went straight to his bed after their quarrel.' I caught the sudden hope in William's eyes and had to force myself from crying.

Matthew Reith turned to the crowd with both palms in the air. The silence was instant as his voice turned to steel. 'But it does surprise me, Mrs Burrow, that you have no recollection of whether Mr Cotterell's boots were on the rack or whether you were up…or had gone to bed, because Mr Berryman is quite insistent that you were there when he arrived. You have, I believe, a very fetching nightcap and rather delightful embroidered slippers. Perhaps, you might show them to the court if Mr Cotterell gets falsely accused because your memory has played you false.'

Shivers ran down my spine and I grasped the pressed clover to my heart.

'Ye did it, Elly. Ye did it. They've got to clear him now.'

I hardly heard Billy. The jury began talking across each other, nodding, frowning, shaking their heads, but I kept my eyes locked on William. He looked so proud and dignified and my heart burned with pride. I loved him so much it hurt me to breathe. He had stood up for himself and his beliefs. He had not let himself be intimidated or bullied. He had kept his pride, his manners obvious for everyone to see. He was better than all of them. He was noble and honourable and my body ached with a fierce, overwhelming love that felt like pain.

The court was settling, but Matthew Reith was still on his feet, the forefinger of his right hand raised in the air. Sir Thomas breathed deeply. 'Another question, Mr Reith?'

'I ask that we hear the testimony of one further witness. I believe the jury needs to hear this evidence before they make their decision.'

There was a commotion at the back of the room and everyone turned. Mr Hearne was making slow progress through the crowd. He bowed to Matthew Reith. 'Mr Hearne, good, you made it. I was worried there for a moment.'

Both men nodded thoughtfully, exchanging hurried words, and I turned round, expecting to see Ruth or Nathan. They were nowhere to be seen, just the respectable figure of Tobias Hearne, dressed in his minister's clothes with the long white bands hanging from his neck. I had never spoken to him but liked him on sight. He was a tall man of stocky build with a ruddy complexion, his forehead creased by years of concern.

Matthew Reith waited while the constable called for silence. 'I would like the jury to hear the testimony of Mr Tobias Hearne, lay preacher of Porthcarrow – a man known to many for his compassion and charity.'

Tobias Hearne took the stand, towering above the jury as he swore his oath, his voice soft and compassionate. 'I believe 'tis my duty to speak – though what I've to say may offend many. I've a difficult task ahead of me, a difficult path to tread. By seekin' to defend one man, I may be the ruin of several women and I'd like the court to know that I don't do this lightly.' He took a deep breath.

The jury leaned forward, trying to catch his words, and Sir Thomas put his hand to his ear. 'Speak up, if you please, Mr Hearne.'

Tobias Hearne coughed. 'There's no way to dress this up so I'll speak plainly – what I have to say is that Mr Drew sought *comfort* in the linhay as many men do. He was a regular there, so to speak...an' I know this, because I take food to the women at night. My wife comes with me...to try an' make them change their ways. She's seen Mr Drew there many a time...an' so have I. 'Tis only right the court should know.'

A member of the jury stood up, raising his hand in obvious indignation. 'It's not right. It's improper – you've no right to smear a man's reputation after he's dead.' He shook his head vigorously. 'Speakin' ill of a man who can't defend himself!'

He sat down amidst nods and murmurs and even Tobias Hearne nodded. 'I agree with ye, sir. It's as distasteful fer me as it is fer ye to speak ill of the dead, but I'm not here to judge my fellow men and nor is anyone else in this room.

Only God needs to know a man's business an' I'd not be tellin' ye this if I didn't think an innocent man might hang. Ye see, ye have to pass close to the settlin' pits to get to the linhay – it's dark an' the way's slippery, even more so after the rain or when a ship stays overnight an' plenty go that way. No one goes there by day – it's only at night that the men go up an' there's little or no protection. It's easy to lose yer balance, 'specially after a drink or two.'

Sir Thomas leaned forward. 'Are you saying, Mr Hearne, that a man with poor eyesight might slip and fall?'

'I am, Sir Thomas.'

'And you can swear Mr Drew was a regular visitor to this so-called *linhay*.'

'I can, sir, and plenty alongside me, though I'd like to keep their names back fer want of privacy.'

'Thank you, Mr Hearne. You can step down now.' Sir Thomas reached forward with one last shuffle of his papers. 'Gentlemen of the jury, you've heard all the evidence in this inquest and you must now consider your verdict and come to an agreement. It is a quarter to eleven. This session will resume at eleven o'clock. You may step into another room or you may remain where you are. You have a quarter of an hour to reach your decision.'

Chapter Thirty-seven

The jury nodded their heads one moment, shaking them another. Hunched in the close confines of their bench, a number were getting quite noisy but most seemed in agreement. I watched Mrs Burrow force her way through the crowd and, though I was still reeling at her deception, I was even more shocked at the thought of Mr Drew in the linhay. Mrs Perys had foreseen such an accident; she had spoken so severely yet her prediction had come true.

The constable rang his bell. Sir Thomas and his companions resumed their seats and in the sudden silence I sat clutching the four-leaf clover to my heart, hardly daring to breathe. Sir Thomas cleared his throat. 'Gentlemen of the jury, have you or have you not reached your verdict?'

The florid farmer who had spoken out before stood up. 'We have, Sir Thomas.'

'And was Mr Drew's drowning, death by accident, death by misadventure or death by suicide?'

'It was death by misadventure, sir.'

'And was that death by misadventure due to a person or persons unknown or was it due to the actions of Mr Drew himself?'

'Due to the actions of Mr Drew himself.'

'Thank you, gentlemen,' Sir Thomas's thin voice rose, 'and what, therefore, is your verdict on the guilt or otherwise of Mr Cotterell? Is William Cotterell guilty or not guilty of the murder of Mr Josiah Drew?'

'Not guilty.'

Sir Thomas reached for his pocket watch. 'Thank you, gentlemen.' He scowled at William. 'You may release the prisoner. Mr Cotterell, you are free to go.'

Tears streamed down my cheeks and I did not care who saw them. The noise was deafening, the air unbreathable and I needed to get out. I must not faint. The pungent smoke was thick and nauseating and I needed fresh air. Billy grabbed my hand, helping me through the rowdy crowd, and I stood blinking in the sunshine, gulping down the fresh air. A movement caught my eye, a red shawl. 'Billy, that's Mrs Burrow – no wonder she's running.'

We were drawn to watch her, pulling back against the wall as a man stepped forward. 'Billy, stop. That's Nathan. He must've been in the court.'

He seemed to be offering Mrs Burrow comfort and fury filled me. She had lied to the court – she deserved censure not comfort, yet there she was, shaking her head and crying. Nathan crossed the road, ushering her beside him and they disappeared from view. 'He knows her, Billy...it must have

been him she was looking for…I saw her searching for someone in the court.'

We walked hurriedly back to the carriage and Joseph
opened the door. 'Here, let me help you,' he said, letting
down the steps. 'A very good outcome – Sir James will be
pleased.'

I was grateful to hide, pulling down the windows to
circulate much needed air. The crowd was spilling from
the Market House, pigs squealing in their pens and hens
squawking in their baskets. Pie sellers were shouting their
prices; there were barrows of cockles, baskets of eggs. Sir
James and Matthew Reith were talking to a group of men
but as William walked through the door, they broke free
from the crowd to stand either side of him. Sir James pointed
to his carriage, and just one glimpse of his face made my
heart sink.

'Seems like Matthew Reith hasn't quite finished with
yer Mr Cotterell yet,' Joseph said. 'Now the questioning's
really goin' to start!' He smiled and winked at Billy. 'Best get
atop, lad.'

They looked so severe, William sitting next to me, Sir James
and Matthew Reith facing him as stern as any judge. Matthew
Reith could quell a witness with his frown and this scowl
frightened me. Once had I seen the softer side to him, sitting
in the back of the church with Mrs Munroe and Sam during
his marriage to Alice Polcarrow. He had looked so happy
then, his gaunt face with its severe lines relaxed and smiling,

yet now his frown and dark thoughts filled the carriage with mistrust. It was obvious he did not like William.

Even Sir James sounded unusually cold. 'You withheld the nature of your argument with Mr Drew because you expect us to pay you? Forgive me, Mr Cotterell, but Sir Thomas was right – your arrogance does you no favours.'

William held Sir James' stare, a slight shrug to his shoulders. 'My arrogance is my livelihood, Sir James. You paid a substantial sum of money for Mr Drew's plans yet my plans have more merit, therefore they should be worth more – but I hope you don't doubt that my first concern was the reputation of your harbour. Just the slightest hint that your lock might silt up and your investment would lie in jeopardy. Every farthing you've spent would be wasted. You'd be back to ships having to beach in low tide and you'd lose the lucrative deal you have with Viscount Vallenforth. Mr Lilly will withdraw his interest – he'll not invest in a harbour that dries at low tide.'

'I'm fully aware of that, Mr Cotterell. It's whether to believe you that concerns us. How do we know you speak the truth?'

'Either Mr Drew was not the experienced engineer he claimed to be or he was a frightened man. Our conversation went nowhere. He refused to be drawn when I accused him of using non-hydraulic lime. I told him the lock would silt up if the leats weren't dug deeper and he accused me of meddling.' He smiled. 'I did say I was coming after him. He was to talk to you the very next morning or I would go to you with my fears.'

Sir James raised his eyebrows. Matthew Reith clamped tight his mouth and I felt ripped in two. Matthew Reith had just cleared William of murder, yet William was showing no gratitude. But why should he? He was right. He had the knowledge they needed and they knew it.

'I mean to salvage your harbour, Sir James. The irregularities can be put right but the cost will be substantial. Corners have been cut, sub-standard materials used.'

Their eyes locked, each man appraising the other, and fear filled me. I had not seen this side to William, this disregard for order and position, and part of me was horrified; the other part was thrilled and my heart soared. He was speaking like an equal, like he knew he deserved their respect. 'My reputation as a troublemaker lies in the fact that I'm not one to hold my tongue. If I believe something's wrong, I stick my neck out and say so. I'm not begging you for a job and I never will. Engineers are in short supply…my last wage was a guinea a week and there's plenty left who'll still employ me.'

Matthew Reith had heard enough. 'You're banned from the mines, Mr Cotterell…you've a subpoena against you. You're in contempt of court…hardly the attributes of a man Sir James – or *anyone* – would want to employ. Can you furnish Sir James with references?'

'No. I'm sorry I can't. There's not one man to speak on my behalf. Except Mr Smeaton – I learned everything from him, yet he lies buried these past three years.'

'How very convenient.'

William shrugged off Matthew Reith's sarcasm with another smile. 'Sir James deserves better, Mr Reith. Either

Mr Drew was incompetent or he has been lining his own pockets. I've drawn up a list of what needs to be done – it's a long list and I warn you, it's not easy reading.'

We were on the cliffs above Porthcarrow, looking down at the lock. Masts crammed behind the locked gates, the huge clay wagons hurtling down the hill. I felt sick with nerves. Yet why should William not talk to them like this? Why should he touch his forelock and give them everything for free? After all, I would not give away my gowns and Matthew Reith charged fees for his expertise. Sir James was staring out of the window, a frown furrowing his forehead, yet he did not look cross. He looked deep in thought and pride swelled within me.

William's voice was gentle. 'I'm not insensible to what I owe you, Sir James. You have gone out of your way to help me. I don't want you to think me an ungrateful wretch. My fighting talk is for my work alone…I'm sincerely grateful for your kindness and generosity in lending me these clothes – and for providing my food this last week. I'll get the clothes laundered and returned to you as soon as possible. If I owe you money, I can repay you as soon as I get my belongings back.'

'You owe me no money. The clothes are Joseph's – you can return them at your leisure. I was once falsely charged for murder, Mr Cotterell, as no doubt you know. No man will suffer the same injustice if I can help it. *Innocent until proven guilty*.' His voice softened. 'My mother-in-law speaks very highly of you, Mr Cotterell, and she is a woman I both trust and admire.'

'She is a remarkable lady – most would judge me guilty on my name alone.'

Sir James shrugged his shoulders, a half-smile on his lips. 'Your reputation certainly does you no favours. Your *confrontation* with Viscount Vallenforth made for interesting reading but I have my own reasons for disliking the man. He and his friend Sir Charles Cavendish have tried hard to steal my land. They want my clay. The court cases are only just over.'

The carriage slowed, the horses almost coming to a stop, and we began edging alongside the clay pits, inching past the wagons laden with sawn planks. Poles lay stacked in piles, the men busy digging fences to mark out the new setts. Heaps of spoil lay untidily along the road, the same white dust covering everything. Across the hill, the maidens stood scraping the sand off the dried blocks, their lively chatter reaching us on the wind.

William frowned. 'Sir James, if you'll excuse me, I need to speak plainly. I've no proof – and I believe Mr Reith would discount this as not being proper evidence – but there's something that concerns me...'

Sir James looked annoyed. 'More concerns?'

'A serious concern – I've written to a friend of mine who's a chemist and I've not yet received his reply but I believe someone's putting blue dye into the lower settling pit. If I'm right, this dye has the effect of whitening the clay. It would take time...but I believe there's been sufficient time for the effect to take hold...'

'What?' Sir James looked astonished. 'Someone's been

altering the clay to make it whiter? Is this possible? A blue dye would surely turn the clay blue.'

'That's why I've written to my friend. It's something I overheard but I'm not a chemist...'

'On what grounds do you make this claim?'

'On the grounds of seeing drops of blue liquid in that privy – and a man acting as if he didn't want to be seen.' He pointed to the hut where we had seen the man run in such haste and I bit my tongue, fighting back my urge to speak. Yet why not tell them? Mr Sellick had spoken against William so why should I not speak against him? I drew a deep breath, fighting my nerves.

'Richard Sellick had a dark stain on his breeches that day... and he didn't go to chapel. He won the Wedgwood contract yet I remember Nathan saying there was rust in his clay...it was at Mrs Perys'...we were having luncheon...' I could not believe I had spoken so fiercely, yet I could not help myself.

'Rust?' Sir James' brows contracted. 'We lease our setts as measured plots of land. The plots are randomly selected so no prospective leaseholder can claim we've favoured one man over another. Some of these setts may prove worthless... some may have no clay, some the best clay. Rust is not a good sign, but no one can be sure until they dig six feet underground.'

'And yet the Wedgwood clay agent has chosen Richard Sellick's clay? They must believe it to be the best.'

'Indeed, Miss Liddicot,' replied Sir James. He nodded to William. 'We'll set a watch, see if anyone goes near that privy.' The rise in his eyebrows was followed by a slight lift at the corners of his mouth. Definitely a half-smile. 'Is there anything else I should know about my clay or about my harbour, Mr Cotterell?'

'Everything will be in my report, Sir James – I can have it to you by the beginning of next week.' Matthew Reith sucked in his gaunt cheeks yet William took no heed, smiling broadly now. 'But there is something else I'd like to talk to you about – it concerns your father's old mine.'

James Polcarrow's laugh filled the carriage. 'You have ideas for my derelict mine, have you? You know it's been shut these twenty-five years, Mr Cotterell? Is there no stopping you?'

William brushed his hand through his hair, untidy curls spilling over his face. 'I believe there could still be copper down there. I don't like tattle and I never engage in it, but I've heard talk in the taverns. Some say I'm contrary, but when I hear men saying something's worthless, it gets me thinking the opposite. And all this talk of rust in the clay… well, some say that's evidence of copper.'

The engine house loomed in front of us and Sir James pulled down the window. 'A moment please, Joseph.' We stopped with a jolt. 'A few minutes…'

Sir James opened the door, smiling at Billy who pulled down the steps and we stood looking up at the old engine house with its sturdy granite walls and boarded-up windows. Swallows swooped from their nests and began flying around us. Sir James' voice was full of regret. 'My grandfather opened the mine and it broke my father's heart to close it. It's named after my mother – Wheal Elizabeth. The old engine's been dismantled and sold.'

'A Newcomen engine?'

Sir James nodded. 'They tried everything to keep the mine in profit.'

William held his hand against the glare of the sun, looking up to survey the building. 'It's idle talk, Sir James, but it's doing the rounds. They're saying there's nothing but a tobacco pouch worth of copper left in the mine, but why this sudden talk?'

Sir James shook his head. 'We've been through it with a toothpick. There's nothing we haven't tried.'

'No, I meant why this sudden talk that the mine's worthless – after all these years? There's more talk, too. There's talk of men seeing a green glow – a strange luminosity in a certain light. I'm a miner's son, Sir James, and all my life I've heard talk of mines being haunted or moors having the light. Tarnished copper turns green and the water reflects it. Many say rust indicates a copper seam.' His voice hardened. 'Others know that too.'

'And if they spread rumours that the mine's worthless, those with any shares left in it will panic and sell.'

'Precisely. It's not my business to know how many shares you still own but if I were you, I would hold on to them. Even buy back as many as you can.'

My heart was hammering. William was speaking softly, yet I could tell Sir James was listening. We began walking round the disused buildings; the huge bell was still hanging on its rusty chain, the door boarded up with stout planks. Herbs carpeted the cobbles, the heady scent of thyme crushing beneath our feet. Twenty-five years ago, the mine had scarred the surroundings yet nature had reclaimed her hold; clumps of vetch and thrift grew on the steps, oxeye daisies protruded from the stonework and fluttered in the gutters.

Joseph rushed toward the mine workings. 'Someone's sawn through this chain and eased back this boarding...it must be the vagrants.' He stood by the window, shouting loudly. 'Come out...we'll not harm you. There are barns three miles from here...come out...this is no place to shelter...' He pulled back the loose board, slipping through the window with the agility of a cat. 'There's no one here...but someone's been here...there's a lantern...and the dust's been disturbed.' His voice grew fainter as he walked deeper towards the old shaft and we waited, Sir James obviously in two minds whether to follow.

At last, Joseph came back. 'There's no one there.' He eased himself back through the window. 'The shaft's flooded – it's too dangerous even for vagrants. They've not stayed.'

James Polcarrow nodded. 'See it gets boarded up again. So, Mr Cotterell – a flooded disused mine that no one can make profitable, yet you beg to differ?' If he meant to sound mocking, he failed. We caught the glimmer of hope, if not in his voice, certainly in his eyes.

William put his hand on Billy's shoulder. 'Tell Sir James what's needed, Billy.'

Billy coughed to clear his throat. 'William can build ye an engine that uses *less* coal, Sir James. He knows just how to do it – he's going to separate the condenser and let the steam escape. He's got all sorts of plans, like making the cylinder smaller and bringing it nearer the shaft.'

William cuffed him round the ear. 'No need to tell them everything, lad – we'll keep that to ourselves.' He looked up, his eyes searching each of ours in turn. 'That goes for everyone present – these plans are to be kept to ourselves. My engine will use less coal and be cheaper to run...It was the high cost of coal that made your father stop...not the lack of copper.'

Billy seemed so much taller, a youth not a boy, and I knew I was losing him to the best man possible. I thought my heart would burst. He coughed once again, with no trace of a smile. 'Will thinks you'll need a deeper adit, Sir James – one that drains the water right down to the sea. It'll be the biggest drain anyone's ever seen.'

Sir James looked amused, his usual composure thrown to the wind. 'And how else do you intend to spend my money, Billy?'

Billy smiled, allowing himself a quick glance at William. 'Will thinks you'll need *two* engines, Sir James – one to pump the water out an' one to bring the copper to the surface.'

Sir James Polcarrow rested his hand on Billy's shoulder. 'You honestly believe this mine could prove profitable, Mr Cotterell?'

He had asked him like an equal and my heart flooded with pride. 'Under copper, there's usually tin. Copper or tin – either way, I believe you should buy back as many shares as you can – before Viscount Vallenforth and his consortium grab them all. I think it must be them spreading these rumours. They wanted your clay, perhaps they want your copper, as well.'

Matthew Reith was not smiling. 'Not one person *alive* and willing to give you a reference? Not *one* single person? Do you think us so short-sighted, Mr Cotterell?'

The wind blew William's hair, ruffling his thick black curls. He shrugged his shoulders. 'There's one or two who might – and there's always my mother!' He put out his hand, taking mine. His hand felt strong, clasping mine so tightly, and a flood of happiness made me force back my tears. 'My engines could be in place and ready to start one minute past midnight on the first of January 1800, but more pressingly, my plans for your harbour could be on your desk in just over a week.' He bowed formally. 'Would you mind if we walked from here? I'm restless from lack of exercise and this fresh air smells so good.'

Matthew Reith was still frowning. 'Who *set about you* and stopped you attending court, Mr Cotterell?' His voice was terse, almost hostile.

William held his eye. 'I was going to court to serve a writ of *scire facias* against Mr Watt and Mr Boulton – I intended to challenge their patent and cause them embarrassment and trouble...and expense. They live in fear of being taken to court and they want men like me silenced...But as to my assailants? I've no proof of their identity – they were unknown to me and I hardly saw them. They could just as easily have been Vallenforth's men. I exposed the terrible conditions his tinners have to endure and he'll never forgive me.' He turned to Billy. 'How's this steam going to escape then, Billy? Have you designed us a valve yet?'

Matthew Reith's voice cut through our laughter. 'I've read

every report of your court cases, Mr Cotterell. *All* of them. I've done extensive searches...' My heart began thumping; his look was so fierce, his tone so chilling. 'The last thing I read was a passenger list on a ship called *The Golden Eagle*. It states quite clearly that you embarked on the fourth of June at six thirty that evening. You caught the evening tide for the East Indies – yet here you stand, Mr Cotterell. *Alive and well.*'

I thought I would be sick. Horrible, horrible man, standing there with his ruthless eyes and wicked tongue. His tone was so accusing, like he was threatening William, like he did not believe him. Sir James looked up in sudden shock and I thought I would cry. But Matthew Reith was not finished, he was still speaking. 'It's my firm belief that Mr Drew did *not* die by misadventure.'

There was accusation in his eyes, terrible recrimination in his voice and nausea ripped my stomach. What did he mean? Hateful, hateful man. I must have looked shocked, I certainly was giddy; I had not eaten all day and the heat of the sun was suddenly overwhelming. William held out his hand, drawing me to the cool of the shade and I tried to quell my fear. I could see William was angry; there was tension in his shoulders, a firm set to his jaw. Was Matthew Reith accusing him of murder? Was that what he meant? I searched William's face, desperate for his answer.

His voice remained respectful. 'As it happened, I *did* board a ship that night but not one of my own choosing. I was beaten to within an inch of my life and sold to the master of a Caspian lugger. I'd be sailing her still had I not jumped ship in time.' His voice hardened. 'My name on that passenger list is a fabrication…I don't doubt for one moment someone boarded that ship in my name, but it wasn't me.' He bowed stiffly. 'And I don't blame you for your caution, Mr Reith. Indeed, I admire you. I even agree with you: either Mr Drew was murdered or he took his own life.' He ran his hand through his hair, loosening his neck tie. 'And if he did take his own life, I must live with the sorrow of believing myself responsible.'

Chapter Thirty-eight

We watched the carriage turn and dip out of sight. Billy was still distraught. 'Why'd he say that? Honest, I used to like him but I hate him now. Why'd he go to all that trouble to clear you an' then be wicked like that?'

William squeezed my hand. 'He's not wicked, Billy. He's a good man and I have every respect for him. He's just cautious, that's all, and quite right too. He's Sir James' attorney and he's keeping a close eye on his affairs. Don't be hard on him.'

'Least Sir James likes you – I know he does. And Joseph likes you…he says you're to drop in for something to eat when you return his clothes.' He was walking sideways, skipping in front of us. 'Jenna's a great cook. She learned everything from Mrs Munroe.'

We turned down the drovers' lane with its muddy hoof prints baking in the sun. Birds were singing in the hedgerow, a blackbird perching on a gatepost. My fear was subsiding, my happiness hard to keep in check. Matthew Reith was only doing his job – underneath his stern exterior, he must admire

William, be grateful he could salvage Sir James' harbour. I had no idea of the salary engineers could command and I wanted to pinch myself. I was in love with such a clever man. He was everything I dreamed of – kind, intelligent, beautifully mannered, and he made me laugh and want to dance. I did not know I could feel such happiness.

He had loosened his neck tie, his jacket slung over his shoulders. He was so strong, his powerful strides making me skip like Billy; the three of us walking in loving companionship, Billy pointing to the birds, me stooping to pick a flower; the pair of us loving William so much.

A fallen tree trunk lay as inviting as any seat and William stopped, his smile turning mischievous. 'Billy, if the first lesson's never to kiss another man's woman and the second is never to kiss a woman who won't kiss you back…what's the third?'

Billy scuffed his shoes in the dried mud. 'Don't know… only kiss a woman if you're goin' to marry her?'

William laughed and my cheeks flashed with fire. 'Maybe …but I was thinking more along the lines: *always take a good lookout when you go for a walk*. See that rock over there? You think you'd see everyone coming?'

A thrill of expectation ran through me and my blush deepened. Billy rushed to the rock and William drew me to the fallen log, spreading his jacket wide for me to sit on. 'Once again, I owe you my life,' he said. His voice was tender, full of love. 'Matthew Reith told me of your trip to Porthcarrow. Without Mr Berryman there would have been very little in my favour.'

'Mrs Burrow was lying. I'm just relieved Mr Berryman wrote back in time.'

'Apparently, he didn't. Matthew Reith wanted me cleared – he knew the evidence would come in time for the trial, so he risked it. But it was a sign of his trust. Don't doubt Matthew Reith, Elowyn. I know he's upset you but he's on our side.'

His hand was so warm, his arm slipping around my shoulder, holding me to him, and I rested my head against his chest, relishing the strength of his embrace. I had never expected to be held like this, to feel so safe and protected. I had been mistrustful of men all my life, expecting the worst, yet how wonderful it felt to be so loved and cherished.

He reached into his pocket, drawing out a silver coin that glinted in the dappled shade. It was a sixpence, rubbed smooth by wear and tear, but as he handed it to me, I saw he had rubbed it free of all marks and had engraved it. There was a heart in the centre, our initials on either side; across the top, *I will love you*, along the bottom, *Every day of my life*. It was so beautiful and I fought back my tears.

'It was almost smooth when I got it, but I rubbed it every chance I got. This last week, I'd plenty of time to finish it.' He laughed softly before his voice turned serious. 'You were never out of my mind, Elowyn – every waking hour, every long hard night only bearable because I thought of you.'

I stared at the smoothed coin, at the small hole he had made for a ribbon. On the back he had engraved a beautiful hedge rose with the year, *1796*. 'It's so beautiful…thank you. I've got just the right ribbon for it…' I could hardly speak.

It was more precious to me than any gold or diamonds, and I fought my desire to reach up and kiss him. Yet why not show him the same love, always holding myself in check?

Our lips touched, his strong arm closing round me. His kiss was gentle and I kissed him back, my love so visceral it felt like pain. I, too, would love him every day of my life. Gwen was right when she had said I would know. I did know, with absolute certainty. He drew away, tracing the contours of my face with his fingers. 'I must make amends with your brother, Elowyn. I'll go to your uncle first thing tomorrow. He has to know how I feel about you...'

My happiness drained from me. William had no idea how much Tom hated him. 'Perhaps not tomorrow.' I said it so quickly he seemed surprised, drawing my chin back as I tried to look away. 'Give me a chance to talk to them first...let me prepare them...I don't want you to have to give Tom another dunking...'

His hazel eyes, his smooth, freshly shaven chin. His black curls, the slight lift to his chin. I would do anything to protect him from Tom. I wanted to tell him about my night on the clifftop; I so, so wanted to tell him but what I knew must never pass my lips. Just one word in the wrong ears and Uncle Thomas, Billy and William would be in danger. Everyone I loved at risk of being silenced by those who sought to teach me a lesson.

'It's all right, Elly,' he said softly, 'I know you're protecting him. They're both in it. I've seen your mother's skirts. I imagine they tried to make you do the same.' His eyes held such love and I thought my heart would break. 'No need to speak of it, I won't tell a soul.' He put his finger against my lips and I kissed it softly. He stood up, holding out his hands to help me up. 'I'm going to find lodgings in Fosse. I'm going to look for somewhere so I can start building an engineering works. I'll take what work I can in the meantime, but I'm staying, Elowyn, and Tom will have to get used to that.' He cupped his hands round his mouth, calling up to Billy.

'You were so kind to go looking for Billy's brother and sister,' I said, watching Billy jump from one tuft of grass to another.

'I was foolish, Elowyn. I may have acted in good faith but I must live with the consequences.'

The sadness in his voice made my heart jolt and I searched his face. 'What consequences? William, you did no harm… you did right…'

'I didn't, Elly,' he said, stooping to pick up his jacket. 'It was an act of aggression and I regret it now. I'm not saying I didn't loathe the man, or still think ill of him, but my action was provocative – I as good as murdered him…'

'Of course you didn't.'

'It set the seeds…it made men think…it was all that was needed to trigger that lynching and I must live with that knowledge. But I swear to you, Elowyn, I'll not be so hot-headed again. I have you and Billy to care for now and I'll never put you in jeopardy.' He reached for my hand, putting it to his lips. 'Since my brother and father's death, I've been consumed with anger, my bitter hatred poisoning my thinking. Matthew Reith's quite right. I channelled all my energies into being a thorn in the side of the authorities.

350

I didn't care who I annoyed – in fact, the more I fought, the better I felt. But James Polcarrow is a good, honourable man. He has all the qualities I admire…and I won't have Billy compare me with him and find me lacking. I want him to be proud of me, and I want you to be proud of me.'

A lump filled my throat and I could hardly find my words. 'I wish I'd known your father…and your brother. But if they were here, William…if they could see you and speak to you, surely they'd want you to put aside your quarrelling…?'

His eyes pierced mine. Hazel eyes that held such love. 'I shall never be able to put aside my quarrel with those who hold life so cheap. I think you must understand that about me, but you're right about hatred, Elly. It eats your soul – its bitterness turns cancerous and I know neither my father nor my brother would want that. I could almost hear them saying as much as I engraved your token. It's love I want reflected in my eyes, not hatred.'

His eyes did reflect love and I reached up, kissing him softly on the lips. He smiled, holding me to him. 'It's strange how things work – Matthew Reith has done me a service. I knew I was up against ruthless men, but I didn't realize quite how ruthless. They put my name on that passenger list to account for my sudden disappearance and I must tread carefully. They'll read about this case and know I'm in Fosse. But enough of me, what about you? Have you found a new lease?'

I smiled. 'Lady Pendarvis is going to buy my fabric from me and she's to store it in her attic room. We're going to wait to see if Gwen's baby is a boy or a girl. If it's a boy, Uncle Thomas might buy me a lease as an investment.' Billy had jumped the last boulder and was hurtling towards us. 'Steady on, Billy, you'll have me over.'

William put out his hand to catch him. 'What took you, lad? Elowyn and I can't wait all day.'

Billy grinned, skipping sideways again. 'It's Mrs Pengelly's birthday soon…shall we take her up to the cliffs? We could borrow a horse and cart from Joseph.'

'What a good idea. We can get Mrs Munroe to pack a hamper and Sam and Tamsin can come too. We'll all come. Let's take her where she can watch the seals.' I, too, began skipping sideways, keeping up with William's long strides. 'You can take your sketch book and sketch her…you can make her a garland for her hair. She'd love that.'

Billy jumped a large cow pat. 'We'll bring a rug and Sam can bring some ale…Just imagine her face when you arrive in the cart…'

William's smile deepened. 'Would Mrs Pengelly allow us to sing *bawdy* songs?'

'Course she would, Will – she knows yer song already. Sam sings it all the time.'

I sat by the open casement, pressing William's token to my lips. One o'clock and the night so still, no breeze to take the heat from my cheeks. Owls hooted across the river, moonlight dancing on the water. I would remember this day for ever. Not for the inquest, not even for travelling in Sir James' carriage, but for the sheer joy of walking hand in hand with the man and boy I adored; walking and singing at the tops of our voices. I had never done that before – never sung so loudly or so happily. The words were so beautiful: *Were I laid on Greenland's coast, and in my arms embraced my lass.*

I could not sleep. I was reliving that first night, his naked body pressing so warmly against mine. I was reliving his kiss, the strength of his arms as he held me so tightly.

'Gates shut…'

Chapter Thirty-nine

The Quayside, Fosse
Friday 15th July 1796, 10:00 a.m.

At last, the cart was loaded, my rolls of fabric protected by layers of wadding. It was as much as I could bear to see them go but Billy seemed less perturbed, chatting happily to Jago as he finished his pipe.

Lady Pendarvis nodded, the emerald brooch glinting in her turban. 'I shall be away for two weeks, Elowyn – although Sir Alex may need to stay longer. Hannah has *very* careful instructions – but, of course, she already knows how to keep linen *fresh* and the air *circulating. I promise* she will take great care of your fabrics.'

She reached into her basket and I put my hand gently on her arm, drawing her back to the empty storeroom. I was desperate Gwen and Josie did not see any money change hands. 'Are you happy with the amount – have I done my calculations correctly?'

'Everything is quite correct – though I would have preferred to give you a banker's draft. Forty pounds is a dangerous amount of money to have in your possession.'

'I'm going to give it straight to Uncle Thomas…'

'I am sure Mr Scantlebury will do what is right for both you and your money. He is a good man and will have your best interests at heart. Tell him I am sorry there is no gold. These notes are very flimsy. Mr Hoskins should pay more attention to his banknotes and leave the business of dressmaking to us. Dear Lord – that dreadful woman is here! When I *think* how she used to treat me…'

She swept through to the sewing room, hovering at the door like a bird of prey. Mrs Hoskins was at once fixed by those hawk-like eyes and realized she must curtsy deeper. She went lower still, her arms reaching out for the nearest chair. Lady Pendarvis smiled.

'A bit blustery for a sail but I shall relish the fresh air. I hope you are well, Mrs Hoskins.'

It was all very well for Lady Pendarvis. She could sweep out in her elegant fashion but we had to face Mrs Hoskins' sullen fury. Josie helped Mrs Hoskins back to her feet but it was not enough to stop the backlash. All three chins were wobbling.

'Why are those fabrics in the cart? Has Lady Pendarvis bought them? Well, honestly! You should've come straight to me…I wanted your fabrics…I made that quite clear when I was here last time. Is my money not good enough for you, Miss Liddicot?'

Josie took her cloak, soothing her like a child. 'Oh no… Miss Liddicot don't think that at all. Yer money comes straight from the bank and that's got to be good money.' She smiled sweetly. 'Lady Pendarvis's only storin' the fabric fer Miss Liddicot – on account of us havin' nowhere to go…'

Gwen pushed the dressmaker's dummy forward. 'We're nearly finished...This is the last fittin' – we'll have them done by Monday. What do ye make of this ribbon embroidery, Mrs Hoskins? And look at this gold stitchin'...an' these pearls.'

The room looked forlorn with all the empty shelves and I could barely bring myself to cajole Mrs Hoskins into better spirits. I had been up all week sewing her gowns, my fingertips aching, my neck stiff from sitting so long, but the results were beautiful and even Mrs Hoskins stopped mid sniff to stare at the intricate embroidery. We would get very little praise and next to no thanks but at least we would get paid.

Money used to be my only thought, yet since our walk from Porthcarrow, I could think only of William. He filled my thoughts so completely, every moment imagining what he might say or what we might do. This was our last Friday – on Monday, we would deliver the finished gowns and hand Uncle Thomas back his keys. I should have known how much it would hurt. I wanted it back already. I wanted us to be happy again, I wanted somewhere we could teach Gwen's daughter to sew amidst laughter and singing.

The baby was going to be a girl. Mrs Munroe had seen three sightings of three magpies and she was never wrong. Three magpies meant the dream of owning my own lease was over, four magpies and Uncle Thomas could tell the Corporation he was buying a lease for his sister's grandson. But three magpies, *three* times, I was beginning to see the reality not the dream – Gwen's baby was going to be a girl and the Corporation would block any chance I had of owning my own business.

Thunderous black clouds darkened the sky, soon we would need candles. 'Go home, Gwen...you, too. Josie. It's gone seven and it's too dark. You're both exhausted – I'll just finish this last rose...and I need to speak to Uncle Thomas.'

I watched them cross the courtyard, stretching up my arms to ease my back. My shoulders ached, my eyes beginning to sting. Billy streaked across the cobbles, charging up the steps, and I opened the door, standing back just in time. 'Ye've got to come,' he gasped. 'Now...Honest, Elly, lock the door an' come at once...Will's waitin'.' He rushed for my cloak and bonnet, thrusting them towards me. 'Quick...'

Any mention of William and my feet would fly but this was different; I had never seen Billy in such a state. He rushed me across the town square and along the river road, ignoring my pleas to tell me where we were going. 'You'll see,' was all he said. The man behind me was struggling to keep his hat in place, the wind blowing the tops of the trees, black clouds circling above us. Salt filled the air, the smell of a well-churned sea. There would be thunder soon and lightning and I clasped my cloak tighter.

'He's meetin' us...just along a bit. Come on, Elly...'

He began pulling me behind him, running along the river where the new houses were to be built. There was only the tumbledown boathouse and a derelict forge, and I caught my breath. 'Billy, stop! Where are you taking me?'

As I spoke, William stepped from behind the door of the old forge and came forward, taking hold of both my hands, putting them straight to his lips. He seemed as excited as Billy. 'Come, Elly…come and see this.' He was smiling but his eyes were serious, full of expectation, and I knew this was no joke. Yet why the old forge? It had been in a state of disrepair ever since I had come to Fosse; the gate was banging on its last hinge, glass was missing in several of the windows and a pile of stones showed where the huge chimney had started to crumble.

'Why here?' I asked, laughing despite my astonishment.

'Shut your eyes, Elly.' I did as I was told and felt myself lifted in his arms. He was carrying me across the overgrowth in long, purposeful strides and I leaned against his chest, breathing in the smell of leather.

He put me down. We were on the back step of what must have been the living area and I peered through the open oak door. It smelt musty and damp. Cobwebs hung from the ceiling and bits of rubble littered the floor. Birds were nesting in the beams, the wind blowing through the broken panes. I could see the hearth with its blackened bricks, several rows of hooks and a pair of bellows by the fire. The bread oven looked intact, the surrounding hearthstones dusty but complete. Two doors led to other rooms. 'Don't see it as it is, Elowyn…see it as it could be.' William's voice was thick with emotion.

Billy was exploring the outbuildings and I was alone with William. 'Come, Elly…Take a look at the other two rooms.' My heart was pounding. This was not a joke. His eyes never left my face, and I knew he was deadly serious. He would never bring me out on an evening like this if it was not important. 'Here, Elly, here's where the pipes could come through from a room next door...we'd have running water...*hot* running water, as I intend to build you a boiler – and a pump to pump the hot water through.' He smiled, lifting an old bench to one side. 'You can have steam if you like...steam straight to your iron...and here we'd have a range. It'll be the first thing I make. I'll cast it in iron, like one of my engines...You can have an oven that opens as well as this old bread oven.'

He held my hand, leading me across the dusty floor to the rooms beyond; both were in the same state of dereliction but were large with good-sized windows. In fact, they were perfect dressmaking windows. They faced south and I stared at them, my heart thumping. 'You mean for me to set up my shop here?' I could hardly speak. 'The light's perfect...in this room, we can build shelves for a storeroom...my customers can come through the front door...I'll grow roses round the gate and we'll serve tea from my range. William, did you mean it when you said you could give me steam in my iron?'

'Of course.' He smiled, pulling me forward. 'This wooden staircase leads to another two rooms upstairs. They would be our bedrooms. I'd like to take you up but it doesn't look safe. I don't think we should trust these steps.'

He drew me back to the hearth. 'The lease has run its course, Elly. The old man was the last of his family and he's not lived here for years. It's coming up for auction this Monday night...' The hairs on my arms rose. I could see a fire burning, a rocking chair with a tapestry cushion. There was a table laid for a family. I could see the curtains at the windows, the carpet on the floor. 'It's a flat walk from town but the town will soon extend well beyond here. It's on the main road so there's good access, but the beauty of the place is that round the back, there's a good half acre. There's an old stable and any number of outhouses – it would be a perfect place to build my works. I'll design a new engine – my engine, ready and waiting for when the patent runs out. Watt and Boulton will have no say after that. It'll be *my* engine, built to *my* design.'

'You'll have to take out your own patent – stop them from copying you!'

The hairs on my head tingled; I felt sick with want. Five minutes from Coombe House, ten minutes from Admiral House – a wreck of a building, birds in the rafters, mice in the skirting boards, yet every bone in my body ached to live there. He was staring at me, his eyes burning with love. 'And here…Elly…just here, this is where I'll place your nursing chair…and here…right here…we'll rock our babies to sleep in their crib.'

I could hardly look, let alone speak. Tears filled my eyes and I bit my lips to stop them quivering. He fell to one knee, his hazel eyes with their green flecks, his ruffled hair so precious to me. 'I'm talking years, Elly – three, maybe four. I'm talking of a lifetime. We may not even live here – but somewhere like here. Somewhere where you can have your shop and I can build my engineering works. Your customers coming to the front, mine to the back.' He looked up. 'We'll make it a home for Billy, and my mother will visit…Perhaps

I could convert the old stable so my brother's wife and my two young nephews could have a home?'

I slipped to my knees beside him, not caring about the dust, putting my arms around his waist. He clasped his hands behind my back, drawing me to him, and I knew we were kneeling on the hearth where we would raise our children. 'It's perfect, William,' I whispered. 'I feel it. Deep in my heart, I feel it.' I rested my head on his chest. I could hear chatter and laughter, the sound of banging in the yard. Gwen and Rosie were sewing in the front room, their soft singing breaking out into sudden giggles. 'Billy wants a pig; you know that, don't you?'

'You'll have water piped to your door. I'll design a wheel to turn the mangle – like the spit Billy mended...' He stopped, releasing his hold to reach for my hands, the tenderness in his voice breaking my heart. 'I love you, Elly, I cannot live without you. My destiny was to jump that ship – I could've floated anywhere on that current...I could've been washed up on any beach. When I saw the log, I knew I had to jump but I had no idea I would be found by the most beautiful woman I've ever set eyes on. I meant what I said. I'll always be there for you. Will you marry me, Elly? Will you allow me the honour of loving you for the rest of my life?'

I held his gaze, my love for him so overwhelming I could hardly speak. Our souls had brought us together; our souls calling out across the sea, making one jump, the other take the cliff path at just the right moment. Billy felt it too, the three of us, destined to find each other, just as we would find Billy's brother and sister. I loved him so completely it hurt to breathe. I loved his gentleness, I loved his quarrelsomeness. I loved his strength, his intelligence. I loved his manners, the way he had brought Mrs Pengelly roses, the way he had thanked Mrs Munroe. I loved his sudden smile, the way he teased me. I fought the lump in my throat. 'I'd love to marry you. I think I wanted to marry you the moment I first saw you but I didn't understand it...It's as though my heart knew but my head was against it.'

He smiled, putting my fingers to his lips, curling a lock of my hair with his finger. 'I wanted to marry you the moment I smelt your hair...but when I saw you...Oh, Elly, that first morning by the cave, I could hardly take my eyes off you. I thought I had died and gone to heaven...No, don't laugh, please don't laugh. I know that sounds trite, but I had so nearly died...and there you were...your beautiful voice breaking through my confusion. I heard you, Elly. I felt your soft touch...your compassion and absolute determination I should live. I felt it, Elly – I felt it deep within my heart – and from that very moment, I began to live again.' He bent forward, his lips brushing mine. 'My spirit had died...my reason to live...and there you were, scolding me for nearly dying. I love you, Elly, more than I'm capable of expressing. I think I'm better with engines than I am with words.'

I loved him so much more than words could tell. 'You saved me too, remember.'

There was a cough behind us, a polite clearing of the throat. 'I'm sorry, Will...but can I come in now? I'm getting wet. Good job the old roof's holdin' up.'

Billy ran across the room, sitting cross-legged next to us,

and I smiled back at the two conspirators. 'Would you like to live here, Billy? I don't mean all the time, of course… you'll still have your room at Coombe House and Endymion's always going to want you to share his bed, but—'

'But when I'm home from school? From Truro, you mean? Did Will tell you about the hot water? Can you imagine turnin' the tap an' getting' hot water? Wait till Sam hears about that!'

William shook his head. 'Don't tell him, Billy. Not yet. Tell no one we want this lease – if people know we're interested, others might come looking. Many won't even know it's available – it was Joseph who told me. But though it would be perfect, we must be prepared to see it go. I can't promise to get back from Penzance in time.'

'Penzance? Now?'

'If I'd seen it earlier I could have had everything in place. I'm sure my bank could be persuaded – Father left me a small legacy, which will cover the cost.'

'But the bank won't be open on Sunday and the auction's Monday night!'

'I know, Elly, but it's worth a try. I'll spend time with my mother and go first thing Monday morning. If the coaches run smoothly, I could be back in time.' He looked up. The wind was rattling the window frame, rain blowing through the broken pane.

'William, the roads will soon be impassable…you can't go in this storm – nobody will be going anywhere, let alone the stage coach.'

'Then I'll hire a horse. I'll do my utmost to get back for

the auction, but we must be prepared to lose it…It may not be *this* place we buy, lovely though it is, it might be somewhere like this – somewhere just as promising.'

Disappointment seared through me, gripping me with pain. The light would be perfect. I knew exactly where I would store my fabrics. A shiver ran down my spine, we could not lose this place. I could see Josie and Gwen sitting with their heads bent; I could hear their happy chatter. I could see the crib by the hearth, the toys cluttering the flagstones. A cat like Mr Pitt was watching me from the hearth. We could not lose this, we could not. Chickens were pecking at the kitchen door, Billy chasing a pig round the yard. I could hear him singing – all of us, singing. We could not lose this. Not if I had the money.

'What will this go for, William? What's the guide price?'

'There's a reserve price. Joseph believes round forty pounds would secure it.'

My heart was hammering. 'And what if I *have* forty pounds?'

He smiled, shaking his head. 'No, Elly, never, I'll not use your money – if we lose this, there'll be another.' He rose, brushing the dust from his knees. 'I'll get you home and leave straight away.'

'William, wait. Why not use my money to secure the sale? Then you could go to Penzance and get your bank draft. You'll never get there and back in time – the roads will soon be impassable.' I did not want to plead but I was so sure I was right. Destiny had brought him to me and destiny had made my lease run out. My funds were free. Another half an hour and I would have given my money to Uncle Thomas. I had the money because destiny meant us to live here. I could feel it in my bones, the shivers on my arms, the hairs on my head. 'Please, William, I love this place. I know it's a ruin but it has such beauty…'

He shook his head. 'No, Elly, I can't. It wouldn't be right.'

'Please don't let pride cloud your judgement, William. Just think…even if you did get back in time, who would believe your bank draft was genuine? Everyone thinks so badly of you, they'll assume it was forged. But if you had the money *in your hands*, they would have to take you seriously. They couldn't discount your bid if the money was in front of them.'

Billy's face was as eager as mine. 'She's right, Will. Ye'd not be taken seriously.'

William smiled, shaking his head softly. 'That's two against one. I don't think I can hold out against the two of you. I'll borrow the money to secure the lease – then I'm going straight to Penzance.'

Chapter Forty

The heavy clouds showed no sign of dispersing; the streets were awash, rivulets weaving across the cobbles and pooling into puddles.

'It's not goin' to stop. Honest to God, Elly, we could've had another day sewing.'

We were all exhausted. We had worked day and night to get Mrs Hoskins' dresses finished. They lay wrapped in cotton, ready to be transported, and my frustration was turning to panic. I needed forty pounds, not thirty-six. I had to get the money for these dresses or I would be four pounds short. 'When's this rain going to stop? It's got to break sometime.'

'One drop of rain on that silk — an' she'll blame us. Ye know we've to wait. What's the matter? Ye've been like a scalded cat all mornin'.'

'I have to hand in the key this afternoon — Tom made that very clear! But we can't give them the key if we still have the dresses here. You two might as well go home, Billy and

369

I can wait.' The rooms echoed around us. The bureaux and table were unchanged, but the shelves were bare, the ribbon cabinet stripped of all colour. Josie and Gwen's hearts were breaking but mine held such hope. Hope and panic. The auction was at eight and I could not let William down.

Josie's new spectacles had made all the difference and Jenna had said we could join her school until we found a new lease. Joseph and William had shaken hands so warmly at the wrestling match and Jenna's generosity in lending William the clothes made me feel churlish. She had showed me nothing but kindness and my jealousy was misplaced. Jenna was forthright, that was all – forthright and unforgiving if you crossed her, but fiercely loyal and protective if she liked you.

Josie grabbed her umbrella, making a dash across the cobbles and anxiety twisted my stomach – it was half past one and there was still no sign of a break in the rain. Mrs Hoskins had specified a morning delivery, her reply to my note insisting I deliver the gowns before two o'clock or it would have to be Tuesday. Another glance at the clock and my last hope died.

Gwen gasped, bending suddenly double. 'Oh my God… That was awful…That was—' She blanched again, gripping the back of the chair.

'Gwen, what is it? Is the baby coming?'

She nodded, waiting for the pain to pass. 'That was different…I've had pains on and off fer a couple of days – but that was awful.'

'Gwen, you should have told me.'

'We had to finish the gowns, Elly. 'Tis like perfect timin'.'
Billy's face went ashen.

'Stay with Gwen, Billy…I'll tell Tom to fetch Mrs Benbo.
Gwen, breathe…everything's going to be fine…Billy will go
for Mrs Cousins the moment I come back…' I ran down
the steps two at a time. She had looked so frightened and I
prayed my hardest. *Don't let her die; please, please, don't let her
die.* We had looked forward to this day with trepidation and
now it was here, I felt nothing but panic. I would stay by her
side to the end…until I held the baby in my arms.

Uncle Thomas' pleasure in seeing me turned straight to
concern. 'Elly love, you're trembling. You look like you've
seen a ghost.'

'Gwen's pains have started…Where's Tom?'

'He's in the yard. So, the baby's coming at last – is Billy to
go for Mrs Cousins or shall I send Tom?'

'Billy's going but Tom's to go for Mrs Benbo – they both
said they'd come…'

He held my shaking hands. 'She's a strong lass, Elly. She's
fit and healthy and everything will go well – just wait and
see. This baby will be the first of a whole string of babies.'
We had hardly spoken since William's trial. The gowns had
taken all my time but it was not only that keeping me from
our morning talks. I did not want us ever to argue. I loved
him so much, yet he was so set against William. When he
met William properly, he would realize his prejudice was
misplaced. 'An' good timing on her part,' he added.

Gwen's labour could last all night and I would miss the
auction. But even without Gwen's pains, I was still four

pounds short. William could be outbid – or at the very least, not have enough to reach the reserve price. The bottom drawer of Uncle Thomas' desk lay open, his tobacco pouch nestling against his money box, and my heart hammered in painful indecision. Yet why not ask him for the money? I could pay him straight back. Even as I hesitated, I knew I would have to lie.

'Uncle Thomas...I haven't been able to deliver my gowns...they're wrapped and ready but I've been waiting for the rain to clear. I'm to be paid on receipt, but that leaves me four pounds short for Lady Polcarrow's new silk. There's a merchant waiting for my payment...' I spoke quickly, horrified at the ease with which the lie had sprung to my lips. 'It's just till tomorrow...I can return your money as soon as I've delivered the gowns...'

I had never lied to him before and never felt so wretched. Uncle Thomas' eyes darted to the corner of the room and I thought I would faint. Nathan Cardew was hanging up his travelling coat, his hat dripping with rain. He was smartly dressed, his silk cravat pinned with a silver pin, his jacket and breeches of very fine twill, and my heart hammered so hard I thought I might be sick.

He walked slowly towards me, bowing politely. 'Forgive me, Miss Liddicot, for bein' an unwillin' eavesdropper. Yer uncle had no time to tell you I was here. I'm shelterin' from the rain...Please forgive me if I intrude.' I saw the pain deep in his eyes and a knife sliced through me. I could hardly bear the mortification. If I had seen him, I would never have asked.

Uncle Thomas shrugged, shaking his head sadly. 'You've

372

not come at a very good time, Elly love. I've next to nothing in the box as I've just paid the men. I paid a deal too much for that last batch of hemp and we've just stocked up on varnish. There's been nothing but a steady trickle of money out, but if you come early tomorrow, Wilkes is collecting his trunnels and he's to pay up front.' He shut the drawer, his eyes straying back to Nathan.

My cheeks burned. 'Of course, I understand, I should never have asked.' Tears of embarrassment stung my eyes.

'You've used up all your savings, Elly?'

I breathed deeply, realizing the stupidity of my lie. 'Lady Pendarvis has everything in safe keeping...They've a strong box and she's keeping my savings alongside my fabrics. It doesn't matter...I'm sure he can wait until tomorrow...I need to get back to Gwen – could you tell Tom to go straight for Mrs Benbo?' I turned to go but Nathan stepped quickly forward, his hand reaching inside his jacket.

'No...wait...please, Miss Liddicot. I'd like to think we're still friends enough for me to lend you four pounds.' He opened a large leather pouch, drawing out a thick wad of notes, separating four pounds and holding them out to me. 'I'm to buy a horse but there's more than enough to cover it here. You can pay me back at your leisure. I'd consider it my privilege.'

I could hardly look at him, but shook my head in mortification. 'No...thank you, I can't accept...It's very kind of you to offer...but no. Thank you.'

'Then I shall lend the money to Mr Scantlebury...Here, Thomas, surely you can have no objection to that? Let the debt be yours – you can pay me back the moment Mr Wilkes has cleared his account...' He held the notes for Uncle Thomas. 'Elowyn wouldn't ask for money unless she really needed it – and Lady Polcarrow must have her silk.' His voice softened. 'Please, Thomas, allow me this small service to Elowyn.'

'No...no...please...I should never have asked...'

'Please, Thomas, I insist. Pay me back tomorrow. It would mean a lot to me.'

Uncle Thomas took the proffered money, handing it straight to me, but I shook my head, wanting to cry. Of course, I wanted the money, but not from Nathan. It was wrong to use his money for my home with William. So wrong, like rubbing salt into a wound – his good intentions serving only to help his rival in love. Yet there it lay, the four pounds that could help secure our future.

The notes felt crisp and I took a deep breath. 'I'll bring the money to you tomorrow – this is just until tomorrow.'

Pleasure shone in Uncle Thomas' eyes, a glint of happiness, and I winced at my deception. He believed he was playing Cupid, paving the way for a reconciliation, and that it would be only a matter of time before Nathan became family. 'Go back to Gwen, Elly,' he said, smiling. 'I'll fetch Tom.'

Gwen was sitting by the window, crocheting a baby blanket. 'Billy, come...I need you...' We went through to the empty storeroom and I lowered my voice. 'Go to William and tell him I want him...now...straight away. Tell him to come to the shop…tell him it's urgent. Then run to Mrs Cousins and tell her I'm taking Gwen home.' A sudden cry made me turn round.

'I'm fine, Elly, Mrs Cousins said I was to keep walkin' and talkin' when the pains came.' She drew a deep breath, her lips pursed. 'Tis passin' – but 'tis gettin' more frequent.' She was clutching her walnut birthing charm and I tried to smile.

'I'll get my things…' Rushing through the storeroom, I slid open the secret door and pulled back the carpet. My hands were shaking as I lifted the loose floorboard. All my money was in a silk purse mainly notes but a few sovereigns and fifteen shillings in loose coins and tokens. I added the crisp new notes, reaching inside my basket for William's notebook. I opened the page, once more kissing the four-leaf clover for luck. *Please let our bid be successful*. It was everything I had – all my hard-earned savings, lying in a silk purse tied with a satin ribbon.

'There's someone coming,' called Gwen.

William was standing in the rain, shielding his eyes with his hand. He was looking up at the sign and I waved to him from the window. Gwen looked horrified. 'Dear God, ye're not letting that man in?'

'Gwen, he's my friend and I need to give him something – then I'm taking you home…'

She sat stony faced as William bowed in greeting, his coat dripping onto the polished wooden floor. 'Is there to be no break in this rain?' he said politely, but there was no time for pleasantries and I took hold of his arm, pulling him into the storeroom.

'Gwen's pains have started and I'm going to stay with her…Here…take this…it's the money. I've got just over forty pounds.' I thrust the silk purse into his hands. 'Please get it, William…I couldn't bear it if it went to someone else.' I wanted the old forge so much I could already feel the heartache of losing it.

William drew me closer, kissing my hair. 'We've as good a chance as any. I'll put the lease in both our names – another name can be added as our family grows.' He kissed my hair again. 'It's expensive to add names but if we get it for forty pounds, we'll have done very well.' He released his hold, pulling my chin up, his lips brushing softly against mine. 'Sir James has asked for my plans. His smelting deal's gone through so there's every chance he'll be able to find the funds for my viaduct.'

'Your viaduct?'

'It's the perfect solution – he'll have so much power he won't know what to do with it!' He smiled and I thought my heart would burst.

'But you'll know how to use it.'

He kissed me softly. 'I should say so! A grinder for the ore, a faster flow to the mill and I'll build him a large waterwheel so he can pipe water to every corner of his new town. I've a list as long as my arm—'

From the next-door room we heard Gwen gasp, and I knew I must get her home. 'Be successful for us, William,' I said, snatching one last kiss. 'Get us that forge.'

William bowed to Gwen as he left. 'I wish you every happiness with your baby, Mrs Liddicot.'

Gwen's usually ruddy complexion drained of all colour. She gripped the back of the chair, and not just in pain. 'Ye're never still seeing him, Elly?'

'Of course I am. I love him, Gwen and I'm going to marry him.'

Her eyes widened in horror. 'Dear God, Elly, are you out of yer mind? The man's a murderer.'

'He's not a murderer, he was completely cleared. He should never have been charged.'

'Elly, ye can't be truthful...?' She winced once more in pain. 'Ye're never serious...Of course it were murder. If them boots had been found earlier, he'd never have got off.'

'What boots?'

'The boots found two days back in the rubble behind the hotel. *Large* boots, Elly, completely caked with clay – bigger than most men's feet but they'd fit William Cotterell.' She gripped her belly. 'Jesus...'

I grabbed our hats, plonking them on our heads, throwing my cloak round me inside out. By the sudden panic on her face, it must have been the waters going – dear God, Mrs Cousins had better come quickly. Gwen was breathing heavily, clutching the rail with one hand, her skirts in the other. 'Ye won't forget the locks, promise me, Elly...unlock everything – open all the windows. There's a chest under the bed, make sure ye undo that. An' my silver necklace...don't miss a single lock.'

'I promise...Come...take care, it's very slippery.' I held the umbrella in one hand, ready to brave the rain, but stopped, drawing back as Nathan ran quickly across the yard.

'He's buyin' a horse...an' he's been invited to join the adventurers of Wheal Charlotte. That's why he's bought them new clothes.' There was reproach in her voice, a deep sadness. 'He's a broken man – he told Tom he'll not marry now. Men like that only love once.'

Chapter Forty-one

I unlocked the door, racing quickly upstairs to open the windows, unlocking everything I could find – every cupboard, every chest, every drawer. A gypsy once told Gwen that her birth would go smoothly if there was nothing locked in the house. Everything had to be open and I searched the bedrooms, my heart hammering. Rain splashed through the window, the salty air filling the stuffy room, but everything was unlocked and I rushed back to Gwen.

She was doubled up, moaning. She held a small crucible of lilac oil and was halfway through lighting a candle. 'There's rushes round the back, Elly – and I've a pile of rags in that basket. I don't want to make a mess.'

'Like that matters!' A young lad had gone for Jenna but so far no one had arrived and my fingers fumbled as I tried to light the candle. 'What about changing into your nightdress – that's easily laundered?'

The pains were growing fiercer, certainly more frequent, and Gwen doubled up again, leaning against the table, clasping her head in her hands. 'Jesus Christ…Oh God, Elly, I'm sorry fer swearin' but it's that awful…' She began moaning, reaching for some ale. We had every window open and every door was ajar but the heat was building. Beads of sweat glistened on her forehead and I reached for the sponge to cool her flushed cheeks. 'Where are they, Elly? Why aren't they here?'

I tried to soothe her, though she spoke my thoughts. Jenna would want to boil water for tea – nettle or yarrow, something her grandmother had taught her, so I began working quickly, lighting the fire, laying out the rushes, unfolding the rags. I filled the kettle from the yard, hanging it above the fire, and rushed upstairs to retrieve the pillow Gwen had filled with lavender.

I loved the cottage with its solid granite walls and tiny casement windows keeping it cool in the summer and warm in winter. It was the third in a row, rising sharply from the water's side; Uncle Thomas had lived here with Aunt Peggy and never thought to move. Six months ago it had been my home, Mamm and I in one bedroom, Tom and Uncle Thomas in the other. I rushed to the window, leaning out in the rain, desperate for someone to join us. Jenna was running down the lane, her umbrella blowing sideways in the wind, and I cried out in relief. 'Jenna – quick, the baby's coming.'

When she came into the cottage she was smiling calmly, rolling up her sleeves and reaching inside her basket for a freshly laundered apron. 'I'm sure we've a while yet. What's the time?' She looked at the sturdy oak clock on the sideboard. 'Half past three.' She rummaged further into her basket. 'We'll get these herbs burning an' we'll start with raspberry tea. A cup every twenty minutes…perhaps ye could grate this ginger fer me, Elowyn?'

Half past seven and I could hardly bear Gwen's screams. I held her hand, mopping her forehead, each scream ripping me apart. Her hair lay damp against her cheeks, her flushed face covered in beads of sweat. I had rechecked all the rooms, searched every drawer. She screamed again, squeezing my hand so tightly I thought my fingers would crack.

Tom had tried to get Mrs Benbo but she was detained at another birth and had told him to come back later – the rains had brought the babies, storms did that, and the children born of storms had a stormy temper. It was not what Gwen wanted to hear and Tom stood pale faced and petrified, his clenched fist pounding his mouth, his wet leather boots creaking as he paced the room.

Mrs Cousins clearly wanted him out of the way. 'Try her once more, Tom – an' while ye're passin' the church, tell Mrs Pengelly an' Thomas there's no news yet.'

She waited for him to go, lifting Gwen's nightdress to peer into the depths. 'No change, my love.' She placed her huge hands on Gwen's belly, 'There's a strong kick right here – so it's comin' head down, but we've a long way to go.' She smiled at Jenna, taking hold of the proffered cup. 'Here, love, try an' get that down ye. Ginger will ease the sickness – an' catnip helps the cramps. An' Jenna's got some crampbark so we'll try that next.' She smiled. 'Take a turn round the room,

381

love, then I suggest ye lie on yer side fer a bit. Try an' get some relief by bringin' up yer legs.'

Mrs Cousins was like a favourite aunt. She was similar to Mrs Munroe in almost every way, their speech and mannerisms so alike, they could have been sisters. She had been with Mrs Pengelly at Rose Polcarrow's birth and Mrs Pengelly was adamant she should be with Gwen. Yet Mrs Benbo's professional jealousy had us all on eggshells. Gwen screamed, and the look Mrs Cousins threw Jenna made my heart jolt. Gwen was clearly losing strength and I held her hand, helping her down to the blanket I had laid on the floor. She screamed again, drawing up her knees, writhing in agony.

I felt so powerless, each scream slicing through me, each writhe of agony twisting me apart. I had no idea how brutal childbirth was, nor how loud a woman could scream. Jenna handed me a cup of ginger tea, lifting a stray curl from my face. 'Ye sure ye want to stay, Elowyn? It might put ye off – sure ye don't want to join the others, or sit next door?'

I shook my head. 'I've promised to stay. I'll not leave her.'

Another blood-curdling scream and I knelt on the cushions beside Gwen. She was adamant not to spoil the bed, shaking her head at every suggestion. But we all knew why: the memory of the pool of blood never left her, her mother's pale face, her hand going limp. Our foreheads touched and we clasped hands over her walnut birthing pendant. Her breath smelt of vinegar, her forehead damp. A gust of wind blew through the open window making the candle die and Gwen stared in horror at the thin plume of smoke.

'The candle's gone out…Quick, Elly, get it alight…' Jenna

struck the tinderbox and Gwen clutched my hands tighter. 'Promise me ye'll look after the baby. If anythin' happens, promise ye'll take care of my baby…and stop yer quarrel with Tom. Promise me…' She drew up her knees, her face contorting as she began to scream once more.

'Nothing's going to happen,' I said, soothing her forehead as she lay back, closing her eyes. 'Of course the candles are going to blow out…we'll never keep them alight with all these windows open…besides, you've got to get used to this. Uncle Thomas says it's the first of a whole string of babies.'

'Like hell it's goin' to be.' She kept her eyes shut. 'But I mean it, Elly, please look after him as if he was yer own.'

I wiped the sweat from her brow. 'It's going to be a girl, Gwen. Mrs Munroe saw three magpies, *three* times. And nothing's going to happen.' I glanced at the clock: half past eight and the bidding would be starting. 'Besides, nothing's going to happen because I've seen you sewing with Josie… you were sewing and the children were running round the yard. You were happy, Gwen…laughing with Josie…'

'Ye can't trust dreams, Elly – sometimes they mean the opposite.'

'It wasn't a dream, it was more than that. It was like seeing the future – like knowing how it was going to be. Look, I've got goose pimples just thinking of it. Look at the hairs on my arms. That's how I know it's true.' I glanced back at the clock. 'You'll see.'

'What d'you mean…you'll see?' She sat up, making Mrs Cousins rush forward.

'Ye goin' to be sick, my love? Ye need yer bowels open?'

She plumped up her cushion. 'Ye comfy, love? Thank you, Jenna. Here's a little more ginger…'

Gwen put the cup to her burning lips. 'I do feel sick but I'm not goin' to be sick.' Mrs Cousins resumed her knitting, sitting back on the rocking chair as if she was Mrs Munroe and Gwen clasped my hands again. 'What d' ye mean, Elly? A shiver means the passin' of someone's soul…it's never right to shiver…not here…not now…not with the baby comin'.' She clutched her belly, once more screaming in pain.

'Gwen, I saw it…' I replied as she lay back exhausted. 'I saw it like I'm seeing you. We were all there. I can't explain it…it was so certain. I'm not fanciful, you know that…we all saw it…William and Billy as well.'

She struggled to sit. 'Where…? What are ye sayin', Elly?'

'I'm going to marry him, Gwen. He's buying us the old forge…that's where we'll set up our next shop…that's where I saw us…'

'Not that man, Elly. He's a liar…he's no good, surely ye see that?' She clenched her fists, her scream piercing my ears. Tom must have heard her from the street outside as he came flying through the door, throwing himself on the floor to cradle her in his arms. Tears stung his eyes; he looked petrified, like a rabbit caught in a trap. 'Mrs Benbo's come… I've brought the chair…I had to carry it fer her…but I'm here now…I'll fetch it in.'

Mrs Benbo nodded curtly, taking off her hat with a sniff, flinging her dripping cloak to the back of a chair. 'How far gone?' Her apron was smeared with fresh blood and I could feel my senses swim. 'Get these windows closed…draw the

384

curtains...I'm surprised at you, Mrs Cousins, exposin' this poor girl to all the draughts.' She turned to Jenna, her face falling. 'Oh, it's you. Well, get the chair in an' I'll take a look.'

Tom rushed back through the door, carrying Mrs Benbo's heavy oak chair high in his arms. The central part of the seat had been cut out and I stared at it, my queasiness turning to nausea. Despite the rain, the seat and legs were still covered in fresh blood and there were red smears on Tom's chest where he had rested it against his shirt. Mrs Benbo pointed to where she wanted it put and wiped her hand across her nose. 'Get those windows shut, Jenna Marlow, an' let's take a look. I like to get a feel of the baby's head.' She pointed to her chair. 'Sit on that, my girl...Ye may feel me pushin' a bit. These storm babies never come easy. An' ye can clear away that tea, Jenna Marlow, it's gin she needs...not tea.'

Jenna stood with her arms crossed, glaring at Mrs Benbo from her place by the fire. She had been singing softly while brewing her tea, crocheting a baby's bonnet as she chatted to Mrs Cousins, but now I hardly recognized her. She looked furious, her luscious blond hair waving round her like a lion's mane with a scowl beneath as ferocious as any wild animal. 'I've been Jenna *Dunn* fer nearly two years,' she snapped, 'an' I've just scrubbed that floor clean. An' I don't take kindly to filthy aprons, an' as fer that chair! Look, 'tis filthy – all that blood, 'tis quite horrible. An' 'tis quite crowded enough in here – Mrs Cousins is doin' just fine – an' no doubt ye're tired an' wantin' some rest.'

She pointed to the chair, nodding at Tom to leave him in no doubt she wanted it removed from the cottage. Mrs

Benbo looked thunderstruck. 'Well, I see ye've not changed one little bit, have ye, my girl? Always was one to speak yer mind—'

'Perhaps ye should get a little rest an' we'll call ye the moment we need ye,' cut in Mrs Cousins. 'Ye look fit to drop.'

Tom picked up the chair, resigned he would have to carry it back to Mrs Benbo's cottage. Jenna held her chin high in the air and watched their retreating figures from the open door. 'Jenna Marlow indeed! Who does she think she is? Just because she wanted *her* Susan to marry *my* Joseph! He kissed her *once* – that was all…an' he was only sixteen. Hardly a crime an' hardly an engagement – I bet she sticks pins into a wax doll of me.'

She had her hands on her hips, still frowning. 'She's full of poison, that woman.' The wind blew her hair, not a lion, but a lioness protecting her own, and in that moment I understood my jealousy; it was her strength I envied, her confidence to speak her mind. I always bit back my words, too afraid people might censure me. She smiled. 'Oh, bless his heart, here comes Billy. Honest, that boy – splashin' through them puddles! He might as well be swimmin'.'

Chapter Forty-two

One look at Billy's face and I caught my breath. He flung himself through the door as white as a ghost. 'He never came, Elly. He's nowhere to be found...'

I took his arm, ushering him through to the front parlour with its gleaming brass candlesticks and brocaded cushions. 'Go to his lodgings...maybe he's ill...or fallen asleep—'

'He's not there.' His hands were trembling, his jacket soaking, his hat sitting limply on his wet hair. 'I went there first...he wasn't there.'

I tried to stay calm. 'He must have been detained...Sir James wanted to see his plans and he must still be there. Go to Polcarrow...see if he's there—'

'I've searched everywhere. The auction's over...I've just passed the inn an' they're coming out.'

I felt winded, fighting for breath. 'William knows what he's doing. Perhaps the old forge wasn't in the auction...perhaps William knew that...maybe that's why he didn't go...'

Jenna came through to join us, standing in the doorway as

she held up a towel. 'Come here, Billy, let's get yer hair dry – Gwen won't take kindly to ye messin' up her parlour. An' ye're not to stay long – 'tis no place fer a lad.' She stopped. 'What's wrong…what's happened?'

I could hardly speak. 'William said he was going to bid for the old forge.'

Her face softened. 'And he didn't get it? No, I can see from yer faces he didn't. I'm that sorry – got outbid, did he? There was plenty of leases for the takin'.'

A knot in my stomach twisted, I needed to stay calm. There would be a simple explanation; I must not think the worst. 'The forge can't have been in the auction…it must've been withdrawn…'

Jenna began rubbing Billy's hair. 'It was in the auction all right…'twas first on the list. There were five in all, but the old forge was first. Stand still, Billy, ye're gettin' me wet.'

The knot twisted deeper, my mouth so dry I could hardly speak. 'William must still be with Sir James…he's probably so engrossed in his plans, he's forgotten to check the time…'

'No,' she answered quickly, 'he's not at Polcarrow. Sir James is in St Austell with Joseph…the smeltin' deal's gone through and they're drawing up the contract…Elly, what's wrong?'

Gwen's scream pierced the room and Billy looked as if he might faint. Jenna grabbed him by the shoulders. 'Out ye go, Billy…out…now – go to the church an' tell Mrs Pengelly and Mr Scantlebury there's no news…an' ask Josie fer her mother's smellin' salts…' She ushered him through the door. 'Here, borrow this hat…off ye go.'

Nausea churned my stomach. Someone had to alert the constable – they must find William, quickly, before it was too late. Jenna stood at the door watching my hands trembling against my mouth. Her hands flew to her hips. 'What's goin' on, Elly?'

'William wouldn't miss that auction, Jenna…he really wouldn't. I think he's been waylaid. There are men who hate him and want his downfall.' I reached for my handkerchief, wiping my tears. 'They're ruthless, Jenna. I know they are… They must have caught up with him again. Last time they beat him badly and put him on a ship. He jumped but he nearly died.'

Her eyes widened. 'What are ye sayin', Elly? Talk slowly.'

'There's a court case going on. It's about a patent…it's very complicated and William doesn't *know* it's them because he's crossed so many…but they're ruthless – they want him gone.' I looked up to see Tom standing in the parlour doorway.

He threw off his hat and jacket and rolled up his sleeves. 'Well, I hope they've found him and given' him a good beatin'.'

'Tom, don't say that…he's in danger…we need to alert the constable…'

'Ye think I'll waste a minute of my time on that scoundrel when my wife's havin' a baby? I don't give one toss fer that man.' He shook his head.

'Tom, please…he may be dying…'

Tom's face hardened. 'He'll be where he always is – in the tavern, or down the bothy.' He turned in disgust, going back to Gwen, kneeling quickly on the floor to take her in his arms. She lay exhausted against him, strands of damp hair clinging to her burning face, and I knew I could not leave her. Jenna returned to the fire, wedging the door ajar with the bucket of water. Mrs Cousins looked up from her knitting, raising her eyebrows at the wind blowing through the open casement.

None of them understood the terror I felt, and why should they? We were all facing another terror; one that was real and immediate, not imagined. Jenna handed me a cup of hot ginger and I knew I must draw on her strength. 'We have to find him, Tom. He must be in danger.'

He glared back at me. 'The further he gets from this town, the better. I'll not ask a single person to search fer him.'

Gwen's eyes were closed but she clutched his arm. 'Please, Tom...She loves him...she's going to marry him...please ask the constable to search...' She breathed deeply, screaming once more in agony. Tom blanched, his fists flying to his mouth as he fought his fear. It was gone ten o'clock. Perhaps William had been delayed. Perhaps he was working so hard on his plans he had not noticed the time.

Upstairs a door banged. A sudden gust of wind made the window fling open and the curtains filled like a sail, billowing in the rain. Tom sprang to his feet, spilling water from the pail as he shoved it to one side. He slammed the door, striding angrily across the room to pull the casement closed. 'For God's sake, shut these bloody windows.'

'No, Tom, no...keep them open...don't shut them... please...' I ran after him, following him from room to room. 'Keep them open…' He ignored my pleas bounding up the tiny stairs in three large strides. 'Go back to Gwen… please, Tom…please don't lock anything…leave everything unlocked.'

He stood by the closed window, grabbing my arm. 'Are ye mad, Elowyn? Are ye insane? There's a gale blowing through the house.' He stared at my creased dress and my untidy hair, and I knew I looked a sight. 'Ye're mad, aren't you? He's turned yer head – he's bewitched ye.'

'I love him, Tom. I love him and I'm going to marry him.' I started sobbing, my whole body shaking. 'We have to find him…' He glared back at me in horror and I knew he would only start a search party if he knew about the money. He would shout at me, curse me, probably even hit me, but I had to tell him. 'He's got all my money…' I whispered, hardly able to form the words. 'He was going to bid for the old forge…'

He swung round, his horrified glare making my blood run cold. 'What d'you mean he's got yer money?'

'He's got everything…all the money for my fabrics, all my savings…everything.'

He looked thunderstruck. 'He's fleeced ye. He's robbed ye and ye're so stupid ye never saw it coming! How much?' He saw me hesitate and his eyes sharpened. 'How much? How much money did he steal?'

'About forty pounds…but he's no thief…he borrowed it…I lent it to him until he could pay me back.' I never knew I could feel so wretched. I felt dizzy. I wanted to be sick.

'Jesus Christ! Ye gave that fraudster *forty pounds*? What did

ye do – beg him take it? *Here, have my money...take everythin'*
I've got! Jesus Christ!' His incredulous look was full of hatred
and I turned away, unable to bear his contempt. 'Ye had *forty
pounds?* An' ye just handed it over?' Gwen's scream echoed
round the tiny bedroom and Tom made to leave. 'Ye stupid
idiot. Jesus Christ, ye handed him yer savings – after I told
ye to stay clear of him.'

He bounded down the stairs and I stood reeling from the
force of his anger. Mrs Cousins' sharp command sounded
urgent: 'In the parlour – this minute. Stay there till ye're
called.' I tore round the rooms, re-opening every window.
Gwen's howls filled the cottage and I fell to my knees,
crossing myself in sudden prayer. Her cries sounded so eerie,
so plaintive, like a woman wailing for a lost child, and tears
splashed my cheeks. Suddenly, there was silence and I knelt
there, frozen to the spot. She had stopped screaming; there
was only silence. My heart was thumping so fast I could
hardly breathe but I stumbled to my feet and rushed down
the stairs, flinging myself into the room.

She was lying back against Jenna as white as a sheet and I
knelt beside her, my tears wetting her hand. *Please God, don't
let her die. Please don't let her die. Not Gwen. Not my dearest, truest
friend.* I searched Jenna's face. She was looking so solemn,
nodding only briefly. Her lips tightened as she bathed Gwen's
forehead.

'Not long, now,' Mrs Cousins said, tucking Gwen's nightgown out of the way. 'I want ye to hold back yer pushin'.
Let me guide ye...we've waited this long so we can wait a
minute longer.'

I could hardly breathe. Gwen opened her eyes, her eager smile giving me much needed courage. I kissed her hand. 'All the locks are open,' I whispered, unable to stop my tears. 'Everything's going to be all right…'

Gwen took a deep breath, letting it out in a silent whistle. 'Should be me cryin', Elly, not you.' She took another deep breath. 'I feel like pushin'…I can't stop…I feel like pushin'.'

'Push away,' said Mrs Cousins. 'Ye're tearing, but it's a big baby…good girl…Now push again, my love…push… an' now pant…pant like ye're a thirsty dog…Now push like never before.' Gwen's face turned puce, her mouth clamping tight, and I squeezed her hand almost as hard as she was squeezing mine. 'There's a good girl…Now rest till ye feel like pushin' again…There ye go…push…and here we have him.'

Indignant cries filled the room and I stared in wonder at the puckered red face of a screaming baby. My hands were shaking, tears rolling down my cheeks – a baby boy, a perfect baby boy; a screaming, plump baby with fingers and toes and a shock of black hair. Gwen was smiling, but my heart was too full to speak – a perfect baby, born alive and screaming, and Gwen sitting up, reaching over for him.

Mrs Cousins washed her hands in Jenna's bowl of hot water. She reached for a towel. 'There ye go, my love, like shelling a pea. Ye're born to have babies. I'll get that cord cut – then we've the after birth to get clear – perhaps now we can get these windows shut.'

Mrs Pengelly shook her head, wiping her eyes with her handkerchief. 'I don't know what to think, Elly, but there's nothing more we can do – not now. The constable's searching and we must leave it to him.' I nodded, too numb to speak, and she tucked the blanket more firmly round me. 'They'll do everything they can...Sleep now, my love.' She stroked my hair, the white lace on her nightgown catching the candlelight. 'But love can blind us, Elly. It can make fools of the best of us – ye must prepare yourself for that.'

I clutched William's token to my heart. The constable did not believe he was in danger; I had seen the contempt in his eyes. Mrs Pengelly and Sam and Mrs Munroe had pain deep in theirs, all of them as dazed and shocked as I was. 'There's been no trickery,' I cried, 'William would never think to rob me...he loves me as much as I love him. He didn't even want my money – he was going straight to his bank – he was going to pay me back.'

Mrs Pengelly picked up the candle, her voice breaking. 'Hush, Elly love. Try to sleep. The constable's setting up the search. Hush now, you must get some sleep.'

Chapter Forty-three

The Quayside, Fosse
Tuesday 19th July 1796, 1:00 p.m.

The sun shone in the cloudless sky. No hint of a breeze. Seaweed lay strewn along the banks, tangled ropes and broken barrels lying where the tide had tossed them. Large branches and planks floated in the river, rowing boats, broken free from their moorings, drifting on the fast flowing current. Not a breath of wind, the calm after the storm, yet the storm inside me raged fiercer than ever. Not one of them believed me – they had all laughed at me. They thought I deserved what I got. I could see the gloat in their eyes, as if they thought me too uppity and in need of bringing down, but I did not care what they thought. I just wanted them to find William.

I had watched the hue and cry set off at first light, Sam rushing to join them. They were to notify the ships before the tide turned, circulate William's description. Nearby turnpikes and coaching inns were to be alerted, each coach taking his description to the next inn. But none of them had listened to me, the constable laughing in my face as I told him he should be searching the coves and ditches, the places where a beaten man could be hidden and left to die.

'We'll take Mrs Hoskins her gowns then we'll search behind the tannery.'

Billy nodded, his eyes as red rimmed as mine. 'And the brewhouse – there's a mound of rubbish behind the brewery. But Mrs Pengelly believed you. She didn't like the constable talking to you like that. She was really upset. And Mrs Munroe's been crying all morning.'

The town was busy, men and women turning to stare after me, and I bit my lip to stop it from trembling. Mrs Hoskins had changed the delivery time yet again, but at least it gave me a chance to compose myself. In the courtyard my courage drained. Josie and Uncle Thomas would be waiting in the shop and I had to face them. I must take the consequences of my lie. Billy saw them, too, and put his hand through my arm.

'I'm all right, Billy. Take Gwen Mrs Munroe's calf's foot jelly. Tell her I'll be along later.' I handed him the stone jar, summoning up my courage. I was not all right; my head was thumping, a terrible sickness churning my stomach.

Josie held her arms wide and the tears I had been holding back suddenly flowed freely. I could not stop myself; fierce sobs wracked my body and I gulped for breath. 'Come, my dear, come...Yer uncle's not cross...he's just shocked ye lied to him. 'Twas the wrong thing to do, but 'tis done now an' no amount of shoutin's goin' to put that right. We've to find him, that's all...'

Uncle Thomas sat with his head in his hands. Dear Uncle

Thomas, unable to scold me even after I had lied to him. He shook his head and I ran to his side, kneeling on the floor to beg his forgiveness. 'I'm so, so sorry...I should never have lied to you...never.' He put out his hand, resting it on my shoulder, but he could not speak. He shook his head again. 'I can pay you back...I'm going to Mrs Hoskins now...I didn't lie about that.'

'You lied about your savings,' he said softly.

Tears poured down my cheeks and I laid my head on his outstretched arm. My dearest, generous uncle, the man I loved and trusted. I should have told him, never lied to him. I should have taken William straight to him and told him our plans. He would have understood. He would have liked William. 'I needed forty pounds and I only had thirty-six. William's not a thief...he was going to buy the old forge...' My heart was breaking. This gentle man who had done nothing but offer me wise advice, who had taken me in, given me everything. 'William has his own legacy...he was only borrowing the money...he was going to give it straight back.'

He looked up. 'Ye did wrong, Elly. Ye should have told me everything.'

'I know...I know that now...'

'You trusted a complete stranger with your money and not your uncle? With that amount of money, I could have got you a lease – set you up for life.'

'But I thought Gwen's baby was going to be a girl and I thought you'd want to put Tom's name on my lease.'

'You thought wrong, Elly, but you didn't think to ask?'

'I was too scared of Tom knowing...scared you'd suggest I should help him get the yard instead.' I wanted to tell him about Mamm and her list. How she had me lying awake at night. How neither of them could be trusted but I could say nothing. I knew I had to keep silent.

He shook his head again, his hand warm on my shoulder. 'It's not your fault, Elly, it's me to blame. I should've been more watchful – these villains work like that. They divide a woman from her loved ones...sow seeds of mistrust, make you believe they're right an' *they're* the one to trust, not the family who love you. William Cotterell knew very well what he was doing.'

Pain cramped my stomach. 'William's not wronged me ...he's a good man. It's others that wrong him...others want his downfall.' I was in such turmoil, wanting to tell him about the brother I no longer trusted, about the vicious clubs and Mamm's brandy, the watch they set at night. Yet if I told him they were no longer a family I could love and trust, my very words would bind him. List or no list, I still lived in fear.

His voice hardened, his eyes almost unrecognizable in their sternness. 'Billy told William Cotterell exactly how much you were worth. He told me last night. William knew right down to the last farthing how much you could lay your hands on. You had Billy count your money, remember, Elowyn?'

I felt sick, unable to breathe. 'William wanted me to use the money to buy back my fabrics...'

'I can't go along with this, Elly. He's robbed you, an' I think, deep down, ye know that. If he'd have been half decent,

398

or half serious, he'd have come to see me. A decent, honest man would have come to me and made his intentions clear.'

Outside, horse's hooves came to a stop, a man was dismounting. Josie went quickly to the window. 'It's Mr Cardew. He's talking to Tom. He's tying up the horse an' they're comin' up.' She walked swiftly to the door.

'No, Josie...I can't face them. Don't let them come up. Please not Nathan...not Tom. Please, Uncle Thomas, stop them from coming in.'

'I can't, lass – you must hear them out.'

I stood up, reaching for my handkerchief, watching in horror as Tom strode angrily up the steps. Nathan followed, grim faced and serious.

Uncle Thomas stood up at their entrance. 'Tom, you're to keep a civil tongue. No good will come of shouting – Elowyn's upset enough already.'

Tom flung round to face me. 'So she should be. The man's an imposter. He's not William Cotterell and never has been. He's a lyin' toad, pretendin' to know about ditches an' locks an' engines but he's nothin' but a fraudster – he's done this before. He pretends to love someone an' steals their money. Tell her, Nathan.'

Nathan stood clutching his riding whip, awkwardly twisting it in his hand. Everything about him showed discomfort, the way he kept his eyes to the floor, the way he stood half facing the door. 'I'd rather not...if it's all the same to you, I'll wait downstairs. Elowyn's too distressed and I shouldn't be here.'

'You should be here and she needs to know. Tell her, Nathan.'

Uncle Thomas nodded. 'If you know something, please tell us. Elowyn's distressed but she must know the truth. Speak gently, Nathan – tell us what you think we should know.'

Nathan shook his head, clearing his throat. He seemed nervous, ill at ease. 'It was after the wrestlin' match – one of the sailors from Plymouth said he hardly recognized William Cotterell.' He coughed again, glancing nervously in my direction. 'I knew I had to be careful, I knew my own impartiality might blind me. I was on difficult ground, but I put out word, askin' if anyone knew anythin' about him.'

He tapped his whip anxiously against his thigh. 'Ruth had money stolen from the collection an' the only person who'd been near the barn was William Cotterell...Then I started hearin' back. People's things were goin' missin' – clothes from lines, knives...picks and shovels. A man answering William Cotterell's description was seen sellin' them in Fosse an' I began askin' more questions.' He stopped, looking down, swallowing his discomfort. 'I found out that William Cotterell had left for the East Indies on the fourth of June. Matthew Reith was just as suspicious – no one knew William Cotterell here...none of us would recognize him as an imposter.' He stopped again. 'I'm sorry. This is too painful for Elowyn. I don't think it's the time.'

'Tell her, Nathan. Tell them both.'

'A man came forward, this mornin'. He's a sailor, workin' on the coal ships. He was there on the night of the quarrel but sailed that night. He heard the argument – Mr Drew was angry, tellin' William to pack his bags an' leave. I've questioned him further an' he's prepared to swear, under oath, he

400

heard him say the word *imposter*…an' he heard William say he'd be *coming after him*.'

Tom glowered at me across the room. 'Do ye see what Nathan's sayin'? Either Mr Drew knew William Cotterell or he knew the man claimin' to be him. Either way, his challenge proved his undoin'. The man's an imposter, Elowyn, a murderer – if those boots had been found *before* the inquest, he'd not have been acquitted. Only a murderer hides his boots. Mrs Burrow hadn't seen him that night because he *wasn't* there. He'd put his boots on the rack an' climbed out the window. Tell her the rest, Nathan…'

Nathan shook his head, his glance full of pain. Concern creased his brow. 'Elowyn's heard enough. There's nothin' more.'

'Tell her.'

He shook his head, turning away. 'There's nothin' more, Tom.'

Tom shook his head. 'Elowyn needs to know. How d'you think this imposter knew where to murder Mr Drew? Well, I can tell you. He knew he'd be in the linhay – and ye know why? Because he's been there every night, that's why. Yer so-called love bird, spendin' his nights in the linhay—'

'Tom, that's enough. I said keep a civil tongue.'

I could take it no longer and rushed into the storeroom, clinging to the empty shelves, thinking I would faint. I could hardly breathe. I thought I would be sick, bile filling my mouth. I was shaking, I needed the privy. I needed air, everything spinning round me as I fought to keep control. Josie ran behind me.

'He should never have said that…ye poor, poor darlin'. 'Twas a wicked thing to tell ye, even if 'twas the truth…'

Someone was ripping my heart from my chest, the pain so unbearable, I wanted to howl. It was not true, it could not be true. They were lying, making up lies, William loved me. I fell to my knees, curling up in a tight ball. That slight hesitation when he told me his name. No proof of identity. He had been in a fight. He knew I had money. None of that was new to me. They forged the embarkation record because they had thrown him on another ship.

Through the open door, Nathan's voice was a whisper. 'He must've been a close associate of Mr Cotterell – someone who knew him well. Someone who saw him board that ship to the East Indies. Perhaps one of the miners he worked with—' His voice broke. 'I feel it's my fault…I should've taken greater care of her…I should've warned you the moment I had my doubts…but I thought it was my jealousy. I thought you'd think me vindictive, tryin' to blacken another man's name so I still stood a chance…'

'We should all have been more watchful – I thought it was just *one* kiss…*one* dance…I'd no idea she was in so deep.'

Tom's voice was gruff, rising with his anger. 'Where'd she get that sort of money? Honest, Thomas, she's been given every chance an' she's just thrown it away. I could've used that money to secure the yard…I work every hour God sends me an' I've little to none put away. Now the baby's here an' I've next to nothin'—'

Nathan's voice cut him short. 'Ye can depend on the yard, Tom…I owe it to you. No strings attached. Sir James looks

402

favourably on your application an' it's yours for the takin'. I've let you all down an' it's my way to make amends.' There was a pause, footsteps to the door. 'I must take my leave. I'm to go to the adventurers' meetin' and dinner tonight. It's an honour to be invited to invest with them. They're openin' a new cost book an' I'd be lying if I said I'm not tempted. My father's bricks are sellin' well an' we've secured the contract for the new granary.'

Uncle Thomas sounded cautious. 'You're thinking of investing in the mines?'

Nathan's voice dropped to a whisper. 'The investors are seeking new members — there're worthless shares to be bought. It's not common knowledge but now's the time to buy.' The door opened. 'Oh, I nearly forgot — I've asked Major Trelawney to widen the search — his men are combin' the moors where a man's been seen answerin' to Cotterell's description.' His voice hardened. 'He'll not get away. We're goin' to find him.'

Chapter Forty-four

Billy laid the gowns carefully in his barrow, the bright red paint gleaming in the sun. Three years ago, Madame Merrick had designed the barrow to advertise her business, her name painted in large gold letters down either side, and we had left it as it was. Billy had delivered every new gown in that barrow, walking proudly through the streets as if wheeling a barrow of gold. Yet now the gold was gone.

He put his hand on my arm. 'Ye all right, Elly? Only she said four o'clock so we'd best hurry.'

The streets smelt fresh after the heavy rain, the sewers flushed, and I breathed deeply to steady myself. People were drifting away from the market stalls, sellers packing up their unsold wares. A man threw Billy an apple, another handed him a handful of plums. Everyone loved Billy and I swallowed back my tears, the pain of this last delivery almost too much to bear.

'Wait, Billy…let them go.' I pulled him back behind a pile of empty crates.

A group of well-dressed men were gathering outside the Ship Inn; some I recognized as members of the Corporation, others I did not know, but one face was very familiar – Mr Hellyar. Mr Hoskins was in the centre, ushering the others through the door before him. 'They're forming a consortium to buy up worthless mine shares. Nathan's thinking of joining them,' I said, waiting until the door closed behind them.

'I don't like Nathan, Elly. I've never liked him. William says he's got detestable self-importance.'

I fought the cry that rose from my heart, the terrible lurch at the mention of his name. He had spent every night in the linhay. Every night. I needed to be sick again and ran to the gutter. Billy watched me wipe my mouth. 'Ye all right, Elly?'

I shook my head. 'I don't think I'll ever be all right again.'

Mrs Hoskins' house was along the shore road; a fine house, well befitting a prosperous new banker. It was recently built, positioned to catch the fresher air and long sea views, with eight large sash windows, iron railings and steps leading up to the front door. Smaller steps led down to the servants' entrance but I stood on the top step, grasping the brass knocker firmly in my hand. Mrs Hoskins would not like it but we could not carry the gowns all the way down those steps and through the kitchen.

The maid ushered us up the wide staircase to where Mrs Hoskins was waiting in what she called her *boudoir*. She had been watching us from the window and stood pointing to where we should lay the gowns. She looked surprisingly happy, even greeting us with a smile. Billy bowed politely, going back to the barrow to eat his fruit, and I began undoing the cotton wraps, wondering how I was going to manage to get through the fitting.

'Thank you, Elowyn. And have I got news for you?' She seemed as excited as a child. 'Mr Hoskins has secured us our new premises. He bid last night an' the Corporation's that pleased he's got the shop. 'Tis a prime location...in Fore Street, though it's goin' to take some time to prepare – we're to refurbish it. Of course we'll need to remove the old furnishings but I'm that delighted. I'll send for you – after the wedding.'

My last delivery and my future in ruin, I had to breathe deeply, stop myself from crying. It was the shop Lady Polcarrow had thought to lease and I knew it would be perfect. Mrs Hoskins hardly stopped for breath; she was talking happily, struggling out of her clothes, the maid running round her like a timid mouse. I should have been delighted. She looked beautiful, even dignified, the dress complementing her, making her look soft and feminine. The ribbon petal of the roses looked perfect, the pearls catching the light. Yet I was filled with numbness, a terrible feeling of loss. I could hardly smile back as she swirled in front of the looking glass.

'Ye've done well, Elowyn. A mother shouldn't outshine her daughter but I think ye've done me proud.'

All my savings, I had nothing left. 'There's nothing I can see that needs changing...the fit's perfect. Is the wedding next week?' I managed to say.

She smiled, not wanting to take off the gown, but there was the second one to try. It was a cluttered room, the furniture too heavy, and I fought back my tears. She would offer me a job and I would refuse. I would work with Jenna and save every farthing to buy back my fabrics. I had to believe in myself. I was Elowyn Liddicot…I bit my lip, forcing down my nausea. The linhay, he had spent every night in the linhay.

How could I have been so wrong? I was not stupid, I was wary. I never let merchants cheat me. I mistrusted men, forcing my way past the hands that tried to grab, the slap on my bottom, the brush against my bosom. I was no longer the daughter of a drunken fisherman that men felt they had the right to touch. I had got away, found respect and love. I was a good judge of character. I knew how to read people, dress them well. My gowns exceeded their expectations. William had seen that, he had given me the confidence to believe in myself.

'We're to leave first thing tomorrow. Two days ago, we'd lost all chance to travel, yet the sun's already dryin' up the ruts. We're off at first light to reach Exeter before dark.'

I would be out of here soon. I took a deep breath. 'With any luck, the weather's set to hold.'

Mrs Hoskins' good humour showed no sign of abating. 'We've all the luck we need,' she said, still admiring her figure in the mirror. 'Ye've heard of four-leaf clovers, have you? Well, there's a thing…I know the journey will go well – even my daughter's marriage.' She walked briskly to the mantelpiece but I barely saw her. 'Can you imagine?' she said, holding up a delicately pressed four-leaf clover. 'There's a sayin' that if you find a four-leaf clover, you can wish on it.'

407

I could hardly breathe, cold shivers running down my back. It was William's four-leaf clover – exactly as it had looked when I had placed it between the crisp new notes. My last wish that William would be successful in his bid. I could hardly speak. 'Where did you find it?'

'I didn't *find* it, as such. Mr Hoskins gave it to me – it was among some banknotes he was counting. Such a lucky coincidence…he knows how nervous I get about travellin' so he brought it straight over – not that a good Christian woman like me believes in such nonsense.'

'This morning?' I managed to say.

She nodded happily. 'Elowyn, are you feeling faint? You look awful.'

'It's just the heat…I've been rushing…I need some air.' I had to stop the room from spinning. 'Does he know who deposited the money? Perhaps they wanted something very badly?'

'No, of course not,' she said, her chins wobbling as she laughed. 'It all gets put together. Honest, Elowyn, you don't think my husband keeps money boxes with everyone's name on them, do you?' She laughed again, turning once more to catch the back of her new gown. 'It's not like that at all. The money gets put together and my husband invests it. Money makes money, Elowyn – it's not kept in someone's money box!'

Her joy was uncontained. She reached for her purse, pulling free the ribbon. 'And Mr Hoskins brought my money to pay you. I have it here – four pounds, I believe.' She held out the crisp new notes and I caught my breath. They were identical to the notes Nathan had held out to Uncle Thomas, the same crisp feel in my hand and the same icy hand gripped my heart. I fought to keep calm. 'Does Mr Cardew bank with Mr Hoskins? Only I've just seen them together – going into the Ship Inn.'

'I've no idea. All the best merchants bank with my husband. Certainly Sir James does and most of the Corporation. My husband advises on investments. In fact, he's advising the adventurers as we speak – they're openin' a new cost book... I believe they've hit a rich new seam. Course, I shouldn't be tellin' you that.' She giggled, going back to the looking glass to admire her new gown.

'Mrs Hoskins...I'm sorry...I do feel rather faint. May I leave you now?'

She smiled back at me from the mirror. 'By all means. I'll contact you when I return. Of course, I'll need to make certain *economies*; expenditure will need to be curtailed and wages kept reasonable – Mr Hoskins is not made of money, though many think he is.'

I left her laughing at her own joke and tore down the stairs, rushing through the door to grab Billy's hand. I hurtled him round the corner.

'What is it, Elowyn? Ye look like ye've seen a ghost?'

'William was robbed. My money was put in the bank this morning...I know that because my four-leaf clover was among the notes – Mrs Hoskins's just shown it to me.' Was I being too fanciful? Just because the money looked identical did not mean it was the same. All Mr Hoskins' notes looked the same, all of them with the picture of the ship, the words

409

I promise to pay the bearer one pound. Yet the more I stared at the notes, the more my heart raced. 'Billy, do you think Nathan can have anything to do with the theft?'

His eyes widened. 'Nathan? Why do you say Nathan?'

'Because I think he might bank with Mr Hoskins. Yesterday he gave me the exact same notes.'

'A lot of people would give you the exact same notes – even Mr Scantlebury.'

'But what if Nathan's not really what he seems? What if on the surface he's all goodness and charity but underneath he's lying?'

The shock was passing, my mind clearing. What if Nathan was pretending he did not want me to know William spent every night in the linhay? What if he was lying to make me think ill of William? The barrow was blocking the pavement, people looking strangely at us and we needed to step aside. 'Nathan's said things that aren't true, Billy...he said he had to persuade Sir James to open his barns for the vagrants but that's not true – Sir James was more than willing – and he told Sir James we were engaged.'

Billy shook his head. 'But that don't make him a thief, Elly.'

A few lies were nothing, besides, no one would believe me. No one had seen me with my four-leaf clover, they would think I was making it up, and even if they did believe me, Nathan regularly deposited money into Sir James' harbour account – anyone could have given him the four-leaf clover tucked between their notes.

Billy's eyes sharpened. 'We need to know *when* Mr Hoskins found the four-leaf clover and *who* put the money in the bank.

Only Sir James can get that sort of information…he might be back.'

We left the barrow, running through the empty market square and round past the church, climbing the steep cobbled road to the gatehouse of Polcarrow. The huge gates were shut, the tall crenelated wall encircling the large estate. Billy knocked on the gatehouse door, annoying the gatekeeper with his repeated banging. 'Hush, Billy, ye'll wake the dead. 'Tis not like ye to knock so rudely. Learn some manners, lad.'

'I'm sorry,' I said, fighting for breath, 'but we must speak to Sir James. Is he back?'

The gatekeeper shook his head, the gold brocade on his livery embroidered by Jenna. 'He's in St Austell – expected later tonight. Lady Polcarrow's in…'

The more I thought about Nathan Cardew, the more scared I became. It was as if my instincts had been warning me, the icy hand my heart's recognition of his deceit. His excessive vulnerability, his lost-boy looks and nervous expectancy could all be a sham – used to entrap me, to make me feel I was the only woman he could love. It was like blinkers falling from my eyes.

'We need to go to Porthcarrow – Nathan's in a meeting… then he has a dinner. We've got just enough time to search his office.'

Billy swung round, his face incredulous. 'Ye can't mean that?'

'I need to see his rent books. I only caught a glimpse of them but they didn't make sense. The cottages are doubled up. He's

411

charging each family rent yet there's only rent recorded for one family. I saw it, Billy. His accounts are a mess.' I started walking, breaking into a run. 'I thought he was in a muddle... but what if they're designed to confuse? When I said I'd help him, he snapped at me.'

'Ye mean he's cheating Sir James?'

I nodded. 'Quick...I need to speak to Bethany.'

Chapter Forty-five

Billy helped me over a stile and raced ahead, both of us flying along the cliff path as if we had wings. I had never run with such purpose. Sweat clung to my back, my shoes and hem ruined by the muddy puddles where the sun had not reached. We were making progress, walking hurriedly through the narrow parts, running like the wind when the path opened up.

A slight breeze blew from the east, ruffling the waves in the bay as it arced in front of us. It must be more than coincidence. Nathan had been spending money on new clothes and horses. He was about to invest so surely he would put the money in his bank to swell his funds.

The same cold hand clutched my heart. Nathan was never going to give me up. He wanted to control me, make me jump to his commands. He wanted me on his arm; he wanted to see the envy on other men's faces. He must be having me watched – that man I had seen clinging to his hat must have been following me. He must have known about the old forge and he must have seen William leave the shop. He had rushed across the courtyard only moments later. I stopped to catch my breath, doubling over with the stich in my side. Billy was breathing hard, his cheeks flushed. 'Why talk to Bethany? What's she got to do with it?'

I gasped for breath. 'She can't look me in the eye. She did at first – before she knew I was courting Nathan – but then she changed. She became fearful, looking everywhere except at me…and the women in the cottages looked at me with such loathing…but I think it's Nathan they loathe, not me. But it's not just that…Oh, I hardly know what to think but it doesn't make sense…'

'What doesn't?'

'Nathan's put oil lamps round the harbour – they're everywhere, yet he doesn't have one outside his door. Why keep the alley outside his door so dark? Why when there's bread to be had and women are walking alone in such darkness?'

We started running again, round Penwartha Point, cutting across the clifftops, the gorse snagging at my shawl. I had never run so fast, the screeching of the gulls echoing the screeching in my heart. What if William had walked out of my shop and straight into Nathan's trap? Billy seemed to read my mind. 'They'll change their search if we find some sort of proof. They'll believe us then.'

Mamm's back door was closed, the dry path easy to run down. Once clear of the gate, we caught our breath, confident we had not been seen. It must be well past six o'clock, the evening sun just visible over the surrounding cliffs. Ships were making their way into the lock, the sea lapping gently against the rocks beside us. I hardly glanced at the pier houses, running quickly past the hateful cottage where Nathan had planned to imprison me.

Bethany's door was open, the evening sun flooding the hall. She had the baby on one hip and a huge basket of laundry on the other; one look at my face and her smile disappeared. She came forward tentatively, shutting the door behind her, her cheeks ashen with sudden fear.

'Why do you hate Nathan?' I asked as she hurried me away from the house. She did not answer, tears filling her eyes. She bit her lip. 'Who were you running from that night? You'd no need to be there…the hotel's in the opposite direction… You'd already gone for bread.'

She said nothing, putting down the basket, rushing me round the corner and out of sight of the cottages. She crouched on the ground, the baby wailing in her arms. She was hiding her face, her sobs so pitiful they wrenched my heart. In that moment, I knew. Bile rose in my throat, disgust tearing through me, and I had to stop myself from retching. Neither of us could speak, neither move, nor even look at each other. Billy looked at us open mouthed and I reached for the baby, passing him over. 'Take him over there a moment.'

I knew to keep this to myself. Bethany looked up, pleading in her eyes. 'Don't tell anyone, please, please…Samuel must never know…Please don't judge me.'

'You think I'd judge you? It's him that needs judging. I'll give no names…There are others, aren't there?'

She covered her head with her scarf, kneeling in the dust in a crumpled heap. 'I don't know…' she sobbed.

'Believe me, there are others – I've seen them in his ledgers: rent rescinded, rent revoked, like he's some guardian angel, letting you off.' I put my hand to my mouth, fighting my nausea. 'Others are doing the same. You think other women wouldn't use the only thing they have to keep their children from starving?'

I pulled back her scarf, wiping her tears with my handkerchief. 'I'll not tell a soul but I'll expose his cruelty. He makes you come to the stables, doesn't he? He keeps it dark so no one sees you come or go. I'm going to expose him – Sir James will know of his deceit.'

'No…no…you can't. You can't touch him…Miss Liddicot, you mustn't. Don't tangle with him. He's evil…you'll not win…'

Billy followed as I strode furiously down the hill. Nathan had seen me visit Bethany – that look I had witnessed had been a scowl of dislike. He did not love me, he loathed me. William was right. He needed me to cover his tracks. He wanted me like a shield on his arm, deflecting any suspicions. Sir James would never suspect him if he was married to his wife's friend. What other fraud had he committed? I hardly saw the ships, nor heard the men shouting across the lock. All I knew was that I had to search those ledgers and we had to find William. Suddenly, I stopped.

'What is it, Elly?'

'Nathan's sent Major Trelawney out to the moors – he said there'd been a sighting…but he'll have sent them on a wild-goose chase. William must be still here. He must be somewhere close.'

The alley was deserted, the stable empty, and I stared at the locked door, my despair mounting. 'Can you break locks, Billy?'

'Not that one.'

'Can you kick it in?'

'No one can kick that in.'

'Then what are we to do?' The windows were round the front and even if we found a ladder, we would be spotted climbing in. Time was running out. Nathan would be at the dinner but he would soon be back to supervise the unloading of the ships.

Billy was smiling, his grin widening as he backed away. 'It's a stable, Elly. Every vagrant knows there'll be a trapdoor leading to the hay loft.'

The stable was stuffy, dusty cartwheels lying against the wall. Coils of ropes and an old harness hung from hooks, wooden buckets and a broken cart littered the floor, but the stalls were still intact and Billy reached up, swinging his legs from side to side as he pulled himself up. He stood looking down at me, balancing on the wooden stall as if he had done it all his life. 'There's a trapdoor all right.'

I stared into the shadows, looking up at a small square door in the rafters above. It was half hidden, the rough wooden planks merging with the beams around it. Billy held his hands flat against the wooden planks. 'It's lifting, Elly. It's well used...it's as silent as a grave.' He reached further. 'There's nothing but a rug on top.'

He gripped the edge of the trapdoor, springing as high as he could, heaving himself up by his elbows, his legs dangling momentarily before he turned to peer down. 'I'll reach for you. Take my hands, give a good spring up.'

I tucked my shawl round my thighs, tying it tightly. It was not breaking but it was certainly entering and I did not give it a second thought. I swung up on the wooden stall, balancing along the top, reaching up for Billy's hands. His grip was strong, pulling me firmly, and I gave a huge push, at once lying sprawled across the floor of Nathan's office.

'He should have it nailed up,' said Billy. 'Anyone can get in.'

The last rays of the sun streaked through the window. There was no need for a candle but we knew not to stand up. Until it was darker, people might look up and see us – we would crawl on our hands and knees. The table and chairs were in the corner, the desk on the other side, and I made my way across the rough wooden floor. There were the same profusion of bills and receipts, the piles of ledgers, and my mouth tightened – evil, evil man, subjecting those poor women to his brutal deception. They stood no chance against his threat of eviction.

I opened the first ledger and my heart froze. Everything was neatly entered, no crossings-out – the dates, the amounts, the sums neatly added. Not even a smudge. I turned the pages in mounting panic – ten cottages, with the rent entered neatly by the side. No *fines*, no rent *rescinded* – everything immaculate. I reached up for another ledger. Again, the same thing. No crossings-out. No smudges, everything neat and readable, the outgoings listed down one side, the incomings down another. A perfect set of accounts.

'What is it, Elly?'

'It's not what I saw before...when I came last time, the accounts were a mess...these are too neat. There are no fines or rescinded rents...' I stared at the entry by Samuel Cooper's name. The rent was paid, just like all the others. Ten cottages at two shillings a week.

Fury filled me, a terrible anger sweeping up my throat, burning my cheeks. 'He must have two sets of accounts – one for himself and one for Sir James. He must be expecting Sir James...or maybe Matthew Reith's been looking through them. We've got nothing on him...there's nothing here.'

'Ye sure, Elly?'

'Billy, I saw them with my own eyes. He's an evil man and we need to find them.'

I began pulling open the drawers, lifting out the contents and sifting through them. Each drawer contained piles of accounts, references, proposed work and tenders for business. Putting each drawer carefully back, I lifted up the tobacco pouches, pipes, boxes of spare candles. There was nothing there. But the drawers were too small for the ledgers, they were big books and I knew we must look elsewhere. 'Search next door – there's a small room he uses to sleep in. There's a couch and wash things.'

Outside, I heard shouting, the gatekeeper giving the command to close the lock. The sun was dipping below the cliffs, the harbour darkening. We did not have much more time.

'Quick, Elly. Ye better see this.' Billy was kneeling by the makeshift couch, a small chest open in front of him. I rushed to his side and stared incredulous, a wave of fear making me catch my breath. My blood turned to ice. The chest was full of clothes; a black jacket, a pair of black breeches, a heavy black cloak and a large black hat. Beneath the hat lay a leather mask and a thick black scarf.

It was Nathan who had followed me, Nathan enjoying inflicting so much fear. Nathan dressed like a demon, subjecting poor Bethany to unspeakable horror. Nathan waving me goodbye, his cat-and-mouse game over. Nathan next morning showing me such concern. The ledgers were under the clothes, a whip lying across them. 'Dear God,' I whispered, my hands shaking, 'Bethany said Nathan was evil.'

Billy stared at the clothes. 'Why, Elly? What sort of madman is he?'

I opened a ledger and saw a letter tucked between the first two pages. I held it up, hardly believing what I saw. It was addressed to *Mr William Cotterell*, dated Thursday 16th June.

Dear William,

How relieved I am to hear you are avoiding further mischief — at least for now. The dye you speak of is most likely ultra-marine blue — no doubt ground very fine from lapis lazuli and made into a tincture. I believe the effect of this substance in a settling pit could well be to whiten the clay, so your suspicions may be founded in truth. I will take your question to the Worshipful Society of Apothecaries and let you have their considered opinion.

I trust your mother is well. Please send her my sincerest regards.

Yours in friendship,
Hugh Lefroy

The letter trembled in my hand. Nathan had kept it, never given to William; he knew about William's suspicions but to keep the letter and not alert Sir James? I could hardly take in the implication.

Billy stared in horror. 'Why not give it to William? What's he doing, creeping round the harbour at night, hiding behind his mask and long cloak?'

'He's watching people – that's what he's doing, using everything to his advantage. That's why the trapdoor doesn't squeak. He slips in and out in the dark. They think he's working at his desk but really he's prowling round, watching. He must know everything that's going on. Perhaps he's blackmailing people. Perhaps that's the real meaning behind the word *fines*.'

I picked up the ledgers. If I was right he would have known about the clay in the flour. He would know everything. There would be an entry under Mr Sellick for the blue dye, an entry under Jack Deveral for the clay in the flour. Who else had been *fined*? The ledgers were just as I remembered, the blotches, the crossings-out, the cramped rows of names under the heading *Money Owing*. I flipped back several pages, trying to make sense of them.

'Here...look: Jack Deveral, John Polkerris – thirty pounds. The date's Sunday the twelfth of June – surely that's before Matthew Reith started his investigations? Nathan knew all along who'd contaminated the flour – look...here, he must have *fined* them for his silence.'

The light was fading yet we could not light a candle. I picked up the two ledgers, taking them to the floor beneath the window. The docks were busy, wagons loaded up with coal. Time was running out, Nathan had bought a horse and his return would be swift.

'I need to check something…it's something I remember. Mr Drew said it was the builders who do the work, not the engineers…It sounded strange at the time and I'm not sure what he meant…William said the work was shoddy – what if Nathan's cutting costs and creaming off the money, putting in expensive bills yet using the poor quality materials? If he's cheating with the rents, he's bound to be cheating on the costs.'

I was thinking so fast I could hardly say my words, all the while turning back the pages, trying to make sense of the entries. 'That first day when the cows broke through the new fence, Nathan was furious but what if the wood was sub-standard? What if he was using rotten wood?'

'Elly, it doesn't make sense. Nathan would never risk that. Sir James would find out and he'd lose his job. He wants the power…he wants the control…he'd never let Sir James' harbour fail.'

I stared back at him, hardly able to breathe. 'But what if he *does* want the harbour to fail?' I was thinking so quickly, my mind in turmoil. 'What if there are others as well – what if it's Viscount Vallenforth who wants Sir James to go bankrupt and he's paying Nathan to build everything badly?' My hands were shaking. 'Billy, look at this: Nathan's fined Mr Sellick thirty pounds…here…that must have been *after* he read William's letter about the dye, but look, it's been rescinded. Why would he suddenly stop blackmailing Mr Sellick?'

'I don't know…Elly, we can't stay here. He'll be back soon. We'll take everything with us – the clothes, the ledgers… but we must be quick.' Billy looked petrified, and with good reason. I had never felt such fear.

'No…leave them here – put them back exactly where they were. Sir James must find them. If we take them there's no proof they came from here.' I slid the letter between the pages, handing him back the ledgers. 'Wait…one last thing…I need to check…'

My heart was pounding. *Don't let me find it…please don't let me find it.* Yet there it was: yesterday's date – John Polkerris and Jack Deveral: *fine rescinded*. I could hardly read it for the tears rolling down my cheeks. The slate for adulterating the flour had been wiped clean – paid in blood money. 'Oh God, Billy…they've killed him. They've used their clubs on him… two huge men against one…he wouldn't stand a chance. Billy, they've clubbed him to death.'

I was shaking uncontrollably, staring blindly at the ledger. Billy took it from me, hurrying back to the makeshift bedroom, putting everything back exactly as it was. I could not speak but fell forward on my knees, gasping for breath.

'Elly, we have to go…quick. I'll check no one's down there then I'll lower you down. Come, Elly, please. I'll leave this rug the best I can…Elly…can you hear me? We've got to get away – our lives are in danger. Come…'

I could not move; a shiver had taken hold of me, a terrible chill. I felt as cold as a grave, ice-cold tentacles running down my spine. 'William's body will be in the tunnel…' I whispered. 'They'll take him to the cave. The storm stopped them getting a boat out last night but they'll do it tonight. They'll smuggle him out and he'll vanish without trace. I want him back, Billy. I want to bury him...I need a grave...I need somewhere to lay his flowers...' I shivered again. 'Billy, that night Nathan followed me, he reached the cliff almost as quickly as I did. He was a long way behind but suddenly he caught up with me.'

'What are you saying?'

'Nathan knows about the tunnel – there must be a whole network of tunnels leading to the cave. One moment he was on the slipway, the next he was behind me on the cliff. He must have run through a short cut.'

Chapter Forty-six

The huge cranes were lifting the heavy sacks high into the air. I grabbed some discarded sacking to use as a cloak. It was filthy and damp but my yellow dress was acting like a beacon – one glance at the dockside and Nathan would see me. The dock was teeming, the oxen carts waiting in line. We kept to the edge, stepping over the ropes, ducking under the chains as they swung above us. The lock was full, the ships lying two abreast against the quay. Billy pulled me back, hiding behind a hogshead. 'Wait...Mr Perys is looking. Wait till he turns his back.'

The water was no longer blue but grey and murky. The sun was dropping, the light from the oil lamps gradually taking hold. Men were unloading the ships, some singing, some silent; a group of boys were calling down to them as they worked. We were at the end of the lock, crossing the slipways of the new boatyards. The first boatyard was already taking shape, the second still a wasteland, full of rubble and grassy mounds. It was to be the boatyard Nathan had promised Tom.

'Billy, wait!' I stood stock still.

Nathan had been on this very spot when he had petrified me so completely, slipping in and out of the lamplight playing his cat-and-mouse game. We were under the lamp now, the first store with its thick iron grille facing me. The store was in shadow, the thick grille locked like a dungeon.

'What is it, Elly?'

'This is where I saw him last. He was right here. The tunnel must lead from somewhere very close. We need to search that store.'

'You sure? How d'you know?'

A terrible instinct was leading me. I was inside Nathan's mind, thinking the evil he would think. I understood his power, the enormity of his reach. It was not just Mamm and Tom wanting me to have that boatyard, but Nathan as well; all of them lining up the perfect route to keep it in the family. No need to anchor, no need to row out to the ship. Bring the ship in and pretend it needed repairs. Lady Polcarrow's friend married to the Piermaster so no one would suspect. My heart was racing. Nathan had organized the cart, he knew all about the bladders. I was to become one of them. And Gwen? When were they going to tell Gwen?

'We're in luck,' whispered Billy, standing by the grille. He reached into his waistcoat, pulling out a fine silver hat pin. 'There's two, but one's not locked. This one's easy.' He started poking the hatpin into the huge iron lock, holding it steadily.

'Billy, where did you get that?'

'Found it on the street. I didn't steal it. I could sell it, mind

426

– it's worth more as a lock-picker than a hat pin. Most grain stores have these locks – or something like this. You have to be gentle, take it slow. You just keep going round one notch at a time. If you miss it, you need to go round again.' He looked up, smiling. 'My dad taught me. Chicken coops have locks like these. They all open in the end.'

The grille was shadowed by the overhang of the road above, directly below the pier houses Nathan had built. My heart was pounding but I knew not to hurry Billy. Even hidden by the shadows, we might still be seen.

'Make it look like you're just waiting. Sit on a barrel, swing your leg – make out you're waiting for someone on the ship.'

I sat on a crate, the filthy sacking covering me. It barely made sense – if Nathan was one of them, why did he fine Jack Deveral and John Polkerris for the clay in the flour?

'Billy...what if Nathan knows about the smuggling...but what if they went behind his back and hadn't told him about sending the clay to the flourmill? What if he was watching them and found out? He'd be furious, wouldn't he?' Cold fear clamped my heart; it suddenly made sense. 'Nathan must have absolute charge. He must run the cartel.'

Billy looked up. 'If he's running the smuggling, then of course he wants Sir James' harbour to fail. He wants everyone gone – he wants it back to how it was.' He turned the hat pin and the lock opened. 'I'll leave it so it still looks locked.'

The store had been dug deep under the road, long and narrow, the furthest end hidden in darkness. Barrels lined the walls, hooks hanging from the ceiling, pulleys on rusting wheels blocking our way. Chains lay in heaped coils, empty wooden crates stacked against the side. It smelt musty and damp, of old rope and tar. Lanterns hung unlit on the walls, deep recesses reaching back into the shadows. We would have to search in darkness.

We walked deeper into the store, feeling our way along the rows of barrels. The light from the entrance was fading, the darkness beginning to engulf us. We would have to feel for the way out – a small arch or a trapdoor. Billy walked in front of me, falling to his hands and knees to search the floor. Despite the sacking, cold penetrated my gown, making me shiver. It was as cold as a grave and William was down there.

We reached the end wall and could go no further. Barrels lay stacked neatly in front of us, another pulley on wheels next to the hogsheads. They were too heavy to lift and would be loaded onto a trolley to be pulled by a donkey. Each barrel crammed against the other – there was no gap, no secret passage. The floor was neatly swept, no sign of a trapdoor. 'Search again, Billy. There's a way out of here – there must be.' I tried to sound brave, but my heart was crying. He would be lying face down. He would have his skull smashed in. He would be wrapped in heavy sacking, ready to be thrown overboard.

Billy picked up a shackle and began tapping every hogs-head. 'That's liquid in there – says limestone on the sides but if you tap them you soon know.' He tapped each in turn, all sounding the same. He tapped the corner barrel. 'There you go,' he said as a hollow ring echoed round us. 'This one's empty – Father found one just like this in the vaults under the church…and this one's empty…and so's this.' He reached up, edging the empty barrels away from the wall.

I helped him move them aside and a tunnel stretched in front of us. Diffuse light lit the darkness, everything merging together in the half-light and I put out my hand, running my fingers along the wall – it was brick, about eight feet in height with brick arches lining the route. The floor was mud, bricked in places. The light grew brighter as we walked. 'There must be a lamp hanging round the bend – there might be someone there,' I whispered.

'Or they've left a lamp burning because they'll be back.'

I stared down the tunnel, knowing we should turn back and seek help. Sir James would be returning from St Austell, we must tell him all we knew. Yet as I stared into the half-light, something drew me on. 'He might still be alive, Billy… he might be lying there dying, all alone. He might be in great pain…hoping we'll find him…'

We must have gone sixty yards, no more. The lamplight was getting brighter, shadows flickering against the wall. A bend lay before us and we stopped, straining our ears for the slightest sound. The silence was eerie; no sound at all, just the stillness of a grave. Billy edged forward, nodding for me to follow.

Tall pillars stood on granite bases, rows and rows of them, arching across a vast cellar. A rush lamp was burning against the brick wall, the soft light flickering over the barrels stacked against the side; a vast collection point, right under the houses. Another two tunnels stretched into the darkness and I pointed to the one on the right. 'That must lead past Mamm's cottage and down to the cave – I saw them enter the privy that same night. I saw three men go down... Mamm's involved, Billy. She's been smuggling brandy under her skirts...she swore me to secrecy.'

'I know – bladders under their skirts – I saw that.' He smiled. 'I keep my mouth shut, same as everybody.' He looked across the vast cellar to the other tunnel. 'That must lead up the St Austell road. They'll need a barn or something...wagons to distribute the stuff.'

I dreaded finding him, dreaded not finding him. I began searching the shadows, desperately looking for a roll of sacking or a heavy canvas, anything that might be hiding his body. These were old tunnels, well used by generations – Cardew bricks, made in their kilns right above us; hundreds and hundreds of bricks made to line the tunnels that would bring such reward – the Deveral and Polkerris families in league with the Cardews. No wonder Nathan's family had prospered.

'He's not here – he might be in the cave...or somewhere down that tunnel,' I whispered.

Billy turned sharply. 'There's a lamp – Elly, hide – there's someone coming.'

A faint light flickered in the tunnel leading from the cave and I ran to the largest hogshead, squeezing silently behind it. The sacking was just what I needed and I drew it over me, peeping from under it to see where Billy had thought to hide. I caught my breath, hardly believing my eyes. He was standing as bold as brass, hands on hips, staring straight down the tunnel. The light was getting brighter, muffled footsteps approaching, yet he stood staring straight ahead, his black hair lost to the shadows, his eyes defiant. 'Billy,' I whispered, but he took no notice. The shadows were taking the shape of men, the same silhouettes we had seen in the cave – huge men with thick necks and heavy tread. 'Billy, hide!' Men who killed without thinking, bludgeoning anyone to death if they threatened their lucrative trade. I felt giddy with fear. They would kill him, I had to stop them.

John Polkerris held the lamp high in the air. 'What the bloody hell are ye doin'?' He was a huge man with shoulders like an ox. He was bearded, his head shaven beneath his hat. Jack Deveral was right behind him, glowering at Billy with murder in his eye. Anger distorted both men's features. They stepped forward, drawing daggers from their belts. The daggers glinted in the lamplight, huge killing blades as sharp as razors.

'I needs to speak to Jack Deveral or John Polkerris. Take me to them if ye please.' I hardly recognized Billy. He stood so assured, facing the two men as if he had done it all his life. They stopped suddenly, their sideways glances showing their surprise. 'I needs to speak only to them.'

John Polkerris took a step forward, holding the lamp above Billy, his dagger thrusting forward. 'What are ye doin' here?'

'I'll speak to no one but John Polkerris or Jack Deveral.'

'Speak, fer Chrissake…' The dagger flashed and my heart missed a beat.

'Nathan sent me…says ye've not done yer job prop-erly…' Billy sounded so assured, as if he had every reason to be there. 'Says he saw William Cotterell not three hours since – alive an' well. He was walkin' down the street in Fosse. Nathan's that angry – says yer to explain yerself—'

Jack Deveral reached forward, grabbing Billy's collar, his dagger pressing against his jacket. 'I don't like the look of ye…ye smell of trouble…I know ye…ye're Elowyn's shadow.' He shifted the dagger to Billy's throat. 'An' I've seen ye with that William Cotterell. What are ye doin' here?' He gripped Billy's collar tighter, the dagger glinting.

Billy's voice did not waver. 'I work fer Nathan – I report back…I tell him everythin'. That's how he knows what's goin' on. Elowyn tells me stuff, an' I pass it on. He told me to make friends with William Cotterell because he wanted to know what's goin' on an' I told him. I'm no friend of either. I do my job an' I get paid. Now, he's sent me to fetch ye. Wants to know why ye haven't done what he asked.'

Fear made me tremble. I was petrified, yet if I showed myself they would know he was lying. They were both scowl-ing, their faces furious. 'Ye're a lying little bastard, aren't ye? Lying, weasel little bastard. Nathan didn't send ye.' He grabbed Billy's arm, twisting it behind his back. 'Yer snoo-pin' fer the revenue…Ye've made a big mistake – a very big mistake.'

'It was me Nathan sent to the cave – that night when ye was shippin' the clay. I work fer him. Else you'd be swingin'. Nathan says ye're to explain yerselves.'

'Ye snivelling little spy – ye don't speak to me like that.

Ye don't come down here an' ye don't speak to me like that. Swingin', ye say? I'll give ye swingin'. Ye need a lesson… ye need teachin'.' He wrenched Billy's arm high behind his back and Billy winced with the sudden pain. 'I know just the place fer ye.'

John Polkerris put down the lamp, reaching quickly for a coil of rope. Billy began struggling, lashing out, kicking frantically as they began binding his arms and legs; huge, killing hands, intent on doing their work. Billy twisted his head. 'Nathan saw him…clear as day…walking down the—' A gag bit deep, Billy's words lost to the red scarf being tied so viciously. Once tied, they pushed him to the floor and I fought my nausea.

They were not men; they were demons, possessed by evil. They stood poised with their huge boots in the air, laughing as they saw Billy wait for their kicks. I nearly cried out; I was screaming inside, peering between the barrels, desperately thinking what to do. But they stopped laughing, dragging him instead along the floor to the base of a pulley, the large chain dangling in the air above them. 'I'll give ye swingin' – ye can swing here.' They worked quickly, as if they had done this many times before, turning the wheel to hoist Billy high in the air.

Billy swung above them, dangling in the darkness. 'We'll soon see if Nathan sent ye.' They turned, heading back towards me.

The lantern was on the floor in front of my barrel and John Polkerris retrieved it, placing it on a hogshead not four feet away. He was muttering, straightening his hat, and I held my breath, grateful for the heavy sacking. 'What if the boy's not lyin'?' He took hold of a barrel, turning it to its side.

Jack Deveral reached for another. 'The boy's lyin'.'

'What if he's waitin' fer us?'

'Oh fer Chrissake, the man's seein' things – 'twas bleedin' flooded.'

'Praps we should go – then deal with the boy if he's lyin'.'

'The boy's lyin'. Fer Chrissake, no one climbs out of that shaft.'

They turned angrily, leaving their lantern, walking grudgingly down the tunnel the way we had come. I hardly saw them leave – William was down a shaft. I could hardly breathe, the same shivers running down my spine. They had thrown him down the old shaft to drown. Yet he could never drown – he was alive. He was still alive.

'Billy,' I whispered, reaching for the heavy wheel, 'he's down the mine – they've thrown him down the old shaft, expecting him to drown – but he'll never drown. Never.' I pulled the wheel with all my strength; we had to hurry, they would soon realize they had been tricked. The pulley began to move, the chain slowly lowering Billy to the ground. He lay looking up at me, his gag so tight I could hardly untie it. 'We can still save him.' My fingers fumbled with the knots, my nails breaking as I managed to get it lose. The ropes around his wrists were just as tight, cutting into his flesh.

'Quick, Elly.' Billy reached down to untie his feet. 'Bring that sacking – we'll bind it with these ropes, it's so dark they may not notice.' His wrists were bleeding as he twisted the sacking and bound it tightly with the ropes. He hoisted it up into the shadows. 'That other tunnel must go up to the road – either way, we'll have to use it.'

I nodded. 'We'll take their lamp.'

Chapter Forty-seven

The tunnel remained bricked and arched, twisting into the hillside like a long black snake. The ceiling was getting lower but it was still the height of a man and we ran easily on the packed earth. The air smelt dank, the lamp showing patches of damp, but we were definitely rising, our footsteps echoing down the tunnel, our shadows following us along the wall. We stopped, gasping for breath. There was a choice where to go, a passage opening out to the left. 'Where d'you think that leads?' Billy held the lamp higher. 'D'you think it goes to the inn? It looks flat – the other one's still rising.'

'Perhaps it leads to the brickworks – think how many wagons leave those kilns.'

'Then we've to go higher,' he replied. 'Let's hope they think we've gone to the cave. All right to go on?'

I nodded, racing behind him. The tunnel was narrowing, getting markedly steeper. They would be behind us; they would know someone had heard them say the word shaft. We had to hurry, we still had a chance. William was not dead when they threw him down – he would be bound and gagged but he could still be alive. They must have set a trap – sent him a letter from Sir James. Nathan knew both Sir James' writing and his signature – perhaps he had forged a letter, asking William to meet him at the shaft. Thoughts jumbled in my mind – perhaps they used a pistol. Perhaps they swung him from behind with a club.

A stitch snagged my side and I had to bend double to catch my breath. Ahead of me, Billy stopped suddenly and held up the lantern. 'That's it. That's the end.' In front of us stood a set of sturdy wooden steps leading up to a trapdoor and I stared at it, gasping for breath. 'I need to snuff the wick, Elly – they mustn't see our light.'

A row of lanterns hung on hooks behind him and I watched him turn down the wick, plunging us into darkness. I heard him hang the lamp up on a hook. 'You all right, Elly?'

With the light, it had been bearable but in the darkness it was like a tomb and I fought my panic. What if it was locked and we had to make our way back in total blackness? I heard Billy climb the steps, heaving against the door with his shoulders. A crack appeared, a glimmer lighting the darkness. 'It's shifting,' he whispered, his outline beginning to show against the trapdoor. He opened it a little more, peering tentatively round. The scent of hay filled the tunnel, the smell of manure. Straw fell onto the steps and he pushed the door further. 'It's a barn – no, it's a stable,' he whispered.

I glanced out of the tiny window – we were in the stable next to the granary where dogs patrolled at night, the watchmen armed with pistols to keep looters at bay. Nathan's power was absolutely terrifying. He was guarding his tunnel like he guarded the cliffs. 'Billy, if the nightwatchmen are part of it, who else is involved?'

He looked as frightened as I felt. 'We can't trust anyone, Elly – only Sir James.' The stable was built of brick, the door bolted from the outside. Billy glanced up at the small window. 'Reckon you can squeeze through that?'

Dusk was falling, the sea growing blacker by the minute. Lamps were shining in the town, the lock hardly visible in the growing darkness. To our right, the tall chimney of the engine house stood dark against the greying sky and all hope drained away. We would need help; we could never haul William up by ourselves, neither did we have any way of knowing if Sir James had already passed – and what if who we called worked for Nathan? What if they were *all* working for Nathan, *all* their names on the list – their children only safe because they obeyed his every command?

I could at least call to him; my voice penetrating his torment, demanding he lived. I could shout to him, tell him how much I loved him – tell him he had to stay alive and that we were coming to save him. He had heard me before and he would hear me again. We started running along the lane, cutting back across the rough grass towards the old mine buildings. A shape was taking form on the road ahead, hooves scattering the stones. Someone was coming, the horse getting nearer. In the fading light I stood too petrified to move. Nathan had seen me. He was coming straight over.

I fought to breathe, watching the horse canter to a fast stop. Nathan swung himself out of the saddle, walking quickly towards me. 'What are you doing up here?' His eyes were speaking for him, his words a mere formality. They pierced me like daggers, stopping my heart.

Billy was some way ahead, nowhere to be seen. 'I'm walking home,' I stuttered, looking quickly down.

'From where?' He glanced towards the stable, his shrewd eyes taking in the hay still caught on my hem. He began slapping his riding whip against his outstretched palm, slowly, the same rhythmical tapping, each beat getting harder. No sign of lost vulnerability or boyish charm. It had been in his face all along, the hard lines around his mouth, that sudden glare of displeasure.

The mine buildings lay shrouded in dusk, the breeze blowing the scent of the flowers. I could see the boarded-up windows, the doors barred by planks of wood. In the dimming light, I could just see Billy dodge behind the old horse whim to hide. We were so close – so nearly with William. Nathan stood beside me, offering me his arm. 'What are ye doin' here, Elowyn? Perhaps you need help? Perhaps you need me to take you home?' He did not bother to keep the cruelty from his voice. His whip slapped his gloved hand even harder.

The outline of the bell was just visible in the growing darkness; the old bell, used by the mine captains to ring out danger. It was our only chance, and Billy was just by it. 'Ring the bell, Billy…' I shouted as loud as I could. 'Ring the bell…'

Nathan swung round to see Billy dash across the old stones. The bell began ringing, louder and louder, the urgent clanging sweeping across the hills, echoing down to the town, and

Nathan thrust me aside, pushing me to the ground as he ran towards Billy. I picked myself up, clutching my skirts high, tearing after him. Billy had the rope in both hands and was using all his strength to swing it from side to side. The bell had not been used for twenty-five years but it rang out loud and clear, the urgency of the ringing an unmistakable plea for help.

Nathan reached up the small set of steps, grabbing Billy's legs and I flung myself forward, pulling him back. Nathan kicked me free, sending me flying, but I was not done. William was right; I had the strength of an ox. I fought when needed – I fought them all off, every last one of them. Hands that grabbed, the lust in their eyes – none of them got what they wanted. I stood in front of him as his arms reached round Billy. I knew how to aim my knee right where it hurt. I was Elowyn Liddicot, daughter of a drunken fisherman, able to fell a man with just one thrust.

He lay curled on the ground, writhing in agony, and I stared down at the town, praying for people to come. The old bell was doing its job. Lanterns were swinging, men shouting, and tears began streaming down my cheeks. William would hear the ringing. William would know we were coming. He had to stay alive. In the growing darkness, I ran to the old shaft. They had boarded it up again, the nails well hammered, and I screamed against the boards, tears flooding my cheeks: 'We're coming, William…we're coming.'

There was nothing I could use to break open the planks. I began tearing at the wood, gripping it with both hands. No pickaxes. No shovels. No crowbars. Nothing I could use. I ran to every window, shouting against the thick wooden

planks. 'We're coming, William. Don't die. Don't die on us.'
Please let him hear the ringing. Let him hear the ringing.

Men were running towards us, huge men from the granary. 'What's wrong? What's the trouble?' They stood, gasping for breath.

'Someone's fallen down the mine.' I stared down at Nathan, still writhing on the ground. 'Mr Cardew's done all he can, but he's injured. He wants everyone to come and help.'

More men were arriving, their shouts adding to the sound of the bell; a donkey cart stopped and Mr Hearne jumped quickly off. He stared down at Nathan and I took a deep breath. 'William Cotterell's been thrown down the old shaft. Please, you've got to save him.'

Mr Hearne stared at me in horror and turned quickly, shouting to a group of men. 'Get ropes – we'll need to lower a man. Get those boards off – we'll go in from there. Get the lamps together – ye two – go back down fer stronger ropes – take Nathan's horse – then we'll use the horse to pull him up...Mr Cotterell's a heavy man.' He reached into his cart. 'Here, try this...or this.' He must have had his tools with him, his cart was laden. 'Who's goin' down? I need a lighter man to volunteer – yes, you. Take off yer jacket an' tie this rope round yer waist.'

I sat hugging my knees, the wind blowing my hair. Dusk had given way to night, the huge moon rising above us. A man shouted, the boards ripped quickly away; men held their lanterns high, all of them rushing to crowd round the shaft. Billy forced his way between them. 'Let me go – I'm the lightest...'

441

'No, lad. Stay back. We need someone to tie strong knots –
we've got just the man we need. Steady does it…slowly,' he
shouted. 'If the rope's not long enough, we'll bring ye back
up. Take yer time.' I watched the backs of the men as they
peered down the flooded mine shaft, their hands grasping the
rope firmly as they lowered the volunteer down.

'Ladder's rotten – the rungs have long gone,' I heard one
say.

''Tis the storm water – all that heavy rain…'

Behind me, Nathan's horse returned and a man jumped
off, struggling to lift a huge coil of rope hanging from the
saddle. Mr Hearne rushed forward to help, his shirtsleeves
rolled to the elbows. 'Get one end around the old whim…
get the horse harnessed an' let's see if it still works. William
Cotterell's a large man – he'll need winchin' up. See what ye
can do, lad.'

I sat resting my chin on my knees, listening to the men
hauling on the rope. *Please, please, let William be alive. Please,
please, don't take his soul.* William could not die, he must not.
He must never die thinking I thought ill of him. I started
shaking, tears rolling unchecked down my cheeks. He was
the only man I could ever love. The only man I could ever
marry.

Across the darkness, two lamps were swinging in time and
I stood up, staring into the blackness. It was a carriage: Sir
James had not already passed. The sleek black horses came to
a stop and Sir James flung open the door, jumping quickly to
the ground. He walked briskly over to Mr Hearne. 'What's
going on, Tobias?'

'William Cotterell's body's been found. They're just hoisting him up from the shaft. I'm afraid he's dead, sir — drowned. He's been bound and gagged, with a nasty blow to the head — it's the devil's work, an' no mistake.'

I doubled over in pain. Joseph Dunn must have heard my sudden gasp and came running over. 'Elowyn...Elowyn?'

I could hardly hear him. I could not breathe, the pain so excruciating, I thought I might be sick. We were too late. He had died all alone, never knowing we were searching for him. I began howling, sobs wracking my chest, the pain ripping me, slicing through my heart. Nathan Cardew must pay. They all must pay.

'Tell Sir James, Nathan's cheating him,' I whispered. 'Tell him he runs a vast smuggling cartel...and he's behind Mr Drew's death.' I looked up. Nathan was nowhere to be seen. 'Nathan was here...he's gone...Quick, tell Sir James the false ledgers are in a chest under his bed in the office...the tunnels run from the first store near the new boatyard...there's a cave under Penwartha Point.' My hands were shaking.

Joseph stripped off his jacket, putting it round my shoulders. 'Stay here,' he said.

In the strengthening moonlight, I saw James Polcarrow look up sharply. He came quickly over, looking tenderly at me through those eyes that knew suffering. 'They've brought William's body up,' he said softly, his hand on my shoulder. 'I'm so sorry, Elowyn...I liked him — we were going to go ahead with his plans.' His grip tightened. 'Nathan Cardew, you say?'

I nodded, my mouth hardening. 'He's been cheating you

– pocketing half the rents – he blackmails people. He gives you false accounts...the real ones are under his bed in his office – he's got a makeshift bed...they're in a chest under that. If his door's locked, go up through the trapdoor.' I reached for my handkerchief. 'Jack Deveral and John Polkerris did the murder – they jump to Nathan's command.' I stared into his incredulous eyes. 'They probably all do – except Mr Hearne and Ruth.'

Mr Hearne's voice carried from the door of the building. 'There's two more bodies – we're bringin' them up now. One's very decomposed, the other's just about recognizable.'

James Polcarrow's face hardened, he nodded to Joseph. 'There'll need to be an inquest. Dry William as best you can and bring him over. We'll keep him at Polcarrow.' His eyes softened; he was kneeling in front of me, his hand on my shoulder. 'I'm so sorry, Elowyn. Why don't you take him back to Polcarrow in my carriage...Henderson can see to him... We'll keep the other bodies here...but, you and Billy...ride with him to Polcarrow so you can say goodbye.'

Goodbye. The word cut me like a knife. 'I'd...I'd rather take him home to Mrs Pengelly if you don't mind...They'll want him there...Mrs Pengelly, Mrs Munroe...Sam and Tamsin... they'll all want him home...it's where he belongs.'

His grip tightened. 'Of course. Take him home, Elly.' He turned to go.

'Sir James...what if it's not just Nathan? What if there are others who want your harbour to fail? What if they're paying Nathan to build your harbour so it silts up and crumbles?'

Sir James stiffened in sudden anger. 'Viscount Vallenforth!

444

Of course, who else would it be. He assured me he'd put all thoughts of building his own harbour to one side. He almost begged me to allow him to use my harbour. Yet all the time…'

I wanted to scream with the pain. They had killed William because he knew too much. It all made sense now, a powerful man sweeping aside those in his way. 'What if Viscount Vallenforth's behind the dye in the clay as well? If your mines are discredited, you'd lose everything. Mr Sellick must have got the money for the lease from somewhere…Nathan stopped blackmailing him about the dye…perhaps he realised Viscount Vallenforth was behind that, as well?'

Sir James put out his hand, gently helping me to my feet. 'Come, Elowyn, let me help you. Joseph and Tobias have put William in the carriage; the driver's ready. Take him to Coombe House – we've time enough to talk.'

Chapter Forty-eight

His body lay in our arms, Billy and I holding him so
tenderly. Joseph had closed his bruised and swollen
eyelids, a vicious cut showing above his left eye. The carriage
was swaying, the huge moon lighting the moor around us.
They had taken off his wet shirt and wrapped him in the travelling rug. Another large gash sliced across the back of his
head, a huge lump the size of an egg in his hairline. His cut,
swollen lips were bloodless, his face blue-grey. He must have
put up a terrific fight; his knuckles were swollen and bruised,
huge purple bands stretching across his chest and abdomen.

I pushed aside the curls falling over his forehead. 'He was
sent to us, Billy. Sent so I wouldn't fall into Nathan's trap – so
Nathan's treachery was discovered…so that you would go to
Truro and become an engineer. You've got to do it – for his
sake…You've got to study his plans and make sure you carry
them all out – everything, just as William wanted.' I bent to
kiss William's cold cheek and a sudden shiver made my spine
run cold. The passing of his soul – he felt so close, as if he was

446

watching us. 'Mrs Munroe says the soul stays with the body – she says it waits until it's the right time to say goodbye. I think he can see us, Billy. I think he's saying goodbye to us.'

The carriage was swaying, the coach driver urging the horses on. Moonlight streamed into the carriage, lighting the tears on Billy's cheeks. 'If you hadn't put that four-leaf clover with your money, we'd never have found him.'

I clamped my mouth tight, fighting back my tears. 'I was so sure, Billy...so, so sure. I saw us living there...I just saw it.' The shiver was back, the hairs rising on my arms. 'I can't explain it, I just saw us.' I blew my nose. 'It was Nathan's greed that led us to him...if Nathan hadn't banked that money, we'd never have been alerted. I told Sir James I thought Viscount Vallenforth might have been behind the dye in the clay.'

'Perhaps they were going to claim it was Sir James putting it in?'

I nodded. 'I suspect that's right...William died because he knew too much, just like poor Mr Drew. They had to kill him before he noticed the building was sub-standard. His eyes were bad...he might not have noticed for a while longer but they had to kill him after William confronted him.' I shivered, ice-cold tentacles stabbing my heart. 'Mr Drew was always going to have to die. They're evil, evil men and William suspected it.' I traced the contours of William's face. 'I'm never going to marry now. I'm going to build up my savings and start again – William's given me the courage to do it. He made me believe in myself – just like he taught you to believe in yourself.'

'Ye know he was right – he was always right.'

'Right about what?'

'About the not drowning.'

I sat bolt upright. 'What d'you mean?'

'He didn't drown. He died from the bang to his head – I heard them tell Sir James he was caught by his collar. Once the flood waters went down, he was left hanging there – by his collar...he didn't drown...Elly, what is it?'

I stared at William's lifeless face, putting my fingers straight to his neck. 'Lie him flat, Billy – lie him flat. Now.'

William lay half stretched on the seat and I put my hands against his chest, spreading my fingers wide. There was nothing – no movement, just the terrible cold of a lifeless body. I put my ear against the mass of tight black hairs. 'William, come back...' I shouted. I put my hand against his chest, shaking him violently. 'Breathe, William, breathe. Don't you dare die on us. Come back to us...come back.' I began shaking him, my heart racing.

Billy looked horrified. 'Elly...don't...that's horrible... Elly, what is it?'

The movement had been so faint, just the smallest intake of what could have been a breath, but there had been something – definitely something. 'Quick, Billy, get him warm. Take off his breeches...hurry.' I put my cheek to his nose, feeling for a breath. He was as cold as ice and I freed my shawl, shaking it so Billy could help. 'Here, use this. Quick, rub his chest. He's not dead...it's just like last time...it was the cold of the water killing him but he hasn't drowned ...they just assumed he had.' We began rubbing, shaking him, the carriage lurching from side to side.

I put my cheek against his nose. 'Breathe...William... breathe.'

The faintest breath caressed my cheek. 'He's alive, Billy. He's alive.' I laid my head against his chest, the pounding in my ears making it almost impossible to hear. There was the faintest movement, the softest of beats. 'He looks dead but he's alive.' My hands were shaking, tears streaming down my cheeks.

We knew exactly what to do. He needed to be stripped of his wet clothes and dried completely. The coach was warm, but not warm enough – we needed to use the heat from our own bodies. 'Get these breeches off him – get him stripped.'

Billy looked under the seat. 'There's another rug. Here, lie down and I'll cover us.'

Once again, we lay down against William, Billy on one side, me on the other, lying against the man we both adored. He had heard us calling, he was coming back. When the shivering started, we would not be afraid. We would see him through the shaking and the convulsions. The parched throat and terrible headache. We would bathe his wounds, apply copious amounts of arnica salve and witch hazel. He would work his way through any number of Mrs Munroe's pies. There would be buttered buns, lardy cake and huge pots of calf's foot jelly. Sam and Billy would sneak brandy into his room; Mrs Pengelly would close the shutters against the chill of the night.

I laid my ear against his cold chest. His heartbeat was getting stronger, already he felt warmer. I had glimpsed our future. I had seen us in the old forge, seen the iron arch laden with yellow roses. William had spat on his hand and shaken. He had promised to be there for us and he would never break his promise.

Next to me, Billy began to sing:

> *Were I laid on Greenland's coast,*
> *And in my arms embraced my lass,*
> *Warm amidst eternal frost,*
> *Too soon the half year's night would pass.*

I joined him, the two of us singing loudly so William could hear.

> *And I would love you all the day,*
> *Every night would kiss and play,*
> *If with me you'd fondly stray,*
> *Over the hills and far away.*

We were taking William home.

I opened my eyes in sudden panic.

'It's all right, Elly. He's still sleepin'.' Jenna reached across the bed, her hand on mine. 'His breathing's easier an' his heart's stronger.'

'Oh dear…I didn't mean to fall asleep…' I felt stiff, my arms tingling from where I had been holding William. 'He looks better, he's got more colour.'

The smell of comfrey filled the room, Jenna's arnica salve and Mrs Munroe's finely sliced potatoes still bandaged against William's chest. The bruising on his face looked purple in the morning light and I reached for the sponge, dabbing it against his swollen lips.

'Ye needed yer sleep – just like Billy needed his.' Jenna's face softened as she looked down at the curled figure on the floor. 'He wouldn't leave neither – sleepin' like a babe, bless his dear heart.' She reached for the strings on her apron, untying them swiftly. 'I'll leave ye now. I'll go back to my boys but I'll be back with some more comfrey. Mrs Pengelly will be awake soon, an' Mrs Munroe said she'd be up at five. Ye'll not be alone fer long.'

The clock on the mantelpiece chimed four. 'Thank you, Jenna...thank you so much.'

She smiled as she opened the window to let in the air. 'There, that's better. Ye know, don't ye, that the old forge didn't reach the askin' price? Joseph told me there were two bids, but neither was high enough – it's still available, Elly... Ye could still get it.' She stopped, peering suddenly down to the street below. 'Goodness, that's Tom...what's he doin' pacing about like that?' She frowned and leaned out. 'Tom... up here...What's wrong? It's not Gwen, is it?'

'No, Gwen and the baby are well. It's Elowyn I need to see. Can ye let me in?'

I heard him bound up the stairs and he stood in the doorway, his eyes wild with fright. 'Elowyn...oh God, Elowyn.' His hair was rumpled, his clothes dishevelled. He stared at William. 'How is he?'

'He's warm but he's not woken. He's talking but his words don't make sense. He's not opened his eyes yet.'

Tom crossed the room, slumping on the chair left by Jenna, staring across the bed, his hands shaking. 'They've been questionin' me...Major Trelawney had me arrested. I was in handcuffs but Sir James let me go...Elowyn...Oh God, Elowyn...' He put his head in his hands, crying piteously.

'I know what you're talking about. I saw you...that night on the clifftop, I saw you with that club in your hand. And it was you loading clay for the flour, wasn't it? I saw that as well.'

He looked horrified. 'Elly, they made me. Nathan...Jack ...Mamm, they all made me. At first, I thought I was only to do the ship repairs...then I realized I was in their books. You don't understand...you've no idea...They've got lists of everything they ship, everyone they deal with...lists and lists detailin' every last run...but they're not true. They draw you in an' threaten everyone you love. Once I'd done those repairs, Gwen was in danger...Uncle Thomas...everyone...'

'I know. Mamm threatened me just the same. I'm in their books, too.'

His eyes widened. 'Elly – if Jack Deveral and John Polkerris get caught we're like to hang.' His hands shook as he held them against his mouth. He reached for a bowl, fear making him vomit.

He was voicing my own fear, the threat that never left me. 'I take it Mamm's gone with them?' I saw his sudden panic, the hesitation in his eyes. 'Tom, you know where they've gone, don't you?'

He stared back at me. 'I overheard them a while back. There's a cottage in Mevagissey…in Shore Street. It's got huge cellars – it's where they store stuff. But, Elly, don't you see? I *can't* tell Sir James. If I tell him, we'll all hang…innocent people will die. They've covered their backs…no one will talk.'

'Tom, you know Jack Deveral's cottage well enough, you must be able to think where they'd hide those lists.'

He looked as if he might be sick again. 'Elly, ye think I haven't searched everywhere? Ye think I haven't spent my whole time trying to find them? They're not in the cottage, and even if they were, Trelawney's men are there. He's got men everywhere.'

'What about somewhere down the tunnels? Or the cave? What about in one of the barrels?'

He grasped his head in his hands. 'No, I've looked… believe me, I've searched and searched. I had to go along with them. Nathan's become so powerful…he made me do things I never should've done. Elly, I never should've said those things about William. He was never in the linhay… those boots were planted by Nathan to sow doubt in your mind – but I didn't know that at the time.' He looked at William's bruised face. 'I wronged him, Elly…I wronged him and I wronged you.'

Into my mind came the shadowy figures of three men furtively crossing the back yard. 'What about the tunnel leading from the privy?'

'There's no tunnel leading from the privy.'

'But…there's something under there.'

He shook his head. 'No, there's nothing under the privy.'

My heart began thumping. 'There is...there's something big enough to hide three men. I saw them enter the privy and not leave – three of them. I thought it was a tunnel but there's definitely something. The books must be in there.' I rose quickly, reaching for the tinder box, gathering as many candles as I could. 'Take these, hurry...use the cliff path and get to the privy. Find the trapdoor...search everywhere.'

'You really think there's a stash under there?'

'I'm certain of it...especially now I know they kept it from you. The books have got to be there. Here, take this lamp oil and burn everything you find. When everything's burned, tell Sir James about the cottage in Mevagissey.'

He stuffed the candles and vials of oil into his pocket, his hands shaking. 'They threatened Gwen would come to harm...they threatened my new-born son.' He wiped his hands across his mouth. 'I wanted to tell you, Elly, but I was too scared.'

I nodded. 'I wanted to tell Uncle Thomas but I was too scared.' I felt my mouth harden. 'Has Nathan gone with them?'

'No, they used the rowing boats in the cave. I watched them go. They didn't see me but I saw them. Mamm and Lowenna were with them but not Nathan. He's somewhere in Porthcarrow. He's hiding – Sir James's searching every-where.'

'Tom, has Sir James got the ledgers?'

'He's got everything – except Nathan. He missed him by minutes. Sir James disturbed him and he ran down the alley. It was too dark to see where he went.'

Our voices must have woken William. I saw his eyelids flickering. 'Quick, go…find those lists.'

Anyone could be hiding Nathan. There would be plenty in his power to call on. I heard Tom run down the stairs and leapt to the window, throwing open the sash. 'Tom… Tom…' I called. He looked up. 'Nathan must be somewhere near his office, somewhere next to the alley. Tell Sir James to search Mrs Burrow's lodgings. Tell him, Nathan's got a hold over her — he made her lie in court and her lodgings are right by the alley. Tell Sir James he could be hiding there.'

I had shouted loudly and looked round. William was restless, his head turning from side to side, and I rushed back. His hand was moving slowly beneath the sheets, reaching out as if wanting to touch me and I slid my hand under the soft eiderdown, our fingers meeting. His hand slipped slowly over mine. His touch was soft, just the slightest pressure and a shiver ran down my spine. 'You're safe,' I whispered, my heart soaring, 'but you need to lie still and gather your strength.'

I forced back my tears. His touch had been so gentle, the merest squeeze of his hand, and I knew he was trying to thank me. I began thanking the shadows for giving him back to me and reached for his pulse — it was full and steady, a comfortable rhythm. 'Are you all right?' I whispered.

His cracked lips parted in a slow smile. 'I've felt better,' he whispered. 'I've a head from hell.' His throat sounded sore, his voice parched.

Billy woke at the sound of William's voice, immediately rushing to his side. 'Are ye hungry, Will? Only Mrs Munroe's made ye some chicken soup? She had it ready last night but ye didn't wake up. Shall I go down and get it? There's potted crab as well…'

William smiled, wincing in sudden pain. He lifted my fingers to his swollen lips, kissing them softly. 'Chicken soup sounds perfect, Billy…let's leave the potted crab for later.' His voice was hoarse, his lips barely moving and we stood smiling down at the man we adored. His eyes slowly opened, his smile broadened, 'I take it you both saved my life…?'

Billy shrugged, forcing back his tears. 'Will…I've been thinkin' about that valve for Sir James' new engine. It's got to have some sort of suction…it's got to let the steam out but not let it back.'

William shut his eyes, his voice cracking. 'A vacuum… we'll create a vacuum.'

'How will we get a vacuum, Will?'

William smiled, his hand squeezing mine. 'The steam's under pressure…when it cools, a vacuum will form…that will snap the valve shut.'

My heart was aching with love, with joy for the future. 'Billy, there's time enough for Sir James' new engine. Let William rest now – go and warm up that soup.'

Billy ran down the stairs, waking the household and William returned my fingers to his lips. 'I love you, Elowyn Liddicot,' he whispered.

I bent to kiss his smiling lips. 'And I love you, William Cotterell.'

Dawn was breaking, the first tentative calls of the cockerels echoing across the water. I pulled the eiderdown around him, protecting him from the fresh sea breeze. Soon, he would belong to everyone, but for the moment he was just mine.

'I can't live without you, Elly,' he whispered.

'So it seems,' I replied, bending to kiss him again. 'How about I get you a whistle?'

He shook his head painfully. 'How about I never let you out of my sight?'

Acknowledgements

This is my third novel and, once again, I would like to extend a huge thank-you to my family and friends; to my agent, Teresa Chris, for her unwavering encouragement, and to my editor, Sara O'Keefe, for her invaluable help and expertise. A big thank-you to the whole team at Atlantic Books, and to all of you in Truro Records Office for making my search for original sources so much fun.